book should be returned/renewed by the
' date shown above. Overdue items incur
₃s which prevent self-service renewals.
contact the library.

'worth Libraries
' Renewal Hotline
₃3388
✓andsworth.gov.uk

Wandsworth

THE DARK ARTS of BLOOD

BOOK FOUR
of the
BLOOD WINE SEQUENCE

FREDA WARRINGTON

TITAN BOOKS

The Dark Arts of Blood
Print edition ISBN: 9781781167106
E-book edition ISBN: 9781781167281

Published by Titan Books
A division of Titan Publishing Group Ltd
144 Southwark Street, London SE1 0UP

First edition: May 2015

2 4 6 8 10 9 7 5 3 1

CPI Group (UK) Limited, Croydon, CR0 4YY.

For Mike with love: husband, best friend and guardian angel.
"May the road rise with you."

CONTENTS

PART ONE

CHAPTER ONE

LADY OF THE MOUNTAINS

SPRING 1928: LUCERNE, SWITZERLAND

B lood was imperative.

The hot ruby fluid of life… Charlotte caught the scent and stopped mid-stride. Around her, a maze of lanes wound between timbered houses. Rain drizzled from the night sky, shrouding the meadows and mountains above the town. Although she had fed once tonight, the waft of salty, musky warmth arrested her.

She rarely scented blood in the open air, unless a human was injured.

There and gone. The miasma blew away on a rainy gust of air.

She sensed motes of human life inside the medieval houses of the Aldstadt, but the alleys were silent. This lull between one seasonal festival and the next felt uncannily quiet; the noisy parades of *Fasnacht*, meant to drive out demons before Lent began, were over. The ritual herding of cattle up to the Alpine meadows was some weeks away. How eerie the town seemed when the drumming stopped and the hollow turnip lanterns went dark.

Although a passionate vampire, Charlotte wasn't voracious. She loved to walk alone at night, savouring the life around her without wanting to devour every drop.

Now she sensed someone walking parallel with her, a street or two away… perhaps a trick of her too-vivid imagination. The impression lasted a few seconds, then – like the blood-scent – it vanished.

She reached the end of the lane where it opened on to the banks of Lake Lucerne. A few hundred yards away, the old wooden Chapel Bridge crossed the river Reuss, connecting the old and new sides of town. The water was black obsidian, full of wavering reflections from the town lights. Two men leaned on a railing with their backs to her. They shared the same slight, elegant build, blond hair and matching dark overcoats.

One of them turned and came to greet her with a smile.

"Well, my sweet friend," he said, taking both her hands and kissing her cheek. "What a delightful coincidence. What brings you here?"

"Stefan," she said, embracing him. They exchanged a light kiss on the lips. Stefan gave his usual flirtatious grin, as if to say, *Ah, if only...* "What brings me here? I could ask you the same. I felt too languid to stray far from home, but I thought you were in London, so...?"

He drew her under the eaves of a big hotel that faced the lake. Niklas followed. He was Stefan's twin, identical except for his eyes – Stefan's were blue, his pale gold – and for the fact that he never spoke. He only echoed Stefan's actions, like a mime.

Charlotte kissed Niklas too. Although he didn't react, she always acknowledged him because she knew this pleased Stefan.

"A pleasant night's hunting?" he asked.

"I would never call it pleasant," she said quietly, "but I would call it my own business."

"You and Karl are so strange, still hunting separately after all this time. Eccentric." Stefan's white smile grew broader. "But we like you for that. Don't we, Niklas?"

Niklas gave a faint smile. His eyes stayed unfocused.

The brothers had been vampires since the eighteenth century. Stefan still preferred the fashions of his own time, when circumstances allowed. Charlotte thought modern dress never looked right on them, but it was essential for camouflage. Her own taste was for silk and lace in subtle colours, but tonight she wore a black coat with an enveloping fur collar and a cloche hat that half-concealed her eyes.

Better for disappearing into darkness. For hiding stray blood splashes.

"Sometimes we hunt together," she said. "But we never plan it,

12

because… well, it can be unsettling. Almost too intense."

"Ah." Stefan's eyes shone with wicked knowledge. "Of course. I can imagine."

"I would prefer you not to imagine anything." Charlotte tried to sound haughty, but he only smirked.

"Forgive me. However, as the world's greatest proponent of pleasure, I can only state my view that the more… *intense* a shared experience, the more cause for celebration, not shame."

"And for discretion," she said.

"Oh, I am all for anything secret, clandestine." He slipped a friendly hand through her arm. "Are you on your way home?"

"No, my night isn't over yet." Charlotte fed sparingly, careful not to kill outright, but this meant she needed more than one victim. "Yours?"

Stefan shrugged. "You won't spend the rest of this beautiful, wet evening wandering with us? Lucerne is the loveliest of towns in all seasons. Have you seen the Christmas parade, where Santa Claus has a terrifying demonic companion who goes around threatening to punish the bad children?"

"Yes, I've seen that." She gave a small grimace. "They call him *Krampus*, don't they? Or *Schmutzli*? I'm glad I didn't grow up here. I should have been terrified."

"Now we *are* the demons," he said. "Will you stroll with us?"

"I'd love to, but not until…"

"Other needs are satisfied. I understand. In that case, I'll let you go on your merry way. But you always see through me, don't you?"

"Usually," she said, her eyes narrowing. "Why? Were you looking for me?"

"Guilty," said Stefan. "We tried your chalet but no one was there. However, you were easy enough to find. Hardly fifty miles away, in one of your favourite towns… The lovely warm trace of you was like a sunlit cloud-trail through the Crystal Ring."

"That's a poetic way of admitting you were pursuing me." *I can never be annoyed with Stefan,* she thought. *Not for long, at least.* He'd perfected the art of being a complete rogue, so charming that she couldn't help but love him.

Also, he was one of the vampires who'd helped transform her. However difficult the memory, that created an eternal bond.

"We have news."

"Oh, is something wrong?"

"Not at all. Niklas and I have taken a house beside Lake Lucerne. It's beautiful." He pointed across the water, where a scattering of distant lights gleamed. Mount Pilatus was a vast pale shadow in the night. "You can't see from here, but it's outside the town, near the water's edge, like a fairytale chalet surrounded by forests and meadows... Why are you frowning?"

"It sounds idyllic," she said, "but you know perfectly well Violette has opened her new ballet academy here."

"Yes. So?" He looked innocently confused.

"You know she won't tolerate a houseful of vampires so close to her dancers!"

"Hardly a houseful. Only Niklas and me."

"And your guests. After all that happened recently, she sees danger everywhere, and I don't blame her."

Stefan drew a half-circle on the air with his forefinger. "The house is by the lake, at least ten miles away, even by boat."

"That's still close. She won't be happy."

"That's not my concern. You're one to talk – here you are, hunting hardly a mile from her new premises?"

"I know," she said with a twinge of guilt. "Not my cleverest idea, but I won't make a habit of it. I'm always drawn to where she lives, even when she's away."

"We won't trouble Violette," said Stefan, "but she certainly won't dictate where I choose to live. You know Niklas and I would never touch her dancers, and besides... is there any power on Earth that *could* make Violette happy?"

"You have a point," Charlotte said softly. "It's only a bare few months since her heart was broken."

Violette – who believed herself too damaged to fall in love – had found someone precious, only to be cruelly bereaved. Beautiful Robyn, a human woman caught between Violette and an even more dangerous lover, had preferred to die rather than become a vampire.

"And her reaction was to work like a maniac on a brand new tour, new theatre and school, all at the same time?"

"That's her. Anything to distract herself, rather than moping. Pain like that is so raw, I don't think it ever heals."

They stood without speaking for a while, listening to raindrops pattering into the lake. Charlotte felt rain penetrating her coat, but cold and wet meant nothing to a vampire. Last year she'd staged her own death and funeral – for her family's sake – and afterwards she had crawled up through heavy clay to escape the grave. The experience would haunt her forever. Rain, storms and snow were nothing in comparison.

"I know." Stefan shivered. "I can't imagine such loss. I'm not devoid of feelings, you know. Behind this ice-cold, manly exterior I'm as soft-hearted as you, my beloved friend."

"Ice cold and manly?" she exclaimed. "Stefan, you do this every time."

"What?"

"Make me laugh so I can't be angry with you."

He grinned. "Well, I came to say that you and Karl are welcome at our new house whenever you wish. Will you break the news to Violette, or shall I?"

"I'll tell her," said Charlotte. "She's away, touring America again. I'm not sure when she returns. Within a few days, I think. Don't worry, I'm used to handling her with the softest of kid gloves. Heaven knows, she's always been temperamental. These days she's stronger, but in some ways... stormier than ever."

"Never predictable. Tell me you don't find that a little thrilling?"

"That's one word for it."

Stefan clasped her hands. "If anyone can soothe her grief, it's you, Charlotte. Enjoy the rest of your... stroll. Come, Niklas. We'll see you later, perhaps? Back here?"

Charlotte resumed her walk, climbing a narrow street between rows of timbered houses. She felt pensive now, eager to feed swiftly and return home to Karl. The upper storeys seemed to lean in towards each other, turning the lane into an eerie corridor. Rain fell through the gap to flow down the cobblestones in a shining stream.

Was Stefan being mischievous, taking a house so close to Violette's new academy, or did he simply want to be near others of his kind? If the house was only for him and his twin, there would be no problems – but Stefan loved company, vampire and human alike. He lived for parties and decadence, luring his victims with the temptations of glamour, music, drugs and sex – not to mention the most addictive narcotic of all: Stefan himself, with his hypnotic charm and his nearly painless bite. All kinds of people would be drawn there, like wasps to honey.

No, Violette would be displeased, on a scale from exasperation to fury. Charlotte trusted only three vampires in the world: Violette, Karl – and Stefan, despite his reckless lifestyle.

Or if she had to choose between them, just Karl.

A fresh conflict between Stefan and Violette was the last thing they needed.

Charlotte had met Karl five years ago, when he'd asked to study science with her father in Cambridge. A year and an ocean of heartache later, she had joined him in his strange dark existence. Her short vampire life so far had been fraught with feuds, danger and bloodshed.

Karl and I want the same thing, she thought. *A quiet life. Love. Is that so much to ask?*

The notorious tyrant, Kristian, was dead, but he'd left multiple shadows over them. Others had tried to take his place. They had failed, but not without causing chaos and anguish.

Meanwhile, Violette had found Robyn, only to lose her.

Charlotte tried to console Violette, a task akin to nurturing a wounded, raging panther. Comforting a vampire was never easy, still less one who was an avatar of Lilith.

Violette was powerful, embodying a dark goddess who killed or cured by bringing her victims face to face with the stark truth about themselves. But that did not make her invulnerable to pain.

Charlotte's head came up: there was the tantalising blood-scent again. The smell was richer, more complex than that of ordinary spilled blood. Ripe, almost sexual… a fragrance that might fill humans with disgust. To a vampire, though, it was intriguing, delicious.

Her senses came into acute focus. She followed the scent as if it were a visible, crimson mist-trail.

A few yards on, a young woman came stumbling out of a side lane towards her.

She wore a pale coat and hat, button-strap shoes grey with rain.

She staggered, bent nearly double and clutching her abdomen. The hour was long past midnight and there was no one else nearby. Charlotte paused, wondering what to do. The pull of blood was irresistible but she held back, moral sensibility overriding her animal thirst.

She said in Swiss German, "Are you all right? May I help?"

The woman stopped, propping herself with one hand on a wall. She appeared to be in her early twenties, with a sharp, striking face, brown eyes, dark curls showing beneath her hat brim. She looked familiar, although Charlotte was certain they'd never met before.

The woman's brow creased. "*Ja. Nein.* Do you speak English?"

"Yes." Charlotte hurried to support her with a hand under her elbow. "I am English."

"Thank goodness! Sorry – I can get by, usually, but the words have all gone out of my head."

The ripe blood smell rose from her, overpowering. Charlotte's mouth watered and her tongue touched her lips... but she forced back her fangs. Not that she'd never fed on someone in pain, but an instinct stronger than blood-thirst held her back.

"What's wrong? Let me help you. I'm Charlotte."

"Amy. I – really, I'm all right, just..." The girl swayed and her legs buckled. Charlotte let her sink gently to the ground. The pale coat fell open and she saw the source of Amy's blood: a red stain, soaking the fabric of her dress between her thighs.

Charlotte's breath stilled with a horrible blend of shock and excitement. The thought of plunging her head down to taste the blood was hard to resist. At the same time the act was unthinkable. A trace of human, puritan restraint stopped her cold.

Or common sense, she thought. *I am a vampire, but not a beast.*

"Oh... oh dear, don't worry. I'll get help. Nature is often not kind to women, is it?"

Amy took a few breaths. Her accent was upper-class English, a familiar one to Charlotte's ears. She shook her head. "No. It's not... I can't explain. I'm so sorry, I feel such an idiot, but..."

"I should take you to a hospital, or find a doctor."

"No!" Her face lost all colour. "No doctors!"

"All right. But I won't leave you here... Amy?" Her eyelids fluttered down, opening again as Charlotte tapped her cheek.

"Do not pass out. Do you live nearby? Is there somewhere I can take you?"

She pointed with a shaking hand towards the top of the steep lane. "I'm staying at a house, up there at the forest edge, with my uncle. There are lots of people staying with us. They will take care of me."

"And call a doctor?"

"Yes, if they must. But I'll be quite all right. I just can't manage to climb…"

"Hush, don't worry. I'll take you."

"Thank you," Amy whispered. "Thank you so much."

She was too faint to walk, so Charlotte lifted her in her arms and carried her up the steepening incline. She kept one arm beneath Amy's thighs and let the coat hang free so that the blood wouldn't soak into it. All through the long climb, the ripe blood-scent tormented her, while Amy sobbed quietly into her neck.

"It's an awfully long way," Amy said after a while. "I'm sorry. We can get motor cars up to the house, with great care, but I don't drive."

The town ended and there was only Alpine pasture ahead, a thin rutted track growing ever steeper, rustling forests.

"Amy?" said Charlotte. "There's nothing here."

The woman raised her head. "Along the path. Just a little further."

Fifty yards on, Charlotte glimpsed light through the trees. Around a curve in the track she saw a white edifice: a newly built house in the stark modern style, like a marble monument with tall windows framed in black. The house was so imposing, with its straight lines and brutal facade, that Charlotte could not decide whether it was ugly or beautiful.

"I didn't know this place was here."

"Isn't it grand?" Amy said tiredly. "You can leave me at the door."

"No, I want to be sure there's someone to take care of you."

A few vehicles were parked on either side: a mixture of sleek expensive models, old boxy cars and vans, motorcycles. Light fell down the broad shallow steps. Charlotte saw figures moving behind textured glass panels that flanked the front door. She helped Amy to stand, taking almost her whole weight, and rang the doorbell.

The woman who peered out through a narrow gap was a matronly type dressed in dark brown, greying hair plaited around her head. Seeing Amy, her round, stern face furrowed with concern. She spoke German with the local accent. "Miss Temple? What happened to you?"

"Nothing, Gudrun. I felt faint," Amy said, smiling weakly. "This is Charlotte. She's been awfully good... I'd be lying on the street if she hadn't picked me up."

The woman paused. Her nostrils flared; the blood-smell was strong even to a human. Perhaps she already knew the nature of the problem.

"Bring her in. Miss Temple, you should not have gone alone. What were you thinking?"

As Charlotte helped her over the threshold, a few drops of blood splashed on the pristine marble floor. *God, the gorgeous red blood...* She could scent it on the older woman too, a subtler smell overlaid by sweat and perfume, and wafting from dozens of other people elsewhere in the house... The temptation was unbearable.

"Nothing," said Amy. "I just need to rest. Don't fuss."

Charlotte gave her into the care of Gudrun. There could be any cause for her bleeding. Mere nature: heavy menstruation, perhaps a miscarriage, or – God forbid – an injury of some kind. Also, she knew that unmarried English girls sometimes took a quiet trip to the continent to end an unwanted pregnancy, although they generally went to France... Such matters were never discussed in public, but that was life's reality. It wasn't her place to speculate or judge.

"She should lie down," said Charlotte, "and perhaps a doctor—"

"We thank you for your aid, Fräulein," she said brusquely, "but everything is in hand."

In the background, Charlotte glimpsed a handful of young-looking men and women, but the sight was brief. Guiding Amy, Gudrun turned at an angle to block Charlotte from going any further into the vast hall. She was being dismissed. Even as she stepped outside, the high black door swung towards her face.

Although startled, she was grateful to be severed from temptation.

"Thank you, Charlotte," Amy called as the door slammed between them. "Thank you so much for your kindness."

* * *

Well, that was bizarre, thought Charlotte.

Walking downhill towards the town, she breathed deeply of the fresh, wet Alpine air. From this height she could see the ruined city wall with its ancient watchtowers, the twin spires of the church, and rows of handsome houses clustering down the slopes.

How easy it would have been to take both women! To stupefy the matronly Gudrun with the mesmeric gleam of her eyes, then to lap blood from between the girl's thighs as if licking clean a wound... finally cleansing her palate with a few sips from both their veins.

If other humans had come running to stop her... the grand marble hallway might have become a bloodbath.

But she hadn't.

"Oh, dear God," she groaned, leaning on the wall of the first house she reached. *What am I, that I could even think it? Well... I know what I am. So, I'll keep walking. Fast.*

She carried on towards the heart of town. The strip of cloud above continued to unleash a steady downpour. She turned her face to the sky, letting the rain wash her clean. One thing she'd learned from Karl was self-control. He hunted by striking fast out of the dark, never looking at his victim's face if he could help it.

Charlotte, by contrast, was inclined to befriend people before she fed. Even though she knew her desire for mutual affection was deceptive, she found the impulse hard to resist. Winning their trust, only to betray them.

"We all find our own ways," Stefan would say with a shrug. "We're vampires. Accept it. If you agonise over every pang of conscience, you may as well put yourself to eternal sleep in the *Weisskalt*."

Charlotte could only imagine how desperate someone would have to be to seek that terrible frozen realm, the outermost shell of the Crystal Ring. The *Weisskalt* did not even guarantee true death: some vampires had come back after years of hibernation. Some claimed to remember every moment.

Perhaps she would find Stefan again, as he'd suggested, and tell him what had happened. *Even if*, she thought, *he only finds the tale amusing, as he always does.*

Although her hunger was acute, her desire to sate it had vanished.

Sometimes the prospect of a too-lavish feast could kill the appetite.

Then a man stepped in front of her.

She was startled. Normally she sensed humans before they appeared, but she hadn't been paying attention. The stranger was walking up from the town, where there were hotels and bars along the water's edge. He was drunk, judging by his unsteady gait and the insolent way he confronted her, forcing her to stop. He reeked of stale beer. Jacket undone, hat askew. His clothes were nondescript: a plain suit that gave no hint of whether he was a tourist or local, rich or poor.

Not that his station in life meant anything. Alcohol could turn aristocrat or peasant alike into a brute. To a vampire, this meant nothing.

Blood was blood.

He addressed her in Swiss German, slurring his words as he propositioned her in the crudest of terms. As a human, she would have been terrified. Now, however, he had no idea what an extreme risk he was taking.

But she had no desire to hurt him.

She made her expression icy as she distanced herself and began to walk around the drunken pest. Unfortunately, he lacked the sense to let her go. He slipped and staggered on the cobbles, arms flailing for balance. Giggling, he circled in front of her again. Charlotte's gaze became flint.

"Let me pass," she said in German.

She side-stepped again, but this time he seized her arm. "No, come on, a beautiful girl all alone? Want to talk to you. Not good enough for you, Fräulein, is that it?"

His grip was strong. He might be an ex-soldier, one who'd guarded Switzerland's borders during the Great War: he had that tough, weather-worn look. His hair was cropped short, his face red and sweaty. Not much taller than her, he was heavy-set, with muscular arms, blood vessels throbbing in his thick neck.

Charlotte preferred to avoid fights, unless pushed to the limit. However reckless or determined the man was, if he planned to overpower her he would be in for a shock.

"Let go," she said, her voice a sword-blade.

The drunk responded by gripping both her upper arms. A

slight tussle began. She was startled by his strength – as he was doubtless surprised to find her immoveable, like a tree.

"Don't be unfriendly, darling. Just a kiss. Look at those beautiful lips. You ever been kissed before? Bet you haven't. Not like this. And I've something else for you, a real surprise…"

Over his shoulder, Charlotte saw Stefan and Niklas, tiny and far away at the bottom of the lane. They were looking up at her, but Stefan would view this as a moment of entertainment, not a reason to rush to her aid.

"Take your hands off me now or you will regret it," she said softly.

"Ooh." The drunk laughed. "What can you do to stop me, skinny little flower?"

"Let me go and run for your life, unless you wish to find out."

More laughter, witless yet malevolent. He jerked her towards him and made to kiss her. Charlotte brought up her arms in a swift movement that broke his grip. He tried again, this time seizing her around the waist and the back of her neck.

Her eyes glazed, and she struck.

His skin tasted foul with alcohol-tainted sweat but she buried her face in his throat, heard him grunt with pain as her fangs pierced his veins. His body went into a spasm, arms flapping as he tried to push her off. He cursed, still fighting – that was unusual. Victims usually went still and pliant under her spell…

This one went berserk.

She needed so much force to hold on to him, she could barely keep her fangs in his neck, let alone draw blood. From the corner of her eye, she saw a flash.

The glint of a steel blade.

The drunk's elbow hooked back and plunged forward. Charlotte felt the blade go hilt-deep into her abdomen. The sensation was like a punch. Then a terrible throbbing discomfort began to spread from the wound.

He slurred angry words that she could hardly understand.

She gasped, lost hold of him and staggered backwards, clutching at the dagger hilt. It had passed between the edges of her coat and straight through her dress as if through paper. Vampires could be injured and suffer agonies, but they usually healed swiftly, able to ignore pain for long enough to kill their attacker.

This was different. She'd never felt pain like it. The stab-wound felt cold, pulsing as though it was releasing poison through her whole body. She doubled over, trying to pull the knife free. It stuck fast as if held in her flesh by barbs.

Her attacker staggered sideways, pressing one hand to the wound in his neck. Blood oozed through his fingers to soak his shirt collar. Face contorted with shock and rage, he snarled, "*Strigoi!*"

That was the last word he uttered before Stefan caught him.

She wasn't sure what happened next. Her head swam and her sight went dark. She was aware of lying face down on the wet cobbles. There were noises above her: scuffling, footsteps, gruff curses... then silence.

Charlotte half sat up and looked down to see her coat hanging open, the yellowish handle of the knife sticking out of her stomach and her slow, crimson blood staining the pale silk crepe of her dress. She couldn't breathe or think for shock.

"Charlotte, my God." Stefan was crouching at her side, looking horrified. "Can you walk? Don't try to pull out the..."

Knife, he was about to say, when the blade fell free at last. He caught it before it hit the ground, immediately dropped it with a cry.

"It *burns*," he said.

"Yes," she gasped. "Like ice. God, it hurts. I can't..."

"Charlotte? Dearest, I'm sorry, if I'd known what that rogue intended..."

The blade shone, luminous to her sensitive eyes.

"Did you kill him?"

Stefan shook his head. "Couldn't hold him. He ran. Never mind him, you're more important. Can you stand up?"

"I'll try." The dark street whirled around her. Everything was unreal, as if she were slipping in and out of consciousness. It took a far more drastic injury than this to destroy a vampire: decapitation, at least. She knew this was serious, but her mind wouldn't accept it.

"Charlotte?" Stefan sounded panicky now. "Stay with me. What the hell did he do to you?"

"I don't know." She tried to force a smile. "Humans are supposed to succumb, not to fight back."

"I know. How dare they defend themselves?" Stefan tried to joke but he looked as grey and deathly as she felt. "Hold on to me. Niklas and I will take you home."

"Bring the knife."

Grimacing, Stefan picked up the weapon, using his coat sleeve to protect his fingers. Swiftly he wiped off the blood and slipped the blade into his coat pocket. "I have it."

She was shivering violently as he wrapped his arms around her. "I'll be all right in a moment," she said through chattering teeth. She felt she'd split in two, half of her looking down on the scene from above.

"Of course you will," said Stefan. His horrified expression belied his words.

"But tell Karl to find out what the knife is," she added, "in case I can't."

"You can tell him yourself." Stefan spoke through gritted teeth as he drew her with difficulty into the Crystal Ring. Her vision exploded with black stars. The other-realm received them, but it felt wrong, hostile, as thick as wet cement. "We'll take you home, and you'll soon be better."

"But the knife," she persisted, trying to make herself clear while she still could. "Freezing cold, burning like acid. You must find out who made it and why."

"I understand. Keep talking to me. Soon be safe."

She felt herself falling, stumbling. Rain drenched her. Raqia – their other name for the Crystal Ring, the secret astral realm of vampires – had spat them out.

"It's no good," he said. "We can't take you that way. You're too heavy."

"Heavy?" she gasped, trying to make light of the situation even as her vision turned black and red.

"You know what I mean. You're like a willow branch, my dear, but too weak to enter the Crystal Ring. The wound's taken all your energy."

"Yes… God, Stefan, it hurts."

"So, I have a new plan. We'll steal a car and drive you home. Don't worry, it won't take more than two hours at most."

"Thank you," she whispered, unable to argue. "That man was

incredibly strong, too strong for a human. And he said something…"

"What?" Stefan bent his ear to her lips. "I can barely hear you."

"He said, 'I know what you are. Your strength will become ours and you are finished.'"

CHAPTER TWO

THE COLD KNIFE

Karl chose Prague as his hunting ground tonight, travelling there swiftly through the Crystal Ring. On most nights, he journeyed far from the house he shared with Charlotte, a chalet high in the Bernese Oberland. Feed too close to home, and rumours would begin.

Not that they'd always resisted temptation.

He loved Prague's beautiful old buildings with their red roofs and majestic pastel walls, all the elaborate churches. He liked to walk slowly among the night crowds, his mind gradually emptying of all thoughts as his blood-thirst grew.

A group of smartly dressed men and women gathered in the doorway of a hotel, apparently heading out for supper. As Karl approached, one woman caught his gaze and froze, her dark eyes shining. Her attention stayed locked on him as he passed, as if her companions had vanished.

She might see a handsome face in shadow beneath the brim of his hat, some kind of tantalising promise in his eyes. That was a vampire's deceptive allure. Instant, heart-stopping desire for a stranger: he'd seen the reaction so often that it made his heart sink a little.

Now he only had to stop and smile to have his victim for the night. The man at her side might be her husband, but she'd still find a way to escape: anything to be with the dark-haired stranger whose face made her forget to breathe or blink…

Eventually she did blink, languidly, like a cat.

Karl turned and hurried away through the crowd.

Every vampire had their own way of hunting. In the past Karl had been tormented by his conscience, but he'd never let it rule him. Thirst conquered guilt every time. Unlike some, he wasn't inclined to seduce and torment his victims first. He aimed to feed with as little distress to his prey as possible.

He did not always succeed.

He was still a vampire, after all. When the need arose, he could be as soft, emotionless and lethally cold as snow.

In a back street, he saw the silhouette of a young man bent over the engine of a very old motor car. The scent of oil and fuel and sweat twined around Karl as he approached. He seized the man from behind, fed swiftly—

Outside time as blood filled him with delicious crimson flames...

Then he laid the man gently down on to the cobblestones, hoping he would not die, and that his nightmares would not be unbearable. Quick and soundless, Karl walked away without once looking at his face.

"You might have offered to mend his car first," said a familiar male voice from the shadows.

Karl halted as Pierre and Ilona stepped out in front of him, two fashionably dressed dark figures against blackness, outlined by splinters of light from nearby windows. They were arm in arm: Pierre, his wayward friend who'd rarely been anything but trouble, and Ilona, Karl's daughter.

For years she'd rejected Karl in angry punishment for the terrible wrong he'd done her: transforming her without her consent, simply because he couldn't bear to see her grow old and die. That was a mistake he would never make again.

With Charlotte, he'd made very sure she was aware in advance of the dangers and horrors of immortality, as well as the pleasures.

Lately, Karl and Ilona had reached a truce, almost full reconciliation. *Almost*. Seeing them, he felt resigned joy mixed with the sadness of all their past conflicts. They exchanged greetings: a light kiss on the cheek for Pierre, two kisses and an embrace for his daughter.

"What a pleasant coincidence," Karl said softly. "What brings you here?"

Pierre shrugged. "We all have to be somewhere, my friend. And

Prague's one of our favourite cities, as it is yours, so not a very great coincidence."

"You would have to be on the other side of the world for me not to sense your presence, beloved Father," Ilona said with a cool smile.

"Walk with me," said Karl, glancing back.

"Ah, you still like to leave the crime scene as swiftly as possible," said Pierre, rather too loudly for Karl's liking.

"No crime scene, I hope," Karl replied. "Merely a young man who wonders why he passed out. He should have nothing worse than a few days of fever."

"With delicious fever-dreams about *you*, I hope," said Pierre.

The three of them strolled through Wenceslas Square. Rain sifted down, sparkling against the grand ornate buildings. "How is Charlotte, my beloved Ophelia?" Pierre asked.

"Still happier not to be called Ophelia."

Pierre grinned. "Hard luck. If I wish to give her a romantic nickname, I will, especially if it annoys her. Is she well?"

"Very well," said Karl. "We are both alarmingly content and happy."

"That's heart-warming," said Ilona. "And Violette?"

"We've not seen much of her lately. She's busy with her ballet academy in Lucerne, and touring again. She throws herself into work rather than brood, but Charlotte and I prefer a quiet life, at least for the time being. Why do you ask? If you are bored and planning mischief, *please* keep well away from us." Karl spoke with polite menace.

"So suspicious!" Pierre rolled his eyes.

"We might be looking for mischief," said Ilona, "but not here. We thought of trying Russia for a while, just to see how the revolution is progressing."

She gave a sweetly demonic smile.

"And if that's no fun, there is China… India…" said Pierre. "I don't much care where we go, as long as there's mindless amusement to be had, and a rich supply of human blood."

"So we found you to say *auf Wiedersehen*, Father," said Ilona. "It's only for a year or so, I expect. But if you can't find us – assuming you might ever *wish* to find us – you'll know why."

Karl took his daughter's arm and drew her aside. He wasn't particularly shocked by her news, but he was surprised – considering how much trouble Pierre and Ilona had caused in their time – to realise he would miss them.

"Ilona?" he said gently. "All I can say is that I wish you a pleasant journey and a swift return."

"Swift return? I thought you'd be glad to have us out of your hair, dear Karl."

"Only because…"

"We cause you so much grief and disruption?"

"Well, I can't deny that, but I think we've all grown up since Violette came among us. We've no need to fight among ourselves any more."

"True. And I do love you, Father," she murmured. "But all of this new-found wisdom and solidarity among vampires will not stop me having fun. What? Why are you frowning at me?"

"I'm not, but…" Karl glanced at Pierre, who was gazing into the air and waiting with an exaggerated show of patience. "Am I imagining this, or are the two of you going as a *couple*?"

Ilona laughed. "Oh, did I forget to tell you? The wedding invitation is in the post! Will you give me away, Father?"

"Very amusing. You and Pierre don't even like each other."

"Nonsense." She gave an insouciant lift of her eyebrows. "I can bear him for… minutes at a time. Longer, if he's busy pleasing me. He's handsome enough, and surprisingly attentive…"

"Spare me the details," Karl interrupted drily. He knew that Ilona and Pierre were casual lovers, but preferred to put the thought out of his mind.

"Father, he's lonely. So am I, a little. We'll be perfectly happy together, at least until I can't stand him a moment longer. Then I'll take an axe to his neck and find some luscious young Russian Cossack to amuse me instead."

With a teasing grin, she kissed him and went back to Pierre. Karl, finding nothing else to say, only shook his head. His heart gave a slight tug as his wilful daughter began to walk away with the hopeless rogue, Pierre, of all people.

"What shall it be?" Pierre said. "Taxi cab, horse and carriage, train? I'm not travelling through the Crystal Ring." He turned and called back over his shoulder, "*Au revoir*, Karl. Stay out of the other-realm. It's like hell tonight."

Karl ignored the warning.

Later, replete with blood, he drifted through the Crystal Ring above Prague. He felt the cold flow of ether over his flesh, saw his own hands outstretched like claws against the stormy purple cloudscape. The other-realm distorted his human form into a slender amorphous shape, a blend of winged demon and jet-black serpent. After a hundred years and more he should be used to it, but the change still amazed him.

He hoped Ilona would be happy, with or without Pierre.

He undulated through Raqia more as if swimming than flying. He longed to float into a trance – the closest vampires came to sleep – but the Ring was too stormy. Massive thunderheads surrounded him. The void between them was an ocean of thick blue fog cloaking the Earth. He rose and dropped on rough air currents. No hope of rest tonight. Better to make for home before the storm carried him away.

Even his extra-sensitive sight could not penetrate the murk. All that helped him to navigate was the Earth's magnetic field: faint ribbons of light that mapped the Crystal Ring on to the contours of the real world. The seventh sense.

With fearful exhilaration, Karl turned headlong into the gale.

The Crystal Ring was the natural habitat of vampires, but that did not make it safe. Every time they came here, they ran the risk of staying too long, growing too cold and exhausted to escape.

According to Charlotte, Raqia was the massed subconscious of humankind, formed from their dreams, nightmares and myths. As the zeitgeist shifted, Raqia echoed the changes in its own surreal way. Clouds became fortresses, phantom armies marched across the vast sky, angels manifested only to go mad and vanish again. Disconsolate voices echoed from nowhere.

Looking up, Karl saw a clear space in the fog and a dozen columns of red and silver light shooting up from the Earth towards the unseen heights of the *Weisskalt*.

What did that mean?

Sometimes Raqia threw out mirages of pure, enigmatic beauty. Everyone had theories, but no one really *knew*. Was it God, or the

Devil, or mankind itself playing unconscious games?

Full of wonder, mystery and danger, the Crystal Ring was as addictive as blood itself.

All he wanted now was to be at home with Charlotte.

Although he tried not to distress his victims, he had tormented Charlotte beyond reason, thanks to the simple misfortune of falling in love. Eventually, against all his instincts, he'd transformed Charlotte rather than lose her. Karl thanked all the powers of the universe that she'd survived, but he had vowed never to transform anyone, ever again. The initiation held too much danger and pain. Last year he'd witnessed a rash attempt by a power-hungry madman to turn a large number of humans into his own vampire army. The experiment had ended in horrific failure. The Crystal Ring itself would not allow too many vampires to exist.

And that is no bad thing, Karl thought. *We are predators, after all. The Earth needs no more of us, especially if something worse is brewing in the human world. Up here, ever since Violette opened our eyes to the dangers, I sense mankind sleepwalking from one devastating war to the next and there is not a damned thing we can do to stop them. A cynic might conclude that the sole purpose of vampires is to feed on the remains of humanity, like vultures on carrion.*

He fought to stay on course as the storm closed in. Karl could see nothing but wild indigo cloud. When he looked up, though, he saw a new apparition: an ebony mass, flickering with blood-red lightning... A shape that coalesced out of nothing.

As he watched, it dived straight towards him – a coal-black comet the size of a house.

Karl swerved, thrown sideways by turbulence. Hot damp air filled his lungs. Powerful instinct told him that the thing was sentient, and intent on killing him.

With an instant survival reflex, he arced out of its path. His hands formed claws, his fangs unsheathed. He was ready to fight – but the entity went roaring straight past, vanishing into the muddy lower layers of the atmosphere.

Karl took a few moments to recover from the shock. An illusion, no doubt, but the encounter left him with a clear impression of a gigantic death-like figure in a hooded robe, with a huge skull head and a staff like a lightning bolt.

Only an energy-projection, someone's dream. Not really there. Whatever it was, it left turmoil in its wake. Raqia began to roil violently, the storm whipping up into the worst tempest he'd ever encountered. He lost his sense of direction. Couldn't see, let alone navigate.

Enough of this mad, nightmarish troposphere. All he wanted was the firelight of his own parlour and Charlotte's arms around him... *Focus on her,* he told himself, closing his eyes. Focus on Charlotte, a tiny golden beacon so far away...

If only he could find his way back to Earth.

The knife lay in the centre of a small table, gleaming against the dark walnut surface. Stefan and Charlotte sat on either side, studying the weapon. The blade fitted into an ivory haft that appeared hand-carved. The ivory was smooth, with a repeated motif along its length and a ruby cabochon set into the pommel.

Charlotte thought it appeared more of a ceremonial item than one made to cause real harm. Not an army-issue knife that an old soldier might carry, but an unearthly thing with its own glow. Now and then it would tremble, as if someone had knocked the table.

The parlour was lit by a single stained-glass lamp. The home she and Karl shared, a black timber chalet poised on a hill, stood high and remote amid pine forests, surrounded by a wild and lovely green landscape. The Alps floated like monumental clouds, draped with snow. All around were farms and tiny villages where she and Karl tried never to feed. They had no wish to harm their neighbours, but... once or twice, thirst had got the better of them, and that was all it took to start rumours.

Charlotte wrapped her arms around her waist, trying to suppress shivers. She didn't want Stefan to see her in pain or ill. The wound should have healed by now. Still she felt tendrils of cold poison spreading through her veins.

Yet nothing poisons vampires, she thought. *At least, nothing we've discovered... yet.*

Niklas sat on a sofa a few feet away, gazing at the knife without blinking. She wondered if he had any thoughts at all, and simply couldn't express them.

"Have you seen an artefact like this before?" she asked Stefan.

"Many knives, but never one like this," he replied.

"And you are not kicking the table?"

Stefan half-smiled. "I haven't moved."

The knife spun in a slow quarter-turn on the polished wood.

"This is like a seance," he added. "We should put the letters of the alphabet around it, and see if it spells out our doom."

"I assume you're joking," said Charlotte with a grimace. "That's a perfectly terrible idea."

"You should know by now that I'm full of terrible ideas."

When the dagger came to rest, she went to pick it up. As she touched the handle, cold shock numbed her whole arm. The pain in her stomach flared as if claws were gripping her insides.

"Charlotte?" Stefan came to her side and knelt by her, holding both her hands. "Come away and rest." He stroked her cheek. "You look awful. When I held the dagger, I've never felt a force so... repellent. I shouldn't have brought it here. Don't touch it."

"Obviously I *can't* touch it." She pressed against the chair back to steady herself. "But we need to know what it is. And the man who had it, who was he?"

"I don't know, but we'll find out. Will you please rest a while? Until you're restored to health, nothing else matters. Where the devil is Karl?"

His eyes were tender with worry, but she didn't want to be nursed.

"Stefan, dearest, I'm all right," she replied. "The trouble is that resting doesn't help us as it helps humans. It's always blood we need."

"True," he said softly. "You should feed."

"I'm not hungry. Not for blood, at least. I need knowledge."

She stood up, restless, scratching at her arms as if ants were swarming over her. She went on, "No poison harms us. None that we've ever found, at least."

"We?"

"I mean Karl and me. He conducted research in my father's laboratory, when my father wasn't looking." She smiled. Even the effort of smiling made her head spin. "We found nothing except the extreme cold of liquid nitrogen… or of the *Weisskalt*. But this feels different. Weapons are inanimate. They don't shine or move or radiate a force that disables vampires. Someone with too much knowledge has manufactured this, but who, and why?"

Stefan blinked at her, shaking his head. "I've no idea, but…"

"We have a magnifying glass, microscope, other testing equipment set up in the library. If I wrap it in cloth and carry it on a tray, I can take a proper look."

"Yes," Stefan said, frowning, "but surely that can wait? Until you recover, it's secondary."

"Not to a scientist," she retorted. She paced, full of manic energy, talking too fast. "My father was a physicist. He taught me everything he knew. I helped push his experiments further than he would have gone without me. I was a scientist in life; why should that stop, because I became a vampire? The researcher in me is still there."

"A fair point." Stefan caught her arms to stop her pacing. "And she'll still be there once you've fed."

"I'm not hungry," she repeated. "I don't need a victim."

"I'm worried about that wound. Blood will help you heal."

"Will it? I need something, but not…"

Stefan looked more worried than ever, but Charlotte could barely focus on him through the white storm of her vision. She needed to take urgent action, but how?

"Yes, blood," he whispered. "I'll help you to the nearest farm. It will take only minutes."

"No, I need the Crystal Ring." Surely the other-realm would soothe her restlessness.

"We've already tried that."

His voice faded as she tried to step into the hidden dimension. It was like stumbling down a non-existent step. A pale snowstorm whirled around her. Instead of taking flight, she found herself on the floor. There she lay like a melting snow-figure, with no strength to move.

"Charlotte." Stefan was gathering her in his arms, Niklas helping.

"I'm all right," she murmured, aware she was slurring.

"Clearly you aren't. Stop arguing with me!"

Charlotte let Stefan help her upstairs into the large bedroom. Although vampires did not sleep in the conventional sense, beds had other uses. He wrapped a blanket around her, propped her on pillows, and offered her his wrist.

"I don't want it."

Stefan paused, let his hand fall. "It's human blood you need."

"I can hardly move, let alone hunt. What's happening to me? Am I dying?"

Stefan's blue eyes penetrated her. "No talk of dying. Charlotte, I don't know how to help you, but I love you like a sister, with all my heart and soul. I will not allow you to die."

He straightened up, graceful in the candlelight, and stepped away from the bedside. "You'll be all right alone for a while?"

"Of course. Where are you going?"

"To find Karl. Rest. Niklas and I will return as swiftly as we can."

Some called the house ugly. Even his niece Amy had barely hidden her dismay when she first arrived. In her sweet, shy way, she'd ventured that the rooms were awfully big and cold, the ceilings too high. The pure white marble walls put her in mind of a tomb, she said.

Godric Reiniger indulged her reaction. Bergwerkstatt, which he'd designed himself in the modern geometric style, was not to everyone's taste, but it suited him perfectly. A house for the future, containing a workshop, film studio, a screening room big enough to be called a cinema, everything he needed.

His headquarters.

There were plenty of bedrooms to house his film crew – both his inner circle, and his general employees – and big reception rooms where he'd allowed Gudrun to add homely Swiss touches. Although they clashed with the stark minimal decor, he let them stay because they made him nostalgic.

Now he walked slowly through the rooms touching each object with a fingertip as if to claim all it represented. Local embroidery, decorative pails and other items carved of wood, even a cuckoo clock; Godric liked these reminders of tradition around him. Past met future here.

In his office there was nothing cosy. The windows were tall narrow oblongs of blackness. He had no curtains, and as little furniture as possible: one desk, one large bookshelf, and four chairs with tall straight backs that recalled prison bars. They were as uncomfortable to sit on as they looked. Two electric chandeliers, like black metal cages, filled the room with light.

Godric prowled around his desk, an island of chaos in its pristine surroundings. He had so many projects in hand that he could barely keep them in order. Manic creative energy kept him from sleep. Sketches, photographs, scribbled ideas for film scripts, books of Swiss folklore and philosophy... he pushed them around with his left hand as if stirring soup. In his right he gripped a cigarette. No one else would make sense of the mess, but he knew where everything was and what it meant.

He glanced at the clock. Past midnight. A touch of concern nagged him: had Amy gone out for dinner with the others, and if so, had she come home?

He stubbed out the cigarette, went out into the grand hall and climbed the stairs. The house was quiet: his crew were either asleep, or out carousing. Insomnia gave him time alone to think, but he sometimes wished he could turn off the flood of ideas.

Branching out from local newsreels into feature films was ambitious, and meant he'd had to take on a throng of new people, not least actors and actresses. Enthusiastic amateurs. Although they shared his goals, he didn't know them well enough to trust them and his priority was to protect his niece. Just nineteen, she was highly impressionable.

Light shone under the door of Amy's bedroom. He could hear the murmur of Gudrun's voice and the scratchy sound of jazz music, which set his teeth on edge.

Gudrun, solid, dour and loyal, had been his father's housekeeper. After his parents' early deaths, she had brought him up in her no-nonsense way. She was more housekeeper than foster-mother to him – always had been – but he valued her as the archetypal mother-figure that all women should aspire to be.

His older sister, Amy's mother, was already married and living in England when Godric was orphaned at the age of ten.

He thought of himself as an only child.

Now in his forties, he relied on Gudrun more than he dared admit. She was the sturdy heart of his world, but not his intellectual equal. His niece, though – despite the irritating caprices of her youth and gender – was a bright spark in his life, a willing audience for his flights of inspiration.

"Amy?"

Godric knocked, but Gudrun answered and blocked the doorway.

"Why is her light still on? Is she ill?"

"No, sir." She'd always called him sir, even when he was a boy: an imperious, confused, bereaved boy. "A headache. She needs her sleep."

"Well, then, let her rest," said Godric, irritated. "Don't sit fussing over her all night. And make her turn off that damned gramophone!"

"Yes, sir. Isn't it time you retired to bed also?"

Her tone, like that of a school matron, always awoke the child in him. He obeyed.

He was in no hurry, however. On the way to his bedroom he entered the vast meeting chamber that dominated the upper storey: an impressive space that doubled as a film studio for interior scenes. Deserted, the large echoey space felt haunted. He glanced at the framed pictures hung in an austere row along one wall: stills from his movies, drawings he'd made and photographs he'd taken of the mountains, of Alpine farmers and milkmaids, of folk musicians and revellers dressed up in costume for Christmas, *Fasnacht* and other festivals.

At the far end of the chamber, he unlocked a steel cabinet in an alcove. Inside were thirty numbered pigeonholes, twenty-nine of them containing a dagger resting on a velvet pad. The thirtieth, he carried with him at all times.

His father had left him money, but this collection was the most intriguing part of his inheritance. The spoils of a long-ago archaeological dig near the edge of the Sahara.

Godric intended to take out each *sikin* in turn, to polish it with a soft cloth and replace it in its padded pigeonhole. Before he could begin, he felt the air frosting the back of his neck, every hair standing up as if drawn by static electricity. He *felt* the presence before he turned and saw it.

A column of shadow with glaring eyes. *What the hell...*

37

What... Incoherent thoughts slithered through his mind, not even thoughts but currents of alarm.

A woman. She wore plain modern clothes of a muddy colour, brown or olive, with a close-fitting hat, a single long strand of beads. Her skin was dark and her eyes were exotic, beautiful and terrifying, as if green fire glowed behind the brown irises.

Godric saw at once what she was. *Strigoi*. A vampire.

He used the Romanian term because there was no way to consider a vampire except as a foreign aberration: the undesirable alien.

"These *sakakin* are mine," she said. Her voice was low, accented, full of menace.

"How the hell did you get in here?" he said through bone-dry lips. "Who are you?"

"The rightful owner of those knives. I want them back."

For a few breathless seconds, Godric's head whirled with confusion. Although he knew the *strigoi* were real, he hadn't seen one for years, still less spoken to one. *She is going to kill me, tear out my throat.*

Quick courage came to his defence.

He turned, seized his personal *sikin* from its sheath in his pocket and slammed the cabinet shut behind him. He raised the dagger and pointed the tip at her breastbone.

"Is this what you want, *strigoi*?" he said. "Take it if you can."

Her eyes widened. Then she lunged.

He swept the blade at her. She leapt clear so fast he didn't see her move: now she was standing ten feet away, glaring like a snake. Her mouth was open, fangs shining. Neither had broken the other's flesh. He wielded the blade in a figure of eight, as if weaving a shield to protect himself. Trails of silver light hung in the air; he felt the force keeping her away.

She pointed at the cabinet behind him, but he held it shut with the pressure of his back. Nothing would make him give up his father's haul, his precious ritual weapons.

"Get out, demon," he hissed.

Her face twisted with fury and she lunged again. With a cheetah's speed her hands were on his shoulders, her mouth near his neck. Her grip paralysed him. He waved his knife hand feebly, could not get the blade to connect with her flesh. Her fingernails dug in like claws. She paused, uttered a noise of revulsion in her throat, and pushed him away – thrust him back so hard that his shoulders hit the cabinet, making it shudder.

Again she stood feet from him, thwarted and furious. Her face was the most terrifying thing he'd ever seen, a carnival mask.

"What are you?" He was breathing hard through his teeth. She was plainly repelled by the knife so he brandished it all the more, noticing how its light reflected silver from her eyes. She glared back, but made no attempt to get through his defence. "Who are you?"

No answer.

Instead she vanished. The air crackled. Like breath on a winter morning, she was gone.

Godric became aware he was wheezing from pure fear. He regained control of his breathing, checked every shadow to make sure the chamber was empty. There was no one, nothing there.

He relocked the cabinet, then stumbled in shock to his bedroom and bolted the door – as if that could keep her out. The air stayed motionless, lukewarm… ordinary. He stood guard for a long time before he dared let himself believe she was not coming back.

Godric's bedroom was another square, masculine room furnished only with necessities: bed, dressing table and a wardrobe of black wood. He took off his waistcoat, rolled up his shirt-sleeves, sat on the edge of the bed.

A thousand questions crowded his brain but he put them all aside. The apparition had been some kind of warning, a call to battle. No time for fear. He needed power – more than ever, if the *strigoi* planned to come back.

He drew out his knife and, biting a handkerchief between his teeth, set the blade to the soft flesh just above his elbow. He began to cut a small rune: three vertical lines. The symbol represented the three-fingered salute of the Eternal Alliance: the historic oath that had founded Switzerland.

His hand shook, and the pain made him sweat. A familiar dizziness and tingling surged through him, filling his vision with white stars. Before he'd finished the first line, blood streamed out and he fumbled to press his handkerchief on the wound, cursing. He'd cut too deep again.

Reiniger sank back on to the pillows, gasping. The energy rush was incredible, like a drug.

There were blood drops spattered on the white bedcover and the floor. He was usually so careful not to make a mess. Running his thumb down the inside of his upper arm he felt the scars of older runes, and echoes of the addictive power they'd given him.

With a trembling hand he pressed the blade to his skin and began the next cut.

CHAPTER THREE

LAMIA

Karl forced his way through the tornado that blew up in the skull-creature's wake. He was somewhere over Switzerland at last, but the ether was so wild he hardly knew which way was up or down. He was dangerously tired, and knew he must drop to Earth and feed, even if it took him the rest of the night to get home.

Then he saw a faint gold coil of energy below: the trace of a vampire he knew.

Two traces, in fact, nearly identical, wading up towards him through the foggy darkness of Raqia's lower layers.

They were struggling, he realised. Karl swooped down to intercept them. Close to the ground, the world – seen through the distorting lens of the Ring – was a forest of dark, deformed shapes. Karl could not even see the land surface, but had to make a guess as he stepped into reality. The world snapped into three dimensions – timbered houses, lamplit windows – but he was in mid-air, falling, seeing not solid earth but an ink-black lake rushing up to receive him. He braced to hit the water...

Someone seized him. Karl perceived a figure diving through the Crystal Ring, snatching him in mid-air and making an imperfect loop that landed them both in the shallows at the lake's edge. The shock of hard rocks and the water's chill rendered Karl helpless. Hands caught his jacket, then took a firm grip on his arms and dragged him on to the paved bank.

He looked up to find two angelic male faces staring down at him, framed by spun-gold hair.

"Karl?" said Stefan. "I hope I haven't interrupted a midnight swim, but what the hell are you doing?"

"Trying to reach you," Karl answered. "That was less than graceful, but the Crystal Ring…"

"Is in a hellish mood tonight," Stefan finished. He looked uncharacteristically grim, almost panicky. "I know, I've been hunting you for over an hour. You must come home *now*."

Charlotte stood before a full-length mirror, pulling apart the torn fabric of her dress to examine the wound. The bedroom lay in near-darkness, but moonlight revealed every detail to her sensitive eyes. The purple slash near her hipbone wasn't healing. She could separate the edges and see her unnatural vampire flesh inside, glistening crimson. The wound stung, as if drenched in vinegar. A weak, chilly feeling lingered. She felt strange but calm, as though in a lucid dream.

The attack would have killed a mortal, but vampires were more resilient. The knowledge gave her a thrill of awe, mixed with unease. "We are easy to hurt, very difficult to kill," Karl had once told her. What kind of weapon could inflict such lasting harm? Nothing made by humans, surely.

She was still a fledgling in vampire terms. Five years ago, while her lively sisters revelled in a social whirl of parties and debutante balls, she'd resigned herself to a future in her father's physics laboratory. Thanks to crippling shyness and her reclusive nature, she'd had little to look forward to except work, and a reluctant marriage to their research assistant, Henry…

And then she had met Karl.

Her dark angel Karl, who was beyond beautiful, with his soft dark hair and serene eyes… From the first moment they met, he held her fascinated. At first she was terrified, then hopelessly enthralled. He had been her downfall. He still was.

Staying together had proved costly. People had died: some of her own loved ones, and some of his. *She* had died – more than once, in different ways. She wasn't a predator at heart, and yet she found being a vampire effortless. That couldn't be right, she thought. Living on human blood should require a greater struggle, if only with her conscience.

She and Karl tried to move lightly through the world, causing as little harm as possible: but the truth was, they were still vampires.

Small wonder that *someone* might want to destroy them.

But it was a chance encounter, she thought. *Perhaps the knife wasn't made to hurt vampires at all. A coincidence… but if that's the case, what* is *it for?*

"Perhaps I'm dreaming," she said out loud.

Her own voice sounded like a distant echo.

Looking at her reflection, she thought, *At least the myths are untrue; we don't need to avoid mirrors or sunlight or religious symbols.* To approach a looking-glass and see only thin air – well, that would send anyone insane. But how odd… what she'd thought was a mirror was actually a shimmering white veil in the air. She barely recognised the pale creature on the other side as herself.

The moon-white nymph with rippling bronze hair and a mesmeric gaze was separate: a spectre, a lamia floating in the mist…

"Who are you?" she said softly. "If I saw you coming towards me, would I fall into your arms, or run for my life?"

She touched the surface… and the pale creature on the other side copied her action, reaching up so they joined fingertips. When she dropped her hand, the ghost did the same, in blank mimicry, like Niklas.

She stared and the *doppelgänger* stared back, like an accusing ghost that had floated out of its grave.

Then she understood.

She was human again – had been all along. Her twin self in the mirror was the vampire. The knife had split her in two.

Her breathing quickened. Her vision blurred, making the lamia appear covered in white gossamer flowers. Beautiful, deadly. And Charlotte knew in utter terror that she must keep the lamia inside the mirror-veil, contain her so that she could no longer prey on innocent humans… but how?

She no longer had any clear thoughts. She simply *knew* that the two halves of her had come adrift. But she had no idea how to be human again… the knowledge filled her with dumb horror, worse than that of becoming a vampire.

I can't go back. She tried to form words but no sound came out. *Was I ever you, or have I dreamed it all? I cannot go back! Stop tormenting me! What must I do to destroy you?*

The pale mist-demon only stared back, empty-eyed, devoid of compassion.

Karl appeared in the shadows behind her, making her start.

You're back, she tried to say.

He spoke, but she could barely hear him through the rushing sound in her ears. She thought he asked, "What are you doing?"

"Hallucinating," she said, unsure if she'd spoken out loud. "She—" Charlotte pointed at the apparition behind the watery veil, who pointed back. "She is doing this. She's pretending to be me. Or I thought I was her. This isn't real, but I can't make it stop. Give me a pen and paper. If I write this down…"

She couldn't see his face, only a dark figure. A crisp male voice said, "*Gnädige Frau, entschuldigen Sie, bitte…*"

Not Karl.

She stared straight ahead, confused yet deadly calm. She found her voice and answered in the same language, "Who is that?"

A long pause. She caught a scent of human sweat. Something was very wrong, but she was paralysed by the nightmare and could not, dared not move.

"Police, madam," said the gruff voice. "Is your husband not at home?"

"He is not," said Charlotte.

"Or your father, brother, any male friends?"

What a strange thing to ask.

She heard his laboured breath, a mixture of exertion and angry determination. Her nose twitched with distaste at his human stink of sweat and smoke and the earthy scent of the outdoors on his clothes. There was no way for him to have reached the chalet except by a steep climb on foot. His voice, smell and general aura recalled the drunk who'd attacked her… but this was not the same man. He carried himself with authority. He was taller, red-haired and sober.

"No one but me," she answered. The spectre's lips moved with hers. "What do you want?"

"If I might have a word… We can go downstairs."

"I can't," she said.

"Madam?"

"I can't leave the mirror in case my ghost escapes."

Silence. He cleared his throat again, and this time his voice was harder.

"Who are you? How long have you been living here?"

"What is that to you?"

"I know this area. This chalet is long-deserted – or is it? The owner can't be traced. And yet lights are seen in the windows. A peasant woman comes up to clean the place, but won't speak a word about the inhabitants. Music is heard. On occasion, people succumb to mysterious illnesses. When they recover, they speak of apparitions in the forest, a pale beautiful woman or a man... like the *Weisse Frauen*, the elven spirits of the Alps?"

"What has this to do with me?"

"That's what I'm here to find out."

"At night, on your own?"

More throat-clearing. "The police are never off-duty, madam. Ever vigilant."

"You are no policeman," she said. "Who are you? Do you know the brute who stabbed me? How did you find me?"

That made him pause. Then he said in a low voice. "All I want is for you to answer my questions and give me back the damned knife."

She heard his words with the weird feeling that her mind was cut in two; one half clear and rational, the other stranded in a dream.

"If you want to question me, come closer. I can't leave the mirror. Come."

She watched his reflection approaching until he stood just behind her *doppelgänger's* shoulder. Handsome freckled face, serious expression. He, too, had the look of a soldier: an officer. Perhaps he really was a policeman, or used to be.

"My comrade was a fool to attack you," he said. "But the question is, how did you survive, sweetheart?"

His pale blue eyes widened – mesmerised by the lovely mad-woman. She suspected that he was scared: bright, but out of his depth, pumped up with false courage. If his comrade had assaulted her and stabbed her in the gut, what might this man be capable of?

"Who are you?" she asked. "And the knife, what is it?"

He shook his head. "You don't need to know."

"If she comes out of the mirror, you'll die," said Charlotte, pointing at the lamia.

He hesitated, wetting his lips. He clearly thought she was insane.

"That's your reflection, you mad witch," he hissed. "There's something in this house that doesn't belong to you. That's all I'm here for."

"Who are you? I'm dreaming but I can't wake up. Unless you can help me wake up, you'd better go."

"Not without that knife. Where is it?"

"Until recently, buried in my stomach. Do you want it back so your friend can stab the next unfortunate being who crosses his path when he can't hold his drink?"

"Bruno made a mistake," he said. "He's a fool. But if you hadn't bitten him—"

"If *he* had walked away when I asked him to," she retorted. Both their voices sounded far away and fuzzy. Inside the rippling surface, the lamia's eyes were cold and dangerous, like those of a snake preparing to strike.

"Just give me the damned knife, *strigoi*!"

He grabbed her shoulders. The moment his clammy hands touched her, she reacted as if burned. She spun to face him, her mind suddenly focused. The rough fabric of his jacket scratched her bare arms. His touch was an assault.

"Take it, if you can," she whispered.

She lunged, mouth open, forgetting she was supposed to be human again. The man reacted by reflex, thrusting her away with a curse. She stumbled and fell backwards into the veil.

The mirror shattered under her. A hundred glass shards pierced her body as it crashed flat to the floor. The pain was excruciating. Set free, the lamia came flowing out. Charlotte watched in blank amazement as her other-self seized the man with pallid arms, pulled him to her, pushed her face inside his collar and nipped the salty flesh until blood poured over her tongue…

He cried out. He struggled. Damn him, he was strong, and she was still weak from her injury. Their battle took them across the bedroom to the balcony doors before he finally went limp in her hands. Then, in mindless fury, she ran him straight through the closed glass doors and pitched him over the balcony rail.

In a split second he was gone, falling from sight into the darkness of the steep tree-covered drop below.

His blood was foul, tainted. The dual being, Charlotte-and-lamia, bent over the balcony and regurgitated the blood she'd swallowed. It streamed easily out of her, like water from an upended vase.

Then the lamia floated back inside the room through the ragged hole of broken wood and glass. When Charlotte moved, the creature moved with her. They were one again.

"Help me," she whispered.

"Charlotte?"

She found herself sitting on the bed, curled against the headboard with her hands around her knees, staring at the pine-panelled wall opposite. She wasn't sure what she was doing there... writing, that was it. Filling pages with all that she'd seen.

Karl was back at last.

She looked hard to make sure it was really him. The blanket Stefan had left over her was on the floor. She seemed to have thrown off her clothes and replaced them with a silky robe that hurt viciously everywhere it touched her skin. Her dress was on the floor, covered in blood spots.

Karl rushed to her, sat on the bed beside her and took her hands.

"Dear God," he said, "Charlotte, beloved, what happened?"

"Nothing," she said calmly. Stefan appeared in the doorway, followed by Niklas: another reflection.

Seeing her, Stefan's mouth opened in shock. "Charlotte, gods, what have you done? I knew I shouldn't have left you alone!"

"Don't be ridiculous," she said, not comprehending why they were upset. "I'm perfectly well, just... sore. I don't know why. It's nothing."

Karl turned his head and snapped, "Stefan, a moment, please."

Charlotte realised he was dismissing his friend because she was partly undressed. She'd pushed the robe off her shoulders because it hurt so much. Despite everything, Karl's puritan streak made her smile.

"What?" Stefan said, grinning back at her. "It's nothing I haven't seen before. Oh, don't glare at me like that, Karl. I meant half-clothed women in general, not Charlotte in particular."

"Let them stay," she said, adjusting the fabric to cover herself. "Stefan and Niklas are more like… well, sisters to me than anything."

"*Sisters?*" Stefan retorted.

"I meant it as a compliment."

"I know," he said with a wink.

He sat on a low couch at the end of the bed, facing away from her, with Niklas beside him. He put an affectionate arm around his brother's shoulders, whispering into his ear. He hadn't left Niklas behind to watch over Charlotte while he sought Karl, for the simple reason that Niklas was of no more use than a doll. Without Stefan's care, he was as vulnerable as a human child.

Karl looked as serious as she'd ever seen him. She hastened to reassure him.

"Nothing happened," she repeated. "Karl, I'm sure Stefan told you that a drunk accosted me in the street with a knife. Then I had some awful hallucinations. That's all. I'm well again now."

"Hallucinations?" He drew her robe off her shoulder and began to pluck at her skin, his fingernails as delicate as tweezers. She became aware that he was taking splinters of glass out of her flesh. Strange.

She looked down, turning her head to see mirror shards piercing the skin of her shoulder-blades, the backs of her arms and thighs: dozens of tiny crimson cuts leaking blood. No wonder the robe hurt so much. Wherever it touched, it was pushing the glass deeper into her flesh.

"Yes, from the dagger," she said. "Wait, was the dagger real? It's a blur. I can't remember where reality stopped and the illusions started. I decided to write everything down, in case we found a clue…"

She looked down at the notepad lying beside her.

Blank.

Stefan said, "Ah, Charlotte…" and then nothing for half an hour as Karl took every sliver of glass out of her skin. At last it was done, and she was able to sit up and tie her robe properly. She shook her hair free, saw tiny spots of blood leaking through the ivory silk.

"Well, this is ruined," she said softly. "And so is that dress. How did I get all this glass in me?"

"We hoped you would tell us," Karl said gravely.

Charlotte went still. A cool draft blew on to her. While she contemplated how to describe her hallucinations – the lamia in the rippling veil, and the supposed policeman finding her – she sensed another presence in the house: the unmistakable warmth of a mortal. "Oh, no. You brought prey here for me? There's no need…"

"It's all right," Karl said gently. "Tell us what happened."

"I remember trying to enter the Crystal Ring, and collapsing, and Stefan putting me on the bed. Then I imagined I got up and looked in the mirror, only I was human again and my reflection was… the blood-drinking demon part of me. I was convinced I'd split in two. So disturbing. Then a man came into the house, pretending to be a policeman and demanding the knife back." She laughed uneasily. "Could anything be more ridiculous? We fought. I fell into the mirror, and the vampire escaped and fed on the man – or she tried to feed, but the blood was foul, so she threw him…"

"Charlotte." Stefan beckoned. She rose from the bed, unsteady on her feet, and saw the full-height mirror lying flat on the carpet, glass everywhere.

A long spattered trail of blood led to the balcony doors, which hung smashed on the frame as if a bull had charged through them. More glass glittered on the balcony. A breeze blew through the gap. Smears of blood marked the balcony rail.

"Oh, ye gods," Charlotte said softly. "I didn't split in half, did I? The lamia was me all the time. And that man was really here."

She let Karl and Stefan help her downstairs to the parlour, where she sat frozen on the edge of a sofa beside Niklas while the others lit a fire and more lamps.

Presently she noticed a young woman standing in the doorway that led to the entrance hall and kitchen. About twenty-five, with an intelligent face, dark neat hair and a plain red dress, she looked like a schoolteacher.

Karl sat next to Charlotte and took her hands firmly between his.

"Why have you brought her here?" she asked, looking from him to Stefan.

"There's no need to whisper," Stefan said with a grin that

managed to convey apology, sympathy and a sense of the absurd. "Leni is deaf. She and Niklas would make a perfect couple, don't you think? He never speaks and she can't hear! Ideal."

"Can you not be serious about anything?" she said. "I expected you to bring Karl home, but not a human! Why?"

Stefan kissed the top of her head. "Because you are only going to recover with good pure blood."

"Karl, we agreed not to bring victims into our home."

"I know," said Karl. "And we've singularly failed to keep the agreement, haven't we? You and I have both broken the rule for different reasons. I knew you wouldn't want us to capture some innocent milkmaid, so..."

"Leni is a friend of mine," said Stefan. "She knows what we are, she will give her blood willingly."

"Oh, I see." Charlotte closed her eyes for a moment. "One of your harem."

"I'm offended." Stefan sat down, pushing in between her and Niklas. "You should know me by now. Cultivating a group of human friends who trust us and give blood freely – isn't that gentler than seizing strangers off the street? Or throwing mystery men off balconies, come to that?"

"Stefan," Karl said coolly, giving him a look over Charlotte's head. She *felt* the look pass between them.

"So I didn't imagine it," she murmured. "That man tracked me down because the dagger is valuable to him and he wants it back. He had inhuman strength. So did his drunken friend, whom he called Bruno. They both called me *strigoi* – why use that term? It's a Romanian word, not Swiss. And I could smell the poison of the knife in his blood – I couldn't drink it. Oh, and he spoke of local rumours, as if he knows the area. Apparently this is a deserted chalet with ghosts! And, unless I'm still dreaming, I've just killed him and cast his body into the forest."

"Apparently so," said Stefan. "I'll admit, it's out of character for you, Charlotte."

"Not much out of character," she murmured. "It wouldn't be the first time I've lost control."

Karl held her closer. His affection almost made her weep. That she could behave so destructively, and yet he understood and didn't blame her… But they were both vampires: he'd brought her into this, and had no moral high ground from which to judge her.

"All because of this mysterious knife? Can I see it?" Karl asked.

"I hid it in the kitchen," said Stefan. "Wait there."

Stefan came back with the weapon resting across his palms on a folded towel.

"Don't touch it," he said. "Damned thing has a life of its own. I believe it's only dangerous if the blade pierces the skin."

"I'd rather not have been the test subject," said Charlotte. "I went completely mad for an hour or two."

Stefan smiled. "Happens to the best of us. Come on, Charlotte, let Leni help you."

She shook her head vehemently. "No. Take her away. I tried to feed on that stupid brute who was here! The evidence is upstairs, a broken door and a ruined carpet. This is a nightmare. No sooner have I accepted what I am, this happens! There's always something we didn't expect."

"Yes," Karl said gently into her hair. "Always something else."

"Is this how Violette felt, when she thought Lilith possessed her?"

"I don't know. Perhaps."

"It's horrible, being out of control."

"I see that, beloved. But still, let the girl help you."

"It's all right, sweet friend," Stefan added, touching her shoulder. "Leni's blood is very soothing."

Charlotte gave in and let the young woman come to her.

The affection with which Leni knelt at her feet and offered up her wrist made Charlotte want to weep. She bit as gently as she could, and stroked the girl's hair as she fed. And Stefan was right. The rich luscious blood, freely offered, brought her back to her true self for the first time since the ice blade had pierced her.

Later, she and Karl stood on the lower balcony that led from the parlour, looking out at the peaks of the Eiger, the Jungfrau and the Munch floating against the pre-dawn sky. Snow vapour streamed down the slopes and she heard glaciers melting, flood water gushing into clear creeks as spring took hold. She breathed the chilly air, the fragrance of pine resin and meltwater.

Soon the cattle would be driven up to the high pastures to graze, the musical rhythm of cowbells calling in summer. Every change of season was marked by a festival of some kind and she liked that. Rural traditions were as reassuring as sunrise, even though she and Karl were forever outside the human world. Often it was pleasant standing apart, watching mortal activities with the detached interest of a god. At other times, she wanted to plunge among them, lose herself in the whirl of their heat and energy.

Inside, Stefan was playing jazz music on their gramophone and dancing with Leni, showing Niklas the steps then passing her to his mute brother for another dance. Leni seemed to be having the time of her life. She couldn't hear the music, but Charlotte realised she must feel the vibration.

"Dear heart, I'm so sorry," said Karl.

She put her other arm around his waist, closed her eyes in pleasure as his lips touched her forehead. "What for? It wasn't your fault some drunken idiot stabbed me. I'm better now."

"I should have been there to stop him."

"You couldn't have known. But… I've killed before, Karl, but I hate it. After tonight, I never want to do so again. Never."

"I know." He kissed her again, conveying that he understood all too well. How many similar horrors had he faced in the past, she wondered, and how many could any vampire endure?

"All the same, I know I probably will," she murmured. "So I'd better have a *damned* good reason."

"No better reason than defending yourself," said Karl.

"We must find out about the blade before someone else is hurt in the same way. Or worse."

"Stefan will help us. He always does."

"Bless him. Although it feels strange to bless someone for seducing victims with so much enthusiasm."

Karl laughed. "But they love him and Niklas, so they don't go unrewarded."

"True." Charlotte took a breath of the fresh, resin-scented air. She felt normal again – at least physically – whatever "normal" meant. Looking down into the dark treetops, she said, "Somewhere down there is that man…"

"Who had no business coming here," Karl said. "I believe we know how he found you. Stefan stole a car to bring you home, so he had ample time to follow you, most likely on a motorbike. Stefan says he heard an engine in the distance, but thought nothing of it. Did you?"

"I don't remember. Perhaps it was luck on his part that he caught us up. And he said he knew the area."

"So it's unlikely he has supernatural abilities. He was simply quick-witted or fortunate enough to keep you in sight," said Karl. After a silence, he added, "I went down there, while you were with Leni. I found a trail of scent and blood where he fell, but no body."

"You mean he survived?"

"Apparently. He may not have been alone. There are tyre tracks on the path, not made by Stefan's car, and boot prints. Perhaps the drunken charmer Bruno was with him."

"If they escaped… I don't know whether to be glad or horrified."

"Let's hope you terrified them so thoroughly they'll never dare come near us again." The warmth of his lips felt wonderful on her cheekbone. "However, I won't rest until I've tracked these men down. They won't get away with attacking you."

"Oh, Karl." Her heart sank. "Don't place yourself in danger over this."

"They will be the ones in danger, not us," he said. "You know I can't resist a mystery."

Where her hand rested on Karl's sleeve, she noticed a greyish aura surrounding her fingers. It trailed behind when she moved, like an after-image. A small chill went through her.

It hasn't left me, she thought. *I have to overcome it, I must hold on to my true self. I survived Lilith's bite and I'm too strong to let this… this devilry have any power over me.*

She wondered if Karl could see the mist-image. He said nothing, and she daren't ask.

"And now what?" she said. "Glass can be mended, carpets cleaned. We've lived here in peace for a long time… but people are beginning to suspect us, Karl. Even though we hunt far afield, it takes only one or two lapses on our part and there are rumours of Alpine ghosts and demons and *Weisse Frauen*. Mysterious illnesses. And now, this."

Karl waited for her to continue, as if he knew what she was going to say.

"I have loved being here, but I can't stay any longer," Charlotte sighed. "You know that, don't you? It's time for us to leave."

CHAPTER FOUR

SORCERER

The Firebird spun in a blur of blood-red net, feathers and lace. Her body described a perfect bow of torment: head thrown back, arms stretched behind her like wings.

Emil watched her, entranced. He was so lost in rapture that he nearly missed his cue.

At the last second he jolted from his reverie, leapt over the wall and joined her in the enchanted garden. He became Prince Ivan, capturing the magical Firebird who struggled with ethereal anguish to escape him.

He sensed the enthralled audience, unseen in the darkness beyond the stage lights.

He lifted Violette high on his shoulder, twirled, set her down again to balance *en pointe* on one toe. Her other leg lifted in a high arabesque as she strained for freedom... then they whirled across the stage in perfect step, her costume bright scarlet against Prince Ivan's gold and crimson.

Emil Fiorani had joined the ballet only last year and become her male principal six months ago. Everything had happened so fast. The thrill of being chosen by the world's greatest ballerina would never wear off. On stage he was the complete professional – but in a corner of his mind, there was still a boy exclaiming in disbelief, *I'm dancing with Violette Lenoir!*

Tonight, in New York on the last night of their tour, he gave the story every last shred of passion. Prince Ivan stole a feather from the Firebird and released her, in exchange for her promise to help him later... Then he met the thirteen princesses, imprisoned in an enchanted forest by the sorcerer, King Kastchei.

A performer must act as well as they dance. Emil wondered why Ivan would fall in love with an insipid white-clad princess, Tsarevna, rather than with the Firebird herself... but it was a folk tale. Of course the prince must have a human princess to rescue. For him to fall in love with a bird, enchanted or not, would not make sense.

Still, he played Ivan as if he adored the Firebird. Couldn't do otherwise.

Exhilarating music masked the thud of ballet shoes on wooden boards. The audience little guessed the months of gruelling rehearsal that went to create an illusion of mythical creatures flowing weightlessly in a treasure-box of golden light.

Violette's shoes made hardly a whisper. She always smelled cool and delicate, like lilies, and never seemed to break a sweat as did ordinary mortals. This was part of her mystique, of course: one of the qualities that made her a true star, a goddess.

Now King Kastchei prowled the stage, hunched and evil in his skull mask. By this point, Emil was so caught up in the narrative that he forgot it was Mikhail in the costume. He felt a shiver of true fear. Kastchei's black cloak dragged like funeral cloth, and the bone staff in his hand wielded terrible powers...

Then the Firebird returned to help the Prince. She cast her spell over Kastchei's magical creatures, making them dance like puppets to exhaustion, sending all the princesses into enchanted sleep, finally guiding Prince Ivan to destroy Kastchei the Immortal and set free his captives. Violette leapt and whirled as if she would dance herself to death in a tumult of blood-red. All other characters onstage were secondary.

The story belonged to the Firebird.

Of all ballet heroines, she was the least sympathetic. She inspired awe, not affection. Aloof and magical, the Firebird was not of this world. That was her power.

Watching her, Emil went light-headed. The world changed. This was no drama but *real*, as if he'd entered another reality where the Firebird was a terrifying goddess of blood and fire. All the other dancers were ghosts, while Kastchei stalked mankind like the grim reaper...

So horrific was this vision that Emil nearly collapsed. The stage became a frozen tableau full of horror. His sight darkened with panic...

"Emil!"

Mikhail's whisper shocked him back to reality. He'd nearly missed his cue. The audience didn't notice – but Violette would, of course. He flung himself back into the performance, but his heart was pounding, sweat soaking his costume. Stravinsky's music carried him like a flood, through the grand wedding scene of Prince Ivan to Princess Tsarevna, to the end.

All too soon, they were taking their curtain calls to an ecstatic audience.

Relief and triumph eclipsed his anxiety attack. Violette made no comment about his lapse – it had never happened before – yet the unease lingered in the pit of his stomach. *It was nothing,* he told himself. *Last-night nerves, if there is such a thing. A warning against overconfidence.*

When they finally left the stage, Emil was laughing with the rest. He prayed that no one noticed how violently he was trembling.

At the stage door, Emil found himself mobbed. Dozens of women of all ages surrounded him with shining eyes, wide excited smiles – he'd experienced nothing like it before. There were always fans after a performance, clamouring for Violette. Now he realised in amazement that this crowd was waiting for *him*.

They called his name. He heard sighs, gasps, exclamations – every voice telling him how wonderful he was. He couldn't help but laugh with sheer pleasure.

They all looked so beautiful, young and old alike made radiant by happiness. He smiled as he signed their programmes and photographs – they had photographs of him, as if he were a film star! – and tolerated their warm hands touching his sleeves. Some even reached up to stroke his hair.

A member of the theatre staff appeared at his shoulder and chided the crowd, asking them please to stand back and wait their turn. Emil brushed him off.

"Ladies, ignore this old spoilsport," he called cheerfully. "I have ink in my pen for everyone."

Expressions of shocked delight among the older females made him aware of a *double entendre* he hadn't quite intended... but what the hell. He grinned with them, unable to suppress his amusement. A cloud of mingled perfume and soap, beginning to sour on overheated bodies, threatened to suffocate him. He kissed every hand presented to him, every powdered cheek...

A black limousine slid past. Inside, he glimpsed Madame Lenoir's face looking out at him with a cool, amused smile. Half the crowd turned and rushed after her, calling out her name. Surrounded by bouquets of lilies and white roses, she waved like royalty as she disappeared into the night.

Around him, the press of women sighed with bliss and love. Suddenly Emil began to lose his nerve, wondering what he'd started. Then someone pulled out several strands of his hair. The sting of pain made him jump. More than pain, the sheer brazenness of the action shook him. He stepped back, palms raised to say, *Enough*.

A handful of backstage staff came to his rescue, easing him from the crowd's grip and inside the building. Plaintive voices followed him, fading as the heavy wooden door shut. "*Emil, Emil, we love you!*"

Emil stood in the sudden quiet of a brick corridor. His assistant Thierry – a fortyish, dour Frenchman who took care of his mundane needs – said, "Sir, we're bringing your car around to a different entrance so we can deliver you to the hotel without any more fuss."

Emil barely heard him. The wave of adoration had been unprecedented, terrifying... but gods, so exhilarating! He could spare a few strands of his thick golden hair, after all. He threw back his head, took a deep breath.

"Actually, Thierry, I rather enjoyed the fuss."

"Oh, who would not, sir?" Thierry said drily. "But, perhaps a little discretion next time? You know Madame does not care for... too much display."

Emil only laughed. He ran the length of the corridor, leaping in a high *grande jeté* as he went.

* * *

"So, you have admirers," said Violette.

They stood together at the rail of an ocean liner, ready to set sail for Europe. Well-wishers and photographers lined the quay. Violette had ordered all her dancers, musicians and staff on deck to wave farewell under the Statue of Liberty's serene gaze. Their departure would be shown on newsreels in every cinema across the States within a few days.

"Admirers, madame?" he said, unsure whether she was teasing or scolding.

"Yes, I am addressing you, Emil. Your devotees impressed everyone by their sheer number." She looked stern, which was nothing unusual: she could make her face an ice-mask that struck terror into the bravest heart.

Emil reddened. "No, no, madame, they were there for you, for the whole company."

Violette's mouth relaxed. "Dear, I am teasing you. Did you think I was jealous?"

"Of course not. I'd never presume to receive a hundredth, a thousandth part of the admiration that you have earned… but still…"

"It's nice to be appreciated." She raised a gloved hand to wave as the ship slid away from its moorings. "Don't be modest, Emil. You've made a great impression."

"It was a shock, if I'm honest, to find so many people…"

"Swooning as if you were a matinee idol?"

He gripped the rail, braced for a reprimand. "Forgive me if I embarrassed you."

"How did you embarrass me?"

"Perhaps I should not have been so… available. But…"

"It's all right. You're young, and this is very new and exciting." She touched his coat sleeve. "Believe me, I know how heady it is to be worshipped, especially when it begins. First you reel in disbelief, then you become drunk, euphoric. It's natural to reciprocate, but I also know how very frightening such attention can be."

"Yes, that's it," he said softly. "I hate to admit it, but I was terrified. Don't tell anyone. One of them pulled hairs out of my head!"

Violette laughed. "Fear is healthy, Emil. It's when you take adoration too seriously that madness follows. A warning: don't become lost in it. Keep your distance. You know the saying, that familiarity breeds contempt? Do not let your fans too close, in *any* sense."

His eyes widened at her implication. This was more than advice: it was a command.

"I would not dream of it, madame."

"Good. Accept their awe with good grace, cast a few crumbs, then turn away. Think of yourself as a prince, not a dog to be petted. The very crowd that fawns over you one day may lose all reason and tear you apart the next."

He swallowed hard. "I understand."

They made a strange pair, he thought. He was the son of an Italian farmer from Tuscany, she – despite her French stage-name – an English gentlewoman. *Cast a few crumbs, then turn away*: that was exactly how she treated him. Oh, he knew he was good – she'd hardly have chosen him if he wasn't the best – but she treated him like a headstrong thoroughbred colt to be kept under tight control.

Sometimes, in private, he would rage against the power Violette held over him, but common sense always prevailed. She was the master, he the eager protégé. The price of dancing with her was to defer, always.

"By the way, what was wrong with you last night?" she asked coolly.

"Wrong?"

"You made some mistakes. Most unlike you. Do you think I didn't notice?"

His head dropped. *Damn. I hoped I'd got away with it! No such luck.*

"Two mistakes, madame. I'm aware of them and I have no excuse. Our last performance, the exhilaration, the audience…"

"Exactly so. You let the situation go to your head and lost concentration. We must never allow that to happen."

"Madame, I apologise," he said fiercely. "If ever I let you down or behave in an unprofessional manner – on stage or off – you will have my immediate resignation."

She went silent for a moment.

"Emil, I appreciate the sentiment, but there's no need." Her face softened and she looked candidly at him. She was still a goddess, without the Firebird's heavy make-up: lovelier, in fact, with her snowy skin, ebony hair, expressive violet-blue eyes. "The truth is, all criticism aside, I am proud of you. That is all the praise you will get from me, so savour it. Now bid farewell to your admirers. Smile and wave!"

Emil obeyed.

The liner was midway across the Atlantic when the storm hit.

Emil woke from a nightmare to find the vessel lurching and creaking around him. The storm seemed part of his dream and he was disorientated, struggling to comprehend where he was, what was happening. He heard the roar of wind and waves, muffled yet ferocious. He sat up with a gasp.

"Hey," said Mikhail across the gap between their beds. "If you're going to throw up, do it outside."

His queasiness was nothing compared to the intense foreboding he felt. He'd been dreaming that Violette was in danger.

"No," said Emil. He rolled out of bed and pulled on a shirt and trousers, staggering as the ship rolled. "I have to find her."

"What's the matter with you? It's just a bloody storm. If we sink, we sink."

Mikhail's bravado wasn't feigned – or if it was, Emil had never seen any cracks in his facade.

"Sink?" said Emil. More than fifteen years after the tragedy, no one boarded a liner without thoughts of the "unsinkable" *Titanic*. "I must make sure Madame Lenoir is safe."

Mikhail muttered under his breath in Russian, then said, "Sure. She only has Geli and half a dozen attendants to comfort her. Do you know you talk in your sleep?"

"What?"

"Nothing. Do what you like. Neptune can rock me back to sleep."

Emil staggered into the passageway to find a commotion: crew members trying to shepherd alarmed passengers back into their cabins.

"No danger," they kept saying. "Only a squall, ladies and gentlemen. Stay calm. The ship is sound. You're safe below decks."

Emil pushed his way to the nearest stairs, realising he had no idea how to find the stateroom where Violette was sleeping. Most of the dancers were in first-class cabins but these were spread over two decks, and of course the men were always berthed as far as possible from the women. Violette's accommodation was kept secret to guard her privacy, so how could he find her without hammering on every door? Thrown from one wall to another, he grabbed a stair-rail and began to climb to the promenade deck. A steward tried to stop him but Emil pushed past.

Even the crew – surely old hands at such weather – looked pale as they tried to pacify frightened passengers. Emil's head spun but he ignored the feeling as if it were mere stage fright. The ship reared and fell through nothingness. There was no solid ground, nothing to cling to.

The liner was huge and he was soon lost, the storm turning the vessel into a dark wild labyrinth.

He found himself in a first-class lounge, a large salon full of evening-suited men swigging whisky and playing cards, pretending not to be terrified for their lives. Which way to the staterooms? Or was Violette on the deck below after all? Half out of his mind, he crossed the lounge and climbed a broad shallow flight of steps on the far side. The carpet squelched with brine beneath his shoes. He clung to a brass rail as the whole vessel dropped beneath him.

Two more sets of doors, and he was out on deck.

The storm hit him like a hurricane. The wind sucked out all his breath. Far ahead, he saw the prow rise like a mountain, only to drop again in a long, sickening plunge. The wind whipped spume from the waves. Within seconds he was soaked.

He was on a broad walkway, with rails on his left, portholes on his right. Walls of water thrashed the ship: sheets of rain and huge, breaking waves. The gale was a solid force. Heading towards the prow was impossible, so Emil made his way aft, groping for another doorway back inside. This was hopeless. The vessel was like a small city and he had no idea where Violette was. Foreboding forced him on. He was certain that if he didn't find her, something terrible would happen.

In darkness, all he could see was veil upon veil of spray. He skidded as the deck became a near-vertical wall. Then the ship heaved over the crest and plunged into a canyon, sending him sliding the other way.

Emil gripped the rail and clung on for his life, edging like a snail as he rode out each lurch and drop. He was drenched to the skin, shivering, gasping with the effort of keeping upright. Only his honed strength and balance aided him.

Never had he dreamed his ballet training might save his life.

He saw no one, not even crew members. He realised he must be the only soul on the entire vessel stupid enough to venture on deck in such a storm. If the ship were to capsize, could the crew even launch lifeboats in such conditions?

Don't think of that. Find Violette, make sure she's safe...

"Madame Lenoir!" His shout was a faint rasp. Brine sprayed into his mouth.

Emil didn't pause to think that his actions were irrational – that Violette was in no more danger than anyone else – and in any case he was powerless to stop several thousand tons of wood and steel keeling over into the abyss. But...

If the worst happened, at least he would be with her.

He came to an open stretch of deck: an area where, only the previous afternoon, he'd sat sipping cocktails and taking the sun with his fellow dancers. Now the deck seesawed as waves exploded and foamed around his feet. The sheer effort of fighting the storm drove all fear out of him. This was hellish – yet he'd never felt more *alive*.

All was black but for the faint lights of the ship. By this dim glow he saw a figure moving, black on charcoal. Perhaps twenty feet away from him, the figure had a long robe, a staff in one hand and a mask like a giant skull. It looked exactly like Kastchei, the evil sorcerer from *The Firebird*. Hunch-backed, this apparition glided along the far side of the deck as if untouched by the storm.

Emil stared. Had Mikhail donned his stage costume in order to play some mad practical joke? No – Mikhail was in his bunk, with more sense than to risk such a prank. What maniac *would* take the costume from its trunk in the cargo hold in order to parade around in this tempest?

No one.

The moment was like the trance he'd experienced on stage, magnified tenfold. He'd stepped into a shadow world full of incomprehensible horrors. Telling himself that this must be an illusion did not work. There was no sense to be made of this. Reality itself changed, lifting a scrim to reveal a sinister dimension no mortal should ever see.

The figure appeared dry, unaffected by water or wind. It moved without effort as if gliding across a flat stage – or like a character on film. A ghost, then... yet King Kastchei looked as solid as had Mikhail in the role. And he moved with purpose.

In his deranged state, Emil was convinced that Kastchei was pursuing the Firebird herself. He was hunting Violette.

"No," Emil gasped. Sea-water whipped into his face. He wiped his eyes, panting. "Hey, you! Wait!"

He released his death grip on the rail and started across the treacherous, plummeting deck. With every step he skidded and swayed. Twice he fell to his hands and knees. Kastchei drifted on, oblivious to him. Fire appeared to smoulder dark red within the huge bone skull. Then the sorcerer stopped, confronted by a small black figure – Violette?

Emil could barely see through the gusts of rain and spray, couldn't tell if his own eyes were deceiving him, but the two appeared to be fighting.

Both gripped the staff two-handed, wrestling each other for possession. He struggled towards them, fell as the deck leaned, regained his feet. Panting for breath, he pushed wet hair out of his eyes and saw them with brief but absolute clarity.

The sorcerer towered over the small dancer. The long bone staff leaned at an angle between them as they both held on tight, Violette trying to seize the weapon – or to hold him back. An aura shone around them, the red of hot iron. How could she possibly match Kastchei's strength? Although the sorcerer couldn't break her hold, he was forcing her back towards the ship's rail. She dealt a kick to the side of his knee and he staggered, only to straighten up again and roar his anger.

Violette roared back. No – the gale itself sounded full of human voices. Kastchei twisted the staff, trying to throw her off balance. She dug in, her feet in a wide, stable stance, but he raised the staff higher and began to bend her backwards with such power that her body curved like a taut bow.

"No!" Emil yelled, his voice carried away by the gale. "Take your hands off her!"

Regaining his poise, he charged at them. As he ran, the liner tilted and plunged down a cliff-wall of water, flinging him towards the far rail. His momentum carried him at uncontrollable speed. No chance to save himself. The rail whacked hard across his stomach and he tipped straight over, beyond the point of no return. The ocean roiled below, a furious black chasm yawning to swallow him...

Then a pair of small, strong hands caught him.

One gloved hand grabbed his shirt, the other his arm. Helpless, he dangled – then felt himself being yanked back over the rail. He landed hard. Sprawling on the wet planks, he coughed and swore, shaking, nearly convulsing with shock. Then the same hands pulled him upright, hefted him to a bench, and sat him down.

Violette.

No one else was there. No mysterious skull figure, no sign that she'd been assaulted, nothing. Yet she was real enough. And she had rescued him.

He couldn't speak. Violette's face was even paler than normal, glowing with its own fragile light. Her hat and coat were drenched. She sat beside him, staring hard into his eyes. She looked both furious and relieved – the look a mother might have for a child who'd hurt himself through disobedience.

For long minutes they remained there, clinging to the bench as the liner ploughed on through the storm. He felt they were alone on a ghost-ship. Eventually Violette spoke.

"Idiot. Emil, what on earth are you doing outside in this?"

He thought, *I could ask the same,* but no words would come out.

"I know some travellers prefer to be on deck, however rough the waves," she said. "It eases sea-sickness, even at the risk of pneumonia or falling overboard. Is that why?"

"I'm not sea-sick, madame," he managed to say. "I... I was looking for you."

"Why? You must have known I was in my cabin, as you should have been."

"But clearly you were not. I saw…"

"What?"

"I thought I saw someone attacking you."

She went quiet for a few seconds. "Why would anyone attack me? I think the storm made you see things. The rational part of the brain no longer works in such conditions. It's understandable."

"But that doesn't answer what *you* are doing on deck in this weather, madame."

"Emil, I asked first."

He clenched his teeth, caught between the urge to pour out his emotions and the need to show her due respect.

"I can't explain. I felt you were in danger, not just from the storm but something else. Don't ask me how, I simply knew, and look! I was right! I was trying to find your cabin but I got lost. Then I saw a figure, exactly like Kastchei. I thought I saw him attack you… you were fighting… I don't know what I saw."

Violette reached out and took his hand. Her gloved hand was wet and cold, but Emil didn't care. To feel her fingers around his palm was paradise. She was the most captivating, enigmatic creature he had ever known… and here he was, alone with her, their hands entwined.

"My dear, you are brave and impulsive. Also a little crazy, I fear. And now you know my secret."

"Madame?"

"That I sometimes wander at night because I cannot sleep. I like to sit in the fresh air, however wild the weather, and to contemplate the ocean. The infinite, terrible forces of nature. I've grown rather good at sneaking out past my assistants, who in any case have learned not to stop me."

"But the danger! The storm nearly swept me overboard. What if the same had happened to you? If you'd vanished at sea and no one ever knew what happened…"

"Imagine the headlines!" Violette laughed. "Then I truly would be a legend forever."

"Don't even joke about it."

"Emil, calm yourself. This bench is out of the wind, and perfectly safe if you keep still. I've sat here a dozen times… and in worse conditions than this, on other voyages. Give yourself up to the elements and it's almost soothing. Oh, but don't tell anyone."

"Of course not," he said.

He was rendered speechless by her admission, by the simple miracle of her presence. What a night. They sat together until the storm calmed at last and sunrise tinged the cloudy horizon with silver.

"Well, we survived," she said softly. "We shall not speak of this again."

CHAPTER FIVE

AWAKE BY MOONLIGHT

"You idiot." Wolfgang Notz spoke softly, but his voice pierced like a needle. "Have you sobered up yet?"

Bruno brought the motorcycle to a halt amid the parked vehicles in front of the house. The huge structure was luminous in the dawn. *Bergwerkstatt*, read the modest nameplate. Mountain workshop. As Bruno booted down the kickstand, Wolfgang dismounted behind him with a grunt of pain. Bruno was not the one who'd fallen from the chalet balcony, but he felt as if he had. He slumped forward, his forehead resting on the handlebars. Every sinew hurt, every bone felt bruised. His head pounded in time with the raw ache in his throat.

It was a miracle Wolfgang had escaped with his life. Only the steep, peaty slope of the hillside had eased his fall. Then Bruno had been forced to take the motorcycle's controls for their return journey, despite being in no fit state to do so. He'd nearly killed them again, skidding on the perilous mountain roads. They'd taken hours to reach home.

"Get off," snapped Wolfgang, glaring at him. "I risked my life to save your skin. I am the one with cracked ribs and my throat nearly torn out. And you – you have a mere hangover? Feeling sorry for yourself? *Get off*."

Bruno obeyed, cursing himself for drinking so much the previous night. One more beer always seemed a marvellous idea at the time... but his drunken stupidity had led him to proposition a strange girl in the street, and set in motion all that followed.

"They bit me too," he growled. "Her and the other *strigoi*."

He staggered. Suddenly his companion had him round the throat, pressing him into the canvas side of a truck.

"Idiot," Wolfgang repeated. "You must never carry your *sikin* around in public. You never take it from the cabinet, let alone from these premises. You know that – so what were you thinking? That you'd use it to intimidate someone in a drunken brawl? Or to impress a female with your… weapon? What?"

Wolfgang released his grip. Rubbing his bruised voice box, Bruno choked on the words. "Maybe. I don't know what I was thinking."

"Very little, it seems. Herr Reiniger *must* be able to trust his inner circle. Don't you know how privileged we are? You've broken that trust."

"I'm sorry, sir."

"What punishment do you think you deserve? Expulsion?" Wolfgang's voice was low and restrained, thick with exasperation, but Bruno didn't fear him. Godric Reiniger was the only man he feared.

"I don't know. I came to you and confessed: I didn't know what else to do."

"And I, fool that I am, did my damnedest to help you. Rode fifty miles to the middle of nowhere, faced the mad vampire woman, almost died for my efforts."

"I offered to go into that chalet!" said Bruno.

"You were falling-down drunk," Wolfgang said with contempt. "Hadn't you bungled enough? She *would* have killed you, you cretin. And I would have left you in the forest to rot."

Bruno's anger welled up. "You do understand that I stabbed her *only* because I realised she was a vampire? I was defending myself. I don't go around randomly attacking folk in the street!"

"I believe you. Still, drink and weapons are a dangerous combination for any man." Wolfgang's manner eased. He was Reiniger's deputy, but he had a human touch that their leader lacked. Bruno and everyone ran to Wolfgang with their troubles. "This was your problem, and now you have made it mine. Thank you for that."

"What are we going to do?"

"We shall have to face Godric and tell him the truth."

"What will he do to us?"

"That's up to him." Wolfgang's cheeks lost colour. He pushed a hand over his cropped hair. "We need to frame this in a more positive light. Yes, we lost the knife, but think: *we identified actual vampires.* Is that not the most astounding aspect of this?"

"If you say so." Bruno went hot with delayed shock. Wolfgang was right.

"It's lucky the other two, the blond boys, weren't in the chalet, since I never stopped to wonder how I'd fight three of them."

"Is this news going to please him?"

"I hope so." Wolfgang dropped a heavy hand on his shoulder. "God knows what we'll do with you, Bruno. Keep off the beer. Come on, let's clean up, have breakfast before we face the storm. We'll have to hope Herr Reiniger's feeling merciful."

The front door opened, and a slim young woman stood in silhouette against the light from inside. "Is someone out there? Wolfgang?"

"Yes, it's me, Fräulein Temple."

"Is something wrong? What's happening?"

"Nothing. Bruno got into a little fight, that's all. We're coming in now. Ask Gudrun to make some coffee, would you, please? Black and strong."

Godric stood in the centre of his office with folded arms, listening as Bruno and Wolfgang stuttered out their story. Their muddled shock and sheer amazement at meeting an actual vampire irritated him. They were like naughty schoolboys, frightened by a ghost.

His fury was cold and rigidly suppressed, but it ran as deep as mountain roots. Had there been a knife missing from the cabinet, apart from his own? *I should have looked more carefully,* he thought, *but I did not think I needed to.*

After that, the female *strigoi* had distracted him.

Bruno was quaking at Wolfgang's side. He looked ready to pass out or fling himself through a window rather than face another moment of Reiniger's arctic disapproval.

"So you took the cabinet key from my office and stole the *sikin*?"

"No, sir," Bruno answered, sweating. "I'm sorry. I only pretended to put it back after the last *Eidgenossen* gathering."

"Why?"

"I don't know." His chin rose with defiance. "It's a beautiful weapon. And after all, it's *mine*. I like the feeling of power when I carry it. I have no better excuse."

"It's allocated for your use during meetings," said Godric. "That does not make it *yours*, Bruno. You know that. Yet you took it on a boyish whim, and managed to lose it – how old are you, twenty-eight? An eight-year-old would have more common sense!"

"He knows he made a mistake, sir," put in Wolfgang.

Godric Reiniger paused to light a thin black cigarette. The *Eidgenossen* was his hand-picked group of men: thirty, including himself. He'd named the group *Eidgenossen*, meaning "comrades in oath", in tribute to the pact on which Switzerland was founded.

Pacts, federations, compromises – all very fine in principal, but he cherished a higher vision: Switzerland with a single all-powerful leader, a hero of true vision, a god-like fusion of William Tell and Woden.

Most of his men were ex-army – not that Swiss men ever really stopped being soldiers. They were now his employees, part of his film crew, but more than that: they shared his dreams of a powerful Swiss nation. They shared his secrets.

"The *sakakin* are sacred, left to me by my father," said Godric. "There were thirty. Now we have only twenty-nine. Will that make a difference to our rituals, do you think? It damages the symmetry."

"It was a mistake," said Wolfgang. "Bruno acted stupidly and he's prepared to be punished."

"Punishment won't get our missing *sikin* back," Reiniger said brusquely.

"As I explained, we tried. We almost perished, trying."

"Oh, I believe you. You both look like death."

"But – Bruno's actions aside – isn't the most remarkable factor here that we encountered actual vampires? I hike in that area, I have cousins there. There have been rumours for nearly four years and I've proved them true. Isn't that astonishing?"

"Not really." Reiniger sucked smoke between his teeth,

regarding their mixture of fear and excitement with disdain. "I have told you for years that the *strigoi* are real. Elusive, but a true threat. Are you saying that you didn't believe me?"

Wolfgang's freckles stood out like a rash on his blanched skin. "That's not what I meant, sir."

"I always believed," Bruno put in, but Godric was still glaring at Wolfgang.

"What am I, some crazy old man to be humoured?"

"No, sir." Wolfgang's voice hardened. "I wouldn't be at your side if I thought that. I expressed myself badly – of course we believed you, but encountering the reality – the *shock* – and how close we both came to death…"

"I appreciate your heroic efforts, Wolf, but the fact remains that you failed."

"What will you do with us?" Bruno blurted out.

"What do you mean, *us*?" Wolfgang snapped, turning on him. "You're the one who started this! I only tried to clear up your mess."

Reiniger breathed, looking at the smoke swirling above their heads. He was aware of them both shaking, as if awaiting a death sentence.

How to deal with them?

"This is so much more than *just* a film studio, *just* a political enterprise," he said. "I can't sustain our fellowship unless I can trust every single one of you."

"You can, sir," Bruno said miserably, "but if you decide to expel me, I'll go."

Reiniger stepped forward and clapped him on the shoulder. Bruno nearly collapsed. He reeked of sweat and stale alcohol. "No, I don't want to lose you. As one of my inner thirty, it would be a shame to waste your training."

"Truly?"

Godric regarded his pathetic relief without emotion. Bruno was a useful workhorse, but Wolfgang Notz was much more. Godric could not look at him without a sting of resentment at his popularity. Also, his family was wealthy. He needed to keep Wolfgang loyal and under control, if only for the generous financial contributions he made to the cause.

"The *strigoi* are a real and present threat. I need young men of spirit around me, and it's natural they'll want to drink and get rowdy – but last night, it went too far. I rely on you to keep them under control, Wolf. Yes?" Godric kept his tone firm but uncritical. "I rely on you."

"And I won't let you down, sir." Wolfgang stood like a soldier, as pale as whey.

The vampire fed from him, Godric thought with a shudder of revulsion and curiosity. *Was it the same one who came here? No, they said she was fair-haired. I've not seen a* strigoi *for years... and then four are seen in one night? What does this mean? How will this affect us? I have to get the upper hand, but how?*

"Rest, get your strength back," he said in a businesslike tone. "I'll worry about the missing *sikin* later. We have films to make, messages to promote, people to influence. We cannot afford distractions. Get out, both of you. Go."

The pair saluted and made a grateful rush for the door. Godric drew on his cigarette one last time and stubbed it out.

A few minutes later he was in the projection booth, screening a reel from the new film he was editing, *Triumph in the Mountains.* Soon it would be ready for release.

His previous feature, *The Lion Arises* – showing the heroism of a Swiss soldier in foreign lands – had been well received by his private audience. The "lion" referred to Lucerne's famous statue of a dying lion. Godric was proud of the title's obvious symbolism, that heroic, fallen Swiss soldiers would one day spring back to life and victory. The local dignitaries whose support he was cultivating had loved the film.

The Lion Arises was the fourth full-length movie he'd made. Unfortunately, none of his efforts so far had been acclaimed by the public. He had to pay for screening time at cinemas for the films to be seen at all. Criticism stung. *Audiences are used to trash from Hollywood or Germany,* he thought bitterly. *They need to be educated.*

This scene from *Triumph* showed Wolfgang in the role of self-sacrificing hero, vowing revenge on the villains who'd despoiled his bride. She was portrayed by his lead actress, Mariette, swooning beautifully in a blond wig. The Alps made a stunning background. Godric nodded in satisfaction. The drama was far ahead of its predecessor. Yes, the story was basically the same – a brave Swiss German defeating foreign invaders – but what other story was there? Godric would keep finding different ways to tell it until he achieved perfection.

Next he would revive the tale of the ultimate Swiss hero, William Tell. Filming was already under way, even while he kept tinkering with the script. He would not let anyone forget the Three Tells of legend, the sleepers who would one day awaken to save his homeland. His stories would inform everyone that behind every folk story, every traditional carnival – such as the *Fasnacht* procession, with its raucous music and grotesque costumes – there lay a hidden purpose.

To drive out demons.

From the corner of his eye he noticed a woman beside him.

His heart leapt with shock. Dark skin, a simple olive-green dress... she stood there, silent, watching the film with him. Could she hear his racing heartbeat, scent his fear?

He wondered how many vampires he'd brushed past in the street and never even known. Perhaps dozens. You couldn't be sure of anyone.

His own *sikin* was still in his pocket. Recalling how she'd recoiled last time, he took out the knife and held it ready. Only then did he dare look round at her. She appeared real, solid, even though she'd come out of thin air.

"Don't try to use the *sikin* against me," she said softly in French. "My name is Fadiya. Those knives are mine, Herr Reiniger."

"So you said before." He answered in German. "I do not tolerate degenerate languages in my house."

"As you choose," she said, switching. "I speak three German dialects, French, English, Arabic, Spanish and Italian. And I do not appreciate you looking at me as if I crawled out of a pit."

He couldn't identify the lilt of her accent. She might be from any country of North Africa or the Middle East.

"How do you know my name?"

"I've been watching you for a while."

Anger rose in him like bile. "And how did you know the *sakakin* were here?"

"I sensed them from a long way off. I heard them... groaning.

74

Strange. One on its own, I would not have noticed. But several together give out a sort of vibration that calls to me."

Godric had strong nerves, but her presence made sweat ooze from his neck, cast a literal chill over him.

"Nonsense. They were my father's, and now they belong to me. What do you want, demoness?"

"Your father stole them. He looted them from their hiding place. I want them back."

"And I told you last night that you can't have them," he said, straightening to his full six-foot-two and tightening his grip on the dagger. He knew that a male vampire could sweep a human aside or crush his throat with one hand. Perhaps a female could too – but he was pleased to note that she feared the object she claimed to own.

"How can you own something that was buried in the desert for centuries?" he said thinly. "If they're yours, why are you afraid of them?"

"Guns are no less lethal to their owners," she replied. "You don't even understand what they are."

That was half-true, but Godric had documents left by his father. He knew the knives contained strange properties. Although he hesitated to use the term "supernatural", it was hard to define them as otherwise.

It crossed his mind that she might be able to find the *sikin* Bruno had lost. But his pride would not let him admit that he'd mislaid it.

He was certain that this unwelcome *strigoi* had nothing to teach him.

He stopped the projector. The screen went dark.

"I know you are a vampire, yet you clearly have no power over me. You tried to attack me and couldn't. So, if the knives protect me from you, they must be mine by default. If I knew a banishing ritual, you'd be gone by now. You would be dust."

"The word you want is *afrit*," she said, "or *ghūl*, though neither really fits. I would prefer no label at all. We seem to have reached stalemate, Herr Reiniger. You're right, the *sakakin* have given you power and I cannot get past you to take them. Yet you cannot banish me."

"Can't I?" said Godric, icily furious.

"There is nothing you can do to make me leave this place."

He raised the knife, drawing silver runes on the air, but she only vanished and reappeared in the corner of the booth, like a mocking ghost.

"I am not going to fight with you." She walked forward and rested her hand on the projector without flinching at its heat. "Don't threaten me, and I won't threaten you."

"Who are you?" he asked again. "Tell me, or leave."

"I'm not leaving," was her mild answer. "I want my treasures back, but I won't take them by force. Perhaps we can negotiate, instead."

"Negotiate?" he spat. "With what?"

"We both have things we want." Her voice was velvety. "We don't have to explain ourselves, do we? Simply agree to help each other when the need arises. A compromise for our mutual benefit."

He was tempted to stick the dagger into her throat. How dare this foreign female intrude on his territory, forcing him into bargains on her terms?

"I can't tell you what the *sakakin* are," she went on. "The knowledge is forbidden. However, I've seen you using them in your rituals. Each time you do so, you honour the sacred power that made them. That is interesting. And I think it's a good thing."

"Seen us?" Godric gasped, thinking, *What sacred power? We honour no deity but our own strength, as represented by Woden.*

She smiled. "Humans can't hide from vampires. So I'll let you keep them… for now."

"You will *let* me keep my own knives?" He laughed, a sharp bark.

"I'll let you keep them, on condition that you utter the name of Zruvan, Lord of Immortals, when you use them."

"Why in hell's name would we do that?"

"Because honouring Zruvan is the proper thing to do. And because it will increase your power. Try. You'll thank me."

Godric could barely catch his breath. "What do you expect in exchange for this devilish agreement?"

"Hide me," she said softly. "Let me pretend to be human among you."

"Impossible."

"I'm not asking to live here. I certainly don't want your blood. Just the freedom to come and go as I wish. It's hard for me to stay in one place without a plausible reason. You can give me that reason."

His instincts screamed *no*, but he couldn't resist her persuasive voice. He'd told her she had no power over him, but that wasn't true. She exuded a subtle influence that he couldn't define or resist. Her stare weakened him. He could argue with her all he liked, but he was helpless to destroy her.

"And how do I explain your presence? This is a working film-production studio. A lot of people come and go. Important people."

"Then pretend I'm working for you," she replied with the same sweet tone and terrifying gaze.

He tried to stutter that he could not consider employing a dark-skinned foreigner, not even as a housemaid, but the words wouldn't come out.

"It's a very rare mortal who recognises what I am," she said. "I pass for human every day. I know Europe, I know your customs and fashions. Surely a film studio needs someone to help with sewing, hair, make-up?"

"You promise not to interfere with anyone or anything here?" Godric heard his own voice shaking. "You will even... *help* me?"

"Good. You are not deaf," she whispered.

Charlotte stood before a full-length mirror... a different mirror, in a different bedroom lying in moonlight and shadow behind her. A deep, hot bath awaited her, perfumed with rose oil. Between undressing and bathing, she paused to examine the scar. The wound near her hipbone had healed at last to a silver line. Soon it would be gone, as if no blade had ever touched her flesh.

The scars of memory remained. Being attacked was a shock, but she'd got over it. The lasting effect of the knife was another matter. What kind of weapon could make a vampire go out of her mind, if only for a few hours? Something even Karl had never seen before?

She tried to convince herself that the illusion of splitting in two had passed, but occasionally she would move her hand and see a ghost-trail. Sometimes she glimpsed a pale shape from the corner of her eye, or saw a figure in the distance who looked just like her.

Charlotte tried to ignore these illusions, but they wouldn't go away.

Although tougher than humans, vampires were not indestructible. They were susceptible to emotion, to the dark underside of reality. For a long time she'd dreaded the bite of Lilith – a threat made by Violette, in her Lilith guise – but when it finally happened, the experience had been both fearsome and ecstatic. It had left her stronger, more clear-minded.

The stabbing had been the opposite, as if it could undo Lilith's good work. The idea made her angry. Just when she was growing in self-assurance, the wound had thrown her off-balance.

Lilith's bite was a sharp injection of wisdom, but it was not a miracle cure for all maladies of the soul.

Whatever's happening to me, I'll resist, she thought. *Karl's warned me often enough that we can take nothing for granted, least of all the caprices of Raqia.*

They'd come to Violette's new premises in Lucerne. The dancer had extended an open invitation, even while she was away.

Karl had several homes, including the chalet they'd abandoned: apartments in Paris, Vienna, and possibly others she didn't know about. Charlotte wondered what else there was to learn about her vampire lover… But he'd lived for over a hundred and twenty years, so of course he had a past: previous lovers, and experiences both wonderful and terrible that had shaped who he was.

Did she wish he'd met her as an innocent youth who'd never fallen in love until he set eyes upon her? No. He would have been a different person: still beautiful, but shallow. She loved Karl as he was, however dark and complicated. She trusted him. All that truly mattered was trust.

So they could have gone anywhere, but they chose Violette. She was special. Charlotte was the one who'd initiated her from human to vampire, a decision that had brought near disaster. Now she and Karl were bound to the dancer in a thorny tangle.

The theatre was grand, if dilapidated, with a five-storey dance academy attached. The buildings were designed in the curvaceous Art Nouveau style, painted with soft greens and sunset orange. Restoring the facades and interiors to full glory was costing Violette a fortune. Charlotte knew, since she and Karl had made generous contributions.

Last year's unsettling events had convinced Violette to move from

Austria to Switzerland. Lucerne might not be a vast city, but it was popular with tourists, rich with history and gorgeously beautiful.

A fresh start meant a new name. Violette had dropped the name of her previous director, Janacek, and chosen to call the company Ballet Lenoir instead.

She was working manically, touring *Swan Lake*, *The Firebird* and her own ballet *Witch and Maiden*, almost before her dancers' toes could touch the ground. On the surface, this made good use of their time while the theatre was being renovated. Underneath, Charlotte knew, Violette used frantic work to drive out grief.

Soon she would return, and the theatre would swarm with set builders, musicians and dancers in preparation for their grand opening.

At present the labyrinthine building stood empty. Charlotte sensed a handful of human staff as specks of warmth in far-off corners. All around her lay deserted rooms, as if she and Karl were the only guests in a vast, derelict hotel.

"Come to me whenever you wish," Violette had said. "This suite will always be ready for you. And soon it *will* be refurbished to your taste, I promise."

Charlotte caught her own gaze in the mirror. A shiver passed through her... but her reflection stayed in place. No hallucinations, no ghostly succubus to terrify her. While she'd never been vain, with a non-human eye she could appreciate the beauty that others saw in her: a slender curvy form, complexion like liquid moonlight, innocent violet eyes, a fall of golden-bronze hair... all too useful in snaring her victims.

Movement behind her made her freeze. This time she was very careful to make sure that the new arrival was Karl.

He'd been hunting, returning so discreetly that she hadn't sensed him until he appeared from the Crystal Ring. She smiled at his reflection, experiencing a rush of sheer delight at seeing him. Most vampires were attractive – useful bait for their prey – but Karl had the loveliest male face she'd ever seen: coolly intelligent, serene and humorous. A face to make the angels fall in love. Strong bone structure, softened by full dark hair that took on a crimson sheen in any touch of light. And his eyes – such eyes should be illegal, she thought. Seductive, bewitching, they were amber-golden windows on to another world.

He took her off guard every time, as if she'd never seen him before. Karl simply had a dark allure that she could drink in forever and never be sated. Every time was like the first, and even more intense for all their precious shared experiences. A glimpse of him was enough to take away her breath, to ignite a sphere of heat that began below her heart and spread all through her. Her desire to wrap her arms around him and taste his mouth was as powerful as hunger.

"Have we been introduced?" he said.

Charlotte laughed. "Do you make a habit of surprising women in a state of undress?"

"This is an unprecedented delight." He slid his arms around her waist from behind, resting his chin on her shoulder. "You look like Venus rising from the waves."

He tangled his fingers in her hair with such obvious pleasure that she caught her breath. Her body softened with the sensual intimacy of his touch, and frustration at the layers of fabric between them.

"I don't make a habit of admiring myself when you're not here, I swear."

"No one would blame you." He ran a fingertip along the knife-scar. His touch made her gasp, not entirely with pleasure. "Does it still hurt?"

"Only slight soreness... but look, the wound's healed. Sometimes I think it's a shame our scars don't stay."

"For what purpose?" he said, surprised. "As a badge of... dishonour?"

"In a way, but more than that. Scars would be a map of our existence. Our history, engraved on our flesh."

"Battle scars," Karl said thoughtfully. "If that were the case, some vampires would be truly horrifying to behold." He touched his throat. Charlotte's brother David had once hacked him there with a bayonet in a bold but hopeless attempt to protect her. "After all the fights I had with Kristian and others... I would not be a handsome sight."

"I'd love you anyway. No one could scar your soul. Well, I suppose they already have, but I love you, scars and all." She leaned into him, her head resting back in the crook of his shoulder. "Instead, we're all more beautiful than we deserve, as if we're melted and poured into a fresh mould every night by the Crystal Ring."

"Charlotte? Where is this train of thought leading?"

"I was remembering my hallucinations. The lamia. I'm reassuring myself that it's only me in the looking-glass, and not a separate blood-crazed demon with staring eyes."

"And what do you see?"

"I think the demon is me," she said softly. "But I feel as if the knife cut her out of me, so she's floating about, no longer attached. I know that sounds ridiculous, but Raqia plays games, leaving us to interpret what's real and what isn't. Like Violette, thinking she's Lilith. Or our premonitions, when the three of us... when we saw all those visions together. The unearthly marvels we see every day in the Crystal Ring. They're real, yet not real. I mean that although they're visions, they point us towards reality."

"Riddles," said Karl. "It's possible that the knife is an artefact affected by the Crystal Ring. The question is how."

"You've been in Raqia more recently than me. Seen anything... worrying?"

"A few unusual phenomena. Rods of light shooting up from the Earth. Storms, spectres." He gave a slight shrug. "Nothing coherent."

"Nothing specifically dangerous aimed at us?"

Karl turned her to face him. His hands slid over her hair, along her cheekbones, gliding down her neck and over her shoulders. She pressed against him, pushing herself into his touch like a cat. Her breathing deepened. Karl responded, his mouth meeting hers, so delicious... The kiss ended too soon.

"Beloved," he said, "I don't think the strange moods of Raqia have any conscious intent behind them."

"Probably not, but we know the collective subconscious affects us. The moods of Raqia, and the knife, and my hallucinations all seem tangled together. *Something* is wrong, but nothing makes sense."

"We will find those men who attacked you. And answers, I hope. Don't be melancholy."

"I'm not." Her fingers played, loosening his tie and working at his shirt buttons and waistcoat. "But you know me. I never can stop wondering. The attack was so strange and *wrong*. I can't let this rest. I was a scientist in life, and I still am."

"Yes, beloved. Always," he whispered.

"And so are you. Furthermore, you play the cello better than I ever shall, with your miraculous fingers…"

When she'd been a very proper, studious model of virtue – only a few years ago – Karl had lured her into this secret world of passion, but he'd done so with such subtle, irresistible tenderness that she'd never felt they were doing anything wrong. In a society where unmarried intimacy was scandalous, the need for secrecy had made it all the more exciting.

In her own heart, their forbidden relationship had been the most natural thing in the world. The paradox between her duty to appear virtuous, and the reality of their hidden affair, had been unspeakably thrilling.

Until she'd discovered that Karl was a vampire, and the world had collapsed around her.

Not all the pieces could be picked up… but she and Karl still had the one thing that truly mattered: their mutual, obsessive love.

Now their hands slid over each other, caressing smooth milky skin, no area out of bounds. He raised her hand to his mouth, kissed her knuckles then ran the tip of his tongue over each one in turn. Her whole body clenched tight with bliss. Her head fell back. Always, always this heat swept over her, as if they couldn't help but flow together like molten gold. Even when they were maintaining a decorous distance in public, the magnetic pull was there.

Other vampires joked that they could see it: a shared aura, like strands of glowing plasma between them.

She moved his hand to her breast, pressing herself into the warmth of his palm, then drew that hand all down the length of her body to the sweet ache where her thighs joined. Karl gave the softest gasp as his fingers felt gently, deliciously into her. The intimacy made her nearly swoon with joy.

With her free hand, she worked at his clothing until, smiling, he helped her.

"The faster we try to undress, the more everything gets into a tangle," she breathed against his throat.

He laughed. At last he pressed against her, clothed in nothing but his smooth ivory skin: all hard flat muscle, like a dancer, but warm with stolen blood. His hair brushed her shoulders as he bent to kiss her neck. She felt the teasing touch of his fangs. Entwined fingers, hair, limbs... So exciting, the contrast between Karl as the self-contained perfect gentleman, and this secret Karl, uninhibited and sensual and ardent.

She was delirious. Nothing mattered except to feel him inside her, where he belonged, his swollen, eager flesh enveloped in hers, the pulsing focus of all heat, all the wordless passion in the universe.

He lifted her, with her legs wrapped around his hips, on to the bed. He made her wait, sliding lightly and teasingly just where she ached the most, and then he showed her mercy.

The feeling was pure heaven. And he knew how to draw out the sensations, playing, tormenting her, until she was in a different state of consciousness, flying through a cloud of bliss that built higher and hotter towards the ultimate peak... so slow, so exquisite, she almost did not want the journey to end but it must, she couldn't contain this swelling knot of fire any longer...

All those feelings were washed away by a sudden horrible sensation: a silver river drenching her from head to foot, like mercury: heavy, toxic and icy cold. The room spun. She was suddenly *nowhere*, lost in a snowstorm or in the lethal cold of the *Weisskalt*. Her only clear impression was of a white shape oozing from her, as if she were an amoeba splitting in two.

Her ghost-double, the lamia, rose over the bed and floated, gazing down at her from above. Time stopped. The nightmare moment went on forever.

"Charlotte? What's wrong?"

Karl's voice shocked her back to reality. She pushed him away and sat up. Couldn't think or speak or breathe. As their bodies disengaged she was left feeling empty, hot and slippery and unfulfilled.

Karl grasped her upper arms, looking alarmed. She was confused, unsure of what she'd seen. What *he* had seen.

"I don't know," she whispered. "Why did you stop?"

He was breathing hard, making a visible effort to calm himself. "You went deathly white and cold," he said. "You were shaking, pushing me away. Your eyes were blank. Love, you haven't fed enough and I didn't even ask..."

"No, it's not that. Did you see… did you see the ghost come out of me again?"

He shook his head. "I don't think so. Only some mist that might have been anything. Steam from the bathroom drifting through the moonlight? Charlotte, beloved, it's all right. There's nothing there."

She gave a low growl of exasperation, stared into his feverish eyes.

"What if the poison is still in my blood?" she said. "I daren't risk infecting you!"

"If you have some contagion, I'd happily share it," he responded.

"Don't say that. I can't risk contaminating you, even for love."

"Dear heart, I'm sure you're not 'contaminated' in any way. But if you feel… I don't know that 'unwell' is the right term, but I don't think you've fully recovered. I should have realised, before we went this far."

He stroked her hair. They sat close, tense with frustration in body and heart. Charlotte felt torn up with emotion. She wanted Karl desperately, as he wanted her. They always did, like swimmers diving into a hot volcanic pool again and again, craving the glorious sensation of falling into each other.

Karl was too courteous to sate his own desire after she'd called an unexpected halt. Charlotte suspected that if a victim protested just as his fangs pierced the flesh – the point at which the gushing blood became the entire universe – even then, he would stop.

She admired him for that, but at this moment she wished he were not so self-controlled. If he had ignored her strange turn, if he'd let the fever carry them both into the rush of fire and the mutual blood-feast, they would presently be wrapped together, gasping with contentment – not sitting apart, aching with unspent lust.

But.

Karl might now be full of alien venom from her veins. That would have been worse.

Foreheads resting together, they sat gripping each other's hands, anguished.

"Dearest, I do not think…" Karl began softly. "I am certain there's nothing wrong with you or your blood."

She ached all over, with knots of sensation concentrated in the tips of her fangs and her loins. She also felt vaguely ashamed. *I refuse to let the hallucinations affect me,* she'd told herself repeatedly. Yet she was affected. The knife had cut into her psyche, dissected her in some horrible, indefinable way. She couldn't even judge if she was right to be concerned or making a fuss over nothing.

"How can you be so sure?" she said, her voice raw.

Karl let her go and she sat on the edge of the bed, knees pressed together. He rose to his feet and stood away from her: so beautiful with firelight running like liquid gold over his lean muscular body. Still aroused. He folded his arms, and it struck her that the combination of seriousness and beauty and arousal was mildly comical, as if he were some priapic forest god lost in thought.

She bit her lip. Tears ran down her face, hot and wet like blood.

"Charlotte, are you laughing or crying?"

"Both, I think. Karl, I'm s—"

"Don't," he said. "Do not ever say you're sorry. You've nothing to apologise for."

"But you're annoyed, and I don't blame you. *I'm* annoyed. I've been trying to convince myself I'm well, but I'm not. *I do not want to poison you.* Not with blood, or any other bodily fluids. Perhaps it's already too late, since we have kissed rather a lot."

"I'm not angry with you." He sat beside her, his thigh pressed along hers, and took both her hands. "I'm certain you haven't poisoned me, as you put it. I have many feelings, beloved, but not anger. Only towards the men who assaulted you."

She took a long breath, shivering despite the warmth. Feeling Karl so close was killing her. *How long?* she thought. *Have they contaminated my blood forever?* "But if I'm being paranoid, unhinged in some way… You must think I'm being ridiculous."

"I never think that, Charlotte," he said. "I know you. If you feel something is wrong, I take your concern seriously."

His words made her shiver: a disturbing thrill of alarm mixed with the fever-heat of frustration. It crossed her mind that there were other ways to pleasure each other that need not involve any biting or sharing of blood… but no. The moment had passed and it would feel wrong, mechanical, and tainted by the chilly nightmare sensation that swirled around her…

Karl raised his head, looking towards the window.

"What?" she said.

"Listen."

She listened, and caught the faraway whisper of familiar voices. They engaged her mind more than her physical senses, like tiny pinpricks of light touching the inside of her skull. The warmth of many humans, with a single cool presence among them. "Violette and company."

"It appears they're nearly home." He sighed. "We had better dress and try to appear presentable."

"Pretend nothing happened?" she said unhappily.

He touched her cheek with gentle, expressive fingertips. "*Liebling*, we've endured worse than this and survived. Don't worry."

She turned her head to kiss the heel of his palm. Karl never said anything he didn't mean. Almost never. She slid off the bed and went towards the bathroom.

"I'd better make use of the bath I ran before you came home."

"The water will be cold by now." He gave a half-smile as she looked back over her shoulder: a smile full of pain, love and grave humour. It made her feel better in some ways, worse in others.

"That's precisely what I need, my dearest," she said. "An icy-cold bath."

CHAPTER SIX

RUMOURS

"A my, are you still unwell?"

Godric and his niece had positioned themselves opposite the theatre and academy, ready to film the Ballet Lenoir's return home. A bright full moon, streetlamps and the snow-glow of the Alps filled the evening with eerie light. He hoped it would be enough. Amy was ready to start the camera rolling, while Godric prepared to take still shots. A knot of photographers had gathered, both press and tourists.

"No, I'm in perfect health. Why?"

"You look— Will you please move back! We're trying to film!" Godric walked into the road, grabbing the elbow of a man who'd stepped into his line of vision. The man grumbled in French, but moved aside.

"Damned French-speakers, think they own the town," said Godric. "The hierarchy of language is everything. One day I'll make it illegal to speak *anything* but Swiss German in this country!"

Amy laughed, startled. "Uncle, really."

"Oh, it's no laughing matter. I'm deadly serious." He resumed his position at his camera and made adjustments, silently daring anyone else to obstruct his view. "As I was saying, you look pale. Gudrun said you were suffering a headache the other night. I'll make that appointment with Dr Ochsner for you."

Amy snatched a breath, looking alarmed. "There's no need."

"How can you concentrate on work if you're unwell? Do not

allow Mariette and her friends to take you out drinking and dancing until the early hours. I forbid it. You need fresh mountain air, not cocktails and that damnable American jazz. That's something else I'll ban. What is wrong with our home-grown folk music?"

"Well, it's a little… old-fashioned."

"Timeless!" he growled. "If you think you dislike traditional music, you shall listen until you learn to love it."

"I didn't say I dislike it… never mind. Everywhere closes so early here," she muttered, bending forward to look through the viewfinder. "Mariette says we should visit Paris, where they have a *proper* nightlife."

Was she asking permission?

"I forbid you to go to Paris," Godric said thinly. "The actors and actresses I'm forced to employ have only half a brain between them but *you* should be paying attention to learning the history of your homeland, not associating with their like. *Volkskunde*, the study of folklore, our noble history and heroes."

"I can't help associating with your actors, since they're always around the house." She spoke quietly but with touch of defiance he found infuriating. "They're my friends. I really like the new make-up girl, Fadiya."

"Keep away from her too," he snapped.

"Why? Just because she's from another country doesn't mean she's carrying tropical diseases. Really, Uncle. She's lovely."

Godric felt his face flush with silent rage. He couldn't tell his niece that the intruder was a vampire, a *strigoi* or some kind of desert demon, that he would kill if only he could break the strange influence she had over him. When had Fadiya spoken to Amy? How dare she? She'd promised she would not take anyone's blood, but how could he trust her?

"Just do as I say."

"I always do," said Amy, low but impertinent.

Women – as much as he loved his niece – were impossible. *I should marry her off to a suitable husband*, he thought, *rather than let her wander like a lost soul with ridiculous ideas of being an actress.*

"You are barely nineteen." His low harsh tone made her flinch. "They're too old for you. As long as you're living in my house, I am your guardian and you *will* do as I say or, believe me, neither you nor your 'friends' will like the consequences."

Engine noise drowned her reply. Three limousines swept in front of the theatre, followed by a convoy of other vehicles. Amy turned the handle and the camera began its rolling flutter.

"There's Madame Lenoir," said Godric. Excitement swept away his concern for Amy. "Stay trained on her! You have her?"

"Yes, uncle."

Amy might be only a slip of a girl, but she had a way with a cine-camera. He had to allow her that. Obligingly, Violette Lenoir stepped out of her chauffeur-driven car and turned to wave at the crowd.

Godric Reiniger seized his chance. He'd written to her twice in the past few months, but received no reply. She was hopelessly elusive. In ten seconds, she would vanish inside the building.

He rushed across the street, jostled his way through the dancers and staff who were emerging from the convoy, and caught her just as she set foot on the steps. Camera flashes went off. Journalists shouted at him to move aside, but he ignored them.

"Madame Lenoir! Please, madame, one moment of your time. You will have heard of me? Godric Reiniger, at your service."

He bowed. She looked impassively at him, like a snake assessing a mouse. It was essential he made an impression, made her realise how important he was.

"Your name is familiar…"

Her chauffeur, big and broad in his uniform, stepped forward to intervene, but Violette raised a hand to stop him.

"Reiniger Studios," Godric spoke fast, eager and assertive. "I run the film company based here in Lucerne. We make newsreels and documentaries promoting local culture. Also full-length dramas. Your ballet is highly newsworthy. It's set to become an essential part of Swiss culture, and so quickly. This is a remarkable achievement—"

"My ballet is international," she said with a cool smile. "We just happen to be based here."

"Quite so! That makes you *enormously* important to Lucerne, to Switzerland's prominence in the world."

"Well… thank you, Herr Reiniger."

He noticed a man standing behind and to one side of her.

Stunningly handsome, sun-blond – her male principal, Emil Fiorani. Reiniger hoped Amy had him in the frame, since he was growing as famous as Violette.

She began to turn away, only by an inch, but enough to indicate that she was going inside.

"Madame, your arrival home will be shown as part of a newsreel across all our towns and cities."

"Thank you, Herr Reiniger." She smiled. "One more newsreel won't do us any harm. It was nice to—"

He interrupted urgently. "Madame, wait. I've something more ambitious in mind. I'd like to film the ballet from the inside. Your dancers, rehearsals, the finished performance – a film documenting the real life of a ballet company. *Our* ballet company. Think what an historic record it would make!"

Her expression changed subtly from imperious warmth to polite chilliness. She drew back, making it plain he was too close, too eager, too intrusive.

"No," she said.

"No? Madame Lenoir, please."

"You should have written to us about this. I can't grant requests to strangers in the street. It was nice to meet you."

Now the chauffer's firm hand was holding him back, while Violette dwindled into the shadows inside.

"But I did write!" Godric protested. "I received no answer!"

"She's given her answer," said the chauffeur. He gave Godric a small but firm shove that made him bristle with indignation. From the doorway, Emil Fiorani gave a broad white smile and a shrug of obvious, mocking sympathy, as if to say, *Hard luck. The princess turned you down.* Then he followed Violette Lenoir inside.

Godric went back to Amy. She was still cranking the camera handle at a steady speed.

"Stop filming," he said.

"What happened? What did she say?"

"Nothing." Godric felt every muscle in his jaw tighten as he swallowed his anger, like lumps of curdled milk. Finally he added, "She said no, she won't allow me to film the ballet."

"Oh. I'm sorry."

"How dare she say no? Does she not know who I am? Who do

they think *they* are? As if their form of art is any more important than mine!"

"Perhaps you took her by surprise," Amy said quietly. "I didn't know you were going to run after her like that. Don't be annoyed, uncle."

"I am not annoyed." His rage stilled as quickly as it had blown up. "It's her loss. But... let's wait and see if she changes her mind."

By the time Violette came to their rooms, Charlotte was wearing a lace and silk dress in the soft shades she loved, coffee and rose and champagne, complete with creamy stockings and shoes, her hair neatly rolled on the nape of her neck. Not that she and Violette had many secrets from each other, but she wanted to greet her friend with dignity, rather than make it obvious that she and Karl had been in a naked fever less than half an hour ago. It was a question of good manners.

Karl appeared elegant and collected in his dark suit. No one would guess how dishevelled he'd been so recently, nor that their heated encounter had been miserably curtailed. He was well-practised in switching to a state of instant calm. Charlotte, who'd envied this ability, was learning to match him.

A light knock. "Charlotte? Karl? May I—?"

Karl was already opening the door. Violette swept in, threw her coat and hat over the back of a sofa, and embraced them in turn. First Charlotte, with a long warm hug, then Karl more briefly. A subtle lily scent drifted in with her. As always she looked exquisite, draped in silver-grey and faded violet hues that made her snowy skin and ebony hair all the more striking.

"My dear friends." Violette took Charlotte's hands. "When did you arrive?"

"Only two days ago," said Charlotte. "I'm sorry, it was a rush and we weren't sure when you were coming back. If it's inconvenient..."

"Don't be ridiculous." Violette gave one of her rare but heartfelt smiles. "These are your rooms. This is your home, whenever you wish. I don't suppose you've come to choose wallpaper... so what's wrong?"

Karl moved to the mantelpiece and leaned there, his expression unreadable.

"Nothing," said Charlotte, giving him an anxious glance.

"What is this 'nothing' that's making you both so tense?"

"Oh," said Charlotte. "Truthfully, I wish we were here for the pleasure of welcoming you home. But I can't hide anything from you, can I?"

"Very little," said Violette, eyes narrowing.

"Your perception is flawless," Karl said with a half-smile. "There was an incident. Of what significance, we don't know."

"Perhaps none." Charlotte suddenly felt she didn't want to talk about the knife-wound, the lamia, anything. Not yet. "Our lives are always eventful. I needed a change of scenery."

Violette's eyebrows arched. "You will tell me, sooner or later."

Karl added, "Well, there's no hurry, if you're tired from your journey."

"Tired?" She gave him an imperious look. "Karl, my human dancers are tired. Vampire goddesses only grow... thirsty."

"A figure of speech. You must have a great deal to do."

"I appreciate your courtesy, but chores can wait."

She took pins from her hair and unravelled the skeins from a short modern style to an inky waterfall. She dropped on to the sofa before the lit fireplace, unbuttoned her shoes and kicked them off. "Everyone will devour a hot meal and fall into their beds. Trunks can be unpacked in the morning. Actually I do feel drained. Such a long tour..."

"I wish we'd come with you," said Charlotte, sitting beside her. "We went to the cinema a few weeks ago, and there you were on the newsreel! 'The Ballet Lenoir sets sail on another triumphant tour.'"

"We always seem to be waving from a ship," Violette said ruefully. "I've just had a *very* pushy gentleman wanting to film us rehearsing. Introduced himself as Godric Reiniger and claimed he'd written to me. He was highly indignant that I hadn't read his letter, as if I should be grateful for his attention! I sent him away. Something about him..." She paused. "I can't endure such rudeness, but perhaps I was too hasty. Should I have said yes? What we take for granted today will be lost forever in a few years' time."

"That's a sad thought," said Charlotte.

"Mm. Would future generations want to see us leaping about in shades of black and white, an ancient curiosity?"

"Oh, they will, without doubt," said Karl. "How was the tour?"

"Wonderful. We couldn't put a step wrong, it seemed. The audiences went wild." She spoke with self-deprecating pride.

"I never doubted they would," Charlotte said warmly. "How is your new leading man?"

"Emil has been astounding. Oh my goodness, how they adore him! You'd think an angel had descended from heaven to dance with me. I'm so thrilled I discovered him, I can't find words." Violette laughed to herself.

"What's so amusing?" Charlotte asked.

"He's begun to gather worshippers at the stage door."

"Oh... and what does Mikhail think of that?"

"Mikhail is philosophical. He knows his prime is over, but he enjoys playing the villain instead. I'm grateful for his good sense, because the last thing I need is two rival stags fighting it out. He's more like an older brother to Emil. A mentor. Together we'll drill into Emil's head not to take his worshippers too seriously. After all, youth and strength fade and then what is left?" Violette broke off, frowning.

"Wisdom? Achievement? Contentment?" said Charlotte. "If the tour went so well, you deserve to feel proud. So what's worrying you? It's obvious you're fretting."

"Ah, so many things." Violette stretched her strong, arched feet. "I was thinking that as my male partners and corps de ballet grow older, I'll stay the same. For now it doesn't matter: if I were still human, I'd be only in my twenties. But in the future... My dancers will age, and wonder how I remain unchanged. 'Does she bathe in the blood of virgins?' they'll whisper."

Violette gave a smile so chilling that Charlotte had to look away.

"This is the difficulty of living in the human world," said Karl. "But there are ways around such problems."

"You speak from experience," Violette stated.

"Long experience."

"But being found out may have consequences. Such as being decapitated by an angry mob of humans."

Karl didn't react overtly. Charlotte saw his lips narrow.

"I'm certain you'll avoid decapitation," he said drily. "We can usually step into Raqia out of harm's way. And your reactions are faster than most."

"*Usually*," Violette echoed. "But the Crystal Ring is unpredictable. What if a day comes when it refuses to receive us?"

"We had a similar conversation," said Charlotte.

"There must be something in the ether." Violette rose, paced across the room to the window and stood there outlined by moonlight. Although she put on a brave front, Charlotte knew she was still grieving. *She could no more get over the loss of Robyn than I could get over losing Karl. Perhaps in her whole life, her eternal undeath, she will never get over Robyn.*

She went to Violette. Knowing the dancer hated displays of sympathy, she only folded her arms and asked, "What happened?"

"I'm not sure. On the return journey, halfway across the Atlantic... how do I explain? When my company travels, I travel with them. I don't have to. I could take short cuts through the Crystal Ring – but that has dangers too, and I don't want to invent reasons for arriving before them. No, they're my flock, so I shepherd them. But sea journeys are so long... I try to abstain, and usually I can. I don't want rumours of illness and death following the Ballet Lenoir. That's happened in the past, but no more."

"How often have I warned you that abstaining only makes us more dangerous? You don't try to abstain for the whole voyage?" said Charlotte, dismayed.

"I don't claim it's easy. Sometimes I slip. After all, a passenger confined to their cabin by illness isn't unusual."

She stopped, looking out at the night sky. Charlotte prompted, "So, you slipped? Did someone catch you in the act?"

"No. It was far stranger. Halfway through the voyage, my thirst was unbearable. I decided to enter Raqia, travel to the nearest landmass to feed and return to the ship. Simple, I thought."

Karl said, "Simpler to choose someone on board. Why discriminate between a victim on water and one on land?"

"That's a perfectly good point." Violette turned to face him. "You're always so fair and rational, Karl, even while you're drinking someone's heart-blood. I like that. However... I wanted to keep the ship 'clean', so to speak. Unsullied by my needs." She gave a light shrug. "Think me irrational, if you will."

"Not at all," said Karl. "We all have our own codes."

"I often spent the night on deck, since I can't sleep and I've little tolerance for company. I chose a night to enter the Crystal Ring, only to find I could barely move, let alone travel. A storm racked the whole dimension, so violent it threw me back to the solid world, nearly flung me into the waves, and I only just found the deck. But the storm *followed* me."

With calm understatement, she described walls of water breaking over the prow, driving rain, a gale that threatened to push the liner to the bottom of the ocean.

"But storms at sea are common," said Charlotte.

"Two points. When I first tried to enter Raqia, the sea was calm. When I was thrown back, the wrath of hell came with me. Yes, a storm in both planes could be coincidence, but that wasn't how it felt." She drew her arms tight around herself. "Second, something came back with me."

Karl moved to Charlotte's side. She felt his hand on her back as they waited for Violette to elaborate.

"A spectre, possibly a vampire – not human, but perfectly solid and real. I couldn't see it clearly. A tall figure in a brownish robe, the colour of dried blood, with a giant skull for a head, or a bone mask of some kind. He held a long staff, as if he fancied himself a sorcerer – like the character Mikhail plays in *The Firebird*, Kastchei the Immortal – but different. This thing was sinister, hideous... It takes a lot to scare me, but this apparition made me nearly collapse with terror. I felt it was hunting me. We fought. I tried to thrust it back where it came from. The storm was at full force so the fight is a blur. All I remember is struggling for possession of the staff, which felt full of lethal, weakening power, like some form of electricity. It hurt like the devil to hold on, but somehow I pushed the creature back into Raqia."

"Did you see it again?" Karl asked.

"No. Emil appeared. The idiot, he nearly fell overboard. Once I'd got him back on deck, he said he'd been looking for me so that I wouldn't be alone and frightened in the storm!"

"That is sweet," said Charlotte.

"Foolish," Violette hissed. "His heroics nearly lost me my best dancer. Anyway... What could he make of the attack? Who knows what it meant? So we sat together on deck, while I tried to make light of my excuses for being outside in such diabolical weather. We sat there until dawn. And I was hoping with all my soul that I had not inadvertently summoned the power to capsize an ocean liner."

They were silent for a while. Karl stoked the fire. Charlotte lit lamps and closed all the curtains, except those at the window where Violette remained, a statue.

"Were you able to feed eventually?" Charlotte asked.

"Oh, yes. Not on Emil! No, I found a hapless steward, who mis-read my advances but fortunately remembered nothing afterwards. I'm not unhinged through starvation, if that's what you think."

"I wasn't thinking any such thing," said Charlotte. "Yes, the creature *may* have been illusory. But it's safer to assume that it was real."

"Agreed," said Karl. "I've seen it too."

Violette and Charlotte both stared at him.

"A few nights ago there was a wild storm in Raqia, nearly impenetrable. A shape came flying at me like a black comet. A skull-headed spectre, as you describe. It threw me out of its path and vanished towards the Earth."

"Could it have been on the same night?" said Violette.

"Possibly," said Karl, "but the timing isn't significant. Such apparitions may well be seen at different times and places. Sometimes real, sometimes a mirage."

"Haunting me," said Violette.

"Darling, not *everything* is pursuing you in particular," said Charlotte. "It might be... actually, I have no idea."

"If I'm paranoid, can you blame me?" Violette retorted. "Almost everyone, mortal and immortal, seems to have a reason to persecute me. Lilith's fire runs through my veins. Therefore, shouldn't I anticipate all threats and dismiss them with a goddess-like display of power?" Violette lifted her hands in the air. "So much for that! I'm as much in the dark as you. And I'm concerned – not for myself, but for my company. Every moment, every day, I draw danger to them simply by existing."

"Don't," Charlotte said firmly. "You're not a goddess all the time. You're the avatar of a million dreams and myths about Lilith. You can't expect yourself to be omniscient. If there's danger, we'll seek the source together."

"I know why they fear me. Lilith embodies everything women are not supposed to be: wilful, wanton, disobedient. That hasn't changed."

"But we know the truth," said Charlotte. "They're frightened because they don't understand."

"They're frightened because they can't control me," Violette retorted. "And it may take mankind centuries to overcome their fear of powerful females, since it seems I must go around educating them one by one. And some people don't like having the veil torn away. They'll do *anything* to stop me."

"And we'll help you," Charlotte said firmly. "Always."

Violette held her gaze with stormy eyes. Eventually she blinked. "You know something about this, don't you, Charlotte? Come on, tell me about this incident you claim was 'nothing'."

Charlotte exhaled. "All right. It's a tale of a cold knife, shattered glass, blood, hallucinations and near-death. Perhaps you'd like to sit down?"

Emil looked around his modest bedroom, feeling out of place, oddly deflated. The excitement of the tour was over. How strange was the quiet solitude... His mind still resounded with music, bright costumes and stage lighting, the roar of applause. Theatre smells lingered in his nostrils: perfume and sweaty costumes, rosin dust and greasepaint, bad plumbing. Ah, the girls and women swarming at the stage door as if he were some film idol... The other male dancers – not least his understudy, Jean-Paul – trying to bring him back to Earth with sour jokes. Jealous, naturally.

Then the voyage home. Each time he closed his eyes, the storm still crashed and rolled through his head.

He thought of Violette, alone and soaked to the skin, sitting beside him as if the storm could not touch her. Holding his hand until dawn broke and the sea calmed.

We shall not speak of this again.

He was exhausted, but sleep was impossible.

What was Violette doing at this moment? She was in the same building yet he couldn't go to her, any more than a pageboy in a castle could approach a princess. At supper, he'd overheard the cooks whispering of mysterious "friends" who'd come to visit her.

Although he was a relative newcomer, Emil was aware that she had enigmatic patrons who came and went at their own whim. He'd glimpsed them a few times: a striking couple, the woman dressed in subtle warm colours that complemented her hair, the man dark-haired and elegant in black. They were known as Herr and Frau Alexander, but no one could tell him *who* they were.

They had Violette's confidence. For that, he envied them.

Quietly he left his room and trod the corridor, wincing at every creaking floorboard. He hadn't undressed and was still in the white shirt and grey slacks he'd travelled in, feeling rumpled and grubby. He descended stairs to the next level, hearing snatches of conversation behind closed doors. Apparently others couldn't sleep, either, though the hour was past midnight.

Bedrooms and dormitories occupied the highest floors of the academy. Beneath lay practice studios and rehearsal rooms for the orchestra. Violette's apartment was immediately above the main studio, although the entrance was tucked away and the door always locked. Not that he would dream of trying to enter her private quarters. On the lowest floors lay kitchens, dining rooms, staff quarters and costume stores.

Next door was the theatre, newly restored. Soon they would be rehearsing for the Ballet Lenoir's first performance in Violette's own venue. Emil wandered, envisioning his readjustment to the daily routine of practice, rehearsal and performance that would be his existence for the foreseeable future. How strange, to live in this mixture of the mundane and the magical.

If fate hadn't dealt him the good fortune of talent and looks, he would still be in Tuscany, bullied by his grumpy father, a peasant farmer, bossed by older brothers, alternately fussed over and slapped by his adored if aggravating mother. He missed the warm sun shining through the olive groves, the vineyards and wildflower meadows. Even missed his family, a little. He did not miss the arguments. He couldn't have borne the frustration of doing nothing but farming, having a few children with some peasant girl, and growing old in the same village.

He refused to become his father.

A schoolteacher had told him about ballet, showing him photographs of Anna Pavlova and Vaslav Nijinsky. No one could fathom the workings of a child's brain: why you *knew*, almost before you could walk, what you wanted to be.

Emil had been ten when he announced his intention to become a famous dancer. The resulting blow from his father made his ears ring for a week. Life grew no better. Emil was stubborn. The more his brothers mocked him, the more determined he became. The more his father shouted and struck him, the more his mother pleaded, the less he cared.

Years later, he realised that their anger was fired by more than the prospect of losing a son, a useful pair of hands. They assumed that dancing made him something too unspeakable to be named. *Homosexual.* A word not even to be whispered.

As a child, Emil knew nothing of that. The day of his twelfth birthday, he ran away. He found his way to the Ballet Russes in Paris, begged a job as a kitchen boy. Then he sneaked into classes, solicited tuition in exchange for running errands. Through hard work and natural brilliance, he inveigled his way into the corps de ballet – and one day Violette saw him dance, and took him away with her.

Fate.

He'd never been home. His mother might be proud, but his father would receive news of his success in the traditional way, with a punch to the ear. *Quit this nonsense and get back on the bloody farm!*

Emil laughed.

"No thank you, Papa," he said out loud.

Later, he'd heard the horrific news of his older brother, Alfonso: publicly lynched for attempting to assassinate Mussolini. Emil was only too aware it might not even be safe for him to return to Italy. That was what you got for involving yourself in politics: execution. Emil tried to push Alfonso far out of his thoughts.

In a corridor, he tried the door that led through to the theatre. He expected to find it locked, but occasionally the caretaker would forget. Tonight the door opened.

He strolled through the backstage area and came out into the auditorium, a huge space embellished with Art Nouveau fancies; smooth wooden pillars carved into sweeping shapes, lamps held aloft by idealised female forms. Violette had insisted it be restored to its full romantic glory.

A couple of lamps glowed, shining on a figure that sat on the edge of the stage with his feet dangling over the orchestra pit. Mikhail. He turned and saw Emil in the wings, raised a bottle of clear liquid and waved it.

"Couldn't sleep either? Hey, come share this vodka with me."

Emil crossed the stage and sat down beside him. He accepted the bottle and took a swig, wincing at the burn of raw spirit. He was not a drinker. Violette disapproved.

"I'm forty years old tomorrow," Mikhail said glumly.

"*Prost*," said Emil, saluting him with the bottle. "Happy birthday. You dance like a twenty-year-old, still."

"Hah. No need to flatter me. The joints start to ache, the muscles seize up. How many more moments of glory shall I have on this stage, eh? Is it already over?"

"Surely not. You could go on to sixty, or longer…"

"Ah, but do I want to? If I cannot give my best – no. I want to be remembered in my prime, not as a shambling has-been. Do I want to teach the young puppies who come after me? No. Damn them, with their eager faces and long legs like newborn foals. No. When it's over, it's over."

Emil realised he'd get little sense out of Mikhail. Every time he passed the vodka back, Mikhail pushed it on him again. The fourth swallow went straight to his head.

"You're so young, golden boy. Grab the success, enjoy it while you can."

"I intend to."

"Because I was you, once. So never forget – one day it will be you sitting here in my place, with grey stubble on your chin and a bottle of vodka in your fist, having this same conversation with your blue-eyed replacement."

Never, thought Emil. For a while he was too horrified to reply. He took another drink, startled by how fast the liquor took effect. Soon it seemed perfectly reasonable to raise questions he'd never dared ask before.

"You've known Vi— Madame Lenoir a long time," he said at last.

"No one *knows* her, my friend."

"But…" He couldn't stop thinking about Violette beside him on the liner, her hand in his. The thought made him want to laugh and weep. "Is she… Has she ever been married, do you know? Is there someone… special to her?"

Mikhail laughed so loud that the auditorium echoed. "Oh my God! The puppy is in love with her!"

"No!" Emil flapped his hand to hush Mikhail. "No, of course not. I'm just… curious. No one ever mentions it. I won't repeat anything you say. Please tell me."

Mikhail shrugged. "Married, I don't think so. It's said she had something with Janacek…"

Janacek was the ballet's founder. Everyone knew that, though Emil had never met the man. Violette had taken over as director when he'd died two years ago.

"Did she?"

"Pah. I don't believe it. Idle rumours. Truth is, she hated him."

"Really?"

"She hid her feelings well, but he was a bully, as well as a lecher. She'd never let an old goat like that touch her."

Emil felt a jolt of relief.

"Anyone else?"

"Who knows? She's private." Mikhail waggled his fingers in front of Emil's nose. "*Mysteerrious*."

"Do you know her friends? The couple who visit her? They're here now."

"You mean the Alexanders? Karl and Charlotte. Fine-looking pair, aren't they?" Mikhail sniffed, took another drink. "They helped her rebuild the ballet after Janacek died, but no, I don't know them. They are mysterious too. Sometimes they come with two blond men, twins. But it's not done to pry into her personal life, little brother. Not done."

"What about you?"

"What about me?"

"Come on," said Emil, inhibitions gone. "You partnered her for years. I believe that you and I are the only male dancers in this company who prefer women to men."

"You're right. You got that right."

"So close to her, did you never feel… Surely you and she…?"

"What, you're asking if Madame and I were lovers?" Mikhail roared with laughter, even louder than before.

"Yes!" Emil said, exasperated. "Were you?"

"Oh, you've a lot to learn. No, we were not. I had a girlfriend, until she ran off with the first violinist. I had many girlfriends, but Madame never knew. Oh, I'm sure she suspected, but she pretended otherwise. Not discussed. You must know that. Such matters are *verboten*. But – Violette with her dance partner? Never. Never, never, never."

Emil chewed his lower lip. Mikhail was not making complete sense. Did he mean she never *would*, or that she never *had*? His own skin felt too hot and tight, as if he might explode. He pushed his fingers into his hair, groaning.

"Hey." He felt Mikhail's hand land on his shoulder, warm and heavy. "You've really got it bad for her, haven't you? This is terrible."

"I don't know what to do!"

"You don't? This is *very* bad."

"What do you mean? I don't believe you didn't desire her. Can't believe you didn't *try*. Were you too scared? What?"

Mikhail's face clouded. "You're an idiot."

"I can't help it. I love her."

"Of course you do. Everyone loves her."

"No – I *really* love her. On the ship – never mind. You wouldn't understand. I just feel – damn! I have to be with her, or I shall go mad."

Mikhail chuckled. "Don't torment yourself. Sure, you need to be a little crazy to dance in the first place – but let this go, or you'll end up insane."

"But what should I do? I have to tell her. Should I tell her? I can't *not*… but how? It's no good, I've got to, but…"

The older man was shaking his head. His indulgence brought Emil close to hitting him. "Slow down. You're tired, drunk, emotional. Me too. That's another way you're lucky – at my age, takes *so* much longer to get drunk."

"You're not listening. Please. Perhaps Violette – Madame – is alone because everyone is afraid of her. She's still young, she hasn't met the right man yet. But I'm not afraid. I need to be with her. And I'm sure she feels the same, or would if she knew… I have to ask her, but… dare I?"

Mikhail opened his mouth to speak, lips wet with vodka. He paused. Then he gave a broad grin. "You know what? You go right ahead and tell her."

Emil looked up. He felt a rush of hope. "You really think I should?"

Mikhail opened his arms wide, as if preparing for a bear hug. "Absolutely you should! It's romantic, my friend. Ah, my God, so romantic! Go ahead. Pick your moment, and declare yourself. What can go wrong?"

CHAPTER SEVEN

SILENT SHADOWS

The dagger lay on a scarf in the centre of a small table. Violette prowled around it like a cat circling a venomous snake. The scarf, one of Karl's, was black cashmere. The knife shone against the blackness with a yellowish glow. Now and then the blade shifted so that the tip pointed towards the dancer like a compass needle. As if it were following her, Charlotte noted uneasily.

"So you can pick it up, wrapped in cloth?" Violette asked.

"Karl can," said Charlotte. "If I try, it's like seizing a live electric wire. Still, I can withstand the pain for a few seconds. The knife seems to be dangerous only if the blade pierces the skin."

"Do you think it's safe to have kept it?"

"We couldn't dispose of it," said Karl. "Anyone might have picked it up."

"What of the men who attacked you?" Violette turned to Charlotte with an expressive, sombre stare.

Charlotte's heart went sour, as it did every time she thought of that evening. *This is going to plague me forever,* she thought, *unless we find out the truth.* A string of unpleasant memories flashed through her mind, and she clearly saw the lamia, a pale replica of herself, standing beside Violette.

No one else noticed. Something went dark in her mind, like a lucid dream collapsing into fog. The lamia vanished. Charlotte made a careful effort not to react.

"As I said, I thought I'd killed the intruder in the chalet. But his blood was too foul to drink, and the slope must have broken his fall. Karl found no body, only tyre tracks."

"And you've no idea who they were?"

"They put me in mind of soldiers," said Charlotte. "The one who stabbed me, Bruno, might have been a private once. The reddish-haired one who came to the chalet, an officer. Apart from that impression... No idea at all." Everything about that night was taking on an odd mistiness in her memory. Details were slipping away.

"But they followed you from Lucerne, so it's possible they live here."

"If they do, we'll find them," said Karl.

Violette's startling blue-violet eyes fixed on Charlotte. "Couldn't you have chosen a different town to hunt in?"

"It was only once. You know I'd never touch anyone from the ballet, and you weren't even here at the time. I felt drawn here because I missed you... but that's no excuse at all. I'm sorry."

"Is it likely they're still looking for this?" Violette touched the dagger, snatched her hand away. "Would they break in to steal it, or use it against us?"

"Unlikely," said Karl. "How would they know it was here? Unless they have unknown sensitivities of some kind. They may not be vampires, but they could be working for one." Karl met Violette's doubtful gaze. "It's unusual, but not unknown."

"Why would this hypothetical vampire make weapons to harm his own kind?" Violette immediately laughed at her own words. "What an idiotic question! Vampires fight each other. Some made considerable efforts to destroy me, not long ago."

"And a number of vampires died in that conflict," Karl said darkly. "Perhaps someone wants revenge."

"Who?" Violette shook back her hair. Her hands rose and fell in exasperation. "Kristian's supporters were all destroyed or dispersed. There can't be anyone left to come after us, surely? Those of us who remained made peace, more or less. An exchange of blood and kisses."

"I'm certain the stabbing wasn't planned," said Charlotte. "I was in the wrong place at the wrong time. Or he was. And the cut healed. Sent me crazy for a few hours, but I recovered."

"Are you sure?" Violette held her shoulders and spoke softly.

"You and Karl were obviously shaken by what happened. How are you, truly?"

Charlotte smiled, feeling the echo of a hundred memories in her touch. She recalled Violette on stage, entrancing her audience. Violette in despair, when bankruptcy and illness nearly ended her career... Fighting ferociously as Charlotte transformed her into a reluctant vampire. Violette, transfigured into a wild and dangerous goddess with enemies everywhere.

Her fangs, piercing Charlotte's throat. A surreal, enchanted rite as she and Charlotte and Karl lay naked together, joined, swimming in dream-like ecstasy...

Their love-making had been a form of alchemy, transformation. The mystical power of three. Never to be repeated, but always remembered and treasured.

Charlotte recalled the sight of Violette weeping over Robyn's body, her heart shattered.

"I'm perfectly well," Charlotte answered, stroking her cheek. "But I can't waste time agonising over that night. It already seems hazy. What matters is to find the truth."

"Cold logic. I like that." Violette gave her a light kiss on the lips. "However, I'm not comfortable with the weapon being here. I put the safety of my staff and dancers before anything. Can you store it somewhere else? A bank vault?"

"We'll take it to Stefan," said Karl. "I'm sure he won't mind. We'll examine it at his home instead. We understand."

"Thank you. That hostile glow reminds me of the skull-creature's staff. I want it out of my sight." Violette flipped the edges of the scarf over the knife and turned her back. "If you could remove it by tomorrow...?"

"Do you want us to remove ourselves, too?" Charlotte asked.

"God, no. Please stay." Violette's expression became tender, an aspect of herself she rarely showed. "You'll be here a while, I trust?"

"We hope so," said Charlotte.

"Excellent. I'll need your help. I have three existing ballets to perfect, and a new idea niggling at me..."

"You've only just come back."

The dancer shrugged. "That's what I get for being artistic director, principal dancer and choreographer, all in one. How fortunate that I don't need sleep."

"As long as you don't forget to eat," said Charlotte, touching her arm.

"I won't. Where are Stefan and Niklas living, by the way?"

Charlotte's groaned silently. She realised she'd forgotten to pass on Stefan's news. It had been the last thing on her mind.

"I'm sorry, I should have told you." She looked through a window, into the darkness. "He's taken a house on the other side of the lake."

Violette's face went still. "Has he, indeed?"

"It's at least ten miles away. He swears he won't bother you."

"*Stefan* does not bother me. It's the sort of company he attracts."

"Pierre and Ilona are on their travels in Russia," said Karl. "They won't be back for some time."

"But it's not really them I'm worried about. Stefan has other vampire friends, strangers to us. He knows I will tolerate no threat to my ballet."

"I know, I told him. He insisted that no one will trouble you, and he has the right to live wherever he wishes. Violette—" Charlotte stopped. "I don't know why I'm making excuses for him. He's right, it's his business where he lives, and if you're unhappy, the two of you should sort it out between you. I'm just the messenger."

"Well, this is wonderful," Violette sighed. "Storms and strangeness in the Crystal Ring. Skull-headed entities attacking me in mid-ocean. Drunken thugs with foul blood and poisoned blades. And now a houseful of vampires, a stone's throw from my new academy! Karl, tell me, is this a vampire's lot in life? No peace, ever? A layer of reality torn away so that all manner of horrors can invade our lives at random?"

"Well," said Karl, with a rueful grimace. "If you would put it like that, yes. I'm afraid you're right."

"All right. Then let them come." The dancer's eyes lit up like fiery blue stars. "Let them try."

After Violette had left, Karl came to Charlotte's side and placed his hand in the small of her back. His touch gave her a surge of pleasure, mixed with pain. She loved his warm strength beside her, his dark angelic presence. With him, she was where she belonged. She couldn't be anywhere else. He was the home of her soul. A dark whirlpool, forever drawing her inwards.

Karl was never cruel for the sake of it, but he was ruthless. No one could call him *good*; he was a vampire, after all, and didn't try to deny his nature. But falling in love could not be helped.

He kissed the nape of her neck. The touch of his mouth flooded her with desire, to the very tips of her fangs. Charlotte leaned into him, drawing his hands around her waist. She knew it happened only rarely in life that you met the one: the lover who never becomes ordinary.

Being forced to hold back was unbearable. Every time she tried to will the lamia out of existence, the haunting came back in full force. She couldn't shake the conviction that cold silver poison ran in her veins, that if she and Karl were intimate the contagion would eat them both away like acid.

"You're distracting me," she said.

She felt his sigh against her neck, making the hairs stand up. Their enforced mutual self-control loaded the slightest touch or look with painful longing. He hadn't tried to persuade her she was imagining her affliction, because he saw – whether the cause was external or psychological – that something was genuinely wrong.

She was glad of his understanding. All the same, having to abstain was killing her.

He gave her a light kiss on the shoulder and let her go.

"I'll take the knife to Stefan later," he said.

"I must admit, I'll feel easier without the wretched thing here. Ridiculous, but I feel as if it's *watching* us. Let me study it for a minute before we wrap it up."

"I don't think it's watching us," Karl said wryly. He reached around her and flipped the knife over. "Did you see that?"

The handle was carved with a pattern of pictograms. Each was the size of a fingernail, and resembled a labyrinth with an oval in the centre. A face...

"The symbol?" she said. "Yes. It looks like a skull inside a maze. A skull with closed eyes? And some writing I can't decipher. I need to view it under my microscope."

She leaned forward, holding the haft steady although it kicked painfully against her fingertips. She thought, *Why do I need a microscope, when I have vampire sight?* Gripping the knife for as long as she could bear the pain, she looked deep into the carving, right into the grain itself. Trying to understand the nature of its hostile emanations...

Abruptly she let go, easing her numb fingers against Karl's hand.

"The blade wasn't dipped in noxious chemicals. The harm emanates from the metal itself."

"I suspected that," said Karl.

"And the handle is not ivory," she said. "It's human bone."

"All these little scars on your arms and chest: there are more each time I examine you. Would you care to tell me what's causing them?"

"That's a personal matter," Godric snapped. "They are ritual marks, like tattoos, if you will. Ignore them."

"I see. In that case, I cannot find anything wrong with you, my friend." Dr Ochsner folded his plump hands on his desk.

Godric finished fastening his shirt, glimpsing his own skin and narrow ribcage as he did so. In the dull lamplight of the doctor's office, his pale flesh looked yellow. He trusted Ochsner and wanted to believe him, but...

"They told my mother there was nothing wrong with her, two days before she dropped dead of a stroke."

"Truly, Godric. You're as fit as a freshly trained soldier." He peered at Godric over half-moon spectacles. His red-blotched face widened seamlessly into his squat neck. "You're getting over a slight cold on the chest, and you need to eat more. That's all. Have you always had these anxieties about your health?"

"I don't actually believe I am ill," Godric said thinly. He adjusted his tie and sat stiffly upright in his chair. "But I need to be *sure*. I can't afford to fall sick, I have too much to do."

Ochsner opened his palms in agreement. "Indeed. And I am always happy to give reassurance. You were barely five years old when your mother died. Terrible experience for a child."

"I am not anxious. Merely cautious." Godric tapped his fingertips on his knees, suppressing a wave of the odd dizziness that had brought him here. "I'm solicitous of my own health, and that of my staff and friends. That is why I send them to you for regular examinations."

"That's only wise."

Godric did not particularly like Dr Ochsner, who sat behind his desk like a benevolent toad, but that was immaterial. *Liking* was a feminine weakness. In more important ways, they were of one mind.

"I don't need psychoanalysis, just confirmation of my physical health. It's essential my supporters *perceive* me as strong."

"And they do, my friend." Ochsner gave a small laugh. "Think of me as a mechanic, tuning the engine of a powerful racing car. Your occasional dizzy spells are caused by plain overexertion. Get more sleep, and eat plenty of red meat: that will keep you in the peak of condition."

Godric swallowed. "I only eat white meat. Veal, pork, chicken."

"Ah, well, there's your problem. Change your diet. I told your niece the same. Lots of bloody red steak and offal." The doctor lit a cigar, offered one to Godric. He declined.

"What do you mean, you *told my niece*? You haven't seen her yet."

"Ah." Ochsner cleared his throat. "Actually, I have. She came for an evening appointment, well over a week ago. I thought you knew."

More rebellion, he thought, tensing with irritation. He'd wanted Amy to see Dr Ochsner because – he'd learned from Gudrun – she suffered heavy monthly bleeding that left her exhausted; a check-up was in order. Ochsner had suggested he could scrape out the troublesome tissue: a cleansing procedure to solve the problem.

Godric liked the sound of an internal cleanse to purge all that unspeakable feminine mess. That sort of treatment could only improve one's well-being.

Amy, though, had refused to discuss such a private matter with her uncle. But surely her health mattered more than her privacy? They'd argued. Now to learn that she'd obeyed him, but in secret, indicated defiance of a peculiarly underhand nature.

"Well?" Reiniger demanded. "What did you find? Is she unwell, does she have any... problems that should concern us?"

Dr Ochsner shook his head. He poured schnapps into two

tumblers, passed one across the desk. "Nothing irregular."

"What does that mean?" He sipped the liquor. The doctor took a large swig. "Did you examine her properly?"

"I gave her a thorough examination and curettage, an internal stripping, if you will. It may help, but some women bleed more heavily than others. It's perfectly natural. More importantly: she is not pregnant. She has no diseases. She is a virgin. Is that not what you actually wanted to know?"

Godric Reiniger exhaled and sat back in his chair. Yes, that was precisely what he'd wanted to know. Amy was pure, and now nicely cleaned out. Perfect marriage material, ripe to be offered to a man of wealth and influence.

Her life in London had not turned her into some promiscuous flapper. Godric was very determined that she would not *become* a promiscuous flapper.

"Most reassuring," he said softly. "I wish she'd told me. I suppose she was embarrassed. Thank you, doctor."

"You're welcome." Ochsner drew on his cigar and grinned through a cloud of smoke. "Women, eh?"

Godric rose to leave.

"Come to me at any time," said the doctor, rising to shake his hand. "I look forward to your visits. Anything I can do, at any time of day or night: I'm always here."

Their handshake was firm, transmitting an understanding far deeper than his neurotic medical concerns.

Neurotic, thought Godric as he stepped out of the building. The fresh damp air immediately made his head whirl – not true dizziness, but a strange buzz of energy. *Am I neurotic?* A string of thoughts twined around his brain like barbed wire.

He tried not to think about Fadiya. True to her word, she'd acted the sweet obliging helper, painting make-up on to the faces of his actors for the early scenes of his next film. You would never guess she wasn't human. Everyone loved her.

Godric hated her. The hypnotic glow of her eyes unmanned him. Yes, she'd "let" him keep the *sakakin*, and promised him extra power, but he wanted power on his own terms, not hers. As soon as he found the strength to expel her from his house – or even to kill her – he would.

Although Ochsner supported his politics, he was not part of the inner circle. When Godric told him to ignore the rune scar, he obeyed. The doctor would do anything for a price.

Ochsner was, however, a clod of earth, incapable of looking past the mountain horizon. He couldn't comprehend the unearthly powers that coursed through Godric's body. His symptoms were indescribable.

Seeing things. Feeling that he'd gone transparent. A sensation of wild power, as if he could fly. Feeling invincible. Something both nightmarish and wonderful was happening to him and he kept groping for explanations even though he knew the prosaic Ochsner could not supply an answer.

All he could do was seek repeated reassurance that he was not actually ill. That he was not deluded, not sick, but becoming something *other*: a channel for all the gods and folk heroes that had helped to make Switzerland great.

Becoming superhuman.

Of course I am not going to tell her.

Emil held himself upright, lined up with the male dancers at the barre, pushing themselves hard through the warm-up. The rehearsal pianist pounded away as if she were beating a carpet rather than playing music, while the ballet master, Ralph, walked up and down the line with a cane, prodding at misaligned limbs. Emil watched his pacing reflection with narrowed eyes. If Ralph brought that cane near him, he'd be sorry. Emil held every inch of himself in perfect posture, but that made some tutors more determined to find fault.

Sometimes he caught other dancers, male and female, eyeing him with envy. They thought he was growing arrogant, especially after his success on tour. He'd come from nowhere to be celebrated alongside Violette; of course they resented him, but he didn't care. Let them think what they liked. He disdained their jealousy.

They couldn't possibly guess that his princely form hid a love-struck idiot, as gauche as any other youth in love with a goddess. Nor would they ever know.

I know Mikhail's game, he thought. *Tell Violette! He wants me to make a complete fool of myself. Does he think I'm that gullible? Not in a million years can I tell her. But if I don't, I'll surely explode... but how?*

Sober, he saw that it was impossible.

The knowledge made his frustration unbearable.

In the mirror, he saw Violette slip into the room. In the days since they'd returned from tour, he'd barely seen her. Still, it was her habit to vanish and reappear at will.

Without her dramatic Firebird costume, in grey practice clothes and no make-up, she looked smaller and softer. No longer a terrifying goddess, but a lovely, natural girl next door whom he might have met in his home village. A girl he might have married so they could grow happily old, fat and grey together.

Violette, a contented grey-haired grandmother? Never. But which was more desirable, an uncomplicated peasant life or this sharp-edged existence of glamour and yearning?

Everyone stopped and turned to greet her with a small bow or curtsey, as if she were royalty. And she was, to them. She waved a hand, said, "Continue," then whispered in Ralph's ear. He rapped his cane on the floor and barked, "*Jetés*, please. In pairs. Girls first."

As Emil stood at the barre, watching each pair run and leap their way from corner to corner of the studio, Violette came to his side. He felt his heart drumming faster. She smelled delicious, as always. To his own discomfort, he felt himself becoming aroused.

This rarely happened, despite the proximity of agile females around him all day. It was an everyday situation: the novelty had worn off years ago and rehearsals were simply work. Also, the male dancers wore a dance belt, a protective garment that preserved their modesty and hid any potential embarrassment.

Nevertheless, the garment became uncomfortably full. With all his will he tried to make the pounding blood drain out of his loins. *Think of something else, anything – my toothless old grandma...*

"Emil, will you dance a few steps with me after class?" said Violette. "I'm creating a new *pas de deux* and I need to see if it will work."

"Of course, madame." He swallowed hard.

"I spent my spare hours on tour writing a new ballet. It's about a girl who runs away to join the circus. Would that not be fun?"

"I'm sure it will, madame."

"You look shocked. Emil, you've turned red! I know it's different, but we always perform dark stories, tragedies. Wouldn't it be nice to send the audience out smiling instead of weeping for a change? Think of the stage filled with bright colours, like *The Nutcracker*, but with rather more of a story."

"If you want me on a trapeze, I'll oblige," he said, and felt his face flush even hotter.

"Don't rule it out. Of course, we tread a fine line – the ballet must not *actually* turn into a circus."

"Mikhail should be cast as the evil ringmaster."

How pretty she looked when she laughed!

"You read my mind," she said. "Of course, there must be an evil ringmaster."

The last fifteen minutes of the session passed like fifteen hours. Violette warmed up alone in a corner as the class went on, while Emil tried not to watch her. The perfect curve of her arms. The long slender lines of her torso, the small tight buttocks... *God*.

Eventually all the dancers trailed out with towels slung around their sweat-damp necks, followed by Ralph and the pianist. Emil and Violette were alone.

"This will be the central *pas de deux*," she said briskly, "in which the runaway girl and the male acrobat rehearse together and begin to fall in love. So it should be tentative at first, gradually becoming more sensual as they begin to move as one – but that's fine detail. This is just a walk-through, to see if the poses are even possible."

She went into professional mode, snapping out instructions and expecting Emil to interpret what she wanted instantly. Usually he could: as she said, they seemed to read each other's minds. That was partly why she valued him.

But today... it was all he could do to concentrate as she manipulated him like a poseable mannequin. Usually rock-steady, he was trembling.

As they worked, he saw faces glancing in through the glass doors: people being nosey, then hurrying away when Violette scowled at them.

"Let's try this. I'll wrap around you, spiralling upwards. Then

I balance on your shoulder in an arabesque. It shouldn't be hard, but will take practice."

Her eyes shone – not for him, but with excitement about her new ideas.

Emil was compliant, letting her direct the move. What sweet agony this was... She slithered around him like a snake until she knelt on his right shoulder, their hands joined for balance.

"Let go," she said. In the mirror, he watched her rise on one foot on his shoulder to execute a perfect arabesque, her free leg raised high behind her.

"Don't stand like a post!" she said. "Try your feet in fourth position, and do something with your arms."

Trying not to unbalance her, he eased into a more stable and elegant posture, arms raised in curves to complement hers. Not even a wobble; how was her balance so perfect?

They held the pose, both looking into the mirror. Violette frowned. "Now, does that look ridiculous or astonishing?" she asked.

"Both, I think," he said.

"Which is ideal. All right, let me down."

She lowered her raised leg and executed a light spring on to the floor, turning as she did so to land facing him with her hands on his shoulders. He automatically caught her upper arms to aid her landing.

They looked at each other, a little breathless. His conscious brain told him to let her go, but the command did not reach his hands. Now would be the most natural time in the world to lean forward and kiss her...

Oh God. God!

"Emil." Her hands fell and she stepped backwards to arm's length. He had no choice but to release her. "That was a promising start." Her voice went quiet and cool. "Now would you mind telling me what's wrong?"

"Nothing, madame." His voice went hoarse. "Why?"

All his innate confidence evaporated. No one else had the power to do this to him. He was conscious of how rarely he'd spoken to her in private; normally she had a crowd of assistants around her. There were a few times when she first brought him from Paris... Once, on board a ship in a storm... and now.

"You are absolutely rigid," she said.

He went red-hot. He thought she meant the physical reaction he'd fought to suppress – surely she wouldn't notice, let alone draw attention to his embarrassment? Then she shook his shoulder, quite roughly, and he realised she meant his whole body.

"You're as tense as a board," she added, leaning back against the barre. "The more you tremble, the harder you try to control it, which only makes it worse. You seem off-balance. We all have bad days, but if something's troubling you, I should like to know."

"I apologise. My knee…" He stopped. If he feigned injury, she might perceive physical weakness where there was none. And he couldn't lie to her.

"I didn't notice you favouring one knee during practice," she said softly. She stared straight at him without blinking. Her eyes were blue ice. He felt she was staring into his mind as if he were made of glass, drawing all his thoughts and secrets out of him. It was a most unnerving feeling, like that frozen moment he'd had onstage in New York, when the imaginary world of the Firebird had become real.

She knew.

His hands were clammy. Forbidden emotions rose inside him: anger at losing his professional poise. Fear, frustration. Violette standing there in all her impossible beauty, untouchable – yet he was expected to hold her every day and feel *nothing*… This was unbearable.

Emil came from a family where passions were always close to the surface and no one thought twice before they yelled, wept or embraced. Yet here, he was expected to be as self-disciplined and obedient as a soldier. And until a few weeks ago, he'd been so.

"Get changed and come to my office," she said when he stayed silent. "Perhaps you'll be less tongue-tied there."

Emil rushed to the changing room, doused himself in a cold shower, and threw casual clothes on to his still-damp body. Ten minutes later, outside the solid oak door of Madame Lenoir's office, he halted and took several deep breaths.

"Come in," she called, before he'd raised his fist to knock.

He went in, closed the door behind him and gave a nod of deference. "Madame."

"Sit down."

So now she placed the desk between them, a wide barrier cutting off any illusion of intimacy. The window behind Violette outlined her with dusty-silver light.

"There's no need to be afraid of me." She spoke gently, but her eyes warned, *Be terrified.* "Whatever you say will remain between us. But I will not tolerate dishonesty."

He struggled to speak. Finally he managed, "Has Mikhail said something to you?"

She blinked, and didn't answer the question.

"I know my dancers consider me overstrict. For as long as they dance for me, relationships are discouraged. *All* passion must be channelled into work. Some people have left, finding this impossible. I know it seems harsh – but this is the price you pay to become the best. Anyone who cannot accept this condition is free to leave."

Emil clenched his fists beneath the desk, his blood rising.

"But how can we dance without passion?" he exclaimed.

"By expressing it all in our work." Still she went on freezing him with those beautiful eyes.

"But that is exactly..." *All of it, every drop of fire? Nothing is allowed to spill into our real lives?* He bit back his thoughts, but the harder he held back his feelings, the more they threatened to erupt. "That is how I live, by putting my passion into the dance," he said. "But I cannot turn it on and off like an electric light. What you see on stage is all I am!"

This is insane, impossible, he thought. Perhaps Violette *was* insane. With every second he sat under her arctic stare, the less human she seemed – and the more fervently he adored her.

"Emil, I know, but... What is wrong?" she asked, resting her hands parallel on the desk. "I know you're young and impulsive. You're a perfectionist, like me. Of course tempers flare. But this is something more, isn't it?"

"What did Mikhail tell you?" He could imagine the Russian chuckling into her ear, "You'd better watch that one. He has it bad for you, madame, real bad."

"Why do you keep asking me about Mikhail? What has he got to do with this conversation?"

FREDA WARRINGTON

"Because... Damn it!"

Emil got up and paced the rug on his side of the desk. He knew in that ghastly moment that his career was over. He was trapped, desperate. He could lie or tell the truth.

Either way, he was damned.

But – was there no hope at all? How was it possible to feel so strongly if those feelings were not returned? There must be something mutual. Even the tiniest spark could grow, given time and warmth and nurture...

Her eyes sucked the heat out of him. He felt terror, and a dozen other swirling emotions he couldn't suppress.

"I know he's said something. I'll kill him!"

"Don't kill anyone. Never mind Mikhail. Just say what's on your mind."

"Madame," he gasped. "Violette. Would you force it out of me?"

"If I have to, yes."

Before he knew what he was doing, he circled the desk and fell to his knees on the carpet before her. "I can't – how can I – I tried so hard to hold back but it's unendurable. Please – I'm a fool and I ask your pity. But I – is there anyone on this Earth with a pulse who does not love you? I'm only human."

"Emil..." Her protest was weak. Apparently he'd shocked her nearly speechless. "Please, try to control yourself. Are you saying..."

"I love you," he said simply. He became suddenly calm, as if a higher power were directing him. *Have faith in yourself,* said the power. *Open your heart and tell the truth.* "I've adored you since the first moment I saw you: a photograph in a newspaper. I've worshipped you, heart and body, every moment since. Madame, I am in love with you. You already know, don't you?"

"I... suspected. I hoped..."

"I would do anything for you. Don't mistake me. This isn't blind lust or infatuation. I desire you, of course, with all my being – but this is more. It's everything. I would marry you tomorrow if I could. I don't ask for an answer now, of course not, but my offer is there for eternity. I have to be with you."

"Stop. Emil, please. I was going to say that I hoped my suspicions were wrong."

Of course, she was bound to react like this. This was too

sudden, he knew – but the truth was out now. He drew back, sitting on his heels.

"I don't believe you feel nothing in return," he said, as calmly as he could. "I know you do! That night of the storm at sea – you saved my life. You sat with your hand in mine all through that long, terrible night."

He paused to draw breath. Violette remained motionless. Even in his heightened state, he knew better than to lay a hand on her.

"I lay my life before you," he went on, his voice going hoarse. "We should be together. I *have* to be with you. What do I care for your rules, when they bring us nothing but pain? I may be a fool, but better a brave idiot than a coward. You wanted the truth – there it is. My heart is yours, now and forever. I love you."

He ran out of words, feeling drained, unburdened. Not humiliated, but relieved that he'd found the courage to spill his true feelings, for good or ill. His heart clenched tight around the hope that she would soften and whisper, "I need time to think about this," or, "I have been alone for so long…"

After a silence that seemed to last an hour, she said, "Have you finished?"

He nodded.

"Well, I appreciate your honesty. Stand up, return to the other side of the desk."

He obeyed and sat down, holding on to the arms of his chair.

Her voice was gentle and compassionate, but her eyes were glacial.

"Emil, dear, you need to understand that I don't share your feelings. What you suggest is impossible."

He sat staring, his whole being electrified with denial. He was ready for debate, argument, anything but this wall of ice.

"I'm not angry with you," she went on. "We may all develop inconvenient feelings. That doesn't mean they must be acted upon. I am, however, bitterly disappointed. I thought that I'd found a perfect partner whom I could trust."

"You can trust me!"

"Not any more."

"I don't understand."

"Yes, you do." Her eyes seemed to fill the universe like blue-violet suns, casting a terrible spell over him. "You knew the rules when I took you on. Beyond a working partnership, nothing can or will *ever* occur between us. Unfortunately, your outburst has seriously compromised our professional relationship."

"No – it need not," he said helplessly.

"How not? You have a choice, Emil. If you truly cannot control your feelings for me, you must leave."

"*What?* But I am the best—"

"Yes, the best partner I've ever had, and I don't want to lose you. So if you can erase your emotions, and if we can behave as if this conversation never happened – then you can stay. But I'll never be at ease with you again. You do understand that? I'll never confide in you, never treat you as the other half of myself, never trust you. Because of this, I'll always be on my guard. Everything between us will be work, nothing else."

He groaned, his hands dangling between his knees. His turmoil of misery began to harden into anger. He couldn't accept her rejection, couldn't endure it.

"Madame," he said. "I cannot help my feelings. I wish I'd said nothing, but you forced me to speak!"

She shrugged. "I needed the truth from you, whether I liked it or not."

"Affection may grow in time," he said softly. "I will prove myself."

Violette stared at him. She was notoriously intimidating, but never had he seen her as burning-cold and hostile as she was now.

"Enough. Don't make me repeat myself. *I do not share your feelings*. Do you accept this, or shall I look for a new male principal? Jean-Paul is waiting in the wings. He's not you, but he'll do well enough."

"I accept it," he whispered, floored by outrage and misery. Blood ran scalding through his hands and face. Sweat dampened his forehead. He wanted to yell and lash out at fate – what tormenting deity caused him to love this cursed art form, to bring him into the orbit of a goddess he could never have? All those pretty girls at the stage door – he could have had any or all of them. But the only woman he wanted spurned him. How dare she hold such power over him?

"Good," she said. "For the next week, you will attend class, but nothing else. No rehearsals."

"You're suspending me?"

"Not exactly. Think of it as time to cool off. I do not want to see your face again until you've purged your mind of this nonsense and are ready to work. Now go."

"Madame…"

"Are you going to be professional and forget this ever happened? Or are you going to continue composing your letter of resignation?"

"I can't take it back," he growled, backing towards the door. "You asked for the truth. I won't feel shame for telling it. Forgive me for being a mere mortal."

"Forgiven," she hissed. "Now *get out of my sight.*"

Emil stumbled into the corridor, slamming the door behind him. He was half-blind with humiliation and rage, his heart in shreds. The encounter was no more than he should have expected – yet, for a few impulsive moments, he'd dared to think…

"*Idiot!*" he cursed himself.

Turning a corner, he bumped into Mikhail. The Russian grinned, all innocent good cheer.

"Hey, what happened? Mistress give you a dozen lashes of her tongue? What did you do?"

Emil exploded. "You told her, you bastard! This is your fault!"

"I never said a—"

Emil's fist cracked into his jaw and Mikhail hit the floorboards. He was out cold for a few seconds, then stirred, dazed, with blood streaming from his lip. People began to gather in the passageway. Suddenly Violette came striding towards them.

"What the hell is happening?"

She took in the scene, turned with slow menace to Emil.

"Suspension until further notice," she said.

CHAPTER EIGHT

THE MIRROR CRACKED

Karl clasped Charlotte's hand in the darkness. The flat screen came to life with silvery images, ghostly yet over-bright to his dark-attuned vision.

Most human art held some kind of interest for him: even if a play was dull, he would find endless fascination in studying the actors' mannerisms, or the subtle interplay of the audience. Film was different. For some reason he couldn't make any connection with this comparatively young technology. The surreal glimmer of black and grey, the melodrama, the choppy editing and hysterical music, the way the action ran too fast, distorting time – all combined to give him a sense of nightmare.

"Talkies" were on their way. And colour. When critics insisted that these developments would never catch on, he could only smile. Of course they would. Almost every advance caught on in the end.

Charlotte found the cinema entrancing. Wanting to please her, he'd sat through the surreal horrors of *The Phantom Carriage*, *Nosferatu*, *The Cabinet of Dr Caligari* and too many others.

Tonight they were watching *The Lion Arises*, an overwrought fantasy about an Egyptian queen being kidnapped by her own eunuchs, and rescued by an heroic Swiss officer and his trusty friends. The small cinema was packed with British, American and French tourists.

"Charlotte," he whispered, "we saw this last month. It was as terrible then as it is now."

"I know," she said with an enigmatic smile.

A man leaned down from the row behind and tapped Karl on the shoulder. "Excuse me," he said in a low, clipped tone. "Did I hear you say that this film is terrible? Why?"

"It's… well, a little overacted, don't you think? And the action jumps all over the place," Charlotte answered with polite charm. "But the camera work is very good."

"When the action jumps, that is intentional."

"Dream sequences?"

"It's called symbolism," he hissed.

"I see," said Charlotte. "It's very… striking."

The man sat back with a *hmph* noise.

Karl stayed quiet, thinking, *It's the work of an amateur, trying too hard.* All the same, he became mesmerised by the deep grainy shadows, actors with blanched faces and dark-ringed eyes… divinely beautiful in a disturbing way, like vampires.

A desert sword-fight cut abruptly to *Fasnacht*, the pre-Lenten festival when the streets of Lucerne filled with revellers in grotesque masks, musicians marching in ranks like soldiers. The musical accompaniment – a live pianist doing his best to improvise atmosphere – was out of time, so they seemed to pound their drums to a different, unheard rhythm. The effect was disorientating.

Symbolic, thought Karl. *So this refers to what is happening in the hero's head?*

He'd witnessed *Fasnacht* in reality: a noisy, entertaining parade. He was amazed that the grey tones and soundless frenzy could turn a colourful festivity into a scene from a horror film.

Huge white-faced demons with spiralling horns leered at the camera then reeled away. Hideous kings and queens swayed along, eight feet tall. Gigantic gnomes, wolf-faced warriors with straggling hair – on *Fasnacht* Lucerne was possessed by a medieval carnival, as if the inhabitants of hell had broken loose for a few days.

Karl found himself holding his breath, hands turning cold. He didn't recall being so disturbed the first time they'd watched *The Lion Arises.* Now he felt deep, irrational disquiet, almost a phobia; an emotion that belonged to humans, not to vampires. *I cannot be afraid of a film,* he told himself in disbelief. Yet the longer he watched, the more his unease deepened. The monotones, the overwrought action, the faces that were too pale and shadow-ringed like those of mad, animated corpses...

The atmosphere made him think of Raqia at its most distorted and hostile, and of hallucinations he'd suffered when Kristian brought him back from the dead... Times of pure horror.

Fasnacht was both traditional and powerful. Quintessentially Swiss, yet almost pagan. A primeval ritual to scare away demons.

That was the not-so-hidden meaning. The hero was fighting off demons to save the beleaguered desert queen.

"Karl?" Charlotte whispered. "Are you all right? You look horrified."

He blinked, averted his gaze from the screen. The silvery light flickered over her face, making her appear ghostly. She looked just like one of the actresses: pale, beautiful, sultry-eyed. And a twin sat beside her, exactly echoing her movements.

He closed his eyes, gripped her fingers.

When he looked again, there was only one Charlotte.

"Your hand is freezing," she said. "We can leave. Hunt instead."

"No," he said softly. "Fascinating, that light and shadow can have such a profound effect. We'll stay until the bitter end."

"I think it's wondrous, the way they make images move, create a story out of something that isn't really there. I was eight years old when my father took us to our first moving picture. The magic never wore off."

"And I wouldn't dream of depriving you of that magic," Karl replied, "but if you ever make me watch *Nosferatu* again – well, among humans it might be grounds for divorce."

Charlotte grinned. "Don't tell me you were frightened!"

"No. But it was grotesquely inaccurate. And mildly ridiculous. I should add that if ever I saw an *accurate* film about vampires, I'd be truly disturbed."

"I thought the story was moving," she said. "But I promise I won't inflict any more horror films on you. No more *Dr Caligari* or *Hands of Orlac*... but I think they're fun. Shivers down the spine."

"If you would stop muttering," hissed the man behind them, "perhaps you would appreciate what you're seeing!"

"Apologies," said Karl, exchanging a sideways glance with Charlotte.

He couldn't put his disquiet into words. The flat unreality, the flickering grey shadows full of hidden, indefinable threat, afflicted him at a primeval level. *Uncanny*. That was the only word he could find, and even then it was a feeling, not an explanation.

Karl let his attention drift to the audience. The place was full and he couldn't help savouring the heat of so much human blood. So many pulsing hearts. Couples whispered and kissed in the dark, as they never would in public...

Charlotte gripped his hand, jolting him from his trance.

"There she is, look!"

The scene showed pillared chambers, the queen on her couch. She had ash-pale skin, plaited hair and huge smoky eyes. Dozens of paunchy men played her villainous captors, and half a dozen maidens danced in outfits as revealing as the censor would allow.

"The girl at the back, third from the right."

Karl studied the extra. She was attractive but unremarkable. "What about her?"

"It's Amy Temple," whispered Charlotte. "The girl I rescued in the street. I knew I'd seen her before!"

"I should have known you didn't bring me to the same dreadful film twice for no good reason."

Charlotte went quiet as the scene changed. The swaggering hero fought his way to victory and the story played out with such strutting melodrama that the audience began to giggle.

The end of *The Lion Arises* was greeted with audible groans of relief, laughter and calls of derision. The man behind them stood up and began haranguing the streams of people making for the exits.

"Philistines! Do you not recognise great drama when you see it? You laugh because you don't understand, like schoolchildren!"

Next to him sat a woman, pale and sinking down in her seat. She reached up and pulled at his coat sleeve. "Uncle!"

No one responded to the man's protests. They only glanced in his direction, suppressing embarrassed smiles as they hurried out. Charlotte hesitated, as if she intended to speak to him.

The man – tall with a pale, stern face and gold-rimmed spectacles – looked straight at Karl and froze. His eyes widened, his thin lips parted. There were rare humans who would look at a vampire and see clear through the veil of deception. He had exactly that expression.

Dear God, he knows what I am, thought Karl. People were bunching in the aisle behind them, so he broke eye contact and urged Charlotte to move onward. The moment was lost.

Out in the street, they walked until they reached the lake's edge, well clear of the crowd. A brisk wind ruffled the water.

"That poor gentleman," Charlotte said at last. "He must have helped make the film. Perhaps he wrote or directed it. How awful, to sit there with everyone making fun of your work!"

"I've no sympathy with him," said Karl. "If he cannot tolerate criticism, he should not have been there in the audience. Even better, he should not have made the film in the first place."

"You are cruel," she said with a smile. "I was going to say something nice to cheer him up. Then I saw the way he stared at you. And the girl beside him, who called him uncle? That was Amy! I don't think she recognised me. I do hope she didn't hear me whispering about her."

Karl recalled her description of carrying Amy to her house, the blood-scent so evocative that even now he felt a twinge of appetite. "Like a tropical flower that smells so luscious you can't stop breathing in the fragrance," Charlotte had said.

"So she is a film extra. Why does it matter?"

"Because…" They began to stroll across the wooden Chapel Bridge over the River Reuss. Lights danced in the water. "You say, 'Don't get involved with humans, don't look at their faces or ask their names, or they'll drive you mad.' But it's not that, Karl. I just wanted to know why she looked familiar. And I'm so glad I saw her in the cinema, alive and well."

"You don't think that the thug who stabbed you had also attacked her?"

"I don't think so. Surely she would have told me? She only complained of… female problems." Charlotte went quiet for a few steps. "The house I described up in the hills: did you know it was there?"

"No. I'm not familiar with the area. Not yet."

"It can't be more than a year or two old. *Very* modern."

"Her uncle must be wealthy."

"Reiniger Studios," said Charlotte. "It was there on the credits. And Violette told us that the man who annoyed her the other day, wanting to film the ballet, was called Godric Reiniger. The house where I took Amy must be their premises. It would make sense; I saw and sensed people inside. And there were vans parked, working vehicles. I was curious, but I didn't go in. See, I do listen to your advice. I walked away."

"Straight into the path of a maniac," he said grimly, "who is still free to roam the town."

"Karl." She stopped and gazed intently at him. "I appreciate you trying to protect me, but we may never see him or his friend again. There's no point in letting them destroy our peace of mind, is there?"

"No," he said, "but you can't expect me to let it pass, as if nothing happened."

"Perhaps we should."

His hands rested gently on her upper arms, on the velvety russet fabric of her coat. Her mouth was so beautifully shaped that it was all he could do not to kiss her... but ever since that night, they had both controlled themselves. Charlotte's fear that she might infect him in some way still haunted her. Instead they stood touching each other, but holding back.

"But our peace of mind *has* been disturbed," he said. "You were desperate to find out about the knife. Have you changed your mind?"

They rarely argued. Karl was not combative, which occasionally made Charlotte more annoyed with him. Now she frowned, shaking her head minimally.

"No. I don't know. I don't want to think about the lamia, or the attack. When I try, my mind goes dark and nothing's clear any more. Something is telling me that if we forget it happened, it will all fade away, but if we pursue the issue, it will grow into this awful great shadow between us."

Karl exhaled. Perhaps she was right, but he couldn't let the matter drop.

"Two men tried to kill you," he said softly. "They harmed you in a way that we don't even understand. Yet you're suggesting that we walk away?"

"Actually, that's what you have always told *me* to do."

"Dearest, you insisted on sitting through an appalling film *for the second time*," he said mildly. "That is not how I define walking away."

"It's different."

"Is it?"

"I wasn't looking for Amy with revenge in mind, only curiosity."

"You think that I want revenge on those men?"

"Don't you, a little?"

"Very well," Karl conceded. "Yes, you're right, but more than that I want *answers*. And so do you."

"Yes, answers. Always. How do you manage to talk your way round me, every time?" She pulled a mock-angry face at him.

"I call it being reasonable. We both want the same thing, so we've no reason to argue."

"True," Charlotte said crisply. "Then we won't be breaking your rule not to pursue humans for personal reasons. We're searching only for understanding. Pure knowledge."

"Exactly," he said, smiling but serious.

She exhaled. "Aren't we wondrous creatures? Half of me was dying to drain poor Amy's blood that night, while the other half hoped that she would get better."

Karl kissed her cheek, his lips lingering. "As I always felt about my cherished, human Charlotte," he said softly. "Lucky for Amy that she fell into the arms of a vampire she could trust."

"Well," said Charlotte. "Lucky for her I was feeling kind at that moment, and not ravenous. Never trust a vampire."

Stefan's house was a handsome chalet on the shores of Lake Lucerne, with carved eaves, balconies, and a long veranda a few steps above ground level, perfect for his future house guests to sip champagne and admire the sunset. Karl approached through the dusk, watching the last molten glow of the sun swallow its own reflection in the water. Behind the house, meadows rose towards dark pine forests. Mount Pilatus floated in glory, vast and awe-inspiring.

So peaceful, Karl thought, sighing because he knew why Stefan created such homes for himself and Niklas. Spider webs.

"Where's Charlotte?" Stefan asked, opening the door before he knocked.

"Violette wanted to see her. I'm alone," said Karl. He stepped inside at Stefan's invitation and took in the scent of new pine, Persian rugs, spring flowers.

"Oh, I so want her to see our house." Stefan managed to pull a face and grin at the same time. "She could have brought Violette with her. Unless Madame was in a mood to tear off my head?"

"She only tears the heads off those who deserve it," Karl said mordantly. "But she's calmer these days. Your head is safe."

"Truly?" Stefan led him through a number of spacious rooms and downstairs to a living room on the lowest floor. Long windows opened on to the veranda that overlooked the lake. From this vantage point, the building seemed to be afloat on the water. "She didn't go mad when she heard we were here?"

"She frowned," said Karl.

Stefan laughed. "That's all? She really has mellowed."

"Ah, but what was going on in her head? That should worry you."

"As I said, we've no intention of interfering with her or her precious ballet, as long as she leaves us in peace. Have we, Niklas?"

His twin came to stand beside him, as quiet as a cat. Stefan slipped an arm around his waist.

"And as we told you," said Karl, "it won't be you who causes problems, but your visitors. I know you too well, Stefan. You'll fill up the place with idle young rich people as you always do. Other vampires will be drawn here. Ones who are less amenable to obeying your rules."

"Karl, I can manage my household," Stefan said mildly. "There'll be no trouble, I promise. Look, there's no one here yet: we're rather enjoying the peace. Couldn't you spend five minutes admiring the beauty of our new home before you start grousing at me? We call this the lake room. Isn't it gorgeous?"

"It is sublime," said Karl. "And I've finished grousing, as you put it. I trust you."

Red sunset flooded the interior, drenching the three vampires, turning Karl's dark hair blood red.

"You trust me?" Stefan said with a grin. "That's new."

"Unless or until you do something insane."

"Charming. I know I've not been the most reliable of friends. Yes, I used to sit at Kristian's feet and do his bidding... You could accuse me of bending with every wind that blows, but at the time I knew no better, and I was afraid of him. And in awe, because he saved both my own wretched life, and Niklas's. He gave us that precious gift."

"I'm not criticising you for that," Karl said evenly. "We were all Kristian's puppets in those days."

"But I broke away from him, for the sake of dearer friends: you, Charlotte, and most of all Niklas, my twin soul. And Violette. She's a dragon, but who can help loving her? *La Belle Dame Sans Merci*."

"She's changed us all, in one way or another."

"For the better?" said Stefan.

"I believe so," said Karl. "Yes, I opposed her initiation, but Charlotte went ahead regardless, with your help. I believed disaster would follow. For a long time it seemed I was right. Some vampires come out of the transformation insane, and remain that way."

"Kristian," Stefan murmured.

"Quite. But Violette mastered herself. Eventually – though, heaven knows, it was an epic struggle – she found understanding and peace." Karl paused, recalling her description of the spectre that had attacked her in mid-ocean. "As much peace as she can hope for, at least. I admire her strength."

"Well, she's become a figurehead for us, whether we want one or not," Stefan said wryly. "And I truly don't want my presence to upset her. Has it occurred to you that I might just wish to spend some time with Niklas in calm and solitude?"

Karl gave him a sceptical look. "I suppose anything is possible. No parties, then?"

"In time. We're not making any promises. Are we, Niklas?" His brother, a gilded china doll, gave Karl an empty stare and a half-smile. "But for now... rest. Did you bring the, er, artefact?"

"That's why I'm here." Karl drew the bundled scarf from his coat pocket and let it fall open, so the bone-handled knife rested across his open palms. It twitched. He felt its cold energy numbing his hand even through the cashmere.

Stefan stroked the haft, snatched his hand away, then tried again. "Interesting sigils. Do you know what they signify?"

"Apparently a maze, with a skull at the centre. Its eyes are closed, which is anatomically impossible. What it means, I have no idea."

"Any insights at all?"

"One," said Karl. "Charlotte believes the knife to be carved of human bone."

"Oh? Suitably macabre. I do hope she's right."

Stefan took the dagger from him, cupping it in both hands with the scarf beneath, as if cradling a baby bird. He said nothing, only stared at the weapon's yellowish glow with glazed eyes. The sunset deepened to crimson.

"How is Charlotte?" Stefan asked after a while.

Karl hesitated. "In truth, I'm not sure. She says she's well, but I catch her in a trance sometimes... She still thinks the lamia is haunting her, and that I'm in danger too." He stopped, not wanting to tell Stefan the painful details.

"She's suffering from delusions?" Stefan, who rarely took anything seriously, looked alarmed.

"I don't think she is." Karl stared out at the blood-soaked sky. "If it's real to her, then it's real. I think she is still in shock. At first she was eager to find out who attacked her: now she wants to turn away and pretend nothing happened. Yet she seems rational, as sane as she's ever been."

"Which isn't *very* sane, since she consented to run away with you." Stefan gave a wry smile.

"I will find the men who attacked her. She says she'd be happier if I forget them, but I can't." He groaned. "Stefan, I love her with all my soul, but sometimes I wish I had walked away and left her human, after all she's suffered..."

"Don't be ridiculous. Everyone suffers. You know perfectly well that she would endure it all again, and worse, to be with you. And so would you."

"True. She's stronger than she seems. Violette, in the shape of Lilith, showed us fearful visions of the future, but she also helped to release us from fear. Made us more free to be our true selves."

"I should like her to feed upon me again," murmured Stefan.

"Still, I think part of us resists such drastic change," Karl went on. "Suppose you feel guilt for drinking human blood. You think you've shed your conscience, then it comes back in a different guise. Visions, hauntings... anything."

"I don't bother with guilt," said Stefan. "Never have."

"I noticed," Karl said acidly. "But even if you try to be less of a ravening beast, kinder and less lethal to humans? That beast is still inside you. It will find another way out."

"I am rarely lethal to humans," Stefan retorted. "I love them. That's why they give their blood freely, and keep coming back for more."

"For heaven's sake, I am not talking about you in particular. I'm speaking of vampires in general."

"I know," said Stefan with a teasing smirk.

"I should know better than to expect a meaningful conversation about this. Well, are you happy to keep the dagger for us?"

Stefan's face went blank and he made no reply.

"Stefan? What are you thinking?"

"About all the deaths." His tone was unusually sombre. "You think I'm irredeemably superficial, but you're wrong. I'm thinking about our last great battle to stop Cesare and Simon creating a new army of immortals."

"You weren't there," Karl said mildly.

"That doesn't stop me brooding about it. You can't think I was unaffected? Cesare's plan was maniacal, bound to fail. But all those deaths... Fyodor, Rasmila and Simon. All those human apprentices, promised immortality – dead! Sebastian Pierse, taking himself to the *Weisskalt*. Sebastian, of all the heartless devils ever to walk the night, destroying himself over a human! Who would have predicted that? And Katerina. Even Kristian. So many deaths. Does it not make you feel we're hanging on a thread of spider-silk, those of us who remain?"

Karl walked to the windows and looked out at the rippling red lake. "It's unlike you to be so melancholy."

"I know. Frightening, isn't it? But I remember Violette's words, after Schloss Holdenstein was burned to a shell, when we all gathered and made peace."

"So do I," said Karl. "She said our purpose is a selfish one: to live for blood, to bring pleasure and nightmares to mortals. Not to change the world. The Crystal Ring itself won't let us. She said that everything men do is in denial of death. They wish to live forever. But no man can avoid his fate; no mortal can escape Lilith. That's why they invented God: to annihilate the crone of death. But a few take the risk of embracing Lilith and accepting her kiss."

"Yes," said Stefan. "Then Pierre asked if we become immortal, and Violette answered, 'We live a little longer, that's all.'"

"'Man turns his back on the great mother, but she will come anyway, dressed for battle like the Morrigan, and take her revenge for being rejected,'" Karl added. "So Sebastian said."

"And something about us feasting like vultures on their folly?" Stefan smiled, rewrapped the blade and locked it in a desk drawer. "I don't think I'd want that."

"I've already tried it," said Karl. He recalled mist drifting over the mud and trenches of a battlefield. He had moved like a spectre from one dying soldier to the next, as if by taking the last drops of their blood, he could understand their suffering... "It's not an experience I recommend. If we don't stand outside human folly, it will drag us down and destroy us."

"A wise sentiment." Stefan went to Karl's side and rested a hand on his shoulder. "I like humans. I like to tease and bring them pleasure, not death."

"Mm. You are as pleasurable and harmless as laudanum, or cocaine," Karl said acerbically.

"No one's perfect."

"I should go. You're sure you don't mind keeping the knife? If anything strange happens, let us know immediately."

"Like what? Will ghost hands use it to stab me in the night?" Stefan laughed. "You worry too much."

"No, I believe my level of worry is usually all too accurate." Karl smiled. "Thank you."

"Wait, before you go," said Stefan. "Let me offer you a drink. A small token of friendship. A gift."

He pushed back his sleeve and offered his wrist, raising the heel of his hand towards Karl's mouth. Karl hesitated, only for a moment: then he took Stefan's hand, touched his lips to the soft skin, bit down and drank. Accepted the gift.

Charlotte entered Violette's private apartments, a bower of lamplight glittering on crystal chandeliers and mirrors. The colours were silver and grey, with touches of black. Vases of white lilies and roses filled the air with fragrance. The dancer's maid

Geli – a tall, sweet-natured woman who'd been her companion for years – welcomed her, and left her alone with Violette.

"You sent for me?" said Charlotte, mildly puzzled.

"Well, I didn't mean to seem high-handed, but yes. You're not busy, are you?"

Violette was sitting cross-legged on a couch, wearing a man's smoking jacket thrown over her practice clothes. Her face was an ice-sculpture, her eyes too bright. When she turned that look on humans, they would usually flee without her uttering a word.

Charlotte, who knew her well, was less easily intimidated. Violette had a demeanour that suggested, had she been human, she would have been chain-smoking furiously.

"I was about to go out with Karl, but it doesn't matter. He took the mysterious knife to Stefan as you asked. What's wrong?"

"Nothing and everything." Violette's lips thinned. A flush of blood rose to her face.

"You're blushing!" said Charlotte. "You never blush. Come on, tell me."

"Emil." Violette's voice was barely audible, even to vampire hearing. "It's Emil."

"What? Is he injured?"

"Now there's a thought. If he had an injury to stop him dancing, that would take the problem away, at least for a while. The foolish, beautiful boy thinks he's in love with me."

"Ah." Charlotte's reaction was to smile. She stopped herself, not quickly enough.

"I'm glad you find it amusing," Violette retorted. "I think it began after that storm in the Atlantic – good grief, can I truly not hold someone's cold hand after a terrifying experience without my intentions being misinterpreted? Today I tried to rehearse a few steps with him and he was all over the place. So I asked him what was wrong, and the next I know, he is on his knees swearing undying love! The fool even proposed marriage."

Charlotte couldn't suppress a grin. She lowered her eyes. "Oh, dear."

"Oh, dear, indeed. For goodness' sake – Charlotte, this is *not* funny. I told him to keep out of my sight for a week, and he responded by punching Mikhail in the face!"

"What? Why?"

"I think Mikhail has been teasing him. Emil seemed to think Mikhail had told me, but he hadn't. To be frank, I'd already guessed... but I was hoping with all my heart that I was wrong."

"Has he behaved like this before?"

"No, but he's not been with us long. I think our success in America went to his head. I should have guessed... I told you, the idiot nearly fell overboard in that storm while looking for *me*. I should have realised then..."

"I can see he's rather temperamental," said Charlotte. "I'm not sure why you're so angry about it, though."

"I am deeply fond of him, but he seems to have mistaken my fondness for something more. He's put me in an absolutely impossible situation. I *cannot* work with a dancer who is having... feelings for me. If he won't behave, my only choice is to dismiss him – but that would mean losing the best partner I have ever had! Do you wonder that I'm furious?"

"Dear, don't be too hard on him," Charlotte spoke gently. "He's young and you are a goddess. Thousands are in love with you. Only a very select few are ever privileged to touch you... and there is so *very* much touching involved in your dances. It's natural for him to be overwhelmed. Every ballet has star-crossed lovers..."

"It's called acting," Violette said frostily. "Rehearsal is tiring and repetitive: the novelty of having lithe bodies all around you swiftly wears off. It's work. I expect him to be disciplined. Professional."

"I'm sure he knows that, but... all that emotion and sensuality can't be entirely faked, can they? Sometimes feelings must spill into real life. Emil got a little too carried away, perhaps."

"Why are you defending him? Oh, I know why – because you have a gentle heart and think the best of everyone. You don't want me to punish him for having what I suppose are normal feelings. But this – no, it's not so simple and cannot easily be mended."

Charlotte sat beside her at a careful distance, concerned. "Please tell me you didn't feed on him."

Violette's eyelids fell in dark curves. "No. That would have been wonderfully hypocritical – lecturing him on controlling his appetites when I can't control mine? No... since that one time with Ute, I never touch my dancers. You know that. But it took only a few words to break his heart."

"That you don't share his feelings?"

"Yes. And that he must overcome his infatuation, or leave. He must have known what I'd say, but I doubt that made hearing it any easier."

"I can imagine. You must have terrified him."

"I surely hope so."

"But he took it out on Mikhail?"

"That was the last straw. Emil may be hot-blooded, but his attack was unprovoked and I will *not* tolerate such behaviour! The trouble is, Charlotte…" Violette raked her fingers through her unbound hair. "If Emil were a lesser performer, he'd be on a train back to his home town as we speak." She flung off the jacket as if too hot. "But no, he has to possess a sublime talent that makes him indispensable! What am I to do?"

"Has this happened before? You must have dealt with such situations in the past."

Violette gave a short sigh. "You recall that when I was human, and naïve, my ballet director Janacek treated me as his property, a pet to be fondled. I had no power to stop him. The only reason he never forced me into his bed was that he feared impregnating his star. I should be grateful for that, I suppose. But when I met you, it ended. And when I became a vampire – I knew no man would ever intimidate me again."

"You can't compare Emil to that appalling lecher."

"No, of course not, but I have rules. Any man, dancer or not, who dares show me the merest *hint* of over-familiarity dies in the arctic blast of my stare." Violette gave a thin smile. Charlotte laughed, couldn't help it.

"I had noticed. The world has noticed."

Violette's tone became gentler. "Nearly all my male principals have preferred their own sex – apart from Mikhail, but he's always respected professional boundaries. That makes for a perfect partnership. My mistake was to make the same assumption about Emil. I suspected his inclination was for females, but I chose to ignore my instincts because he's so damned brilliant."

"He is. And handsome."

"And knows it." Violette groaned. "Admirers flocking at the

stage door, tantrums because I reject his advances – how do I bring his ego under control before it destroys everything?"

She seemed to be expecting an answer.

"Speak to him."

"I can't," Violette snapped. "I've tried. There's nothing more to say. Every attempt I make, he'll interpret as a possible way in, a sign that I'm softening. Besides, it would be demeaning. I maintain discipline by being the steel empress; I cannot compromise that by running after him and trying to reason with him. No. All I can give him now is a wall of cold silence. But…"

"You're afraid he's so headstrong he might actually walk out?" Charlotte, startled to see Violette at a loss, tapped her foot as she wondered what help to offer. "Would you like me to have a word with him?"

The ballerina's gaze met hers with a flash of hope. "Would you? I've suspended him indefinitely, which means he must attend practice but nothing else, which is damned inconvenient because I need to start rehearsing. Oh, and tell him I don't want him leaving the premises."

Charlotte grimaced. "Violette, when I was human, I was so awkward that I could barely hold a conversation with a male without fleeing in terror – and they were just ordinary young men, probably as nervous as me underneath. I'd never dream of approaching a golden prince of the stage…"

"You seem to manage quite well with Karl."

"That's different. I fled from him too, but he didn't give up. Yes, I'm different now, but those human fears still rear up and spook me sometimes… What shall I say to him?"

"Oh, you'll think of something." Violette gave her a wry look. "Try to make him understand *why* I enforce these rules – you might make a better job of it than me. If he does as he's told, I may reduce his suspension to two weeks."

"You are an appalling tyrant," Charlotte said mildly.

"So I've been told." Violette gave a savage grin. "Charm him. Do anything it takes, within reason."

"I'll try, but I've never really spoken to Emil; I don't know how he'll react…"

"Nor do I, but I need him." Her voice turned low and fervent.

She didn't need to explain that she meant for the sake of her art, the pursuit of perfection. Charlotte knew, everyone knew, that Violette put her ballet before her own life. "Charlotte, I *cannot* lose him."

The lake was black, glittering with reflections from dim gas-lamps along the promenade. Emil skimmed flat stones across the water, an activity that did little to relieve his frustration. In his dark coat and hat, no one gave him a second glance as they walked by. Tourists, mostly. Couples, arm in arm. Damn them.

He knew he'd behaved like a complete fool with Violette. To stop and think before he acted was not in his nature, but now he cursed himself, striking his forehead with his knuckles. She couldn't have humiliated him more thoroughly if she'd stripped him naked, painted him blue and flogged him through the streets. And he'd known this would happen, yet he'd offered his heart for her to trample on regardless. Weeks in the wilderness of her disdain? Perhaps she would never look at him again without contempt.

"I'll never be at ease with you again. I'll never confide in you, never treat you as the other half of myself, never trust you. Because of this, I'll always be on my guard. Everything between us will be work, nothing else." Her words looped around his mind, like razors cutting him to pieces.

The price of dancing with her, now, was that he would be her abject slave forever.

And yet... how to leave?

He couldn't.

How quickly could love turn to hate? He nearly hated her for her glacial dismissal of him. She valued his looks and talent – but his inner life, his yearning and love and devotion, his humanity, were worthless. He thought, *I am just a thing to her*.

Did she have a heart at all, or a lump of black diamond in her chest?

From nowhere, like a spectre taking shape from starlight, a woman moved alongside him. She appeared so silently that he almost jumped out of his skin. Even in near-darkness she seemed to gather every speck of light, her pale coat glowing golden-cream. Smoky amethyst eyes shone under the brim of her cloche hat. The hat was decorated with a silk camellia, rosy-gold like her hair...

He'd seen her often, but never spoken to her. She was one of Violette's special, secret friends. Frau Alexander, if that was her real name.

"Emil?" Her voice was quiet as she leaned on the rail beside him. "I'm Charlotte."

"Madam." He gave a formal bow, not knowing what to say.

She paused, as if she were lost for words too. Eventually she said, "A beautiful evening..."

"If you like it dark and cold," he said sourly.

"Sometimes darkness helps."

He studied her neat, girlish profile as she looked across the water. She was lovely, unconventional and gypsy-like in her beauty, her eyes unreadable as if they held a complex soul a thousand miles deep... but she was not Violette.

"Did she send you?" he asked at last. "Madame Lenoir, I mean."

"Yes." She turned to face him, gave an apologetic shrug. "I'm sorry, I know this is awkward. She's... concerned."

"Is she?" He gripped the rail so hard his hands burned. "Did she tell you that I made a total fool of myself? That I declared my love to her, despite my every instinct screaming against it? *Agh*." The last sound was a grunt of agony.

"No one else knows," Charlotte said gently. "She trusts me. She said... Look, you understand that it's impossible for her to speak to you at present? But if you abide by the discipline she's set out, everything can go back to normal."

"No. Nothing can ever be normal, after this."

"She would prefer you to stay inside the premises." Charlotte's tone grew firmer. "Emil, I know it's difficult, but either you do as she says or you leave. Neither of you wants that, do you?"

He groaned, put his forehead on his knuckles. "No."

"You must understand that she sets these rules for a reason. Romantic relationships between her dancers are not allowed."

"Of course I understand!" He straightened, throwing his hands in the air. "I am not an imbecile! But I cannot help—" Catching his breath, he said, "Madam, forgive me. I don't mean to cause offence, I'm not usually so ill-mannered, but..."

"It's all right. I'm not offended. I know how it is to fall in love, to be so mad with love for someone that you can't eat or sleep or think. It happens to everyone, so they say. But you have the great misfortune to fall for Violette. The sooner you accept that it can't be, the sooner your pain will fade."

Emil was breathing harshly, trying to suppress another outburst against Charlotte.

"Why can't it be?" He kept his voice as low as he could manage. "Why? She is not much older than me. I can prove worthy of her! Am I hideous? Call me vain – I admit it, I *am* vain – but those stage-door girls don't sigh and swoon for no reason. The heavens blessed me with a fair countenance, God-given talent, and I would like to think enough courage, passion and loyalty to last my whole life. What more does she need of me? Is it unknown for performers paired on the stage or film set to fall in love? How would it harm her to be dancing with her *husband*? Are we breaking some law of the land?"

"Emil, I'm sorry." Charlotte looked distressed now. Her face had an inner light, like an angel, and her eyes glimmered... He caught himself, feeling for a chill moment that she was trying to hypnotise him. He looked away.

"Why are you sorry? I know she sent you to talk sense into me, but you cannot *know* she will never change her mind. Even she can't know that!"

"She won't." Charlotte's voice was quiet but very firm. Another chill went through him. "Emil, please believe me. I know this hurts, but it will pass."

"No. You think this is some boyish infatuation? This will not pass."

"Then learn to live with a broken heart."

He glared at her. "How do you know what will be? She sends you, her confidante, to tell me what she wants me to believe – but you are just a... a bystander. Forgive me, Madame Charlotte, but you do not *know*."

"Emil." Again the tone of sympathy that made him want to scream. "I don't know any way to convince you, except to tell you the truth. There was someone... last year... but that person died. So Violette's heart is broken too. Show her some pity, because she has nothing left for you."

He barely heard the last words through the roar of blood in his ears. *Someone else... but they died... Nothing left for you...* Tears burned his eyes.

"No. No."

He began to back away. Charlotte filled his vision, like a painted angel in silver leaf. There seemed to be two of her, or more: multiple reflections of Charlotte. Again the world shifted, as it had when he saw the skull-figure hunting Violette through the ocean storm. The top layer of reality tore away and he saw, with dreadful clarity, as if he'd been drugged, that she was not human... That she had the same eerie, deathly glow as Violette. Beauty sharp enough to kill, like a sword.

"What are you?" he gasped. Her mouth moved, and she reached towards him, but he was backing away. "*What are you?*"

"Emil, wait."

Her voice was faint through the rush of blood as he turned and fled into the darkness.

CHAPTER NINE

FALLEN PRINCE

Godric pulled his hat brim low over his eyes as he followed Wolfgang, Bruno and the rest of the herd towards their favourite beer hall. He rarely went drinking with them – if he did, they would be on their best behaviour – but tonight he was conducting an experiment. He wanted to observe their antics when they didn't know he was watching. By the time they noticed him – if anyone did – it would be too late. Beer would have dissolved their inhibitions.

He wished to see what they talked about, how outsiders reacted to them. The knowledge might even make dramatic material for a future film. However, his main purpose was to watch for signs of sedition. The loss of a precious *sikin* – on the surface, a drunken mistake – might be hiding a more sinister motive.

He had to be sure of his inner circle's loyalty. The merest hint of insurrection would be crushed. Keeping a careful eye on them was simply pragmatic, not paranoid.

Godric also needed a distraction from his own thoughts. His encounter with the male *strigoi* at the cinema had left him struggling to master his emotions. He'd been stunned, furious, agitated – had no idea how to react or what he should do. And every time he recalled the man's deceptively attractive face, the feelings boiled up again and he grew short of breath, dizzy.

This had to stop. For years Godric had sketched and filmed

"demons" as a form of expression, but real evil, apparently, looked human.

The females of his household had gone to a restaurant for a more civilised evening out. They did not carouse with the men. When the sexes socialised together, he insisted on proper behaviour.

One thing he knew: none of this rabble would make an acceptable husband for Amy. Not even Wolfgang Notz: wealthy, brave and well-respected he might be, but still far from suitable.

Godric watched his gang of supporters trooping into the *Bierkeller*. Heat, music and noise billowed from the interior in a noxious cloud. To one side of the open doors, he saw someone hesitating, a man with a cloud of golden hair and the slender, taut build of an athlete. He swayed a little, clearly drunk. He started towards the entrance, then halted as if the wall of heat had physically stopped him.

My God. It can't be, Godric thought. His heart's rhythm increased and he moistened his lips. Such an opportunity must be seized.

He strode up to the man, placed a firm but reassuring hand on his shoulder.

"Sir, a friendly word of advice," said Godric. "I don't recommend that appalling place. It's filthy and full of drunks. People will recognise you. That could be very awkward indeed. We've met before: do you remember? Godric Reiniger, at your service."

"What?" The man looked round slowly. The flush of alcohol turned his beautiful face ugly. His eyes were red-rimmed and bloodshot.

"Allow me to suggest a more elegant establishment. We could take a little supper together—"

"Oh, I remember you," the blond man slurred. "Leave me the hell alone!"

He swung his fist at Godric's head. His aim was wild, and Godric ducked out of the way, staggering back a few steps to regain his balance. He looked up again to see the man vanishing into the fug of the beer hall.

"Fine," said Godric under his breath. "Go in, then, against my advice. Let's see what you make of it, little princeling."

Someone caught Godric's arm, steadying him. There was a shadow at his side: Fadiya.

She was dressed in her elegant but drab style: a cloche hat and expensive-looking coat of dark brown. She appeared, at least to an outsider's eyes, entirely human.

As always, her disturbing presence made him both infuriated and helpless. He didn't want her anywhere near his household, but he could not make her go away. *The knives are mine, but I'll let you keep them*, she had told him, *if in exchange you let me live among you*. Everything about her made him shudder. He had to keep reminding himself that his rituals had strengthened him against vampires. He grew stronger every day. She couldn't harm him.

"What do you want?" he snapped.

"That young man seemed rather upset with you," she said in her calm, velvety voice. "Are you hurt?"

"This isn't a suitable place for women."

"Why should I care about that? If you and I are to help each other, sometimes I need to go where you go. I like to watch humans. Why did he try to hit you?"

He wanted to tell her to go to hell, but her glittering eyes disarmed him.

"I don't know, but he's going to be sorry."

He walked away from Fadiya, towards the light and noise, but she followed. "Who is he?"

"Emil Fiorani. An arrogant youth who sneered at me when I was trying to speak with Violette Lenoir."

"Oh," she whispered. "How interesting."

"He's one of her dancers. Her principal partner. You must have heard of him."

"Yes, I've heard his name," she echoed. "But are you sure it's him?"

"Of course I'm sure," Godric said thinly. "The question is, why is he in a place like this, drunk and alone? Why?"

The conspiratorial tone of her reply made him wonder, for the first time, if she really could prove useful to him.

"Perhaps I could find out for you."

Emil entered the *Bierkeller* – reputed to be the rowdiest in town – and pushed his way through the crowded cellar in search of a seat. Already drunk from a few glasses of wine in a hotel bar, he hadn't yet reached his goal of oblivion. The air was thick with smoke and stale alcohol, with body odour laced with sickly perfumes. Lamps turned the pall to an ochre fog. Music pierced his ears, an obnoxious blend of folk and popular songs, with bursts of discordant singing as customers joined in. His shoes skidded on spilled beer, wet sawdust and God alone knew what else on the floor.

This place was some kind of purgatory. The clientele reminded him of his own peasant origins, a loathsome thought. But tonight he felt loathsome, and craved everything raucous and disgusting, a sewer of depravity to purge him of Violette.

A group of noisy men pulled him down on to the end of a bench beside them. There was nowhere else to sit. A barmaid slammed steins of beer on to the table, laughing off the crude remarks that were shouted at her. These people were enjoying themselves, Emil noted in disbelief. This was his idea of hell, but he swallowed the rank beer as if forcing down medicine. His companions at the long table shouted and laughed – at what, he didn't care. Two beers later, he was reeling drunk.

The music began to sound uplifting. He was tempted to leap up and perform a folk dance on the table. The girls looked prettier... One in particular kept catching his eye. She was sitting across the room, seemingly alone, too well-dressed for her surroundings.

Some minutes later, he noticed Godric Reiniger at a different table. Herr Reiniger was more or less inconspicuous in a shabby coat and a hat that shaded his face, but the glint of his spectacles caught Emil's eye.

He quickly switched his attention back to the woman. She was certainly too refined for this pigsty. She wore an off-white silky flapper dress glittering with beads, and a long pearl necklace. Her dark brown hair was cut to jaw-length and framed her face in the casual, shiny waves of the latest style. Her skin was dark too, like coffee with a dash of cream, a gorgeous contrast to the ivory of her dress. She appeared to be of Middle Eastern blood – only a guess – but it was unusual to see a non-white face in this area. She couldn't help but captivate him.

Her eyes were glorious. Large, lustrous, richest brown, rimmed by natural dark pigment that gave her the look of an Egyptian goddess. And warm! She smiled at him, and her expression was all sweet, shy warmth.

She was Violette's opposite.

Emil looked away. The room swayed, and he couldn't focus on anything without it flickering and rolling like a stuck movie. The male beside him was tugging his sleeve, shouting some incoherent joke in his ear. They all seemed to be shouting at him – teasing, mocking, joking at his expense – how was he supposed to respond? Another full stein foamed in front of him. He was too far gone to care where he was or what any of this meant.

Nothing. That was the point. He wanted meaningless sensation, and here it was.

A man at the head of the table was speaking in a low, firm voice, as if telling his drinking friends something of great importance. He had the look of a youthful but experienced army officer. A shrewd face, handsome in a way, short hair catching the light like a reddish halo. He emphasised every point he made by chopping the table with the side of his hand.

All the men sitting alongside Emil went quiet and listened. Some began to chime in, or to mutter approval.

Emil took another swig of beer and clenched his jaw. Wonderful – they were talking politics, a subject that made his blood boil. They were all of a type, he noticed, no doubt ex-military: young but older than their years, rough around the edges, in shirt-sleeves.

Emil began to feel restless, bored and slightly ill. Not drunk enough yet... time to leave, find somewhere quieter... perhaps a bottle of plum brandy to drink himself unconscious and fall into the lake. Ha, in the morning they might drag his body from the water with a hook.

Ballet star in tragic drowning... How would Violette like that?

"Hey!" shouted someone down the table. "What's so funny, pretty boy?"

"What?"

The man, a coarse drunk not much older than Emil, indicated the speaker, who was apparently the head of this gang of – twenty-five? Emil couldn't concentrate to count them properly. "Herr Notz is speaking. When he speaks, you shut up and listen. You don't *laugh*."

"I wasn't..." Emil felt a flare of anger. Who were these idiots, with their dishevelled clothes and their narrow, bloodshot eyes?

Another jumped up, raising his beer in the air. "Here's to Godric Reiniger! Here's to Wolfgang Notz! Switzerland forever! The world doesn't know what's coming: *we are!*"

All the others joined the toast, their yells deafening Emil. The red-haired man, Wolfgang, raised a calm hand and said, "Sit down and shut up, Bruno."

"Shut up yourself!" shouted a patron from the neighbouring table. "Switzerland doesn't need to turn into Italy. We don't need nationalist talk here. We're trying to have a good time! Can't you find another cellar for your preaching? A coal cellar?"

Laughter.

Wolfgang Notz only gave a slow, menacing smile. His companion, Bruno, started breathing faster, turning red with rage.

Something odd happened then. Emil's addled brain became a lens: distorted chaos around the edges with a small, lucid window in the centre. With perfect clarity he saw Wolfgang go still and glance meaningfully across at Godric Reiniger. Suddenly noticing that the older man was there, but keeping the observation to himself?

Reiniger stared back at Wolfgang and gave a small nod.

Then Notz stood up and leaned on the table with both hands. His voice was measured but penetrating enough to silence the musicians.

"Have you all forgotten your history, your proud heritage? The heroes like William Tell who fought to make this glorious country what it is? That is all under threat from every side! You in this place, you want to live your tiny lives surrounded by gypsies and thieves, degenerates, homosexuals and cripples? That is your choice. But if you are young and strong, and would like a better future – give us a fair hearing. Switzerland needs to protect herself. Why should we take in refugees, the dross of the world, every time war looms? We need to expel the enemy within. We need breathing room for our pure Swiss nation. You all know what I'm talking about! We could all be strong together. Protect our borders and we become stronger! No more threats or compromises with the nations around us. A new world in which Switzerland stands above all others! This new world has no place for weakness, no room for effeminate aristocrats or those of inferior idle blood ."

Emil saw that Reiniger had a small movie camera on the table; he was filming Notz's performance. Reiniger's mouth curved in a small, proud smile.

"Look at me and remember this moment," he added. "Our founder, Godric Reiniger, knows the secret of power. We know it too. Do you?"

The room went silent. A different voice called out, "If that's what you want, clear off to Italy and march for Mussolini. Lick his boots clean while you're at it."

"It's easy to mock Mussolini," said Notz. "There is a leader with *almost* the right idea. We can do so much better. Come on, we all know that Switzerland is the finest country in the world. It's our duty to protect her!"

This brought cheers, but Emil was enraged. He staggered to his feet, head throbbing. "Mussolini's an arrogant, bloated bastard!" he spat.

A staff member, apparently the landlord, signalled frantically at the band. The music started up again, with the desired effect of drowning the argument. The folk around the edges of the cellar were losing interest. But Wolfgang, Bruno and their band of supporters all turned to stare at Emil.

"And who are you?" said Wolfgang.

"No one. But I'm telling you he's a maniac, a brute."

"He saved Italy."

"I *am* Italian. He spouts fine words, like you, but he'll ruin us! And if you want to ruin Switzerland the same way – you are all gullible fools!"

Emil was panting for breath, struggling to get the words out, beyond caring what he said. The loudmouth, Bruno, stood up again and pointed at him, red-faced.

"See this creep who insults us? He looks like a girl with his golden hair. He's one of those ballet dancers. Don't you recognise him?" Bruno made an exaggerated flouncing gesture. "He's one of those we'll be exterminating, when our time comes. Italians are scum, no better than gypsies and Slavs. You – you're the worst of all worlds! Homo. Queer. Communist. You should be chained up in prison, not prancing on the stage!"

Emil was unsure what happened next. He was dimly aware of lurching forward, striking out at Bruno, missing, nearly falling over. A male server grabbed his arm. Then a fight broke out – Bruno and his comrades exchanging blows with a group of men who'd been heckling them – but the scene retreated into the distance as Emil was hustled towards the doors.

All a blur.

Even through the beer-fog, he knew the only sensible response was to leave. The next he knew, he was thrust outside into the cold and dark. Chilly air hit him, turning the world into a carousel.

He made his way down the side of the building, hanging on to the wall, until the roar of voices and music faded. No clear thoughts in his head, only a swirl of rage and anguish. The alley swayed and rolled like a ship in a storm.

Long fuzzy seconds later, shadows began to gather around him. A voice said out of the silence, "Hey, queer."

"I failed," said Charlotte, sitting on a chair arm in Violette's living room. Karl, back from visiting Stefan, leaned on the chair behind her. "I'm so sorry. I tried to explain…"

"What?" said the dancer.

"That you're grieving for someone else. He must accept that a relationship is impossible. I don't know what else I could have said."

"You could have tried a little hypnotic glamour, Charlotte. It worked on me: it should certainly have worked on an impressionable colt like Emil."

"I did try. I don't even like to do so, because it's usually so easy… but Emil didn't respond. Or rather he did, but in the wrong way. He told me, not politely, to leave him alone, and he bolted into the darkness."

"Wonderful," said Violette. "Where is he now?"

"He made off towards the Aldstadt. I don't think I'd have put things right by chasing him. Violette, he is terribly upset. Don't you realise how badly he's taken it? I'm sorry."

"Oh." Violette dropped her head. "Well, you tried. If I can't bring him to heel, who can? Is this his 'hot Latin blood' or just an excess of… energy? How much truth will it take to convince him?

'I never have relationships with my dancers. In any case, I prefer women. Oh, and I'm a vampire. How many more reasons do you need, Emil?'"

"Dismiss him," said Karl. "If you can't work with him, it's the obvious answer."

"Anyone else, I would," said Violette, shaking her hair back over her shoulders. She looked ragged, forlorn. "But on stage... he is perfection, Karl. I cannot lose him. Not without a fight. And I'm worried. He nearly flung himself overboard in a storm! What else might he do?"

For half a minute, no one spoke. Then Karl gave a quiet sigh.

"Let me go and look for him."

Karl's hunt for Emil took him through medieval streets, between throngs of tourists and locals, past hostelries spilling light, music and the stink of cooking food. The church-going, hard-working nature of the locals meant that revelry tended to cease early, but it was barely nine o'clock and foreign visitors had an appetite for late-night carousing. The less appetising smells masked the aroma of human blood.

Nearly all humans had an aura, but some gave out more distinct signatures than others. Although he knew Emil only by sight, he'd noticed the dancer's strong energy field, easy to sense from a distance. Karl tuned out all the other humans around him and locked on to Emil's bright gold and red outline.

Discreet in a dark overcoat, he slid into the Crystal Ring at ground level. Here the world became compressed and insubstantial. Human beings no longer appeared solid, but as silhouettes outlined by spindly light rays. Every now and then he caught Emil's signature, only to lose it again. But he was nearby... somewhere.

Karl felt like a spy or a bloodhound, performing this duty for Violette. Not that he minded, apart from mild exasperation at Emil's behaviour. *If I were Violette, I'd leave him to his own devices,* Karl thought. *He's a grown man, not a child.*

Unless it was the revelation of *what* she was that had sent him out of his mind.

Most humans were easily influenced by vampires. Curious, that

Emil seemed immune to the power of Violette's will. Charlotte was no less persuasive, but even her mesmeric gaze had failed to calm him.

Surely Emil couldn't know that Violette and her friends were not human? However, that didn't mean he hadn't sensed *something*. Once a human saw through a vampire's mortal pretence, the truth was difficult to unsee.

I only hope he'll listen to me, Karl thought, *because I've no intention of using physical force. If he refuses to come back, I'm not going to fight him.*

Karl caught Emil's aura more strongly. In his mind's eye he touched the fire-bright energy... and although a hundred other auras glowed around him, the signal was steady amid the shifting flow.

The pall of a seedy *Bierkeller* drew him.

Karl entered and pushed his way through the sweaty beer hall crowd. People were leaving, others arriving, causing a constant press of bodies. The air was thick with smoke and the stench of stale beer, sausages and sauerkraut and humans, overwhelming. Raucous folk music, voices yelling along with the songs. He'd been in far worse places, muddy battlefields where young men lay dying in shell craters... in comparison, a room full of rowdy drunks was nothing.

Their blood held no temptation, although Karl might have felt differently if he'd been hungry. He detached himself, imagining the chaos sealed behind a glass wall.

But where was Emil?

His aura had drawn Karl here like a magnet, but now it was gone. One group of fifteen or so, seated at a table near the band, appeared isolated from the other merrymakers. Slightly shabby, fairly drunk, there was little laughter or talk among them. Instead they were all paying attention to one man, who resembled a schoolmaster.

He was tall, and sat as straight as a sword. His mousy hair was shorn, catching the light to give the impression of pale fire cloaking his head. A strong, bony face, light-blue eyes behind spectacles...

Karl recognised him as the heckler from the cinema. Godric Reiniger, the amateur film-maker.

There was power in his blade-straight posture and his air of sheer confidence. The men sitting along the table were all leaning towards him, like courtiers attending a king. Beside him sat a handsome fresh-faced military type with freckles and shorn gingery hair... disturbingly similar to the intruder described by Charlotte. Not distinctive enough for Karl to be sure. Any of them could be the one who'd stabbed her.

If only Stefan were here, Karl thought. *He would identify the culprit for certain.*

Reiniger was speaking of the glory of Switzerland, its rich folklore and heroic history. Nothing wrong with that, but his low, fervent tone made Karl's heart sink. Even here, in a supposedly neutral federation and refuge for free thinkers, there were extremist groups. Some, with powerful connections in the military, had wormed their way into government.

There was something different about Reiniger, though. A kind of desperation, mixed with high-minded goals. Karl realised that he was reprimanding his companions.

"No use shouting about politics in a drunken frenzy. Our approach needs to be subtle, through film and art, poetry and song," Reiniger murmured. "A stealth attack. We can't force a new leader upon them. First we must make them *yearn* for the new leader, one they don't even realise they want until we show them. They must *plead* for him. Only then..."

As he listened, Karl caught another nagging undercurrent. The group gave off the same sour odour that the intruder had left in their chalet... and on Charlotte's clothes. Those aromas mingled here, faint but distinct.

It would make sense, Karl thought, keeping very still, resisting the strong urge to launch himself at them in rage. *If they drink regularly in here, then stagger home – some in a group, some alone – the guilty men could well be among them.*

Being a vampire did not make him all-powerful. He was perceptive, but not psychic. He couldn't slaughter every man here, in public, in hopes that he'd got the right ones. That wouldn't lead him to the truth behind the eldritch dagger. His skin prickled with tension, but there was nothing he could do... yet.

He noted that the benches along the table were a third empty. Then he caught Emil's aura again – no longer inside the building, but somewhere outside in the night.

As he turned to leave, he and Reiniger caught each other's eye. The brief glance froze Karl. Again the look held recognition, a challenge.

Reiniger's stare seemed to say, *I know what you are. I will not forget your face.* And Karl thought, *Nor I yours.*

Outside the crowds were thinning, establishments closing for the night. Men were pouring out of bars, singing at the tops of their voices. Karl caught the red-gold smudge of Emil again. He wasn't in the street but somewhere behind the beer hall.

From the general noise, Karl separated out the soft, horrible crunching sounds of fists and boots pounding into flesh.

He flew through the Crystal Ring to reach the place in seconds. In an unlit alley behind the building he came upon ten thugs, brutalising a hunched shape on the ground. They uttered obscenities, even spat on their victim.

Karl strode to the gang, seized the nearest brute by the shoulders and flung him hard against a nearby wall.

The others stopped their attack in pure shock. They were all of a type, like the ones inside: short-haired, thick-set, hard-eyed. Karl wasted no time on verbal threats. He simply let them *see* what he was: dropped his human persona, let his true nature shine out like white fire. He almost took on his demonic form from the Crystal Ring, but with a pale glowing face, blood-red eyes – enough to warn them either to flee, or die.

The gang broke up and ran. Their pounding footsteps made the walls ring. He'd never seen a bunch of men vanish so fast in his life. Ugly laughter echoed after them.

Then Karl dropped to his knees beside the groaning bulk on the ground.

Emil was a mess. His lip was split, both eyes black, blood trickling down his face. He winced with pain as Karl helped him to sit up.

"Is anything broken?" Karl asked.

"Don't know. God, my ribs…"

He cried out as Karl probed his ribcage, trying to ignore the blood aroma. Masked by the stink of beer and sweat, it was not all that tempting.

"You are just bruised, I think. How did this happen?"

"*Bastards,*" Emil spat.

"All right, tell me later. Let me help you. I'll carry you if you can't walk."

"I can walk! Get your hands off me!"

Karl stepped away, as asked. Emil struggled to stand, finally swallowing his pride and gripping Karl's arm before he could climb to his feet. He was even drunker than his attackers. Not quite so princely now.

"Come on, Emil, let's go home. You know who I am, don't you?"

"Herr Alexander. Another of her friends. I s'pose she sent you to fetch me back?"

He vomited three times before Karl hauled him to the end of the alley. After that, he sobered up a little, and began to weep. Karl aided his slow, staggering progress through the streets, across a bridge to the newer side of town and towards the theatre.

"Bastards," Emil said again, wiping his mouth with the back of his hand. "You know why they beat me up? They thought I was homosexual. Just because they recognised me from the stage – they assumed – the names they called me! Obscene."

"I'm sorry," said Karl.

"What are you sorry for? You stopped them killing me."

"Why were you in there? There are pleasanter establishments."

"Who are you, my father? I was there to get drunk, that's all. I got into an argument with them – that idiot, Notz, was spouting rubbish, praising Mussolini – so I put him right. A fight started – think I was thrown out, don't remember. But once I was outside, some of them followed me. They called me a filthy poof. Me!"

"I could call the police," said Karl. The thought of hunting down each thug individually and tearing out his throat was tempting, but he dismissed the impulse. His main concern was to deliver Emil safely back to Violette.

"No, not the police. I don't want to bring scandal to the ballet – although why should I care any more? She doesn't want me. I can't go back there."

"You might as well. Just go to bed, sleep it off, see the doctor if you need to. Violette will not be happy at the state of your face."

Emil gave a short, harsh laugh. "What does she care? I suppose she told you – has she told everyone what a fool I made of myself?"

"Emil," Karl said firmly. "She told only Charlotte and me."

"Mikhail knows, so everybody knows."

"It doesn't matter. And you haven't made a fool of yourself. You love her, but she doesn't love you? I know it feels like the end of the world, but it isn't."

"Easy for you to say. No one understands how this feels. All the beer, the screeching racket they call music, girls smiling at me, all those boots in my guts – *none* of it made the pain go away. What will make the pain stop? Why can't she…?"

He stopped, gasping for breath. Karl let him pause, concerned that he'd punctured a lung.

"What is it? Can you breathe?"

"Yes. I'm all right. But I remember what Charlotte said to me… that Violette loved someone who died. When she told me that, I felt her grief – Violette's grief. That's why these stupid tears won't stop. But then I thought – who was the lucky man she loved? And if she's capable of love, why can she not love me? I could comfort her. She doesn't have to live alone, grief-stricken, without love."

"Come on," Karl said. He put his arm around Emil's shoulders, as much to soothe him as to help him walk.

"Did you know him? Who was he?"

"She," Karl corrected. "Emil, you don't know Violette at all. No one does, really. She doesn't love easily, it's true. But when she does, her affection is only for other women."

"No." Emil reeled, would have fallen if Karl had not held him up. "You're lying!"

Karl shook his head. "You must have heard rumours. It's true. You deserve the truth."

The theatre rose in front of them, its facade a glory of Art Nouveau curves, with pillars carved in the shape of goddesses trailing fruit and vines from their hands.

"No. Liars, all of you!"

"The sooner you accept the truth, the easier it will be. You are going to look and feel like death in the morning," Karl said briskly. "I'll take you to your room, and bring you water and aspirin. I know this heartache feels as if it will never pass, and you won't get over it in a day – so I suggest that you don't even try.

Just sleep. I'll come back and see you tomorrow."

"Why? Who are you, anyway? She sends her lackeys after me!"

"Half dead on your feet, and still so belligerent?"

"Hide me from Violette," said Emil. He missed his footing as Karl took him through a side door into the academy, collapsed like a dead weight and began sobbing. Karl had never seen a man cry so excessively. "I don't want her to see me like this."

"She values you more than you know," said Karl, hefting him to his feet and closing the door behind them.

"It's not enough."

"It will have to be enough, because that's all she can give."

CHAPTER TEN

CAPTURING AN IMAGE

Emil woke, blinded by daylight, feeling as if a tank had run over him.

The ballet's doctor, a short balding man of sixty or so, was leaning over his bed. Everywhere his fingers probed, fresh waves of pain throbbed through Emil. He slapped the doctor's hand away with an inarticulate growl of rage.

"Get off me!"

The doctor scowled and stepped away, pulling down his rolled up sleeves and refastening his cufflinks. Then Emil saw three figures standing inside the doorway: Karl, Charlotte and Violette. He groaned.

"Cuts and bruises," said the doctor. "And when a healthy young man who never drinks decides to tip beer down his throat – this is the predictable result. He'll live, madame. I recommend a week's rest, and then light practice to regain his fitness."

"Thank you," said Violette. "Come back and check him again this evening, will you? Thierry – he's the assistant assigned to Emil – Thierry will pay you."

Her face loomed over Emil, shell-white, her sapphire eyes large and unblinking. Her lack of expression was more terrifying than anger would have been. Never in his life had he felt so low, like a soldier close to death in the bottom of a trench... so sick, depressed, and humiliated that he was sure he would die of it. Charlotte and Karl stood behind her, looking over her shoulders.

"Karl told me what happened," Violette said softly. "I don't know whether to yell at you for getting into that situation, or give thanks that you weren't murdered. For pity's sake, Emil!"

He turned his face away on the pillow.

"Well, I see there's no point in me saying anything until you feel better," she went on. "Who were the men who attacked you?"

"I don't know."

"Emil! Are you proud of being the most exasperating person who's ever worked for me? Tell me what you remember, and I'll leave you in peace."

Gritting his teeth, he managed to prop himself on his elbows.

"Madame, I was disgustingly drunk. They were talking politics, which I despise. I got into an argument with them. A fight broke out... the next I knew, I was outside. Some of them came after me, started using me as a football, and then Karl arrived. That's all I know."

Karl said, "I saw Godric Reiniger inside. He was talking with some men very similar to the ones who attacked Emil. I believe they were all part of the same group."

"Reiniger, who fancies himself a film-maker?" Violette looked puzzled, then dismissive. "He didn't look the type to associate with inebriated idiots, but I suppose you never can tell."

Karl said nothing more. The three stood gazing down at him. Their faces weren't unkind; they all looked grave and concerned. But as they stared, something changed. Again Emil felt his mind shift, a membrane of reality tearing away to show the truth beneath.

The three faces were not human.

Their skin was radiant, with an eerie glow like pearl. They never seemed to blink. Karl's face was too serene, his eyes like amber fire beneath the sooty shadows of his hair. Charlotte – so pretty and warm, with amethyst eyes that would mesmerise the very soul out of you, lips that would kill with pleasure. And Violette – Snow White, ice maiden, witch, enchantress...

"I'll send Thierry in to look after you," Violette was saying, almost kindly. "I wouldn't have had this happen for the world, but – it's done. Rest."

He heard her words as if from a great distance, as if she were looking at him through rippling water. All he could see clearly were their three mermaid-pale faces, filling him with unutterable terror. He couldn't form any clear idea of what he was seeing, yet he knew.

None of them are human.

"Like hell will I rest," Emil told himself angrily, fists clenched under the covers. An hour or so had passed. His head had cleared to some degree, but the horrible illusion he'd suffered only left him agitated, determined to leap out of bed, shake off his weakness and forget the whole episode. The sooner he returned to normal, the sooner this madness would leave him, and he'd prove to Violette... what?

That he was stronger than she dreamed. She would never look at him with pity again.

Thierry, who fussed like a grumpy mother hen, had gone to bring him some tea. While he was out of the room, Emil got up, splashed water on himself and pulled on his practice gear. Out in the corridor he bumped into Thierry, exchanged a few harsh words, and pushed past. Minutes later, he entered the studio just in time for class to begin.

Everyone stared at him.

His reflection in the studio mirror was ghastly: bruised eyes, battered face, mouth swollen like a balloon. He moved as stiffly as an eighty-year-old, wincing with every step as he approached the barre. This morning the session was being supervised by the ballet mistress, Joelle, who was even more intimidating than Ralph with her long, thin figure, heavily powdered face and orange-dyed hair. She rapped her cane on the floor and said, "What's this? No."

"Have you never seen a black eye before?" Emil said coldly. "A minor accident, that's all."

"I do not think Madame Lenoir would wish you to risk further injury by dancing unfit."

"I'll be the judge of whether I'm fit or not. Ignore me, and proceed."

For the first time in his career, he outstared her. At last Joelle gave in and turned away. "Very well. Your decision, your fault if you hurt yourself. Begin," she snapped.

Emil had never suffered such excruciating pain in his life. Ribs, kidneys, head, every part of him hurt – this was worse than the beating itself. Yet he pushed himself through each exercise, giving his injuries no quarter, refusing to let anyone see his agony.

And the others... did any of them know that Violette and her friends were... different? He glanced around at the intent, innocent faces of the other dancers. Was he the only one who'd *seen*... or was he the only one who was *not* in on the secret? Jean-Paul, Mikhail, Ute – all seemed to be laughing at him behind their blank expressions.

He felt he was going mad. There was nothing to take his mind off the madness except work, however brutal the pain.

Halfway through class, accompanied by an agitated Thierry, Violette entered. Emil kept his eyes to the front and ignored her. To his amazement, she said nothing, only watched him. He could *feel* her gaze scorching him. But by the time class ended, she had vanished.

What was he to make of that?

He'd expected a scene, forceful insistence that he return to bed at once. Instead... nothing. Was she now refusing to acknowledge his existence? Perhaps he'd only imagined that she was there, watching.

"What the hell happened to you, my friend?" In the changing room, Mikhail slapped him so hard between the shoulder-blades that he nearly collapsed. "You want ice on that face. Makes the swelling go down. Ice worked for *me* after you knocked me down yesterday."

"I apologise," said Emil, his voice thick through his split lip.

"Looks like you got your come-uppance, or whatever the phrase is," said the Russian. "No hard feelings, but that must have been a spectacular fight. Who won?"

"No one. Isn't it all over the school, my... misadventure?"

Mikhail shrugged. "Speculation, that's all. Lots of gossip. You want to tell me?"

"Not really," Emil growled. "I got drunk. Some thugs set on me. That's all. It was my own stupidity – which, as you see, I intend to put behind me as fast as possible."

"Ah well. Shattered hearts make us all go crazy. Did you make peace with madame?"

"Violette is not speaking to me. She sends her mysterious

friends after me instead. She doesn't want me, yet she wants to control me? She cannot have it both ways!"

"Ah, that's where you're wrong," Mikhail said, low and confiding. "She keeps all of us where she wants us, under that steel thumb. Accept it, or kiss goodbye to your glittering career."

"Not me," Emil said under his breath. "She won't break me."

At dusk, Emil walked along the lake shore promenade towards the town centre. A cold breeze rolled off the mountains, but he barely felt it. He wore a heavy coat, and a hat pulled down over his eyes to disguise both his identity and his bruises.

His mind writhed and clawed, unable to be still. He was supposed to stay on ballet premises: to hell with that. Rest? Soldiers in the Great War had fought on and on in the trenches with far worse injuries than this. Violette spurned him... the knowledge cut his heart with a thousand knives of agony and humiliation, but if that's what she wanted, he would spurn her in return.

He thought of her with Karl and Charlotte, staring down at him, haunting him like *streghe*, like spectral beings that pinned you down in the night and sucked out your life energy. Pretending to be human, thinking he hadn't noticed their masquerade...

He intended to get drunk again. He couldn't face the beer hall, but there was a big hotel by the water's edge. The tables outside were lit with candles, hardly anyone there but a few tourists wrapped up in coats and hats, looking out over the water. A pleasure steamer chugged its way from one side of the lake to the other.

He sat down and ordered a bottle of schnapps. He'd drunk a third of it when a woman walked past him, stopped, and backed up to look at him.

"Hello again," she said lightly.

He glowered at her from beneath the brim of his hat. The last thing he needed was a gushing devotee to see him in this sorry state. When he said nothing, she added, "You don't remember me? Forgive me. I saw you in the *Bierkeller* last night, but... well, it was so crowded..."

She was wrong. He knew her at once. She was the dark-skinned beauty who'd kept catching his eye. Tonight she was wearing an olive-green coat trimmed with fur, a hat of the same colour. The brim flared slightly around her lovely face and the crown glittered with green crystals that caught every spark of candlelight. A woodland creature, all brown and green... Her German was perfect – better than his – with an accent that he presumed was of her homeland.

"I remember," he said. "No place for a woman, or any civilised human being."

"Those brutes did this to you?" Her voice was warm but not pitying. He liked that. "I saw you arguing with them – brave, though not a good idea – but I thought you had left..."

"They caught me outside."

She took a seat opposite him. "Perhaps if I'd come to speak to you, it might never have happened." She leaned her chin on her hand, looking up at him, foiling his attempt to hide his face beneath his hat brim. Her eyes shone with a mixture of regret and teasing good humour. "I'm Fadiya. Spelled F-a-d-i-y-a."

"Emil." In normal circumstances he would have kissed her hand, made some flirtatious gesture, but he wasn't in the mood. "Perhaps you're right," he said. "You know why they set on me?"

"Every community has its troublemakers. It's never a good idea to argue with them."

"That was my first mistake. Then they decided to punish me for what I do."

"Why, what do you do?" She sounded innocently puzzled.

"You don't know who I am?"

"No. Should I?"

He thought, *Thank goodness. Someone with no ideas about me!* "Only if you go to the ballet," he said.

"I don't," she said bluntly. "I like jazz music. Not the terrible stuff they were playing in the *Bierkeller*. That was torture to the ears."

He smiled. "Then, no, there's no reason for you to recognise me. I don't know what you were doing in that dreadful place."

"Oh, I like to try every kind of local culture: never again. My dress was ruined with beer stains." She pulled a face, smiled again. "But you were saying, those idiots knew that you dance with the ballet? Why would that make them angry?"

"Because they assume it means I prefer my own gender: a

defect that entitles them to beat me like a rat in a sack."

"Do you?" Her lips parted, forming an O of disappointment. "Like other men, I mean?"

"No. I very much prefer women. But that was none of their damned business."

"You do look dreadfully miserable, Emil." She brushed strands of hair out of his eyes with suede-gloved fingers. "May I try to cheer you up? I am a good listener."

What could he say to her? That his life had fallen apart, that he couldn't go home because three unhuman spectres waited there for him, determined to control his every move until he had no will left of his own? How could he explain the exquisite agony of loving Violette?

"It doesn't matter," he said. "Nothing matters. I have nowhere to go, nothing to do."

"Oh yes, you do." Smiling, she pointed at the hotel behind him. *Hotel Blauensee*. He looked up at the painted, timbered facade with its quirky roof. "I have a room in there. Shall we go inside?"

He was too startled to answer, too drunk to refuse. When he said nothing, she laughed and took his hand. "Listen, there's a jazz band playing in the lounge. A *good* band. It's very dark and cosy, no one will see your bruises..."

"I'm a dreadful sight."

"You're a beautiful sight," she said. "I want to dance. You know how to dance, don't you?"

Bruno breathed a quiet sigh of relief to himself. He'd passed the test: publicly declared his support for Herr Reiniger and Wolfgang without even knowing that their leader was watching and filming, and played his part in humiliating the arrogant, effeminate ballet dancer. All in all, it had been a good evening.

He liked such brutal, everyday business.

The esoteric side made him uneasy. As Godric Reiniger let the last of his *Eidgenossen* group into the upstairs meeting chamber and locked the doors, Bruno felt a shiver of claustrophobia. The twenty-nine men arranged themselves into three loose, concentric circles gathered around Reiniger. Wolfgang went around the circles putting a plain blue cloak over each man's shoulders. The cloaks had been hand-sewn by Gudrun and embroidered with a small white symbol on the left shoulder: a skull inside a maze.

Godric, who fancied himself an artist, was designing a simplified version to become their party insignia. They were not yet *officially* a political movement. Officially, they were part of Reiniger's film crew. But the chosen men of the inner circle were all aware of their leader's great project: the Alpine Dawn Swiss Democratic Nationalist Party.

Everyone agreed it was a pleasingly grand title.

Each man held a sacred *sikin* knife – except Bruno, who was in disgrace for losing his.

He was in the outermost ring, feeling safe from Reiniger's scrutiny there. Wolfgang gave his shoulder a squeeze as he put the cloak on him, as if to reassure him, *Everything will be all right.*

Bruno wasn't sure why he'd been admitted to the secret circle, except for his utter dedication to Reiniger's dreams, and the fact that Wolfgang Notz liked him. He was no intellectual – but nor were most of the men here.

Godric was the one who did all the thinking. From his followers, he needed seamless agreement, loyalty and muscle.

They were Reiniger's embryonic army. For now they helped him make newsreels and movies to promote his ideals. One day, they would help him form a government.

Godric opened the meeting as usual with the *Alpsegen*, the traditional Alpine prayer sung by shepherds to protect their flocks against all danger. The men joined in, their voices creating an eerie Gregorian-style chant.

When it was done, all raised their hands in the three-fingered salute that symbolised the unity of all the Swiss cantons.

"Lucerne was once, all too briefly, our seat of government," said Godric. "One day, it shall be so again. May it please God that the *Confoederatio Helvetica* shall be governed from this very spot."

"*Amen*," they all responded.

"My comrades of the oath: you've each been entrusted with a *sikin* knife, unearthed by my father at a sacred site in the desert, a site so ancient that its origins remain unknown." Reiniger's voice was thin and hard, like a blade, a contrast to Wolfgang's cheerful, earthy tone. "Fate delivered the cache into our hands. The very Soul of the Universe favours our enterprise. Let us summon the spirit of William Tell, our national hero, and of Berchtold, leader of the Wild Hunt, and of Woden, god of the mountains, and of Zruvan..."

Godric's mouth always made a little sour twitch on the last name. Bruno had no idea why he spoke it at all, since it wasn't Swiss, but he accepted it as part of the esoteric business that only Godric understood. "...Zruvan, Lord of Immortals, Soul of the Universe, to watch over our ritual tonight."

"*Hail, Lord of Immortals,*" the men echoed. Godric switched from Christian to Pagan invocation without blinking. His only true belief was in the individual's own strength: that was his teaching. All gods were there to serve man.

"However, one of our knives is lost," Reiniger continued. "Until it's recovered, can the thirty function as twenty-nine? Will one missing piece make the whole structure collapse? I believe not. I believe our combined willpower can bridge the gap. Each one of you in turn has received the blood-initiation in order to give his power to the group. A painful but heroic ordeal, no?"

The *Eidgenossen* murmured agreement.

"Now, to compensate for the loss of the *sikin*, a deeper sacrifice is needed. This will serve a triple purpose: to intensify the power, to act as a chastisement and to warn against future carelessness."

Reiniger stared straight at Bruno. He pointed his dagger at him, then turned his wrist to point at his own feet, instructing Bruno to approach the centre of the circle.

He obeyed, sweating.

"Sir, what is this?" he whispered. "I thought I'd proved my loyalty."

"Do not argue with me." Reiniger's eyes were specks of blue ice behind his glasses. "Lie down on your back. Wolfgang, expose his chest."

Bruno obeyed. The marble floor felt chilly through his clothes. He looked up with wide, pleading eyes as Reiniger's deputy undid his shirt buttons and spread open the garment. He was wearing a vest, which Wolfgang simply slit with his own knife. His glance in response to Bruno's silent plea was apologetic but firm, merciless.

"We see the scars of initiation on this recruit's chest," said

Reiniger. "Thirty intersecting cuts forming the sacred Eyes of the Soul. I want each of you to reopen the cut you made, one at a time, in the same order. I trust you to remember?"

The group murmured that they did. Bruno could smell their sweat now. They were almost as frightened as he was. Also, unlike him, aroused.

"This time, go deep," said Reiniger. "As deep as you like. Don't mind his cries. This is his punishment for losing his knife. In payment, his sacrifice will fill us with strength. Watch carefully. If you lose the sacred *sikin* entrusted to you – this will be you."

"No," Bruno mouthed as Wolfgang leaned down to make the first cut: a concave arc across the top of his ribcage.

"Hush," said Wolfgang, barely audible. "Take your punishment in silence. You're giving your life for the good of the group." Then he mouthed, "*I'm sorry*."

Tears ran down Bruno's face, but he didn't make another sound. At first it only stung. He remembered his initiation – just like this, but with the blades barely nicking the skin. It had hurt like the devil. Never dreamed he'd have to go through it again. As each man loomed over him, one by one, he felt their blades go deeper, re-carving the sign into his flesh. He saw their panting, excited faces. The pain built slowly, savage, burning. His breathing was high and fast. He felt hot fluid trickling down his chest, smelled his own blood.

Power was building in the air, hot and flowing like lava. He lay giddy and breathless with agony, aware of his heart pumping out his life on to the floor.

Last, Godric Reiniger thrust his knife into Bruno's belly and ripped it from left to right.

"Thirty cuts," he panted, and pressed his own dagger into Bruno's hand. "Make the last one yourself."

For a split second, Bruno thought of pushing the blade up into Reiniger's heart – but he had no strength or will to do so. He knew it was over. How could he kill the man he'd worshipped? *I'm sacrificing my life for the group…*

Wincing, he pushed the tip into the middle of his own abdomen. A weak effort. Then a terrible despair and anger seized him and he made a last, violent thrust.

Reiniger took the *sikin* from his feeble grip. He bent down and touched his tongue to the wound, grimacing. Then he said, "The linen, quickly!"

An oblong of white fabric was placed on Bruno's torso. Reiniger meticulously pressed it down himself, making sure that every drop of blood was absorbed. It began to congeal a little before he finally tore it away, revealing a perfect imprint of Bruno's wounds.

"It's done," Reiniger declared, holding up the cloth. "That's how powerful your blood vow is, your responsibility – in direct proportion to the reward of great power. Do not let me down, unless you wish to lie in Bruno's place."

Bruno's last mote of consciousness hovered near the ceiling, watching the gruesome scene from above. No emotion. He was beyond disbelief, fear, denial, beyond all emotion. And there was someone floating with him: the dark girl, Fadiya, whom no one really knew. She was looking down at the scene, smiling...

Smiling at him as his mind passed into eternal blackness.

The house was monumental, stark, all straight lines with no Art Deco curves to soften its corners. Imperial. Karl took in the building from a distance, impressed by the way the outside lights floodlit the walls to make the edifice appear carved from ice. As Charlotte had described, several vehicles were parked in front. He marvelled that they'd made it up the steep road.

He read the nameplate: *Bergwerkstatt*. Mountain workshop. A deceptively modest house name, he thought, that masked a grander message. *Here we are slaving to make art in the mountains! Admire us!*

Beneath it was a small business plate: "Reiniger Studios."

So this was the lair of the genius who'd made *The Lion Arises*, Karl noted sourly. Also home to a violent gang who'd tried to slay Charlotte and viciously attacked Emil. According to recent newspapers, the eminent local director, Godric Reiniger, was soon to launch his latest feature, *Triumph in the Mountains*, while working on a drama called *Three Tells*, a new project about Swiss heroes of folklore.

I'm sure the world cannot wait, thought Karl.

His higher senses perceived human warmth inside the building. They were hard to count... he sensed a gathering upstairs, thirty men at most, but they were a blur. At least twenty more were scattered in the downstairs rooms.

How best to approach Reiniger? Probably through the Crystal Ring, so he could hide on the boundary between realms and watch without being seen.

Karl stepped closer to the house. He entered Raqia and drifted to the level of the uppermost storey.

Then he smelled human blood. The scent was strong, hitting him in a shocking sensory wall. Yes, blood, but not tempting or delicious. It was a foul smell of contamination, like decaying meat, mixed with dust and metal.

What the hell is happening inside?

Karl made to pass through the outer wall, but could not. A barrier stopped him – not the wall itself, but an invisible force. Wherever he tried to push through, a red glow tingled around his hands, like charged plasma.

All around the house he probed for a way in, but the harder he tried, the more powerfully the barrier rejected him. At last he fell, landing on soft ground at the side of the house. The unseen power throbbed as if generated by some unearthly, lethal engine. It made his head ring with awful pressure, an electric current that rooted him to the ground.

Against that, Karl knew he couldn't get inside. He didn't even want to.

He sat for a few minutes on the peaty earth, wondering if this sense of toxic revulsion had also afflicted Charlotte. If her experience was even vaguely similar, he understood why she was alarmed and haunted. The power came in waves, cold and sickening.

He'd sensed forces like this before, invisible yet as real as the wind. Never had he encountered one so visceral.

Was someone being murdered in there? What kind of murder could repel a vampire, rather than draw him in like a vulture?

Karl had a dizzying impression that Raqia itself was intruding into the world, distorting reality. He'd met only two humans with the power to touch the Crystal Ring and manipulate it in a small way. The ability was incredibly rare, but not unknown. Was there a human here with similar power? Godric Reiniger himself?

He saw transparent but distinct columns of red light rushing up into the sky.

Eventually the power faded. Perhaps he could have entered then, but his instincts screamed a warning to keep away. As the sphere of force dissipated, he became more starkly aware of the danger inside. In his mind's eye he glimpsed a group of men, wild-eyed and blood-spattered, each gripping a knife like the one used to attack Charlotte, and each blade dripping red...

If he went in now, he would not come out again.

Karl stepped away, glaring up at the monumental Bergwerkstatt. He was shaken, mystified. But above all, he was patient.

"Whatever you are doing in there, Herr Reiniger," Karl murmured, "I do not think you are making a movie."

CHAPTER ELEVEN

ISTILQA

Wearing an ink-blue dress to blend with the night, black hair loose to veil her luminous skin, Violette stepped into the Crystal Ring. At dead of night, there were few humans to see or recognise her.

When she first became a vampire, she'd fought the blood-thirst until she was nearly insane. She recalled those days with a shudder – crouching under a shroud of tangled hair, Stefan telling Charlotte in the distance, "If she doesn't feed soon, we may have to destroy her."

Although she had come to terms with her nature – part vampire, part Lilith, part Violette – she still couldn't hunt easily. Unlike Karl, she rarely seized strangers on the street. Nor did she develop affection for her victims, beguiling them as Charlotte did. Not that she *never* did such things, but every vampire was different. Every victim was unique, too, which meant that each encounter had its own singular ambience.

Violette's habit was to travel through Raqia to some far-off town and haunt the rooftops, seeking the subtle auras of those who slept beneath. Her Lilith instinct drew her to those who needed to change.

Perhaps they lacked the will to escape a cruel husband, or to cease beating a child, or to overcome a weakness of some kind. So many reasons. Lilith's wisdom was enigmatic. Violette rarely knew in advance why she must take *this* person's blood in particular.

Only her subconscious heard souls crying out in their sleep, craving the harsh corrective pain of her bite. Violette simply followed.

That didn't make the hunt easy. It was a nightly battle.

Tonight she stood by the bed of a spinster, a plump woman in her thirties. She slept restlessly, fighting bad dreams of an oppressive mother who bullied her to get married when all she wanted was to farm her own plot of land, and write poetry, and to be left alone... These wisps of knowledge came to Violette in her Lilith-trance.

The woman smelled ripe with menstrual blood and the mustiness of sleep, but the scent was not unpleasant. Violette leaned down and felt her fangs extend, hard and sharp.

"What?" the woman groaned. Her eyes opened, shining white in the darkness.

"Hush," murmured Violette, falling to her knees beside the bed. She put her cold hand on the woman's hot forehead, held her gaze. The victim went calm and still.

"Just a moment of discomfort. Nothing to fear. Tomorrow you'll wake feeling as light as air, unafraid to follow the path you desire."

Afterwards, sated, Violette felt calm again, warm, almost human. She vanished – leaving her victim with the memory of a strange dream – and drifted upwards through Raqia's amethyst clouds until she reached clear air, with bronze hills rolling beneath her and vast fiery chasms above.

She wished she could love Emil as he wanted. It would make their lives simpler – but it was impossible on every level. Her nature sought solitude and independence. The one time she'd fallen in love had cost her more than she could bear. She still couldn't see a certain shade of chestnut hair without her heart ripping itself from her chest.

Even if she had desired men, she and Emil were mentor and student: unequal in experience, emotion, attitude, everything. And even if that could be set aside, there was the greatest barrier of all. He was human, she was a vampire. And he must never know.

Violette saw a coal-black cloud hurtling towards her, a dark meteor. It looked distant and took a long time to reach her, but whichever way she turned, it was still there.

Heading straight for her.

She braced herself to fight. The blackness resolved into a figure with dark red robes, a huge skull-shaped helmet over its head and a long staff glowing in its bony grip...

It was huge, twice her height. She struck out, only for her hand to go straight through as if through smoke. The apparition floated in front of her, staring from the black empty pits of its eye-sockets.

Did she see stars in there? She was looking into the infinity of space, as if its eyes held the whole universe.

Illusion.

Violette had never been so afraid in her life. She felt as if Lilith actually *fled* and hid deep inside her. She was simply human Violette again, suspended like a child in front of this terrible being.

"What are you?" she demanded. "Another messenger from God, trying to tame the rebel demon? I am not your instrument. I bow to no one, I belong to no one!"

The creature only stared, wordless.

The thought occurred to her that there was nothing inside. It wasn't really there at all, but – as Karl had said – some kind of projection.

A projection of what?

A worse idea struck her. *What if I am creating it myself? Karl and Charlotte tell me that such things happen. Anything can appear in the Crystal Ring. Nightmares become real. So if I'm creating this Kastchei-apparition myself, I'll never be rid of it!*

"Who are you?" she cried again. "Kastchei? What do you want?"

No answer. Instead it swooped at her. She couldn't move fast enough to escape its path. The skull-creature went straight through her, and she *felt* it – a horrible, glacial rush that stole all her strength.

It was gone. Nothing had happened, because there was nothing there. Only a mirage. But the shock sent Violette tumbling towards the Earth, numb, unable to stop herself falling down into the muddy darkness.

Emil woke in a strange bedroom full of carved dark wood. His whole body ached... but the pain was dull, nothing compared to the previous day. The bed was empty beside him. The sheets were rumpled, though, and a woman in an oyster silk chemise stood at the window.

He felt as if he'd surfaced from the thick black silt at the bottom of a lake.

"Oh my God, what happened?" he groaned.

She turned to him with a charming white smile. Fadiya, that was her name.

"Sadly, my dear, nothing," she replied. "You toppled on to the bed and fell asleep. I could not compete with the charms of unconsciousness, it seems."

He remembered… just. Dancing with her downstairs in the small public lounge… stumbling upstairs, just drunk enough to find everything hysterically funny, but not enough to start any more foolish fights.

And he recalled kissing her before he'd passed out: a brief, delicious sense-memory of her lips on his, warm and eager.

Panic paralysed him. Could she be a prostitute? The thought hadn't crossed his mind last night, but there had been very little in his mind at all. Or too much. All he needed now was a furious Violette, Thierry or Karl to burst into the room… Fadiya said nothing had happened, but she would still want her money.

"Why are you staring at me like that?" she asked, frowning. "Maybe I don't look so nice in daylight."

She knelt on the edge of the bed, knees parted, the contrast of pale silk on her coffee skin breathtaking. Her messy, wavy hair was the same rich brown as her eyes.

"You look glorious," he said.

A small bathroom led off the room, the door only three feet from where he lay. He got up dizzily, entered and locked himself in. He was still wearing trousers, but no socks or shirt… There he drank a glass of water, washed himself at the sink, cleaned his teeth as best he could with a fingertip dipped into some mint-flavoured tooth powder he found on a shelf. Then he stood glaring at his reflection in the mirror. The worst of the swelling had gone down, but he still looked dreadful, his eyelids livid brown and purple. His eyes were vacant, dead.

Was this to be his future, without Violette? Drinking himself into oblivion, being pummelled by thugs in alleys, waking up next to prostitutes?

Wait. He couldn't assume she was anything of the sort. Surely a whore would have described what a wonderful time he'd had, and what a shame he couldn't remember. She would not have said, "Nothing happened." Nor was she a stage-door worshipper who'd been dazzled by his athleticism on stage. She'd only seen him as an inebriated wreck.

Perhaps she simply pitied him.

"Emil?" A tap at the door. "Are you all right?"

"Yes." He unlocked the door and went to sit on the bed, leaning back against the carved headboard. "Why did you bring me here?"

"I don't know." She looked sombre now. She knelt facing him, picking at the edge of the quilt. "I have never done such a thing before. I was married – my husband died three years ago. We met in Algeria. He was a French soldier, stationed on the Ruhr after the Great War ended... a fever took him. I've been alone since. I don't know... I saw you, and I thought... that you looked kind, and lonely. Like me."

"I'm in love with someone else," Emil said harshly. "She doesn't want me. That's why I was drunk and miserable. I can't love you, I'm sorry."

"Oh. Well." Her lovely dark eyelids fell. "I wasn't expecting love from someone I met yesterday. But... that doesn't mean we can't comfort each other, does it?"

She crept forward as she spoke, let her hands steal over his abdomen to caress his bare chest. Emil surrendered, blood rushing through him, delicious sensation turning him to molten sunlight... She kissed him and he clasped her head, sensual memories of the previous night becoming warm reality. Almost at once he was hard, and struggling with the dilemma of wanting to keep his hands in her hair as her tongue eased between his lips... to tear off what little clothing she wore, and to free his own swollen flesh so he could feel her nakedness against him.

"God, I should have eight hands," he murmured, and she laughed.

"We have four between us. Slowly. One thing at a time. I'll guide you."

Did she think he was a virgin? In truth, he was inexperienced. A village girl or two, a cabaret dancer in Paris... then he'd joined the Ballet Lenoir, and barely had time to think of anything but work. Months of frustrated passion filled him now. As a dancer, he was finely attuned to every sensation of his own body in a way that no ordinary mortal could understand...

There was no more talk.

He set his jaw, fighting to control the sensations building in his loins. Beneath animal impulse, he kept enough intellectual control to know that he must hold back. His pride insisted that he prove himself a good lover, not an inept youth. He held his breath as her fingers worked at his buttons and freed him from his trousers and undergarments. His phallus sprang free, engorged above his muscular thighs. He fought hard to control his pressing need for climax; held back to enjoy a greater pleasure, Fadiya's expression of wonder as she admired his physique. She actually gasped out loud.

He knew he was splendid, and vain – why not? He'd worked damned hard to look like a sculptured god. He felt like laughing and weeping in sheer joy that this gorgeous exotic woman was astride him, appreciating his body like a work of art. As if she'd never seen anyone to compare.

She sat upright, rolled her chemise over her head and tossed it aside. The sight of her slim brown body as she arched her back and threw back her head was magnificent. Her hair was a mess, her eyes glistening. No longer brown but jade-green, like a cat's. The pale eyes against her dark skin were enchanting, maddeningly beautiful. And then she eased into close contact, hot and intimate... he groaned, pushing up to meet her. Her hands were on him, guiding him inside her as she enveloped him a little at a time, rising again to torture him, sliding deeper... rising and falling on him until he floated in sea of mindless bliss.

How long? Time didn't matter: the minutes seemed to go on forever. Her hands explored the muscles of his arms and thighs. A hot, slippery, agonising ache built between them, welding them together. She rose and fell on him, faster and faster...

Her breathing quickened, her movements grew convulsive and her cries so loud that anyone nearby must have heard. Her obvious pleasure was enough to trigger an explosion in him, so violent it was nearly a fit. He gripped her hips. Every touch of yearning he'd ever felt, he poured into Fadiya.

She collapsed on to him. He traced her back with gentle fingers, learning every detail of her spine and shoulder-blades and ribs under the lovely flesh. She attended to his chest with kisses, touches of her tongue and light scrapes of her teeth. After a long time he realised...

He had not once thought about Violette.

Emil looked at the bedside clock. If it was correct, he had precisely forty minutes to reach the academy in time for the pre-rehearsal warm up...

"Am I keeping you from somewhere?" Fadiya asked. She lay across his chest. They were both too warm and languorous to move.

"No. There is nowhere else I wish to be."

She raised her head, resting her chin on her hand. She must have heard an edge in his voice. "I don't believe you. Tell me the truth. Tell me about this woman you love."

He was silent for a while, reluctant to speak. Yet somehow she coaxed the words out of him, and in his unguarded, relaxed state, he told her everything.

"I was mad to think she could return my feelings. I should not have told her, but I couldn't *not* tell her – do you see what an impossible position I was in?" He gazed at the ceiling without focus.

"She sounds cruel," said Fadiya. "It's love you need, not cruelty. You deserve love."

"No, it's not her fault. I did this to myself. Her friends told me that she... she only likes other women, and that she loved someone who died. But that's none of my business, is it? I thought I knew her, but I don't. I had this fantasy in my head that I could be her soulmate, possess her as she possesses me... but it can never happen. I cannot go back to the ballet, Fadiya. But if I don't – what am I? Nothing. A dancer, *her* partner, is all I ever wanted to be. But I've thrown it away. I can hear my father's laughter now."

"Well, your father sounds cruel, too," she said. "May I give you some advice, Emil?"

"If you must."

"Go back to the ballet."

"What? I can't!"

"Yes, you can." She rose on braced arms. Her face underwent a change from sweetness to hard-eyed determination. "That's why you were looking at the clock, isn't it? There's something you should be doing."

"Nothing. Practice. It doesn't matter."

"Yes, it does. Do you know how self-pitying you sound?"

"I *what*?" His blood rose.

"Go to your practice. Face her. Perhaps you can't have *her*, but you can have your career. You still have your pride."

"Too much of it, according to some."

"Dear, beautiful Emil, if you spend enough time with me, I promise you will have no amorous thoughts left over for your ballerina." Her face softened into a sparkling, wicked smile. "But you must go back to the ballet. You cannot walk away! Go back and prove to her how magnificent you are."

"Why does this matter to you?"

"Because I see clear through you. You, Emil Fiorani, were created to be the greatest dancer in the world. And there is no one else in this room to tell you but me."

He caught his breath. She was right. Damn it, he would go back. He sat up. "If I go now – if I hurry, I can be there just in time."

"Then go!" She got off the bed. Laughing, she began to pick up his clothes and throw them at him. He dressed in a rush, hopping as he tried to fasten his trousers and put on his shoes at the same time.

Emil made for the door, only to stop and turn back. He caught Fadiya around the waist, buried his face in her neck and felt her body arch against his.

"When can I see you again?" he whispered.

Charlotte and Karl rose floated through Raqia from the dim lower levels to the rich blue air above. Sunrise lit the cloud-mountains from bronze to honey. A sharp cool breeze carried them gently up and down, like seaweed on an uneasy sea.

Charlotte felt strange. This was the first time she'd entered the Crystal Ring since the night of the stabbing. It took energy to enter the other-realm, and she'd been too weak, and Raqia too wild with storms.

"Thank goodness it's calm at last," said Karl. His voice was more in her head than in her ears.

Raqia changed perceptions. Their bodies became a hybrid of dark angel and dragonfly, tiny in the void. Joined by their entwined fingertips, they drifted above a vast golden-cream plain of cloud, like swimmers floating face down on a clear lagoon. Vampires did not sleep – least of all in coffins – but they needed the subtle replenishment of the Crystal Ring as much as they needed blood.

It's another way of feeding off humans, Charlotte thought. *Absorbing their thought-waves and dreams.*

"How are you, beloved?" Karl asked.

"I didn't realise how much I've missed this," she said. "It's like diving into a mountain stream after being locked in a stifling cell for days. Like stretching out in a clean bed after trekking across the desert."

"Rest," he said. She heard a slight catch in his voice. Then she slipped into the divine waking trance...

Odd, she couldn't properly remember the previous night. She recalled trying to reason with Emil, but everything after that was vague. She'd been restless... Karl had taken her to hunt, and she remembered feasting upon a slim young man, shorter than her and so light that she'd actually lifted him off his feet as she swallowed his delicious hot blood... And being with Karl in their living room, listening to Strauss on the gramophone... dancing together, pressed close, aching with the blissful pain of touching yet still holding back.

At one point, Charlotte had thought, *To hell with this, I can't bear it, what harm would it do if we fell into bed after all.* Wanting Karl so desperately that she simply didn't care any more. Only for the lamia to appear and seep between them like a wall of icy fog. Mindless, emotionless, simply staring at Charlotte like the reflection of a corpse.

Every day she insisted she was getting better. Every day she tried to convince herself that the poison was leaving her system, but she knew the truth.

The lamia would not go away. Perhaps it never would.

Worst of all, the idea no longer upset her as much. She was beginning to accept it, as a dying human accepted death.

She barely remembered Karl bringing her into the Crystal Ring, but what a relief to find herself here again. It was wonderful, like sleeping after days of insomnia.

"Look," she said, pointing at an uprush of crimson light. The light was not random but travelled in straight columns, shooting from the Earth up towards the *Weisskalt*.

She heard murmuring voices. Felt vibrations, like distant explosions, that made the whole of Raqia shudder.

"How beautiful," said Charlotte. "What is it?"

"I've seen it before," said Karl, stirring from his trance. "Caused by human activity, I suspect. I wish we knew what it means."

"If every human stopped dreaming and thinking altogether," she said, "would we cease to exist?"

"As if that is ever likely to happen." Karl smiled, but his eyes – glowing amber in a coal-dark face – held concern.

Charlotte knew why. She would usually be answering such questions, not asking them. She wasn't herself, and they both knew it, but her real self seemed to have slipped just out of reach and she couldn't catch hold...

Soon the phenomenon faded. No cause, no logic – just the emanation of a powerful mortal emotion or dream.

Presently they descended and stepped back into the real world. They were always careful to do so somewhere secluded, away from humans. Today they returned to Earth in the edge of a forest near Lake Lucerne. A church clock struck eleven as they walked arm in arm along the shore. The day was blue and green, almost too bright. Although they preferred the subtlety of dusk and night, sunlight did them no harm. And in spite of everything, she felt calm and relaxed, almost ecstatic.

"You look happy," said Karl, with a smile that went straight to her heart.

"To be walking with your lover on a perfect morning: what more could anyone want?"

"Nothing," he agreed. He stroked her hair, kissed her hands, leaving trails of rushing starfire wherever he touched her. "We should pay a visit to Stefan," he said.

"Should we? All right, that will be nice."

"Nice?" Karl gave her a curious look. "We could take a pleasure boat across the lake, since there's no great hurry."

"Even better."

As they passed Hotel Blauensee near the lake's edge, Charlotte saw a familiar face. The woman was sitting at an outside table with a cup of hot chocolate. Sky and water were intensely blue.

"Isn't that the girl from the cinema?" said Karl. "Amy Temple?"

"Yes. I wasn't paying attention." Charlotte had been in a reverie until he spoke. Now she recognised the open, attractive face, small pointed nose, light brown hair cut in a bob. She recalled carrying Amy up to the huge white house, only to have the door shut in her face. The memory was odd because it seemed to have happened years ago, a long-forgotten event.

"I'd like a word with her," she said to Karl. "Go on without me. I'll catch you up."

"As you wish." Karl raised one eyebrow in the subtlest possible warning.

"Don't give me that look. There will never be another Violette. Trust me, for once."

"I do trust you, dearest," he replied softly. "I'll meet you at Stefan's."

With a brief, affectionate kiss, he walked away. Green dappled light through the trees moved over him as he wove through the folk strolling on the lakeside. She smiled to see their heads snap round as he passed: Karl drew attention without trying, and not only from women. Charlotte didn't blame them. His dark, serene beauty always stopped her heart, too.

And not daring to make love is killing me. I can't even remember why it's so dangerous, I only know that it is because I feel like a leper...

She pushed those thoughts firmly aside.

"Hello, Amy," said Charlotte, sitting beside the other woman. "How are you?"

"Quite well, thank you." Amy looked calm and poised, if pale. "I didn't expect to see you again, my rescuer. What a pleasant surprise."

"I'm Charlotte."

"I remember. May I buy you a coffee, Charlotte?"

"No, thank you. I only wanted to make sure you'd recovered from that night."

"Completely, thank you. I'm sorry they were so rude at the

house – I can't tell you how embarrassed I was, nor how relieved that someone friendly found me. It wasn't what you think."

"I wasn't thinking anything, except that you needed a doctor."

Amy stirred her chocolate, making patterns in the foam.

"Yes, you were. Wondering, I mean."

"Are you here on holiday?" asked Charlotte, trying to sound less curious than she actually was.

Amy gave a hollow laugh. "Not exactly. My uncle Godric... My life is rather a mess, to be honest. Look at the sunlight on the lake! How can anyone be miserable on such a beautiful day?"

"It is lovely. Is your uncle Swiss? You sound English."

"Yes, but his sister, my mother, married an Englishman. She's quite a lot older than Godric so they hardly know each other. I was brought up in London, but my dear father ran off with another woman when I was eight and my mother was rather horrible to me after that. Now I'm grown up, we *really* don't get along. When I told her I wanted to be an actress – you'd think I'd announced I was going to sell myself on the street! So I came to stay with my uncle last year. He makes me feel useful, at least."

"He has a very grand house," Charlotte remarked.

"Yes, he's quite rich. He was an army officer during the War, but he'd already inherited money from his father. Then he worked in a bank for a while and got to know all sorts of important people who helped him set up his business. He makes films. But you know that."

"Reiniger Studios," said Charlotte.

Amy stared at the table and sighed. "I saw you at the cinema the other day, but I daren't say hello, because uncle was furious at the audience for laughing. I could have *died*."

"It wasn't your fault," said Charlotte. "May I confess something? I recognised you from *The Lion Arises*. I was watching it for the second time, to make sure."

"Oh, lord." Amy bit her lower lip. Charlotte watched the lip redden, and felt a stir of appetite. Her blood smelled so enticing and wholesome, and it would be easy to gain her trust... She crushed the impulse. "You sat through it twice? Wasn't it perfectly dreadful? I was only in the background. I'm amazed you noticed me."

"You looked lovely. Your uncle should give you better roles."

Amy smiled, colouring. "No need to flatter me. My dancing is dreadful, and as for my acting – the truth is, I can't act to save my life. I wish I could afford lessons. No one would give me a part at all, except my uncle, who makes the worst movies ever seen! Oh, don't tell him I said that."

"I wouldn't dream of it. I'm sure he'll get better with experience."

"Good heavens, he would hit the roof if anyone suggested he wasn't an expert by now!"

"Is he making more?"

"Oh, he's always working on something. *Triumph in the Mountains* is next, and we're shooting a new one about William Tell, and he's writing three more scripts at least. *The Lion Arises* was his fourth; the earlier ones were even worse, if you can believe it. We're a tiny company – it's hardly Hollywood – but he keeps us busy. We all muck in, making costumes, working the lights and cameras, being extras…" She sighed again. "I can't go back to Mother and admit my career's a disaster. It wouldn't be so bad, but Uncle Godric – well, his films aren't what I expected. He likes brutal stories about women being kidnapped, soldiers, ghosts, madmen, villains having their heads cut off. I wouldn't mind if they were *good* films but he can't see that they come across like pantomimes. He gets so irate when the audience starts giggling."

Charlotte paused, studying Amy's troubled face and the glint of tears in her eyes.

"The most difficult people are those who think they're brilliant, but aren't."

"I know, but no one dares tell him – not while he's paying their wages! Anyway, it's not just about the films. It's all for a higher purpose. To stir up patriotism and general fervour; he loves all that. And the more he flatters wealthy people and makes newsreels about them, the more money they give him."

"That sounds quite cunning," said Charlotte.

"Oh, he is. He's always holding secret meetings with his clique of favourites. Men only. The womenfolk are only there to cook, sew and look decorative. I am a little tired of it all."

"What will you do?"

"I don't know. Uncle Godric's fond of me, and he seems to like me being here. Most of the time he's kind, but sometimes… he can be a dreadful bully."

"A bully, how?"

Amy took a while to answer. "I have a difficult time some months, if you know what I mean. Uncle insisted I go to this dreadful Dr Ochsner, a friend of his – he treats all Uncle's friends and staff – and I didn't want to go, but he was so insistent that I got annoyed and ran off to see the doctor on my own. Gudrun, the woman who shut the door in your face – I do apologise – she's our housekeeper, or should I say sergeant-major? Anyway, she was supposed to go with me, but I made an evening appointment and sneaked off alone. The thing is, I knew I needed to see a doctor. I was just so *embarrassed*. I wanted to keep the whole business as private as possible."

"What happened?" Charlotte asked gently.

"The doctor was horrible." Her voice went very low. "First he asked if I'd had any boyfriends – I haven't, but I was *mortified*. Then he poked and prodded me so aggressively, inside and out, that I was crying, but he told me to stop making a silly fuss. I swear he was enjoying it. It seemed to go on forever. Essential to scrape out some excess tissue, he said. It was *so* painful – is that normal, Charlotte, do you know? – and so rough that he made me bleed."

"He did that to you without any kind of anaesthetic?" Charlotte gasped.

Amy gave a small nod. "It was unspeakably humiliating. Then while I sat there bleeding all over his couch, he said there was nothing wrong with me but anaemia and to eat more steak! Afterwards, I just wanted to hurry home and hide in bed, but I was so lightheaded… If you hadn't been there, I dread to think what would have happened."

Charlotte took her hand, feeling her warmth, her pulse.

"I'm so sorry. Did you tell your uncle?"

"I couldn't." Her gaze fixed on the mountains. "I told Gudrun, but even she said I shouldn't make a fuss. I was far too embarrassed to tell Uncle Godric. I'm sure he meant well, but… He thinks Dr Ochsner is marvellous. He would never believe me, so it's best I stay quiet." Amy stared at the boats crossing the lake. Eventually she said in a small voice, "You know, I wouldn't mind a sweetheart, even marriage and a baby or two, one day… But I'm afraid it will never happen. What if all that digging with metal instruments has damaged my insides?"

"That so-called doctor's treatment doesn't sound right at all," Charlotte said softly, pressing her hand. "Don't go to him again, in any circumstances."

"I won't. I'll warn Mariette and the other girls to keep away, too."

"Good idea. And don't worry, Amy. I'm sure you'll be all right."

"Thank you. You're so kind, Charlotte. Do you have children?"

"Er, no." The question took her by surprise. "I can't, and in any case, I would make no fit mother."

"How can you possibly know? You're barely any older than me." Amy sipped her chocolate. "Forgive me, I'm being nosey. But you're so nice, I feel as if I've known you forever."

Nice, thought Charlotte, *as I sit here imagining how exquisite your blood would taste…*

"I've had a thought," Amy said, brightening. "Some of us are going to Paris, the weekend after this, just for fun. Would you like to come with us?"

"Er… I'm not sure." *Because if I do,* she thought, *I will want to take you into a dark corner and taste your throat and…*

"Don't look so alarmed!" said Amy. "It's only a handful of us. The leading lady Mariette, and our friends. There won't be anyone from my uncle's close circle; they're all too keen on talking politics and drinking beer. Such a bore. Only fun people are invited."

Charlotte laughed. "I'm tempted."

"The main reason I'm going is that Uncle Godric has forbidden me to go," Amy added with a wicked smile.

"Forbidden you? Why?"

"Because there will be American jazz music, and debauchery, and foreigners, and nightclubs open until the early hours! At least, there had better be. And I'm sick of being told what to do."

"Good for you," Charlotte said softly, thinking, *If I spent a day or two away from Karl, it would free us both from the endless temptation. I know we're going to give in, and if we do…*

Something terrible would happen. She tried to recall what the danger was, but it slid out of her mind's grasp like ice.

"It's only a suggestion," said Amy. "My treat, a thank you for cheering me up. Bring someone, or come alone: it's up to you. But if you do decide to tag along – you know where I live."

* * *

Violette looked up and saw, with amazement, Emil's bruised face staring at her through the glass panel in the door.

She was in a side-studio, trying out moves for the new ballet with Jean-Paul. He was good; if she'd never met Emil, she would have considered him an excellent partner. But compared to her protégé, he was so ordinary it hurt. A workhorse… a dancer who was eager to please, executed every step she demanded to perfection, but without a trace of Emil's flare.

"All right, that's enough for today," she said gently, noting the resigned expression on Jean-Paul's face as he slung a towel around his neck and left.

"Madame Lenoir, may I speak with you?" Emil said from the doorway.

"Yes," she said tiredly. "Of course. Come in. Where have you been?"

"At practice, with Madame Joelle."

"I meant before that."

"Resting, as you asked."

"Indeed?" She knew full well he hadn't spent the night in his room, but decided to let the issue pass. "The doctor said rest for one week, not for one class."

"I know." He spoke formally, standing as straight as a soldier and avoiding her eyes. "I wish to apologise for my behaviour. I've been extremely foolish. I – can only say that I'm deeply sorry, and that it will never happen again."

Violette hadn't expected this. She paused, wondering how best to respond. She caught the taint of stale alcohol on him and guessed he'd been out drinking again, against her instructions. At least he appeared not to have come to any harm this time. Would his rebellion end, if she forgave him?

"Emil," she said, keeping her tone balanced: not too cold, not too forgiving, "thank you. I appreciate your apology. I don't know that you need my forgiveness. We all do foolish things, and you hardly deserved to be set upon by brutes…"

"All the same, I am sorry, from the depths of my heart."

"Does this mean you're staying?"

He cleared his throat. "If – if you will permit me, yes."

"Well, I will need you to agree to some rules."

"Of course."

"Perhaps I've been too harsh. I can't keep you under lock and key; you're a man, not a child. So I'll just say that I would *prefer* you to stay on ballet premises, for the sake of your health and fitness – but if you do go out, that is your decision. You must bear the consequences. Just try to keep out of trouble."

"Madame." He gave a sharp nod.

"Take as much rest as you need, until your injuries are fully healed. If you must attend class – well, I admire your dedication, but I'll be most unhappy if you do yourself any more damage. So don't push yourself too hard. And no more arguments with Mikhail or anyone else!"

"I understand."

"And once you are fully fit – I expect your usual dedication. Complete professionalism, both in the studio and outside. Do you agree?"

"Yes, madame."

"Then it's possible we have a future," she said softly. "This will not be easy, but we're both strong."

She thought, *I cannot control his inner life. I can't control him at all. Something's happened to him… other than my rejecting him. What, though?*

"Anything else I should know?" she asked.

He hesitated. "Your friends, Herr and Frau Alexander… They told me that you suffered a bereavement not long ago. I had no idea, or I would never… My deepest sympathies, madame."

Violette only nodded. Charlotte had admitted that she'd told Emil, although he didn't know the details and never would. He was part of her professional life. Her private life, her other existence as Lilith, the loss of Robyn – none of that was his concern, and would remain concealed from him forever.

"I know that pain," he added. "I've suffered it too."

"Have you?" Their eyes met for a moment, then he looked over her head again.

"Someone in my family… My brother Alfonso… I can't say any more."

"Well, who hasn't lost a loved one?" she said gently. "We are partners in pain, then. We can take that on to the stage, and make the audience weep with us."

"Thank you." Tears shone in his eyes, and a spark of his old energy, almost a smile. "Thank you for giving me a second chance."

Charlotte arrived at Stefan's house and found him with Karl in the lake room. This was her first official visit, although she'd seen the place from afar: a fairytale chalet, with steep forests and mountains behind, Lake Lucerne shimmering in front. A narrow lane ran along the forest edge, just wide enough for motor cars. Charlotte arrived on foot, having taken a short-cut through the Crystal Ring.

Stefan kissed her cheek; Niklas half-smiled from where he stood near the windows.

"Sorry I was delayed," she said. "What a heavenly view of the lake!"

"You can admire it all you like, later," said Stefan, "but I expect you're keen to get to business?"

"What business?"

Charlotte had an odd feeling of dislocation, as if she'd just woken up and lost track of time. She recalled speaking with Amy, then travelling through the misty violet lower regions of Raqia… but she had no idea what Stefan meant.

"The knife?" he said. "I thought you were eager to examine it."

"What knife?" said Charlotte.

Why were they looking at her so strangely? Why was Karl coming towards her, frowning?

"This," Stefan said, puzzled.

Across his palms he held a thick folded scarf, a dagger lying on top. Its carved bone handle was set with a ruby, like a giant blood drop. Charlotte had no idea what she was looking at.

Then the memories came back in a violent rush. She backed away until she collided with the far wall, so cold with shock she thought she might pass out like a human. The air shuddered and she saw her double floating in front of her: the mindless, mocking lamia. She felt the sting of glass shards in her back.

"No," she said. "*No!* Take it away from me."

Through a snowstorm, she heard Karl say, "Charlotte?"

CHAPTER TWELVE

BLOOD SISTERS

"How could I have *forgotten*?" she said for a third time, stricken. "How?"

Everything came back now in a clear flood: being stabbed in the street, her nightmarish hallucinations as the self-styled policeman intruded on the chalet and nearly lost his life at her hands. The spectral double. Karl, plucking glass slivers out of her flesh...

And yet, somehow, her mind had wiped out the entire night.

"It must be to do with the knife itself," said Stefan. "Can you remember when you last... remembered what you've forgotten, if you see what I mean?"

"I'm not sure." Charlotte rubbed her brow, glad of Karl's arm around her. "It's been fading for a few days. This morning, when we came out of Raqia, it had gone altogether. But I didn't *know* I'd forgotten until I saw the knife again. I only remembered Amy when I actually saw her, and then only the events that involved her. What's happened to me?"

"As Stefan said, a side-effect of the knife-wound," said Karl. "Why would it cause forgetfulness? I have no answer... Beloved, at least your memory has come back."

"I almost wish it hadn't. Am I going to keep forgetting and remembering? It was... absolutely horrifying." She went to the window and rested her head on the glass. "A cold knife cut me in half and I'm drifting in two separate pieces, untethered. No one else sees it, not even you, Karl. You're all concerned that

I'm in shock, but not that it's real or serious. And I don't want to make a fuss, because only I can help myself and I don't know how yet."

Reflected in the glass, she saw Stefan touch Niklas's arm.

"It's not so bad, having a double," he said.

"It's entirely different!" She turned on him. "Mine isn't a separate physical twin that I could choose to love or destroy. It's me but *not* me... like a living ghost, mocking me... I can't explain. I can't touch her, but she won't go away. What is it? The manifestation of all my guilt about choosing to become a vampire, befriending Ilona even though she killed Fleur, and all the hurt I caused my family?"

"Shed your conscience, or learn to live with it," Stefan said brightly. "I've told you that before. There's no other way."

"I thought I had shaken it off, long ago." Charlotte folded her arms. "I never suffered much guilt at all, to be honest – yet it's there, in my shape, following me around. I'm sorry."

"For what?" said Karl. He looked so beautiful, so concerned and helpless that she hurried forward and embraced him, feeling that she must comfort him, not the other way round.

"Being overdramatic. I'll be all right, I promise. No more strange fits."

"Love, try to keep that night in the centre of your mind," Karl said gently. "The memory will lose its potency, but not vanish again. I hope."

"I'll lock the knife away," said Stefan. "Forgive me, Charlotte, I had no idea this would upset you."

"No, bring it back!" she said. "Put it on the table there. I'm better now, and I do want to examine it again."

Karl passed her a magnifying glass. Bracing herself against the painful shocks to her fingertips, she turned the knife over and studied the carved pattern. A maze, a death-mask with closed eyes in the centre... And another detail, the tiny inscription just below the ruby pommel. She'd forgotten that, too.

"There's a word," she said. "It looks like Arabic. I can't read it."

"Nor can I," said Stefan. "What's the use of immortality, if not to learn every language on the planet? If only I wasn't so damned lazy."

"Let me see," said Karl.

He studied the word for a while. Eventually he said, "I think it reads *Istilqa*."

"What does that mean?"

"I'll find out for certain," said Karl, "but I believe it means 'sleep'."

Later, they sat outside on the edge of the veranda, watching pleasure boats and yachts drift past. Delicate spring flowers danced in the grass. The peaks on the far side of the lake floated like white lace against the sky.

Charlotte related her encounter with Amy. Stefan was leafing through a catalogue of *Spring Fashions, 1928*. She knew he was paying attention to the conversation even though he pretended nonchalance.

"I've still learned very little about Godric Reiniger," she said, "except that he fancies himself a *great* film director and likes to court favour with important people. But didn't you see him in the beer hall, Karl?"

His eyes were intent on her, as golden as two setting suns. Still watching her for signs of mental derangement? She broke eye contact, trying not to mind.

"Yes. And the thugs who attacked Emil were similar to the men Reiniger was talking to inside. Part of the same group. They had a similar aura, a pale yellowish glow. Very faint, but somehow painful to the eyes. And all had an odour like the men who attacked you. Not alcohol, but something noxious in their blood."

"At least I wasn't imagining all that." Charlotte hugged her knees. She checked that her memory was still intact, and recalled how much happier she'd been when it had vanished for a while.

"Perhaps you should go and speak to Herr Reiniger," said Stefan.

"It's not so easy," said Karl. "I tried last night."

"Karl!" She glowered at him. "You didn't tell me."

He met her gaze, blinked. Again she saw his subtle look of concern.

"Charlotte, I did tell you."

When she found her voice, it was rusty, faint. "Did you, really? Last night is blurred... but I felt so tranquil in the Crystal Ring, Obviously I was tranquil because my mind had gone blank."

Karl and Stefan turned their heads to look at each other. She added, "If you two exchange one more of your 'Poor Charlotte's gone mad' looks, I shall bang your heads together, I swear!"

"Sorry," said Stefan. "We're worried, that's all."

"Well, I did not get inside the house," said Karl. "That was the strangest thing. I tried to enter through the Crystal Ring but there was a force around the entire building, physically driving me away. Like a sphere of red energy, a barrier I couldn't breach. And a powerful aroma of blood."

"Pleasant or toxic?" asked Charlotte.

"The latter. Whatever they were doing inside seemed rather more interesting than making movies."

"You didn't think to knock on the front door?" said Stefan. "Too obvious?"

Karl hesitated. "It would have been difficult to explain why I was there. Also, I was sure that if I did get inside, I'd never escape. Every time I've seen Reiniger, he's stared at me as if he knows exactly what I am and is about to produce a sharpened axe."

"Are you sure he wasn't simply admiring the view?" said Stefan.

"Absolutely certain," Karl said drily. "That's why I meant to observe, rather than confront him. As things stand, we still know almost nothing about him."

"Amy mentioned secret meetings," said Charlotte. "Selected men only. She said nothing about... occult practices involving blood, or whatever they were doing. *Her* blood smells wholesome, so she can't be part of it."

"So her uncle doesn't tell her everything," said Karl. "I think I should pay him another visit."

"Must you?" said Charlotte. "I've such a bad feeling about him. You forever warn me not to get involved with humans."

He touched her cheek. They looked at each other, forgetting Stefan and Niklas were there. "I know, but that's because I'm bad at following my own rules. Otherwise I would never have asked your father to teach me about science, nor grown so dangerously close to you."

"You warned me then that you have no morals. I know that isn't true; you have your code of behaviour, but you don't hesitate to break it when necessary. Is that a fair assessment?"

"Perfectly fair," said Karl. "Every incident of late seems to have emanated from that house. The bone-knife, the gang that assaulted Emil, Amy fainting in the street..."

Charlotte tensed with anger. "Did her uncle know the doctor he sent her to was a sadistic old pervert? Does he even care? Poor girl."

"Be careful," Karl said softly.

"I know," she said. "Tender feelings towards a human are deceptive. Sympathy turns into thirst before we know what's happening. You don't have to remind me."

"That's not what I was going to say, but... never mind."

"Karl, I've had enough lessons to know I'm unlikely to change, but still, I promise I have no intention of feeding on Amy. She invited me on a weekend jaunt to Paris. I told her I can't go, but perhaps I should, if only to protect her. She said her uncle's forbidden her to go. I'm worried she's in more danger from him than from me."

Karl looked out across the blue water, his eyes turning thoughtful. That serene stare, framed by dark brows and lashes, had always captivated her. Sweet torment.

"All the more reason for me to visit Herr Reiniger, while you do whatever you must, *liebling*. But let us both be careful. I think I'll do as Stefan suggested, and simply knock on the front door. Do you remember those red columns of light we saw in Raqia?"

"Yes," said Charlotte. "Shooting up towards the *Weisskalt*. You said you've seen them several times?"

He met her gaze, said in a subdued tone, "And last night I saw them emanating from his house. They vanished when the red sphere faded. It's alarming to think he's capable of creating so much energy. I wonder what he's trying to do, and how much he knows."

Charlotte went quiet with shock.

"Do you like this one?" Stefan interrupted, passing her the catalogue and pointing to a sleek evening dress.

"Why? We're trying to have a serious conversation."

"Too serious," he said. "I'm planning a party. I want to treat you to a new outfit."

"What's wrong with the ones I have?"

"Too many bloodstains."

"There are no... apart from the dress that was ruined when I was stabbed..."

"Exactly. You need a replacement."

Charlotte began to laugh. "Stefan, I swear you think I'm some life-size doll for you to dress up! I don't care about fashion."

"Nonsense. Listen to this." He read out loud from a magazine, "'Gone is the flapper. In her place has come the young woman with poise, of soft-toned and correct speech, soberly dressed, and without closely cropped hair. Miss nineteen twenty-eight is much more subtle and polished, and she wears black satin instead of cerise. This year's style in young girls is to be quiet, conversational and terribly in earnest about careers.'" Stefan laughed. "There, Charlotte, you're already well ahead of fashion."

"'This year's style in young girls?' Heaven help us," said Charlotte, pulling a face at him. "I'm so glad I was never part of that world. Are you sure you wouldn't like to try some of these outfits yourself?"

"Well, perhaps I would," Stefan retorted. "Would it not be fun for Niklas and I to dress as women, and pass ourselves off as your twin sisters?"

Charlotte imagined the scene. "Actually, yes. May I wear one of your suits, and a fake moustache to complete the picture?"

"No moustache, but a top hat! Think how glamorous you'd look! See, Karl? Your shy beloved has discovered a taste for mischief."

"I should be used to your sense of humour by now," said Karl.

"We're stuck on this Earth for eternity, as near as makes no difference," Stefan remarked. "A little frivolity helps pass the time. I live in hope that you'll take undeath less seriously, one of these days."

"Karl isn't always serious," said Charlotte. "I love him the way he is, and the same goes for *you*, Stefan, so don't taunt each other."

"It's my fate to be misunderstood. You assume I'm wandering off the subject, while I'm actually trying to help you and you haven't even noticed."

"How?" said Karl.

"A party is the perfect thing to lure Godric Reiniger and his friends out of their lair, isn't it?"

"That's actually quite a good idea," said Charlotte.

"Or a potential disaster," Karl added. "I doubt he'd come, though. He doesn't know us. I suspect he considers himself too important to respond to invitations from strangers."

"Well, you never know." Stefan gazed at the sky. "Oh, we should make it fancy dress!"

"Don't," said Charlotte. "You might put people off coming. Anyway, you and Niklas look wonderful in whatever you wear. Everyday suits, eighteenth-century finery, anything. Be careful, if you don't want to become the playthings of some rich widow..."

"Oh, we have been." Stefan's eyes gleamed. "I've lost count of the dowager duchesses who have doted upon us. Not to mention dukes and counts, princes and princesses... Until they become *our* playthings in return."

"You're perverse, Stefan," said Karl.

"You're jealous. We have fun, don't we, Niklas? And we offer so much pleasure in return. Why not spread it as far and wide as we can? All we take in payment is a sip of blood."

"A sip?" Charlotte raised her eyebrows. Stefan winked. "I thought we were discussing the matter of my party dress." She pointed to a flowing design of golden-fawn and rose hues with handkerchief points, all silk, lace and sequins. "I do like this."

"Only the most expensive item in the catalogue!" Stefan grinned. "It is very *you*, though. Excellent choice."

"I'll pay for it, in any case."

"No, you won't." Stefan picked up her hand and gave it a tender kiss. "My party, my treat."

"What's amusing you?" she asked Karl, who was shaking his head.

"Nothing," he said. "I'm just glad to see you smiling again."

Dawn came, splashing the Alps with fire and turning Lake Lucerne to liquid gold. Godric had not slept. His house guests slumbered – those who were part of the *Eidgenossen* no doubt restless with bad dreams – but he had prowled the quiet house all night. Run through several movie reels in his private cinema. Scribbled a few pages of his new script, sketched some ideas for scenes and costumes. Sleep was impossible. He wasn't even tired.

The mood after Bruno's death had been grim. His followers' blood-lust had swiftly faded to a kind of sombre guilt.

Godric guessed every thought in their minds.

What have we done? Will that be me in Bruno's place, if I put a foot wrong? Oh, but the thrill of taking his life. The rush of power.

He'd dispatched Wolfgang and a couple of others to sneak the body into a van and drive it deep into the forest for burial. Anyone who asked would be told that Bruno had gone back to his family. He was not especially popular. No one would really notice or care that he'd left.

Spying upon them in the beer hall had somewhat reassured Godric of their loyalty, but had not made him complacent. Their terror kept them under his control.

In his office, Godric held up the piece of linen imprinted with Bruno's blood. Dazzling flecks of sunlight gleamed through the weave. Rather than the delicate streaks made by the shallow cuts of initiation, the blood was so copious that the symbol was almost lost, just one great random splodge of brown-red gore. Once it was properly dry, he would frame it.

Paradoxically, blood revolted him, but he endured his revulsion for the sake of power.

When his father's daggers drew blood, something magical happened. Godric had discovered the phenomenon years ago, from his father's papers and his own experiments. He'd never felt anything like the flood of energy generated by the blades entering flesh. Grudgingly, he acknowledged that Fadiya's instruction – to add the name of "Zruvan" to the ritual – made the power even more potent.

When Bruno died, the moment released lightning-bolts through every cell of Godric's body. Somewhat painful, highly exhilarating. The energy continued to flow in delicious pure white currents. It made sleep impossible. Unnecessary.

His inner circle had absorbed some too, but Godric had taken the main share.

He was ecstatic, ready to explode with new-found confidence. He *knew* he was something more than human now. Exactly what he was becoming, though, he was unsure. A touch of unease gnawed at him, as it had since he'd begun to experiment with the *sakakin* in his youth.

With every ritual meeting, every new rune, his strength grew.

But what if he couldn't control the process? What if he was actually destroying himself? Some nights, feverish, he would pace and pace and forget to eat. His strange sensations, hallucinations and dizzy spells often alarmed him.

That was why he kept asking Dr Ochsner, "Are you sure there is nothing wrong with me?"

Now he thought, *To hell with Ochsner. Nothing in his medical training can explain this. As he said, he's just a mechanic.*

"Godric?"

Her voice made him start. Fadiya appeared from nowhere, as if a piece of shadow had come to life. As she came soundlessly towards him, he felt his usual irritation at her presence, accompanied by the hateful sense of being in thrall. The room darkened around her.

Perhaps his ever-increasing strength would enable him to kill her soon.

"I watched your little ritual," she said huskily. "I have never seen the *sakakin* used quite like that before. It was… interesting."

"You seem to struggle with the concept of privacy," he said sharply. "If I'd wanted you to observe, I would have invited you. Members of my *Eidgenossen* only."

She only smiled. "The forces you raised were impressive, but you can't keep me out. They are my knives: I only let you borrow them. Do you even know what you are doing?"

The question made him go still. He *thought* he knew. He dared not consider the possibility of being wrong. But his plans were none of her business, so he didn't answer.

"Oh, Godric," said Fadiya. She came too close and pressed her fingertips into his cheekbones – an overfamiliar gesture that made him recoil. Still, there was a definite note of awe in her voice. "What have you done to yourself?"

"None of your concern."

"But it is. The daggers were not meant to be used in human rituals. I can't *make* you tell me your intentions, but I am sincerely interested. I still say that we should help each other, not fight." She fingered the edge of the linen. "Why do you make these blood patterns?"

His fresh confidence and expanding perceptions made him want to boast, and who else dare he talk to? *I refuse to be afraid of her. If seeming to trust her makes her more inclined to help me, why not?*

"Symbols have power," he said. "I hesitate to use the word 'magic', but they can change reality by focusing minds."

Fadiya nodded. "And why do you want power?"

"Who doesn't?" He laughed. "This small country may seem nothing to you, but it's the most glorious place in the world to me. It's the very heart of Europe. If I could bring all the cantons under my control – well, then, I'd make Switzerland such a force that I'd be regarded as her greatest ever hero."

"I wish men would not insist on being kings or gods over everyone else," she said softly, to herself more than to him.

"Being a *hero* is different," he retorted. "I'll use my position for good. My *Eidgenossen* comrades know that. They would not support me otherwise."

"It's persuading everyone else that's the trouble."

"I can do it. My films will sway them. And once I'm in power, no one, *no one* will ever dare to laugh at my work again!"

Fadiya smiled, beautiful yet impassive.

"What if I could bring you Emil Fiorani?" she said.

"What do you mean, bring him?"

"As a star for your new movie. If anyone could make people love your work, it's him."

"I have a star. Wolfgang is proving an excellent leading man."

"But no one knows him. Emil is famous, and as beautiful as a fair Valentino. Audiences would climb over each other to see him."

Godric bit the tip of his tongue until it hurt. He fumbled for a cigarette. "I don't need him. He and his employer Madame Lenoir have treated me with a level of disrespect that I can't easily forgive."

"I heard she's difficult. But they receive all the acclaim and love, don't they, while you only attract… laughter."

"I have powerful friends," he snapped.

"And I'm one of them," Fadiya said in the same smooth tone. "If I could part Emil from her, they'll both be weakened, which will make you stronger."

Godric sucked a lungful of smoke and held it. She had a point. He'd wanted to film Violette's ballet to increase his own prestige, but she and Emil had dismissed him as if swatting a gnat. So, to gain some advantage over them, perhaps to have her *begging* him to send Emil back in exchange for free filming access... That would put him, Godric, effectively in control of her public image.

"It's a thought," he said, releasing a wisp of smoke. "Interesting."

Fadiya gave a slow, cat-like blink. "What do you actually want, Godric?" she asked.

"I've already told you."

"No," she said, "what do you *truly* want?"

He exhaled the rest of his breath in a billowing cloud. When it touched Fadiya she vanished, as if she'd dispersed with the smoke.

"I told you about the strange episode with my memory, yet you still trust me to do this?" said Charlotte, standing in the silvery bower of Violette's living room.

"You seem perfectly rational to me," said the dancer. "There's no one I trust more."

"I hope you appreciate that I'm extremely uncomfortable about it. I thought we were friends. Blood sisters. Equals."

"Of course we are." Violette rested one hand on Charlotte's upper arm.

"And yet I find myself being used as a spy."

Violette had the grace to look remorseful. "I know, and I'm sorry – but who can I trust, if not you and Karl? I can't ask my human assistants without compromising Emil's dignity – he needs to stay private and untouchable, like me, at least to outside eyes. And who can observe him without being noticed, better than a vampire?"

"I understand. I'm simply telling you that I'm not happy."

"Your distress is noted, my sweet friend," Violette said mildly. "It won't be forever, or for very long, I hope. I said I'd prefer him not to go out, but I didn't *forbid* him, so I've only myself to blame if he does. I admit, I'm disappointed he chose to ignore a clear hint. But, since he persists in defying me, I *must* know what he's up to. Have you anything for me?"

"Er... yes." Charlotte wondered how to phrase the news so Violette would not hit the roof. Nothing for it but the plain truth. "He's seeing someone."

"Who?" The blue-violet eyes shone with anger.

"I've only glimpsed her from a distance. A young woman, very striking and fashionable. Dark hair, darkish skin – I think she might be Arabian, or perhaps Persian or Egyptian: I'm not sure."

"How many times have you seen them together?"

"Three times in the last week. Once, walking arm in arm by the lake. Another time, going into a restaurant. And once, entering the Hotel Blauensee by the lake."

"A hotel. So he's sleeping with her."

Charlotte shrugged. "I can't tell, without following them into the bedroom – and I draw the line at that. I assume he is, though."

Violette's eyes glittered. She looked incandescent. She let her hand drop from Charlotte's arm but otherwise stayed motionless, like a cat about to pounce. "He certainly got over me swiftly."

"I'm sure that's not true. She's consolation, that's all."

"Well, it has to stop."

"Does it?" Charlotte moved away and perched on a chair arm. "Why?"

"What do you mean, why? You know my rules. My dancers are required to abstain from relationships, whether it's with each other or with outsiders."

"Is this a ballet company or a monastery?"

"There's no need for sarcasm. Dancing isn't any job, it's a vocation. If we are to be the best in the world, I require complete dedication – and, yes, sacrifice."

"And of course, no one has ever dared disobey you," said Charlotte. "Not one of them has *ever* had a secret dalliance under your leadership. No one, ever, not once."

Violette's lips thinned. She gave a slow, emphatic blink.

"Very amusing, Charlotte. All right, perhaps my rules are unrealistic, but it's a matter of discipline – yes, precisely as if they were in the army or a religious order. But I'm not naïve. No doubt half of them are breaking the rules as we speak. The point is…"

"Not to be found out," Charlotte finished. She smiled. "My Aunt Elizabeth taught me that. We're governed by the conventions of society, but how people *actually* behave is rather different. Yet the truth can't be admitted openly. So her other piece of advice was that, if a person *is* found out, everyone should act as if nothing has happened."

Violette laughed out loud.

"How British. So when you were caught out with Karl, your family sat down over a nice cup of tea and said nothing beyond, 'Pass the sugar'?"

"Well... yes and no. They expressed every shade of shock, disapproval and rage you can imagine, and I deserved it. If it had been an everyday scandal, they would have forgiven me in the end. I think even Henry would have harrumphed and ignored the whole thing – it's dreadfully bad manners to notice that your wife's having an affair! But they knew what Karl *was*, you see. That was the difference."

"Oh, that's the line, is it? You could have fallen from grace with a poet, a gypsy, a coalman, a jazz musician..."

"But really not with a vampire who has drunk your blood and inadvertently nearly killed your brother's best friend," Charlotte said in a low voice. "To be fair, my aunt stuck to her principles: she was the only one who more or less forgave me, as if to say, 'Oh well, it's not the first time in history someone's fallen for the wrong man.' If anything, she seemed to like me better after I'd disgraced myself."

"Interesting. A guilty conscience of her own?"

"Probably, but she was a realist. We're straying off the subject. What I'm saying is this. If I were you, I'd turn a blind eye. Let Emil have his secret affair. If he's found an outlet for his... feelings, he's less likely to be fixated on you, isn't he? Then, when he's with you, he can put all his energy into dancing. Isn't that what you want?"

Violette paced to the window and back, drummed her fingertips on the back of Charlotte's chair. Her expression went through subtle changes – anger, exasperation, resignation – as Charlotte looked up at her, waiting for a response.

"I appreciate the theory. But I can't make rules, then allow an exception for Emil because he is special."

"No one need know."

"I will know."

"So pretend you don't! I wish I hadn't told you."

"Then you would have been lying to me. Neither of us wants that, do we?"

"Absolutely not. But please... try leaving him alone for a while. Stop trying to control his every move. He might settle down and start behaving himself out of pure shock."

Violette roved the room for a few seconds, stiff-backed. "I'm not at all happy about this. However, he's fiery and hot-headed enough to hate me as easily as he claims to love me. I don't want that. I simply want my perfect, professional partner back. Maybe you're right."

"Really?" Charlotte tilted her head in hope. "I'm not claiming this will solve all your problems, but it must be worth a try."

"It had better be," Violette said thinly. "I only hope I can still rehearse with him, without wondering where his hands have been the previous night…"

Charlotte stifled a laugh. "Darling Violette, you *can't* be that squeamish."

"Oh, you'd be surprised," said the dancer with an icy smile. "All right. Let him enjoy his dalliance, while I blank all knowledge of it from my mind. And this conversation never took place. Let him have a secret wife and a dozen children, if it allows me to keep him!"

"Steady on." Charlotte stood, and gave Violette a light embrace.

The dancer said into her ear, "*But*." The word snapped like a whip.

"Oh, what now?"

"I must know who she is. I can't let him loose with a complete stranger. Charlotte, I need you to keep watching them for me."

Darkness fell, clouds hid the stars and drizzle blurred the streetlamps. Charlotte waited, but to her relief, Emil stayed in his room. Apparently he had no assignation with his lady love tonight.

Once she was certain he was going nowhere, Charlotte went hunting on her own behalf.

The doctor's office was easy to find. Amy had let slip his name: discovering his address was straightforward. Now Charlotte stood outside a creaking old brown building, gazing at his name on a brass plaque among those of other doctors, solicitors, accountants.

She sensed only one human presence inside. One window on the fourth storey shone with dim lamplight. No point in bothering with human charades such as making an appointment, or even ringing the bell: she simply stepped into the Crystal Ring, passed through the walls, drifted up narrow staircases and materialised in his office. The room was shabby and stuffed with bookshelves, reminding her of her father's house.

"Dr Ochsner?"

He sat with his back to her, reading by a desk lamp: a short heavy man with a thick neck, thinning hair combed over his scalp. As she spoke, he went from a study in motionless concentration to a flailing chimpanzee, scattering papers, pens and books everywhere. She half hoped he'd expire of a heart attack, but now he stood glaring at her over half-moon lenses, red-faced and panting with shock, one hand held to his chest.

"How the devil did you—"

Charlotte, in a black coat and cloche hat that hid her hair, sat on the edge of the examination couch. The room was sepia and had an unholy smell of tobacco, schnapps, whisky and disinfectant. She wasted no time, but stared into his eyes, unleashing the full power of her vampiric glamour in order to hypnotise the truth out of him.

"Did you examine Herr Reiniger's niece, Miss Temple?" she asked softly.

He stammered, his terrified expression darkening to a scowl. She read him: a cold man, short on principles, more interested in books than patients, too long in his profession to care about them any more. "Who are you?"

"I've come from Herr Reiniger," she answered coolly. "He is displeased. Were you aware that after Miss Temple left your office, she began bleeding so heavily that she collapsed in the street?"

"What? No! That's none of my doing..."

She was no longer Charlotte, passionate and sympathetic and fair-minded. At this moment she was pure vampire: coldly angry, an avatar of Lilith, like Violette.

She would make him pour out the truth, and he wouldn't even know what was happening.

"Was it not? Isn't it the case that you injured her in a cruel and invasive procedure that should have been performed in a hospital, if it was needed at all? You hurt her. You did so deliberately. Her uncle is deeply displeased."

"But – but—" He looked furious, but his eyes were locked

on hers. "Herr Reiniger knows perfectly well my methods as regards... intimate matters. Internal examinations are of necessity likely to be painful. Sometimes it's essential to be a little rough."

"A little rough? On purpose? *Why?*"

"To teach her a lesson!" Dr Ochsner's face distorted into an ugly expression. "To teach all these foolish young girls a lesson. To make sure she behaves herself in future, that's all. Leave her in no doubt that if she acts the whore, she'll be punished. A young man comes to me with some venereal disease? The treatment is *exceedingly* painful. It's no different. It is a moral lesson, harsh but fair. It was for her own good."

Charlotte stared without blinking. His cruel, fleshy face lost its colour. "And Herr Reiniger pays you to do this?"

"We have an agreement. He sends patients to me. I sponsor his films. I support his political ambitions: a strong proud Switzerland. No one in their right mind could object to that."

"I see," she said coldly. "I've met many good doctors, but you are not among them. Come closer."

Helplessly in thrall, he obeyed. She put her hands on the shoulders of his never-washed old suit jacket. She smelled his sweat, his whisky breath, his terror... but beneath that, the rich, red, throbbing flow of his blood.

She paused.

"Godric Reiniger," she said softly. "Is he your patient too? What secrets does he tell you?"

Ochsner grunted through his constricted larynx.

"He's a hypochondriac. He pays me handsomely every month to tell him there's nothing wrong with him. Even a strong man has his weaknesses. My job is to keep him strong, a role I undertake with pride."

"Anything else?"

"He works too hard, doesn't eat properly. That's all. Please..."

Please spare me? Please feast on me? Charlotte didn't know what he was asking, and didn't care.

Her fangs dropped from their sockets as she parted her lips. Usually she liked to flirt and coax affection first, but now she was as clinical and swift as Karl. Beneath her raven-black coat, she became the lamia from the mirror.

"Well, here is *my* price: that you never torture and humiliate Amy, or any other woman or man, ever again."

She struck. Her prey struggled frantically in her grip but she barely noticed, wholly caught in the rich red stream of his life as it flowed deliciously into her, too luscious for her to hold back. For once, she did not even try to stop. She seemed to be floating outside the window, watching her ghost-self feasting...

Too late, she realised what Karl meant when he'd said, "Be careful."

CHAPTER THIRTEEN

A STUDY IN RED

This time there was no unnatural barrier to keep Karl out of the house. Bergwerkstatt was as intimidating as he remembered, but the atmosphere was quiet, normal. Not even a breeze hampered him as he went up the wide steps to the front door and rang the bell.

To his surprise, Godric Reiniger himself answered. Before Karl had a chance to speak, the man's face lengthened and he blinked in obvious, startled recognition. His inner reaction was perceptible only to a vampire: skin paling a shade, heart rate accelerating.

"Ah. This is unexpected."

"If my visit is inconvenient, I apologise. I'm Karl Alexander."

"How may I help you, Herr Alexander?"

"I heard you speaking in a beer hall." Karl stared straight into his eyes, not pretending any warmth or friendliness. "You seem a man of interesting views. However, some of your companions attacked an acquaintance of mine that night. He was badly hurt. I wondered what you have to say."

The man said nothing for ten seconds. Karl expected the door to be slammed in his face. Godric had the same fish-eyed stare as when he'd first seen Karl at the cinema, but this time he was quicker to mask the reaction.

"And you are here in what capacity?"

"As a concerned associate of the victim."

The cool blue eyes looked him up and down. "Associate?"

"I'm not here to cause trouble. I hope a quiet talk between us will ensure that nothing similar ever happens again."

Another long, wary pause. "If any of the men from the beer hall were involved in a fracas – I know nothing of it, nor can I be held responsible for their actions. They're high-spirited, they drink too much: I am not their guardian."

That was a fair point, Karl thought, if disingenuous. He said, "Still, you appear to have influence over them. If it's good, wise influence, it's within your power to dissuade them from mindless attacks on strangers, isn't it?"

The tip of Godric's tongue appeared and moistened his thin lips. "If I discover the perpetrators, I'll have a very stern word. But won't you come in?" He gave a sudden, alarming smile. "I'd like to make your acquaintance too, Herr Alexander."

"Indeed?" Karl, surprised by the invitation, stepped into the hallway.

He sensed no bristling waves of power pushing against him. The atmosphere was peaceful. Voices chattered in far-off rooms. All the same, he caught remnants of stale rusty blood, and a bitter scent like an extinguished fire. He thought, *Someone has died here.*

"So you heard me speaking. I know you've seen my work. Therefore I assume that this is about more than a backstreet fight. You are intrigued by my political views? Something resonated."

"You could say that." Karl noted how Herr Reiniger flattered himself without any prompting. He decided to play along, as the easiest way to keep him talking. Above all, he wanted to ask what Godric knew about the *Istilqa* knife, but that seemed the most dangerous question of all.

"You described *The Lion Arises* as 'terrible' – and yet you are here."

"Forgive me if I caused offence. The message beneath the overacting was... intriguing."

"Good, I'm glad you perceived it. You appear to be a perceptive gentleman. Intelligent. Different."

He put special emphasis on the last word. Karl was in a state of calm wariness, his distrust of Reiniger was mixed with curiosity. Karl found all humans interesting: occasionally one held him fascinated. For some reason, to his dismay, this gaunt, ethereal eccentric seemed to have that disturbing hold on him.

Karl followed him through the grandiose hallway to a vast, stark reception room. An office? The walls were pure white marble. No curtains hung at the tall windows. The room held little furniture: only a desk, bookcase and some tall chairs, streamlined and austere in style. Electric lights lit the room like sun glaring on snow.

The smell of sour blood was particularly striking here. Karl longed to ask what they'd been doing to create a force so powerful. He recalled rods of crimson light hovering between Earth and the *Weisskalt*. A force strong enough to affect the Crystal Ring? Now and then he glimpsed Godric's strange white-yellow aura.

Herr Reiniger closed the door and stood in the centre of the bare white room. He didn't offer Karl a drink or a seat. They were strangers, yet Karl felt they knew each other. They circled with the delicacy of rival scorpions.

"An impressive house," said Karl, thinking that Charlotte would hate it. Even Violette, who might suit an ice castle, liked some luxury in her surroundings.

"Isn't it splendid?" Godric responded with a flash of unguarded enthusiasm. "Took two years to build. I finished it in twenty-six. My own design. The architecture represents the world to come: modern, simple, pure and audacious."

"Threatening," said Karl.

"Really? You find it intimidating?"

"Very much so. It's almost... imperial. Isn't it designed to intimidate?"

Godric laughed. "Absolutely! If one is going to be powerful, one had better start by *appearing* powerful. A quaint old chalet wouldn't impress anyone."

"Whom do you wish to impress?"

The man shrugged. "Those brave enough to share my ideas for a better future. Men of vision. Those who stand apart from the masses."

"Ah, what are we to do with ordinary people?" Karl said aridly.

Godric flipped open a gold case full of thin black cigarettes and offered one to Karl. He declined, but watched with interest the meticulous way – like the precision of a doctor preparing an injection – that Godric selected a cigarette, took his time lighting it and savoured the first delicate drag. No doubt this fussiness might become annoying to anyone who lived with him.

Godric blew out the smoke in a pencil-thin stream.

"They have their uses," he said. "As foot soldiers, workers. However, you must agree that the human race could use improvement."

"I couldn't say," said Karl.

"Couldn't you?" Again the man gave him a long, shrewd stare. "You don't think society would be better without degenerates running amok?"

"Perhaps," said Karl. "But how do we judge who is degenerate?"

"Oh, that's the easy part. It's all there in my films. Much plainer than the Bible, with all its 'meek inheriting the Earth' nonsense."

"I gather you aren't happy with the way Switzerland is governed?"

"Not really. Cooperation and sharing of power *appears* fair, but it makes us weak. Whenever there's a war, we're expected to absorb the detritus fleeing from the countries all around us. Too many compromises. *Someone* needs to stand for strong leadership. I have the means and wealth to do so, so what else would I do? I'm making my films to fill Swiss German hearts with passion until they finally *understand*."

"What do you want them to understand?"

"That this land is special, that it's *theirs*. The mountains are full of gods and heroes just waiting to be awoken. There's a clear hierarchy of race and language here, and we stand at the top: the heirs of Woden, of Berchtold, of all our great folk heroes. My circle of supporters grows every day."

He regarded Karl with narrowed eyes through his thin clear spectacles. Passion burned beneath the cool exterior, and he clearly wanted to share it.

I wonder why he's being so open with me? Karl thought. *He's fearless and wants to show off? If he truly recognises me as unhuman, he's either stupid, or he believes he's as strong as a vampire. And he does not seem stupid.*

"I suppose making movies is a more peaceful road to power than raising an army," said Karl. "However, your followers made the rather disastrous mistake of assaulting the male principal dancer of the Ballet Lenoir."

Reiniger sat back on the edge of his desk, one hand cupping his other elbow and the cigarette poised near his jaw. "As I said, that was not my doing. But I don't know what a male dancer is, if not degenerate. An Italian communist homosexual who prances on stage is fair game, I'm afraid."

"Do you seriously believe that?"

Godric shrugged. "Tell him to stay out of beer halls."

"I don't think Emil is a communist…"

"Did you know that his brother was executed for trying to assassinate Mussolini?"

"No," said Karl, startled. "I don't blame Emil for keeping quiet about such a thing. Even if it's true, it's a very flimsy excuse for your gang to assault him."

"I have no 'gang'. But, who knows, perhaps one of my friends saw Fiorani take a swing at me."

"He tried to hit you? Why?"

"For no reason at all," said Godric. "I saw he was drunk, I tried to stop him going inside for his own safety. He responded badly. That's all. It was an unfortunate misunderstanding and I… I can only wish him a swift recovery." When Karl didn't answer, he added, "Will you tell him?"

"He doesn't know I'm here," Karl said softly.

"Did Madame Lenoir send you, then? If you know him, you must know *her*."

Karl noticed the blue spark in his eyes when he spoke her name. "Yes, I know her."

"Indeed?" A long pause. A finger of ash fell on to the pristine floor. "She is very much a celebrity, a local goddess, but I'm afraid I offended her. I would *so* like to film the ballet, but she turned down my offer flat. I should like to make amends, to apologise…"

The faint corona that surrounded Godric flared bright, like acid-yellow flames – a brew of excitement, hope, anger, savage determination.

What is going on in this man's head? Karl thought. *If only I could read his mind. All I see is that he wants to control everything and everyone, and is burning with resentment that he can't. He's mortal, so why does he have this shield around him that protects him from vampires? How?*

"I understand that it would be prestigious for you to work with her," Karl said carefully. "It would increase your fame to have your name linked with hers."

"You think I want to meet her out of self-interest? Reiniger Studios is successful in its own right, and every bit as 'prestigious' as the Ballet Lenoir. If anything, it would benefit her more than me, to have her ballets filmed and brought to a wider public. I think she should reconsider. How well *do* you know her?"

"I can't promise to plead your case to Madame Lenoir." Karl evaded the question with a rueful smile. "I don't know you well enough, Herr Reiniger. And she didn't send me. No one did."

"Mm. So you are *really* here about something else? Interesting. Do you want to join our cause, Herr Alexander? Have I inspired you?"

Reiniger's shoulders began to shake with laughter. His lips flattened and tears shone in his eyes.

"What's so amusing?" Karl asked.

The tears spilled as Reiniger went on giggling, making a wheezing sound. He looked down at his own shoes, apparently so lost in the private joke that Karl felt inclined to leave. Then he regained control, dried his eyes and cleaned his clouded spectacle lenses on a handkerchief.

"Oh, more than you know," he said. "My beer-hall friends are part of my film crew. They hold strong and sincere opinions, and when they've had a drink or two, they tend to express themselves rather too loudly in public. Sometimes they go too far and need discipline. But I wouldn't want to rein in their high spirits – and don't you find human behaviour fascinating?" Reiniger, still grinning, fingered a messy stack of papers on his desk. "I was observing, in order to see how outsiders react to them. Do they heckle, or are they inspired to shout their support? And to judge how such a scene might work in a film. Nothing is wasted, creatively. Not even a regrettable street brawl. Don't you agree?"

Karl felt Godric was trying to draw him into some sort of complicity he didn't want.

"Well, I agree that mob behaviour is interesting. Are your supporters trying to clear Switzerland of 'degenerates' one at a time, starting with Emil?"

Godric's thin blond eyebrows rose. "You disapprove of violence? You, of all people?"

"Why do you say, '*Me*, of all people'? You don't know me."

Reiniger watched the curl of smoke he'd exhaled. Karl perceived an indefinable, sinister shift of the atmosphere. The moment was charged with insinuations that he felt he should understand, but did not.

Instinct whispered to him, *Kill Reiniger now and leave.* Yet he couldn't. Karl's curiosity equalled his thirst for blood: some called it a weakness. He was not like Kristian or Pierre, Ilona or even Violette, able to crush the problem and walk away. Perhaps life would be easier if he could, but he couldn't destroy Reiniger without understanding who and what he was.

This was why he warned Charlotte against getting involved. He knew the dangers.

Godric gave a short laugh, a jerk of his shoulders. He stared at Karl with his searing gaze. Eventually he said, "You don't recognise me, do you? I remember you, however."

Dull foreboding snagged Karl's heart.

"Forgive me," he said. "My memory is usually excellent, but you're right. Other than the occasion when we passed in the cinema, I don't recognise you. Where could we have met?"

Godric gave a thin, grim smile.

"If you don't know, I'll keep you guessing for a little while. I didn't know your name then, Karl Alexander von Wultendorf. I didn't realise that monsters *had* names. But I am older and wiser now, while you have not aged a day."

Karl said nothing. Apprehension sank through him. Surely not a past victim… He hunted at night, feeding and abandoning prey before they had a chance to see his face. The attack tended to cloud their memories. Fang-wounds healed swiftly. A few days of madness or fever might follow, but the attack itself would be a blank. A frightening chasm into which they dare not look…

But there might be exceptions. Moments of carelessness.

Godric Reiniger stared through his gold-rimmed lenses. "May I assist your memory?"

"If you must," Karl said steadily.

"I never forgot your face, you see. Like a painting of an angel, too handsome to be real with those lustrous eyes: beautiful, if such a description can apply to a male. Do you notice that people almost break their necks, swivelling their heads to follow you? Quite tiresome, I imagine. Your fine looks are memorable, even in the half-dark. See…"

Godric reached into a desk drawer and took out a sketchbook. He placed it on the desk and opened the cover, angling it for Karl to examine.

Karl did not want to look. He disliked being manipulated, but his innate good manners and thirst for understanding overrode his apprehension. He studied the first picture. A drawing of a man's face in red crayon…

The lines were crude and immature, clearly the work of a child. Yet, without doubt, the face was Karl's own.

"Please, look at the rest," said Reiniger.

Reluctantly, Karl turned the pages one by one. A faint, familiar rusty aroma wafted out of the book. Every drawing was of him, and all were executed in red; crayon at first, then scarlet pastel, red ink, and then a dark red paint that had crinkled the paper. With each portrait, the style grew more sophisticated, moving from a child's to an adult's. Some were full face, others showing the figure from the side, half in shadow. The last three sketches were looser, more impressionistic, almost angry in their rough energy – but all, without question, drawings of Karl.

"Can you see yourself in a mirror?" asked Godric.

"Yes, of course."

"So you know whose face I was trying to capture?"

Karl didn't answer. If this man knew he was a vampire, why wasn't he afraid? He wouldn't be the first human Karl had met who considered himself too powerful, too worldly-wise and clever for fear, or even sensible caution.

"How old do you think I was when I drew the first one?"

"I don't know. Twelve, thirteen?"

"Ten," said Reiniger. "Not bad for my age, don't you agree?"

"Remarkable," Karl said softly. "You were a gifted child."

"Drawing is not my strong point: I'm better with photography and film, but I do my best. The others are from memory. One a year, on average… usually around the anniversary. I would have dreams, you see, and feel compelled to purge your face out of my mind yet again. The most recent" – he waved his cigarette at the page that lay open – "I drew yesterday."

Karl traced a fingertip over the scrubby, red-brown lines. A smell like iron and raw meat rose strongly around him; the taint of dry, dead blood. A human would not notice, but to a vampire it was overwhelming.

"You paint with your own blood?"

"It seems appropriate. How do you know it's mine?"

"The scent," said Karl. "Every human is different."

"Ah, like wine." Reiniger flipped the book shut and snatched it away. His eyes sparked with sudden rage.

The smell was far from appetising. Only blood pulsing through a living human was enticing to vampires. But he hadn't come here to attack Godric Reiniger. Karl couldn't identify the pollutant in his blood, but it made him imagine biting into a ripe peach and receiving a mouthful of vinegar.

"What anniversary?" he asked.

"Of the night you killed my father in front of me."

In the horrible silence that followed, Karl found nothing to say. No point in denial. He still couldn't remember anything, but why would Reiniger make such an assertion if it wasn't true? Shadows stirred in the back of his mind, nothing he could grasp. He only stared at the man without emotion. What did Reiniger see? A monster with the face of an angel, eyes like fiery amber holding no trace of remorse?

"I was surprised to find *strigoi* so civilised, so... human," Godric said after a minute, resting one hand in his trouser pocket. "But glad, too, because it means you have some comprehension of the atrocities you've committed."

"I can't answer this accusation," Karl said very softly. "I have no idea what you're talking about."

"May I assist your memory?"

"Perhaps it's best if I leave."

"I can't stop you leaving, it's true. Nor can I stop you killing me, if you've a mind to end all this – although you might find it harder than you imagine."

Reiniger brought his hand out of his pocket. In it he held a small bone-handled knife, nearly identical to the one that had wounded Charlotte. The blade glittered. A sharp unpleasant tang hung in the air. Karl stared at the silvery after-images as Godric wove patterns with the knife-tip.

It was the strangest feeling. The knife seemed to emanate a deadly vapour... but nothing was poisonous to vampires, was it? *Except this*.

Karl took a step forward, only to find it was not his imagination playing tricks. He felt dizzy and had to move back.

Worse, the feeling was familiar. Not because of the *Istilqa* knife he'd left with Stefan, but something older, so deep and vague he could make no sense of it. Formless, ancient dread.

"What is that?"

"Our defence against you," said Godric. "You've never seen a *sikin* before?"

"I think I would have remembered," Karl said, evading the truth.

"One may not be lethal to your kind, but all my men know how to use them. Just so that you know."

"How many?"

"Enough."

Karl raised his palms. "I swear, I have not come here to threaten you. You can put the *sikin* away. I came to talk."

"Good," said Godric. The knife vanished back into his pocket. "Now, if you would bear with me, there's something I'd like you to see. An explanation. Will you?"

He held out a hand to usher Karl out of the room and upstairs. Karl was puzzled, weirdly entranced by Reiniger, and now apprehensive. But he craved an explanation more than anything.

"We have quite an efficient operation here," Reiniger said conversationally as they went. "We mostly use Bell & Howell cameras, but we're trying the new Bolex models, made in Geneva. I prefer to support the home economy, naturally. We have darkrooms and an editing suite. This is not Hollywood. I cannot afford to employ hundreds of technicians. So, everyone must master several skills. There's nothing I ask my assistants to do that I can't do myself: filming, lighting, processing, even costume and make-up. But all the story ideas, all the scripts, are mine."

"And you direct?"

"Write, direct, edit and distribute. Aside from my supporters, who double as extras and crew, this is a one-man operation. Mine. Reiniger Studios."

The room to which he led Karl was a small private cinema, with tiered seating, a projection booth at the rear and a huge screen veiled by black curtains in front. There were prints along the walls that looked like Japanese calligraphy.

"My screening room," said Reiniger.

"Impressive."

"Take a seat, anywhere you like."

"What are you doing?" said Karl.

"Just humour me. Sit."

With a sense of dread, verging on claustrophobia, Karl took a seat in the back row. Reiniger left him there. A few moments later, the lights went down and he heard the whirr of a projector start up behind him. Karl sat as if chained there. The curtains opened. Beams of light shot over his head and silver grey shadows began to dance on the screen in front of him, playing out a wordless horror story.

CHAPTER FOURTEEN

ROSE AND THE BLACK WOLVES

Emil was drowning. Walls of water hit him, one after another. All was black, the world upside down. In the far distance he saw Violette, a tiny figure confronting a great skull-headed monster – he screamed her name but brine filled his mouth. He must reach her or the world would end...

"Violette! *Violette!*"

He woke violently and sat upright in bed, streaming with sweat.

"Emil?"

Fadiya's voice was warm and soothing. Odd that every time he woke – gently or suddenly – she was always awake first. He couldn't shake off the night terror and almost wished she were not there to witness his panic.

"Another bad dream?" she said. He nodded. He was gasping for breath, his heart racing so hard he thought he might die. "You were calling out her name. Violette."

"I – I dreamed she was in danger. I dream it all the time."

He felt her hand on his shoulder. Her touch calmed him, and he found his breath.

"Always the same," he groaned. "A figure menacing her. It looks like Kastchei the sorcerer from *The Firebird* ballet, but real, and truly evil. Maybe he represents death, or something worse, I don't know. And I have to save her, but I can't."

"Perhaps that is what the dream is telling you, my dear," she murmured. "You cannot save her from her own demons, so you need to accept that."

"But what demons? Why would anyone mean her harm?"

Fadiya shrugged. "Who knows? We all have burdens to bear, and in the end, we all have to face our nightmares alone."

Her words chilled him.

"I can't accept it!"

"You're still in love with her, aren't you?" It was more a statement than a question. He only sighed. He switched on a bedside light, poured some brandy into a glass and drank it in two gulps. Putting the glass down with shaking hands, he missed the small table and the glass thudded on to the carpet.

"Of course you are," she went on. "You aren't the kind of man who would fall in love and out again so lightly. If you were, I wouldn't be here with you. But I *am* here…"

Her words trailed off as her hands moved over his back, tracing every muscle as her lips began to plant kisses on his neck and throat. The warmth of her body against his was irresistible. Her palms slid around to explore his taut abdomen. His hands found the inner surface of her thighs.

"It was only a bad dream," Fadiya whispered. "Let me help you forget."

He turned to her, found her mouth as they rearranged limbs and lay side by side, pressed to each other. Already he was so strongly aroused that he felt he must be inside her or die… and she guided him, laughing and moaning with her own pleasure. She had this effect on him every time, a hot whirlpool of aching, excruciating pleasure…

Would Violette have been like this?

Emil could not, dared not think of her. There was only Fadiya, all around him like umber fire. He was deep inside her now, thrusting into her comforting heat. A thousand times better than plunging through ice-cold storms to reach Violette.

"I don't want to hurt you," Fadiya whispered into his ear. "I only want to bite you a little. Here." She kissed his neck, her mouth a burning pressure on his skin. He was too far gone to care what she was saying. She could do anything she liked to him, anything. "May be a little sharp… forgive me. Won't be for long but I have to… oh God, I have to…"

He climaxed as she bit him, pleasure overwhelming pain. Then he felt himself sinking into darkness, as if he were back in the nightmare again. He tried to capture images, but the fragments vanished like slivers of ice between his fingers. The fact that she'd bitten him, and broken the flesh, barely registered before it faded from his mind...

They lay sated together, too heavy to move. He looked into her sultry eyes and thought of nothing but the erotic wonder of her warmth. Fadiya... she was so loving, so beautiful.

Perhaps he could love her. At least he could try.

Violette always got her way.

Some would call her manipulative, but her hold on Charlotte ran deep. They'd been through so much together – events both wondrous and nightmarish – that no one else understood the dancer as Charlotte did. Violette was a genius and a goddess. Charlotte's obsession with her had nearly destroyed them both, but love between vampires was rarely simple or painless.

They were tangled together like thorn bushes, with as much anguish as affection, but the truth remained that Charlotte loved Violette with all her generous soul and always wanted to help her.

"Next week we start rehearsals in earnest, so I've given everyone a four-day break." Violette was in a silk robe at her dressing table, Charlotte in her black coat ready to go out. "It will be interesting to see what time Emil comes home – if he comes back at all."

"Wherever he goes, I'll be there, haunting him." Charlotte spoke in an ominous tone, only half joking.

"I suppose Karl disapproves of me asking you to watch Emil?" said Violette. "He thinks I use you, I know he does."

"In the past, perhaps," Charlotte answered. "These days, he's more tolerant. Ever since..."

"Ah, the bite of Lilith, which brings enlightenment," Violette said very softly. "And the death of childish fears, and visions of the future..."

"And mutual understanding. Love." Charlotte smiled, picturing the time she and Karl and Violette-as-Lilith had shared each other's blood and bodies in an ecstatic trinity.

"Unfortunately, it didn't bestow us with omniscience," Violette added.

"Probably just as well. The little glimpses we get are enough to drive us mad at times. Occasionally the firmament tears open and shows us something astonishing or horrific... That's quite enough for me." She leaned down and kissed Violette on the cheek. "Off I go to be your night spy. Don't wait up."

Forty-eight hours later, Charlotte was stepping into a Parisian nightclub called Trois Loups Noirs.

She entered the club through the Crystal Ring in order to avoid attention from door staff, waiters or anyone in the fashionable queue that was gradually shuffling inside. Within the smoky, candlelit space, no one noticed her stepping out of the shadows.

Tonight she was not herself. No flowing satin or lace in subtle melting colours. Instead, a visit to a boutique had secured a disguise: black eye make-up, red lipstick, a brown wig cut in a jaw-length bob. And she wore a dramatic black and white dress, not her style at all.

Violette was right: Emil had absconded for the weekend. Charlotte had seen him and his lady friend emerge from Hotel Blauensee at dawn. Soon after, to her great surprise, the two had been collected in a sleek Hispano Suiza – which made her heart jump, as it was like the one Karl used to own – by none other than Amy Temple, with a dark-haired male in the driver's seat. She recognised him as the hero of *The Lion Arises*.

Three more motors had drawn up, horns beeping exuberantly until people began leaning out of the hotel windows to shout at them. Then the four vehicles set off in convoy towards the French border: sixteen bright young adventurers, chattering in a mixture of French, German and English.

Amy was good friends with Emil's lover, judging by the hugs and kisses they exchanged on meeting. Now Charlotte would have to join Amy's jaunt to Paris, whether she wanted to or not.

To take the famous Emil Fiorani on the trip with them was, Charlotte guessed, quite a prize.

She followed through Raqia, skimming through the ether in her changed form like an eel through the depths of a lake. Reality appeared dim, compressed and distorted near ground level. Keeping the cars in sight was not easy; she would have lost them, had they not made several stops for fuel and food. The journey took the entire day. Darkness fell long before they reached the city.

Perhaps she should have accepted Amy's invitation after all – but that might have meant there was no room in the vehicle for Emil. Worse, Emil would then know that Violette had sent her. Besides, following them unseen was a pleasure that suited her secretive nature.

With the infinite patience of immortals, Charlotte watched as the party checked into a tall narrow hotel. They took supper at a pavement café, then withdrew to their hotel and apparently spent most of the following day asleep. That gave Charlotte time to procure her disguise, to satisfy her thirst in the backstreets, and to wish that Karl was with her.

The following evening, the group finally emerged in glittering finery for a night out in Montmartre. She memorised all their faces and realised she'd seen at least half of them in *The Lion Arises*. The actress Mariette – the Egyptian queen – was clearly the pack leader, but Charlotte's attention was on Emil and his companion. He looked splendid in an evening suit, blond hair brushed back. His lover matched him for beauty, her brown skin contrasted by a dress of pale creamy gold, glittering with sequins. Her eyes were huge and dark beneath a sparkling bandeau. She wore a single long strand of pearls.

Charlotte found their glamour mesmerising. Inevitably she began to imagine how the woman's silken skin would feel under her lips... how she would taste... Her fangs slid into striking position. The sudden pain as one fang-tip nicked her tongue jolted her back to reality.

Concentrate, she told herself. *I'm here to observe, not to indulge.*

Five years ago, she'd been a shy human of twenty, thrust by her Aunt Elizabeth into the bedlam of high society. Hard to believe so little time had passed; it felt like several lifetimes. She recalled a blur of debutante balls, picnics, dozens of events aimed at the ultimate goal: to find the perfect husband. Not an easy task after the Great War.

Looking back, Charlotte appreciated that this wasn't such a bad way of doing things. After all, the London season was supposed to be wild fun. Her younger sister Madeleine had loved it. Charlotte, reclusive by nature, had loathed the entire pantomime.

Over-sensitive, she was all too aware of the deadly serious purpose behind the season. A good marriage, the right friends, the constant reweaving of society's structure lest everything collapse... The relentless burden of *expectation* had made her recoil.

Anyway, that was far in the past. Karl had appeared and opened her eyes to the freedom of being her true self. What if she'd never met him? She might still be leading a quiet, productive life as a research scientist. There were worse fates. But she would have remained an introvert: stoic, competent, broken-hearted but never letting her bitterness show.

Karl certainly had not "saved" her in any sense. Their love had proved expensive, not least to her family. But... the heart would not be denied.

Now her life was full of strange pleasures and pains, roaming the night to feast on blood... In spite of all they'd endured – and even with the lamia haunting her – she would not swap her existence for anything.

Entering the jazz club, she felt a surge of nerves and excitement. The atmosphere was intense; a devil's brew of noise, smoke and body heat. Not the sort of venue her aunt would approve of, although Madeleine had sneaked illicit visits in London. Not wholesome for young ladies...

The place was packed with young ladies, regardless.

She was aware of English voices mingling with the French. There might be people here who remembered her. She dared not risk being recognised, since she was officially dead.

Being seen alive was a hazard that went beyond embarrassment.

An African-American jazz band created a raucous, joyous sound that made her want to sway and lose herself in sensuous rhythm. Couples bobbed frenetically on the dance floor. Charlotte smiled. She and Karl favoured the older, graceful dances. She wasn't sure she could tell the Lindy Hop from the Blackbottom or even the Quickstep, and the idea of attempting the Charleston struck her as faintly ridiculous.

In her disguise, she felt ridiculous in any case.

On the far side of the room, she saw Emil's party taking seats around a table with a white tablecloth, candles and ashtrays. They were all laughing, chattering as if already drunk. A waiter placed cocktails in front of them. Cigarettes were passed around. Charlotte saw Emil accept one, coughing clouds of smoke as if it were his first. Everyone laughed at him and he laughed with them, knocking back his drink in one gulp. Next, the regal Mariette tried to drag him on to the dance floor, but he resisted. Their light-hearted argument grew loud and heads turned to stare at him. All over the club, people began nudging each other and turning to gawp. *"Isn't that Emil Fiorani, the dancer?"*

Violette would be horrified.

Surely one night of abandon wouldn't damage his health? Unless this was how he meant to go on, in sheer rebellion. Charlotte had no intention of intervening. She was only there to observe.

"Mariette, leave him alone!" Amy's voice.

"Oh, don't let me prise you away from Fadiya," said the Egyptian queen, waving a dismissive hand at Emil. Even from a distance, Charlotte heard her clearly.

She pondered how best to spy on the group. *Find a table where I can sit close enough to hear them, but not close enough to be noticed.*

As she worked her way across the club, a group of braying Englishmen in Oxford bags got in her way, waving bottles of champagne and entreating her to join them. She tried to slip past but they were insistent, in their polite yet inebriated way. The old Charlotte would have fled. The new Charlotte had to battle with sudden blood-thirst as their salty heat flowed around her... and it would be lamentably easy, she knew, to lure any of them outside into a dark alley...

She held back, biting down to stop her fangs extending.

"You look just like a film star," one of them shouted into her face. "Clara Bow, that's who."

"No. Lillian Gish. Claire Adams, even lovelier," said his friend. They grinned, swaying in front of her. "Come on, join us. You're aspso..." He giggled, unable to form the word *absolutely*. "So lovely."

Through gaps in the crowd, Charlotte watched Emil.

Mariette had found another dance partner, and Emil was sitting with Fadiya, watching the band. His arm was around the back of her chair, fingers tapping to the rhythm; she was whispering into his ear, smiling.

So Charlotte sat down with the Oxford bags crowd, letting them fuss around her and pour champagne, not guessing she couldn't drink it. Well, she could pretend to sip, even force a little down her throat if necessary, but mortal drinks were as appealing to vampires as pondwater.

All the time she kept her eyes on Emil.

He was still smoking. Empty cocktail glasses crowded the table.

Idiot, she thought, knowing Violette would disapprove. She chewed her lip at the thought of reporting back; she felt like a teacher, asked to spy on ill-behaved pupils. *Am I supposed to report him to the headmistress? What will I be telling her?*

"He drank. He smoked. Yes, people recognised him. Yes, he made a fool of himself in public. Danced on tables, fell over. Then he had wild sex with his girlfriend. And with everyone else too; a veritable Roman orgy..." Charlotte groaned silently. *I shouldn't have to witness this. He's a grown man, and I feel more than a little sordid.*

"I say, I love this one!" said the young man beside her as the band launched into an even livelier tune. "Come along, we're dancing!"

He pulled Charlotte to her feet. She tried to resist but he was propelling her on to the dance floor with cheerful, relentless force. She could have stopped him easily, but not without causing a scene and possibly drawing blood. "It's not optional!" he yelled.

It was, however, a way to edge closer to Emil.

"Really, I'm terrible, I'll tread on your feet," she protested.

"Tread away! You'll be fine. I'm Noel, by the way."

"Vera." Charlotte gave the first name that came into her head.

"You don't look like a Vera." He seemed disappointed.

"Rose, then. Will that do?"

"Rose is perfect," Noel said happily. Next moment she found herself caught in a maelstrom of prancing, twirling couples, with Noel's sweaty hands gripping hers. He was good-looking, well spoken, full of laughter: perhaps the sort of man she might have married, if she'd been outgoing and fun, like her sister Maddy.

Charlotte gave up and joined in. She made a fair job of the Lindy Hop by employing the simple vampire technique of mimicry.

"You lied," he said, breathless as he bobbed up and down. "You're damned good at this."

"I'm only copying you," she said, willing her bandeau to hold the wig in place.

"Like hell. If that were so, you'd be stomping like an elephant!" He winked. "I think you're a bit of a bad girl on the quiet, Rose."

She only smiled, all the time keeping her gaze on Emil and his paramour.

He shone in the smoky gloom, with deep golden hair swept back from his proud, striking face. People kept glancing at him. Even offstage he looked like a fairytale prince, a yellow-haired Valentino. His eyes were bloodshot and he had a slight growth of stubble, but he was young enough to get away with these signs of debauchery. If anything, they made him more alluring.

His attention wandered from the band to the dancers and back. He showed no sign of noticing Charlotte, to her relief. She'd only half-expected her disguise to work, but apparently he was fooled. He didn't know her that well and would not expect to see her.

And his state of mind? Hard to tell. His lips smiled, but his eyes were narrow, restless. He looked like someone so determined to have a good time that he was nearly angry about it.

A ragtime number started. Charlotte found herself manhandled, lifted nearly off her feet, compelled to learn a new, more frantic set of steps. There was much jaunty circling with cheeks pressed together, which at least enabled her to see over Noel's shoulder. Again she turned her attention to Emil's companion.

Fadiya's hair was fashionably short and wavy, her skin warm with a bronze sheen. She was nothing like Violette. Her deep brown eyes were framed by thick lashes and heavy brows. A lovely face with a long, regal nose. And yes, very beautiful. Calm, smiling, affectionate, utterly lovely. She and Emil made a striking couple.

Again Charlotte felt exasperated with Violette's need to control every aspect of her dancers' lives. But, as Violette said, they knew what they were in for. In return for the honour of being chosen, total dedication was the price they gladly paid.

Still… could there be special dispensation for the marvellous Emil? Charlotte wondered if Fadiya's devotion would help him to concentrate on his work, or ruin him?

Charlotte was barely aware of the whirling dance. She focused wholly on Fadiya, like a ballerina spotting a focus point during a pirouette. It was like seeing single frames of a film. Smile. Laugh. Shoulder touch. Blank eyes, no expression. Another smile. Not once did she lift a drink to her lips.

Emil's body warmth rippled from him, a sunset aura. From the girl, though, there was almost nothing. The faintest indigo shimmer, at most. That might mean she was putting on a happy front while guarding her true self in public...

Noel stumbled into Charlotte, making her lose the rhythm.

"Most dreadfully sorry," he said, catching her elbows to steady them both. "I think I'm a bit squiffy. Perhaps we should sit down?"

The band began a slower song in waltz time.

"Oh, one more dance," said Charlotte. "We can prop each other up to this one."

"Splendid," he said, grinning. "You're an awfully good sport, Rose. I rather like you. Where do your folks live?"

"Tell you later," she whispered. Shuffling slowly amid the dancing couples, she pressed closer to him, letting him hold her more tightly, her head resting on his shoulder... easing along his collarbone until her mouth touched his neck. She felt him jump with surprise, but soothed him with her hands, heard his sigh of astonished bliss. She clutched the back of his head to hold him steady and bit into his throat, a swift sharp motion too subtle for anyone around them to notice. Ah, the divine burst of blood on her tongue... the matchless flavours, like thick red berry juices and wine and rare steak... indescribable to humans but utterly divine and addictive.

She felt the red rush through every cell, forced herself to drink slowly, savouring every sip, so that he didn't pass out on her. To counter the pain, he would be confused, dreamy, enthralled as if drugged. Certainly not inclined to fight her off.

When choosing victims, Charlotte was usually more private than this. But tonight, she was someone else.

She was Rose, a bit of a bad girl.

When his knees began to buckle she withdrew her canine teeth, discreetly cleaned the wound with her tongue, made sure there was no visible evidence. Then she led him back to his table.

"I think your friend's had one too many cocktails," she told his raucous companions. Noel only swayed and sat down heavily, grinning, reaching out to her and slurring that she mustn't leave, they were having such a grand time... Charlotte evaded all the grasping hands and ignored their entreaties.

Turning away, she saw Emil still sitting at his table. Fadiya, though, had gone.

Outside, the square was full of music and light from all the restaurants and clubs. Crowds of stylish revellers strolled between street artists. Charlotte savoured the scents of the mild Paris night, wishing with all her heart that Karl were beside her. There was no greater pleasure than walking arm in arm with him through human crowds, sated and glowing inside with fresh blood... well, there were some greater pleasures, but this was among the finest.

She put her yearning aside. Tonight she was here on business.

Fadiya was not easy to find in the crowd. Charlotte fixed on her faint indigo trail and followed until she caught sight of her. She appeared to be walking with purpose, keeping close to the buildings of the cobbled square. She was wearing a coat, so perhaps she was heading back to the hotel, but if she were tired or unwell, surely Emil would be with her? The fact that she was alone suggested a private assignation of some kind.

Fadiya did nothing obvious, like meeting another man or a girlfriend, hailing a taxi or heading towards their hotel. Instead she slid through narrow lanes, holding her dark coat around her until she almost disappeared.

With every step, Charlotte's apprehension increased.

She hung back, pulling her aura tight within her skin. The last thing she wanted was for the woman to sense she was being followed. Presently Fadiya stopped, distracted by a bohemian-looking young man who came weaving along the lane the opposite way. He waylaid her, chattering in French to which she responded fluently. She let him light a cigarette for her, pretended to smoke it. The red tip danced as she flirted. Then it curved down and hit the flagstones as she moved in, her dark head almost disappearing in the folds of his scarf and coat collar. A couple, kissing in the shadows… until his head fell back and he began to slide down the wall behind him. Charlotte caught the luscious aroma of blood, subtly different from her own victim's, like distinct wines. Fadiya stepped from the tangle of his folded legs and walked away as if nothing had happened.

"Oh," Charlotte whispered to herself. She stood frozen, dismayed that her suspicions were correct. "Oh no, please tell me this isn't real…"

A few minutes later, she was back inside Trois Loups Noir. Fadiya was at Emil's side again as if she'd only slipped out to the powder room. As Charlotte watched, the pair went to the dance floor and began whirling in a quickstep. Fadiya's face was enchanting with affection and good humour… and stolen blood.

Emil has no idea, thought Charlotte. *And if she's feeding on others, does that mean she's feeding on him? If not, it's only a matter of time.*

"Charlotte?"

The voice startled her. Amy Temple was standing in front of her, looking puzzled. "Charlotte, it is you, isn't it? What on earth have you done to your hair?"

"Um…" Charlotte spoke in a whisper, pulled Amy into a corner so the group at Emil's table wouldn't see them. "Yes, it's me. It's a wig."

"I don't understand." Amy looked baffled and hurt. "You said you couldn't come. Why are you here, but avoiding us?"

Charlotte drew Amy to a small table with two empty chairs, sat facing her. A waiter approached, and Charlotte waited patiently as Amy ordered champagne.

"I'm sorry," Charlotte said when he'd gone. "I know it looks peculiar, but it's rather complicated. I'm not avoiding you. I'm… watching someone. Dear, can I trust you?"

She looked straight into Amy's small, pretty brown eyes, softening her will with vampire glamour. She felt guilty doing this, but there was no time to waste.

"Of course you can," said Amy. "You saved my life. By the way, did you hear the news? That hateful Dr Ochsner was found dead in his office. I shouldn't be glad, but I am."

"I hadn't heard," Charlotte said honestly. She knew without anyone telling her. "What happened?"

Amy shrugged. "A heart attack, they said. I would like to think that one of his patients leapt off the examination couch and murdered him: is that terrible of me? Apparently he was *known* for being sadistic, not that my uncle seemed to know or care. But people like him never suffer as they deserve."

"No, they never do," Charlotte said softly.

"Anyway, are you going to explain why you're creeping around like Mata Hari without even talking to us? Pardon me for saying so, but that dress really isn't you, and your lipstick's a bit smudged…"

"Is it? Do you have a mirror?"

Amy passed her a powder compact from her purse and Charlotte cleaned away the smudges with a fingernail. It was only lipstick, not blood. As she handed back the compact, Amy asked, "Who are you watching?"

"I can't say, but if I ask you some questions, will you promise not to tell your friends you've seen or spoken to me?"

"Of course. They don't know you anyway, so…"

"I know Emil, a little."

The small eyes widened. "You know *him*? Mariette's the only one among us who's even a bit famous, so I don't think she's very pleased to be eclipsed by Emil Fiorani, of all people. How do you know him?"

"I know some people at the Ballet Lenoir," Charlotte said vaguely. "Please bear with my questions. Your group of friends…"

"They're a nice crowd, but goodness, they love to drink. I can't keep up."

"And you're not allowed to be with them."

"*Absolutely* not." Amy gave a small grin. "I shall be in *so* much trouble when we get home."

"The dark-skinned girl with Emil; are you friendly with her?"

"Fadiya? She's the new make-up artist. Yes, she's charming."

"How long have you known her?"

"Only a few weeks. I don't remember where she appeared from. They say she was married to a French soldier who brought her over from Algeria, but he died... so sad. Do you want me to introduce you?"

"No! No, it's all right. I'm not supposed to be here, remember?" Charlotte smiled. "Do you know anything else about her?"

"Not really." Amy was frowning. "She doesn't live in the house with us. I'm very surprised Uncle Godric employed her at all; he can be a bit... dismissive of anyone who's not of traditional German-Swiss stock. But she's terribly nice – she talks to me a lot. Heaven knows what we talk about!"

"You don't remember?" Charlotte ran her gaze over Amy's throat, but saw no tell-tale silvery marks, no sign of the feverish madness that sometimes overtook a vampire's victim.

But if Fadiya hadn't infiltrated the studios in order to feed, why was she there? Perhaps she was saving Amy for a special treat... Charlotte quickly looked away from the enticing skin.

"Oh, everything and nothing. Gossip, jokes..."

"Did she tell you she'd met Emil?"

"Oh, yes!" Amy's eyes brightened. "Not long ago, only two or three weeks. No one believed her, but she said, 'I'll prove it,' and here he is. I'm a little envious. Who wouldn't be?"

"And did she say how they met?"

Amy shook her head, more in vagueness than denial. "At a café by the lake, I think. Nothing dramatic. She's trying to persuade Emil to meet my uncle, so he can put him into the new film! Imagine that."

"I'm trying." Charlotte looked down at the glass of champagne she hadn't touched, watching the bubbles rise in delicate necklaces. *I can't begin to imagine Violette's reaction to that idea.*

"But Wolfgang won't be happy if Uncle gives the lead role to someone else, and we'd have to reshoot the scenes we've already done... Is something wrong?"

"Oh... just that I don't think Madame Lenoir would be pleased if her principal dancer went off to become a film star."

"So you are spying on *him*?" Amy whispered.

"Yes." Charlotte held her eyes, mesmerising her a little. Enough to stop her asking too many questions. "I had no idea he was coming with you until I followed him. You won't tell anyone."

"You're being very mysterious but no, of course I won't."

"And Amy... Your uncle hasn't behaved very well towards you, has he? Perhaps you should think of returning to England."

Amy dropped her head. Her voice tightened. "Did you have to bring him up? I don't know. Some days I think I can't endure him a moment longer... but then, he's giving me this experience of working in movies, and how else would I learn? I should feel so ungrateful if I left."

"Are you frightened of him?"

"Sometimes. He wouldn't understand. Anyway, I can't afford to go to Hollywood, it's such a long way."

Her gaze turned thoughtful, with a glint that was part angry, part yearning. Charlotte reached across the table and pressed her hand on Amy's warm forearm.

"Could you help Karl and me buy a cine-camera? Show us how to work it? Are they terribly expensive?"

"Depends what you consider expensive. There's a new Bolex model that's designed for home movie-makers, but the quality is near-professional. I could lend you mine, to see if you like it... Why?"

Charlotte shrugged. "We like to try new things. Perhaps we could film the ballet ourselves and not bother your uncle at all. Perhaps you could help, since you know what you're doing and we don't."

"*Bother* him?" Amy stifled laughter, smiling behind her hand. "That is a lovely idea. Uncle would be frantic with rage if I took the project from him. *Frantic*."

"It's not his project. It never was," Charlotte sighed. "Would you help us?"

"Of course. I'll happily lend you my camera, but it's not that simple. Asking my uncle to process the film would be awkward..."

"We'd rather he knew nothing about it."

"And I daren't try to use the lab in secret, because there's *always* someone in there and they're bound to catch me. There are commercial laboratories, but..."

Charlotte shook her head. "We'd rather do everything ourselves."

"But you'll need to create a darkroom, with processing tanks, and all the chemicals, which have to be kept at the perfect temperature and concentration or you can ruin the film in a moment, and it has to be dried, and when you've got the negative you have to go through it all again to make the print, and then there's splicing and editing... Oh, and you'll need a projector, of course. It's not impossible, but it's an *awful* lot of work."

"Don't look so worried," Charlotte said gently. "I used to work in a laboratory. My father taught me chemistry and physics. Karl's a quick learner, too. I'm sure it's not beyond our wit to learn how to develop film. We'll buy everything we need, if you'll just give us a guiding hand?"

"All right." Amy brightened. "If it's what you want, I'd *love* to help."

"I'll hold you to that, when the champagne's worn off." Charlotte smiled.

"If I can sneak out without Uncle asking questions..."

"Stop worrying about what he thinks. And promise me one more thing. Don't be alone with Fadiya, ever."

"Why not?"

Because she might be planning to feed on your blood, you idiot! Charlotte bit back the words. "Just keep out of her way. Some people are not as nice as they seem. They have ulterior motives. Promise me."

"All right," Amy said, submitting to Charlotte's will. "If you say so."

"I shouldn't keep you from your friends any longer."

"You're not. I like talking to you."

Charlotte fell quiet, wondering, *What on earth do I do with this knowledge? Confront Emil, tell him to stop seeing Fadiya? Or confront her? She's shown no signs of sensing me, another vampire, but that doesn't mean she hasn't. I don't know. If I approach her, she'll know her secret's out and there's no telling what she'll do. She might be reasonable, or she might savage me. But I can't leave Emil alone with her... In fact my only option is to spy on them from the Crystal Ring, every moment of the night, and only intervene if she attacks him.*

Charlotte groaned at the prospect. *The things I do for you, Violette...*

She raised her head as a man with slick dark hair swaggered towards them. He was the one who'd driven Amy, Emil and Fadiya to Paris. The male lead from *The Lion Arises*.

"Amy!" he shouted over the noise. "Aren't you coming back to us? What are you up to?"

"Peter, I'm just talking to – oh, that's odd. She was there a moment ago."

Charlotte had slipped sideways into the Crystal Ring, vanishing like ground-mist into thin air. Amy was left frowning at her empty chair, Peter staring at Amy, and to Charlotte, they looked like flattened silhouettes, outlined by needles of fire: the signature of their vibrant human energy.

CHAPTER FIFTEEN

THE MISTS RUSH IN

Violette was practising warm-up exercises in the living room of her private apartment: Charlotte suspected she did so out of habit, not necessity, like a form of meditation. For a time she stood watching the dancer, entranced by the way her raven hair slid over her shoulders as she moved, her sheer unconscious grace and passion. So much potential for love lay coiled inside Violette, but outsiders rarely saw inside the ice shell. *She has so many layers*, Charlotte thought. Her fervour on stage, her cold armour, the grief and vulnerability that she rarely let anyone see, her unending war with herself, the goddess-demon inside her and her core of deep wisdom.

Sometimes she's the most wonderful person I've ever known, and sometimes the worst. Who can fathom her? That's why she holds us in thrall, me and poor Emil and almost everyone who sets eyes upon her.

Charlotte was conducting an experiment: holding in her vampiric aura so tight that she was effectively invisible. She needed to know if her effort was working, so she could judge whether or not Fadiya had only pretended to ignore her in Paris.

Apparently her skills were effective. Violette began to dance in the space between furniture and mantelpiece, and did so unselfconsciously for five minutes before she noticed Charlotte. And then, only when she turned and saw her.

She stopped dead with a gasp of surprise.

"How long have you been there?"

"A few minutes. Sorry. I wanted to see if I *could*, without you sensing me."

"Well, there is your answer." Violette came to kiss her cheek, half smiling, her eyes anxious. "You're alarmingly good at it, although I confess I wasn't paying attention. So, what news?"

Charlotte swallowed, moistened her lips.

"Emil's lady friend…"

"You're hesitating." A familiar, dangerous blue fire lit her eyes. "This isn't going to be good news, is it?"

"No, it isn't. I don't know how to tell you."

"She's a ballerina from a rival company? Or married to a man so famous that the affair will cause a public scandal? Just tell me."

"Worse. She's a vampire."

Violette's face went from ivory to the white of fresh snow. Charlotte expected rage, but Violette was speechless.

When she finally reacted, her voice was hoarse. "Are you sure? This is unbelievable. Is it someone we know? Ilona? No, obviously not, or you would have recognised her instantly."

"Quite. I'd never seen her before the first time with Emil. I should have *seen* at once what she was, but I didn't. She must be an adept at concealing her aura. Only the slightest hint leaked out, deep blue like the night sky, and I thought nothing of it. I was doing the same – shielding myself, I mean – so I hope she didn't sense me either, because I was within feet of her at times."

"All right." Violette sat on a chair arm, hands folded in her lap. "Start from the beginning."

Charlotte described all that had happened.

"I began to suspect in the nightclub. Her odd bluish glow made me wonder. Later, when I followed her outside and saw her take a victim, I knew for certain."

"And then?"

"She went back in to Emil and carried on as if nothing had happened."

"Did you let them go back to their hotel together?"

"*Let* them? What choice did I have? I could hardly barge between them and cause a scene, in public or private. I barely know Emil, and nothing at all of this Fadiya, or how powerful she is. Dear, if I'd confronted her, it could have ended in disaster."

"I know," Violette said tightly. "She might have attacked you, or him. I appreciate the danger, but the thought of him alone with her…"

Violette tended to veer between tight self-control and violent emotion. Since gaining a deeper insight into her own nature, she was more self-aware and focused, but no less dangerous.

"I don't think she's fed on him," Charlotte added. "Or… not much."

"Not *much*? Not at all, if she values her life."

"We'd have noticed signs, wouldn't we? I followed them into their room, but all I saw was… what you'd expect between two humans. It wasn't easy, because I had to stay in the edge of the Crystal Ring, so I could observe without them seeing me." She tried to forget the ache of witnessing their ecstasy, while she dared not let herself lose control with Karl. "Eventually, he fell asleep but she stayed awake – obviously – her eyes wide open, glittering."

"Fighting temptation?"

"I imagine so. I can't know what was in her mind. And I didn't stay all night. This morning I saw the party getting ready to drive back. I still don't think she's touched him, but…"

"It's only a matter of time before she does," said Violette. "To wait so long is strange."

"Is it? I knew Karl far longer before he finally… That aside, I don't like the fact that Amy's also in obvious danger."

"Herr Reiniger's niece? Are you sure?"

"Well, it's unlikely Fadiya won't give in to temptation. But… perhaps she's only interested in Emil."

As she elaborated, Charlotte watched anger and puzzlement fleeting through Violette's eyes. Eventually she added, "I'm sorry to break this news to you. I hoped Emil would be happy with this girl – I never dreamed…"

"Don't apologise. Unless you introduced them, it's not your fault, is it?" said Violette. "But if she can refrain from feeding on Emil – *if* – what else does she want with him?"

Charlotte stared at her. "What did Karl want with me? What did I want with you? Or you, with Robyn? Sometimes vampires fixate on humans. It's love. However twisted, it's still a form of love."

Violette's eyes were so fierce that Charlotte expected them to set her on fire, to scorch anything they touched.

"And look where that fixation has brought us all. You and I, unhuman blood-drinkers. Robyn, dead. Do you think I'll leave Emil at such risk? I must put a stop to it."

Charlotte gave an inward groan.

"I know, but poor Emil – how are you planning to stop them? First you break his heart, then you tell him he can't find consolation with someone else? Are you planning to explain what she is, and what you are?"

"Of course not. He must not find out, ever."

"So what will you tell him? He's going to take this very hard."

"Perhaps I need not tell him anything," Violette said coolly. "I suggest we approach Fadiya directly, and warn her away. If she won't go, then we take more desperate measures. Emil will never know why she's disappeared."

"We?"

Violette dropped her gaze, swept her hair back over her shoulders. "Charlotte, I can't compel you. Usually I prefer to act alone, but since this vampire is an unknown quantity, there's safety in numbers. Perhaps we should recruit Karl, Stefan and Niklas as well. I hesitate to suggest Ilona, because she's inclined to attack first and – well, by then it's too late for questions. And not Pierre, because he's an idiot."

"And halfway across the world, the last we heard."

"True, and I am not setting out to fetch them back."

Charlotte groaned. "As you say, Fadiya's powers are unknown. Once we confront her, she'll know our identities. The alternative – that you seem to be suggesting as a last resort – is to destroy her. You know that killing a vampire is as horrific as killing a human; worse, if anything, because it's so much more difficult. And we don't know her. She may be a monster, but still a thinking, feeling creature, like you and me."

"But what else do you suggest? I could seek her out alone, in full goddess mode as Lilith – that might do the trick, but if she's difficult, I may well tear off her head, and I truly don't want to go back to those dark days."

"Or I could approach her. Make friends."

"Friends? Oh bless you, dearest Charlotte. You're as terrifying as a kitten, but that's your power. Steel claws hidden inside a suede glove."

"I *think* that's a compliment," said Charlotte, glaring at Violette under lowered lids.

Violette gave an enigmatic smile.

"It comes down to this," she said. "If Emil is harmed, I won't be able to live with myself. I'd rather stop her *before* she hurts him than take revenge after."

"I know," said Charlotte, "but I still think this requires subtlety. If Emil finds out I've approached Fadiya, he'll know you've sent me. But... I wonder if Stefan knows her?"

"Worth asking." Violette's tone was quieter, brooding.

"Stefan's toying with the idea of hosting a party and inviting Herr Reiniger and his friends."

"Why would he wish to meet the men who half-killed Emil?"

"Because Karl and I need to know what they're up to. The invitation could include Fadiya. However, they don't know Stefan, so what reason would they have to respond?"

"I don't know," said Violette. "For fun? Some people will turn up to every party going and not even care who the host is. Some people are altogether too fond of partying."

"Not Herr Reiniger." Charlotte paused, eyeing the dancer. "But you know what would make him turn up? If the invitation came from *you*."

"What?"

"Famous people impress him. Let him think you've reconsidered his offer to film the ballet."

"But I haven't," snapped Violette. "I don't know that I want to see him again. I took a dislike to him. And after all I've heard, he certainly will not be filming on my premises."

"He's not the only person in the country who can operate a camera. Karl and I had an idea to try ourselves."

"Really?" Violette looked sceptical, then intrigued.

"Well, why not? Amy said she'll help. We'll just need to set up a processing laboratory..."

"You will *what*?"

"May we use one of the backstage storerooms? No windows,

concrete floor – it will be ideal. I'm sure you can spare one room."

Violette raised her eyebrows. "Since you seem to have it all planned, be my guest."

"Thank you," Charlotte said with a smile. The idea had been hers, but Karl – ever fascinated by new technology – had shown immediate interest. She didn't tell Violette, but secretly she hoped that if Karl were behind the camera, he might overcome his hostility towards movies.

Karl was usually so calm and measured in his reaction to almost everything. She found it amusing, and slightly disturbing, that he had a weak spot after all.

"But this party…"

"It's just an idea, but the point is to lure Herr Reiniger into the open and the only bait he'll fall for is someone glamorous and influential; namely, you."

"I dislike being used as bait," Violette said icily. "However… I'll admit Stefan's idea is a good one. If it works."

"He does have a way with people," Charlotte said wryly.

"We'll see," Violette said wearily. "All I wanted was freedom to run my ballet in peace. After those visions we had, warning that Germany and Austria might not be safe in years to come, I thought I'd found a haven in Switzerland. Instead, this!"

"It never ends," said Charlotte. "As Karl says, 'There is always something else.'"

The night was clear and bright with stars, the mountains standing in timeless silhouette along the horizon. Charlotte breathed fresh air, full of pine and grass scents. Lamps shone in the windows of Stefan's chalet, inviting.

She thought of the visions she'd shared with Karl and Violette. Darkness in Raqia was caused by the massed grim thoughts of thousands, millions of humans. Oppression, death, the thunder of marching boots… yet another war, and worse. But the premonitions had been vague. No names, no timescale, nothing clear, because the future was ever-changeable. Perhaps they'd only felt upheavals that were already happening in Italy, Russia or elsewhere. All those dark human energies made Raqia vibrate with thunder. *Why does the mob subconscious of humankind so often choose horror over peace?*

She thought of the bone-knife piercing her, and the terrible visions: seeing the white lamia as separate, knowing it was part of her yet being unable to exorcise it. She pictured herself as that pale lamia drifting through the darkness of Raqia.

"Is Karl here?" Charlotte asked as Stefan opened his front door to her. She asked out of politeness, but she already sensed the soft red glow of Karl's presence. Karl, although courteous in company, wasn't the most sociable of creatures. He rarely visited Stefan and Niklas, or anyone, for idle reasons.

"In the lake room," Stefan indicated the stairs that led down to the lowest level. "Is something amiss?"

"I don't know. He wasn't at home. I was coming to see you anyway, but I didn't realise he was here until I was close. Why, what has he said?"

"Nothing," said the blond vampire. "Didn't even knock, just wandered in from the Crystal Ring, and sat down without a word. Not like him, so I decided to leave him alone until he feels like explaining. Have you quarrelled?"

"No, not at all. I want to ask you…" She decided to leave the matter of Fadiya until she'd spoken to Karl. "It can wait."

"Go to him. We'll be upstairs. Call if you need us." With a warm, concerned look, he kissed her hand and left.

Charlotte walked downstairs and entered the lake room. The space danced with subtle lights: stars reflecting off the lake, candles in red glass holders on every surface. Karl was sitting on a small couch, light painting his left side with a scarlet halo.

"Oh, Charlotte," he said, turning to her as she approached. He seemed to wake from a trance, took both her hands and pulled her down to sit across his thighs. His hands slid around her and his lips moved in gentle kisses along her neck, her jaw and cheek.

"Karl?" she murmured, returning the embrace with surprise and pleasure. She'd come out without a coat. His hands felt wonderful but cool through the voile layers of her dress. "You're cold. Where have you been?"

"My sweet, beautiful love, I'm so glad to see you." He said nothing else, only continued caressing and kissing her. Charlotte was all too aware that they should not be doing this, but they were both starved of each other and the feeling was so divine that she had no will to make him stop. Instead she let herself bask in his attention, transported until she found her mouth resting on his throat. He stiffened as she bit down and took two delicious sips of his blood.

She stopped, let her fangs retract.

"I'm so sorry," she whispered. "I shouldn't have done that."

"I don't mind," said Karl.

"But I do. If this cold lamia... thing... whatever it is – if it gets inside you, I should never forgive myself."

"I really don't care," Karl said against her neck. She tried to control her breath, to suppress the pulsing urge that was unravelling her self-control.

"Well, if we don't stop, we will soon be naked on this couch *with Stefan and Niklas watching.*"

"I'm sure they'll understand." Karl spoke with a glimmer of humour. "Stefan would sell tickets."

"You're wicked," she said, half-sobbing. "I love you. But you're cold, freezing. You need blood, not me taking yours."

"I'm warmer now," he said. "And you may take everything from me that you need, always." He held her close against him and she rested there, her arms beneath his jacket, enfolding his lean body. She could remain like this forever, with Karl's cheek resting on her hair and his arms around her.

But he had questions to answer.

"Dearest, are you all right?" she asked. "Were you looking for me? I was away longer than I meant to be..."

"For Violette. Yes, she told me."

"Why are you sitting here in the dark, instead of coming home? It's not like you to be angry with me. Not for more than two minutes, anyway."

"Of course I'm not angry with you, *liebling.*" He exhaled, his breath flowing down her neck and shoulder. "You're free to come and go as you please, but while you were away... I wanted to be on my own to think for a while, and Stefan's very tolerant."

"He doesn't pester you with questions, unlike me?" Charlotte half-smiled, touching her forehead to his.

"Well... I had nothing to say to anyone, and I've done precious little thinking, either. But now you're here – I've never been so glad to see your beloved face in my life."

"That's heart-warming, Karl, but you're scaring the life out of me. What's happened? You're behaving as if you've done something dreadful."

She spoke lightly, but his answer startled her.

"Yes, I have. That's nothing new, but sometimes… our misdeeds catch up with us. Can we prey on human life indefinitely and *never* face the consequences?"

She slid off his knee and reclined sideways on the couch, her stockinged legs resting over his thighs. "Tell me."

"I paid a visit to Godric Reiniger. Strange man. Dangerous, perhaps. I intended to warn him that he had better not let his political gang ever attack Emil again. You know I rarely have difficulty in putting the fear of God into any human…"

"Only too well," she said.

"Reiniger showed no fear. He denied responsibility for his friends' violence, and he barely apologised. As good as suggested that Emil brought the trouble on himself. And he's very passionate about his ambition to save Switzerland by taking it over. He believes he can influence the entire populace through his films. However, he is quite bitter that not everyone takes him seriously."

"Deluded?" said Charlotte.

"Not necessarily. People may laugh at him now, but the most unlikely candidates can seize power. And *something* is going on in that house. His aura, his blood, everything smelled wrong… like a foundry, all fire and molten metal. I can't explain, but we'd be unwise to underestimate him. He recognised me as a vampire, but it's more than that. Apparently we've met before. He harbours a deep, personal grudge against me."

"Why?"

"He claims I killed his father."

Silence. After a few moments, Charlotte whispered, "Did you?"

Karl went quiet, his fingertips playing on her ankles. "So it seems. He knows what I am, he even knew my full name. He had a sketchbook of drawings he'd made of me – some with his own blood – from when he was ten years old. Then he took me into his private cinema and sat me there to watch a film."

Charlotte studied Karl's face as he spoke. He was no lover of movies, but now his expression was frozen.

"It was a poor effort, very basic," he went on. "One of his earliest works, he said. A dark room, a bearded man kissing his young son goodnight, sending him off to bed with a stuffed toy in his arms. Then an intruder entering the father's study, pouncing on him. A struggle. The stranger sinking fangs into the man's neck – Reiniger had spliced in close-ups, so effective that they made me jump – and the little boy standing in the doorway, watching, with the toy trailing from his hand. The father fell dead on the study floor. The intruder stared at the child and vanished through a window. The little boy stood there…" Karl stopped, not breathing at all for a minute. Then he inhaled slowly. "The whole movie lasted less than ten minutes. No story, no context. Just an episode – a ten-year-old boy watching a vampire kill his father. Yet it was surprisingly powerful. Horrifying. Something about the grainy grey flicker is like the worst of nightmares…"

"Karl?" Charlotte sat up, moved close to him and took his hand. "You're ice cold. It was only a film. It can't have been real, can it?"

"Yes and no. Reiniger said he couldn't get that night out of his head, so he recreated the scene with actors and filmed it."

"So he claims this really happened, and the vampire in the scene was *you*?"

"Exactly so." He squeezed her hand, as if relieved that he'd confessed.

"But that's ridiculous… isn't it?"

"I wish it were. I try not to kill, but you know full well that I have. You've even witnessed it, although I wish you hadn't, with all my heart. Sometimes even slight blood loss can cause death, if the trauma brings on a heart attack… And the truth is, when I saw the film, I remembered. One small event among several thousand nights of hunting… but Godric had made the movie inside the actual house – it must have been his father's house in the town – and I recognised the place. I remembered. I took an adult victim who died in my hands… and when I looked up, there was a child in the doorway, staring."

"When did this happen?" Charlotte held both his hands, as if trying to keep a dying human conscious. Trying to keep him with her.

"Ah… let me think. Reiniger is about forty, so it would be in the late eighteen-nineties. That's as I remember. The time fits. He'd even got the style of clothing correct."

"So he lost his father at the age of ten?" said Charlotte. "And he remembered your face. Even tracked you down to the extent that he discovered your name? That can't have been easy."

"Not impossible. Perhaps I was too careless in neglecting to create false identities."

"He filled a book with drawings, and made a film," she said. "That sounds a touch obsessive."

Karl sat forward, pushed one hand through his hair. His face lost its faraway look and he grimaced. "Not really. I would say it was natural. Godric waited thirty years to come face to face with his father's murderer."

"Does he want revenge?"

"To be honest, I don't know what he wants."

"Did he attack you?"

"No. And before you ask, I left him alive. Perhaps that was a mistake, but in cold blood, I couldn't harm him. He has… he claims to have a number of the *Istilqa* knives, but it was the force of his personality that held me, more than any weapon. I felt paralysed. I cannot express how horrific it was to see my own actions played out on a screen."

He rose and went to the window, stared out at the lake. Charlotte followed and stood beside him. She said, "I can only imagine. Karl, you're in shock. I won't try to soothe you out of it."

"Thank you."

"But what happened when the movie was over?"

"Nothing. I left. Before that, I felt pinned there – forced to stay and see what he was so desperate to show me. He's a peculiarly compelling man. In effect he was warning me, 'I know exactly who you are, and what you did will never be forgotten. Everything you do, the reverberations go on forever.' What could I do or say in response? Nothing. I am not sorry and I do not feel guilty. Sad, but not guilty."

She put her hand through his arm. "It's unusual for our victims to come after us, but it must happen occasionally."

"Perhaps one day they will all catch up with us."

Karl opened a door and stepped out on to the veranda. Charlotte went with him. The night air blowing across the lake was very cold now. Nothing to a vampire, but she felt a brief shiver. Karl put his arm around her. After a while she said, "I have a confession too."

"Dr Ochsner?"

"How did you know?" She was startled that he'd guessed, but not astonished.

"Not difficult. I know you were furious about the way he treated Amy."

"Other patients, too. Practically torturing them to punish them for their normal human biology, like some sadistic inquisitor – and that's part of Reiniger's belief system, isn't it? He wants to enforce purity and control over the population, starting with his own friends and family? I know I said I hate killing, but – oh Karl, if anyone deserved it, Ochsner did. I know I shouldn't have done it, but... go on, lecture me if you must."

"No lecture. I had a feeling you'd hunt him down. And after what I've done in the past, I'm in no position to criticise your actions, *liebling*."

"The good and the evil, Karl: I accepted it all when I came with you."

"And with such grace."

He went quiet. She'd rarely seen Karl so disturbed. Along with a glacial sense of dread, she felt pure hatred for the man who had managed to crawl under his skin like this.

She had to break the silence.

"Is Godric aware that he already has a vampire working for him?"

At that, Karl's gaze met hers, now sharply focused. "What do you mean?"

"This woman Emil is seeing, Fadiya – she's a vampire. I've just told Violette, who welcomed the news with all the rapture you'd expect."

She described her trip to Paris, adding, "Fadiya appears to be part of Reiniger's wider circle. Amy said she works as his make-up artist. She's been there only a few weeks."

"He said nothing of any other vampire. I sensed no one..."

"Did he explain anything about the knives?"

"Almost nothing. He told me only what suited him, kept the rest secret."

"I need to ask Stefan about Fadiya," Charlotte said. "I think we should tell him and Violette everything."

"Don't expect too much," Karl said with a grim smile. "Stefan tends to flee at the merest hint of danger."

"Not this time. I won't let him."

"Well, let us see if he finds his courage, because we are going to need every friend we have." Karl kissed her temple, rested his cheek on her hair. "Love, I'm so sorry to distress you with this."

"Don't you dare apologise. Heaven or hell, we share it all." She turned her head to study his expression, wishing she could read him as easily as he read her. "You're not afraid of Godric Reiniger, are you?"

"Not as such. He's human, after all. But as you've pointed out, certain humans have power over us. The massed energy of their dreams and nightmares brought us into being, so how could they not? Godric seems to know more than any human should. He wants to change the world. And he might manage it, by subterfuge or propaganda."

"Do you think he's truly dangerous?"

"If he only made bad films, I'd be less concerned," said Karl. "But there's something very dark going on inside him."

Charlotte thought of the Crystal Ring's storms and apparitions. She pictured her lamia, haunting her even as she took Ochsner's life. Reiniger's crew, savagely beating Emil.

"Remember how we feared Violette-as-Lilith biting us, because we knew her bite would change us?" she said. "But when it finally happened... when we surrendered, there was nothing to fear after all. The change brought self-acceptance, not loss of love."

"I know, but this isn't the same. I didn't lose my conscience entirely: I would have turned into Kristian or Sebastian, had that been the case. I don't feel guilty. *Disturbed* is a better word. Are you asking why I'm so troubled by this?"

"Why we're *both* troubled. Perhaps even Lilith's power isn't enough to shield us."

"Not if some fresh demon can force its claws beneath our armour," he said softly. "One thing I know for certain: Godric

Reiniger is a far greater danger than the threat he poses to Emil or to me. The last thing I want is to see him again, ever, but I shall have to. It's time we dragged him out of his lair and into the light."

"You spoke of our misdeeds catching up with us. Is that what's happening?"

No answer. Karl went quiet again, staring at the lake. He held Charlotte's hand folded against his chest, his grip tightening until it hurt.

"So this vengeful adversary waited thirty years to *show you a film*? Terrifying!"

"I'm glad you find this amusing, Stefan," said Karl. "I expected no less."

The twins had been out to hunt, returning rosy and bright-eyed from feeding. As Karl and Charlotte explained, as briefly as they could, what they had already told each other, Stefan went around lighting oil lamps. He trimmed the wicks, then sat on the arm of the couch to listen to the rest of their story. The room brightened from dim red to golden.

"Godric sounds delightfully eccentric," said Stefan. "I'm growing more intrigued by the moment. Aren't you, Niklas?" He stroked his silent *doppelgänger's* cheek.

"Eccentric is an understatement."

"Karl, you have a faraway look in your eyes. Might you be caught in the snare that you're always warning Charlotte to avoid? Becoming entranced by a human?"

Karl gave a soft laugh, no more than a breath.

"Not in the sense that I'm yearning for a romantic relationship with him."

"I'm glad to hear it," Charlotte said with a smile.

"Not even in the sense that I crave his blood – it smells so contaminated that I couldn't touch him. He's intriguing mainly because he unnerves me. I killed his father, ruined a child's life or at least changed its course... and he wants revenge, naturally, but of what kind?"

"So you finally admit that you need my help." Stefan rubbed his palms together. "Did I not suggest the simple ruse of inviting him to a party? You sneered!"

"I didn't sneer. I just don't believe he's the type to attend a social event unless there is something in it for him."

"Is he good-looking?" Stefan grinned.

"What has that to do with anything?" said Karl, eyebrows raised.

"I'm not as fussy as you. I might be able to prise out his secrets."

"I wouldn't put it past you to try," said Charlotte. "But what about Fadiya?"

"She'll have to wait her turn, but yes, I'll happily seduce her too. She sounds irresistible."

"That is not what I meant." She struggled not to smile. It would only encourage him.

"Very well," said Stefan. "She sounds lovely, but no, I have no idea who she is. So let's invite her too, by all means. But can't you just warn Emil about her? If Emil was seeing *me*, I wouldn't trust me, either."

"Of course we can't warn him!" Charlotte retorted. "He mustn't find out what she is, or what *we* are, for that matter. We need to make Fadiya vanish before Emil comes to any harm."

Stefan gave her his charming white smile, eyes shining. She loved his good nature, but sometimes his frivolous attitude made her want to throttle him. "What are you grinning about?" she said.

"The prospect of planning this party. Our housewarming. Has it not occurred to you that it might be fun? Humans become drunk on cocktails, cocaine, vampire glamour, and vampires become intoxicated on humans. I'll invite everyone: Godric Reiniger and his crew, and a few dozen guests to make up a splendid crowd. The sinister Godric and Fadiya will simply add spice!"

"Reiniger won't come," said Karl.

Stefan gave a slight frown. "Not even if *you* ask him?"

Karl laughed. "After our confrontation? He'd think it completely bizarre."

"I know how to make sure he turns up." Charlotte spoke softly, hesitant with a sense of foreboding. She was still uncertain of Violette's cooperation. "If it were presented as Madame Lenoir's party – if *she* issued the invitations – they'll all be too star-struck to dream of refusing. If it means a chance of cornering Fadiya, Violette just *might* agree."

"Perfect." Stefan gave his irresistible, wicked grin. "You read my mind, Charlotte. Wine will flow, tongues will loosen. The lengths I go to, to make you two smile again!"

Emil stood in the grand hallway of Godric Reiniger's house, Bergwerkstatt, gazing up at the high white walls and sweeping stairs. The place was like some dictator's palace, as if Reiniger fancied himself a Roman emperor. Fadiya's hand clasped his arm. He wondered how on Earth he'd let her persuade him to come here.

This was not where he belonged. He felt powerfully that he should be in the ballet studio, rehearsing, yet he couldn't seem to move. Fadiya had woven this honeyed spell over him.

"Here he is," she said.

Godric Reiniger came strutting down the stairs with a couple of other men. Emil recognised Reiniger from the occasion he had pestered Violette in the street, and from the ghastly night at the *Bierkeller*. The freckle-faced man with short red hair on his left was the one who'd spoken passionately about Swiss nationalism, until they'd fallen into an argument about Mussolini. His name... Wolfgang Notz?

The other man was one of the ruffians who'd attacked Emil in the alley. Name unknown. He was short but wiry. Emil thought, *How in hell did I let such a weasel get the better of me?*

"Ah," said Reiniger, all friendly good cheer. "The celebrated Emil Fiorani! Delighted, privileged to meet you, sir! May I introduce two of my key assistants, Wolfgang and Walti?"

"We've met," Emil said under his breath, but Reiniger seemed not to hear.

"I believe I shall have the honour of filming you in rehearsal and performance of Madame Lenoir's ballets quite soon."

Emil stared at him in disbelief, thinking, *No, she turned him down. Has something changed?*

"Isn't he magnificent, Godric?" said Fadiya, eyes shining as if she'd brought home a prince. "Wouldn't you like to try him out in front of the camera?"

Wolfgang cleared his throat. He looked displeased, but said nothing.

"If he's willing," said Reiniger. "He looks as if he'd make a splendid leading man indeed. May we offer you a drink, sir, or will you come straight through to the studio? A little screen test – it will not take long."

Emil stared back, taking a long breath. Eventually he managed to speak. "Are you all mad?"

"I beg your pardon?" Reiniger took off his spectacles, rubbed them on a cloth, replaced them. He looked at Fadiya, and back at Emil.

"You." He pointed at Wolfgang Notz. "You were in the *Bierkeller*, preaching the same nonsense that inflicted Mussolini on Italy. When I objected, I was physically attacked. Herr Reiniger was there, watching. Filming. I saw you!"

Reiniger's eyes went cold. "I assure you, we are no supporters of Mussolini. He's inspirational – in that he understands the power of art to spread his message – but he's flawed. I don't see what that unfortunate encounter has to do with this. Look, men argue after a few drinks. We can set all that aside, can't we?"

Emil pointed at the other one, Walti. "And *he* was one of the gang who beat me to a pulp outside. They spat on me and called me a homosexual."

"Emil is not homosexual, I promise," said Fadiya. She pinched his arm, as if to quiet him.

"One moment I am Italian communist filth, fit only to be brutalised. Now you want me to appear in your movies? Are you out of your mind?"

"If what you suggest happened, it was a dreadful mistake and no doing of mine," said Reiniger. Sweat glistened on his high forehead. Wolfgang Notz looked uncomfortable, but Emil felt pure raging fury.

"What in hell makes you think that Madame Lenoir ever wanted your services?"

"We'll see about that. I have a party invitation from her, which rather indicates that she wants to make peace." Reiniger gave a small, tight smile. "There have been misunderstandings."

"I don't think so," said Emil. "You shouldn't have brought me here, Fadiya."

"Yes, why did you bring him?" said Wolfgang. "The last I

heard, you were a make-up girl, not our casting director."

"I thought... Clearly I've made a mistake," she said thinly.

"Wait," said Reiniger.

"You can go to hell," said Emil. "You can all go to hell!"

With that he made for the door, slammed it behind him, marched down the steps. He heard the door open again. Fadiya came running after him and grabbed his elbow.

"What's wrong with you?" she snarled. "You've made me look a complete fool – I thought you'd be magnificent on screen – what was all that?"

He sank down on the bottom step and dropped his head on to his arms.

"I *met* you covered in the bruises they'd left on me! How can you work for those men? They're evil."

"I only do the make-up. I don't know about their political views. They don't tell the womenfolk anything. We're expected to smile and agree with everything they say – that doesn't mean I care about it. It's nothing to do with me."

Tears came. He couldn't stop them. He began to sob, shoulders heaving.

"Emil? What's wrong?"

He wanted to be angry with her, too, but her arm across his shoulders felt comforting. She was the only friend he had.

"My older brother, Alfonso," he said at last. "I never talk of this. It's not safe. He opposed Mussolini. He tried to assassinate him – and he wasn't the only dissenter who's tried in the last couple of years – well, Alfonso took a shot at him and missed. The crowd lynched him in the street. Before the police even got to him, he was dead, hanged from a tree."

"My dear, I'm sorry."

"*That's* why I despise Godric Reiniger and everyone like him. Once they get into power, anyone who opposes them is scum to be killed like a dog. And no one ever sees the danger until it's too late."

Godric walked high into the hills, alone, welcoming the chill of the wind. Usually the low music of cowbells soothed him, but not today. The green meadows and the dancing wildflowers of spring failed to lift his spirits. He was furious with Amy, irritated at Dr Ochsner for dying so inconveniently, annoyed by Emil Fiorani's ridiculous outburst.

Those concerns were gnat-bites when he thought about Karl von Wultendorf. He could not get Karl out of his mind. Godric dissected every moment of their meeting: satisfied that he'd forced him to watch the film, then seething when he remembered how calm Karl had been afterwards, his face tranquil, his eyes dark and cold. The way he'd left without a word.

Godric had simply let him go. There must be more to say, but what?

Far below, on a patch of grass behind the house, a curl of smoke went up. He had set fire to the movie he'd made of Karl murdering his father. What was the point of keeping it, now the perpetrator had seen it and barely raised an eyebrow?

"I thought that would be the end of the matter," Godric murmured aloud. *I'd show him, then kill him – or he would kill me. But it did not happen. I have not finished with him yet. This feels like a beginning, not an end. A beginning.*

He clenched and unclenched his fists as he stared up at the lace-veiled peaks of the Alps. All his anger fell away and he felt a rush of exhilaration.

"How can this kingdom exist and be anything but mine?"

The power-rush he'd absorbed from Bruno's death had not faded. It felt like bristling white energy, so strong he almost expected it to burst through his skin like porcupine quills. Everything was changing. The *Eidgenossen* respected him more, now they'd seen how far he was prepared to go. They'd always treated him with deference; now they were downright terrified, but that was good. They knew he meant business.

Godric had no intention of replacing Bruno, even if the missing *sikin* was found. In fact, he might have to cull more of them. Each sacrifice would increase his power, until all he had left was a tight core of, say, ten men. His ten strongest supporters.

He paid lip service to the *Rütlischwur* oath of fellowship, the confederation of equal partners on which Switzerland was founded. History was all around him: the *Rütli* meadow in which the vow was made overlooked Lake Lucerne, and the three oath-takers were nicknamed the "Three Tells", the legendary figures from whom he derived the title of his next film.

Secretly, though, Godric had had enough of confederations. He insisted on comradeship between his followers, but in his visions they all turned towards *him*: the glowing white sun at the centre.

Lucerne would become the seat of government, Bergwerkstatt his presidential palace, and Godric himself a new kind of god-emperor.

A very modest, artistic god-emperor whose work will be revered and adored. He gave a tight smile. *Anyone who dares to laugh will himself* become *a work of art, like Bruno.*

A shadow darkened the corner of his eye. Fadiya tended to appear obliquely from nowhere, as if she just happened to be strolling in the same area.

He sat down on a fallen tree trunk and waited with grim patience. She approached like a piece of night intruding on the day, appearing to draw closer frame-by-frame rather than in a smooth continuous motion.

"Godric," she said, sitting down beside him. They looked across the town and the lake, not at each other. "I must apologise for bringing Emil to the house."

"Why did you?"

"I wanted to steal him from Violette. However, I misjudged his state of mind. I'm sorry. It will not happen again."

Godric gave a *hmph* of caustic indifference. "I'm not interested in what you want. Why should you be jealous of a mere human, regardless of how beautiful and famous she is?"

Fadiya paused. Although he had no love for her, she was quiet, sombre company, and he'd grown to appreciate that. All the same, his hand slid around the handle of the *sikin* that he kept sheathed in his pocket.

"I know it seems foolish to you, but Emil loves Violette so yes, I am jealous of her. And I wanted to bring you a gift: Emil."

"A gift for me?" Godric was so surprised that he laughed.

"He would have been wonderful in your movies. I'm sorry it went wrong, but you have no liking for Madame Lenoir, either, do you?"

He shrugged. "I am indifferent to her. However, something odd has happened. She has invited me to a party – invited my whole household, in fact – which suggests she's reconsidered her hasty rejection of Reiniger Studios' services."

"Will you go?"

"Why not? My personal power is all very well, but of no use unless I gain support from, or influence over, every person of importance that I can draw into my orbit. So if she's of a mind to befriend me, you had better not sabotage things."

"I wouldn't dream of it," she said in the same cool velvet tone. "If you want to court her favour in order to advance your ambitions, I support you, completely."

"Indeed?"

"I said we could help each other." Another long silence, then Fadiya asked, "Who was that man the other night?"

"Which one? I have many visitors."

"You know who I mean."

"Do you *ever* stop watching me?" he growled.

"You are not that fascinating. Most human activities are so dull that only one in a thousand is worth a second glance. But when something of interest happens, I am there. Did you know he's a vampire?"

Godric knew, but the bluntness of her statement shocked him.

"Of course," he snapped. And he told her, briefly, the tale of how Karl had killed his father. "He came to find me because he knows Emil. Apparently he knows Madame Lenoir, too. But he had no idea who I was! He didn't remember. I was nothing to him, nothing – until I *told* him."

"That could have been dangerous."

"But I have the *sakakin*. I'm his equal in strength… or could be."

"Be careful," Fadiya said gently.

"I'm not afraid of him. Don't you see *this*?" Godric stretched out an arm to demonstrate the spiky power radiating from his body. Nothing showed in the sunlight. Fadiya blinked, unimpressed.

"I advise you to stay away from him. I've seen him around the ballet, and other vampires too, but I can't go too close, in case they recognise what I am."

"Do you know this Karl?"

"No. I'd never seen him before I came here. But I'm glad you told me, Godric, and I'm sorry about your father. If it's revenge you want… we should talk again. Soon."

Fadiya vanished, stepping into thin air. For a moment Godric saw the hint of another world, all grey-violet mist, so tantalising. The ingress snapped shut behind her but the feeling stayed with him: that if he could only absorb enough power, he could pass through the paper-thin membrane into Fadiya's mysterious world where all knowledge would become his.

Godric got to his feet and climbed higher. Clouds rolled down the mountains, enveloping him. He breathed the thick wet air, pushing out the tendrils of his new power to touch that tantalising other-world…

A shape appeared. Not Fadiya. This apparition was pale, like a swirl of snow and fog, with fair hair rippling to her waist. She had her back to him, but as he stood there, trying to comprehend what he was seeing, she turned slowly to face him.

Clearly not human. Some kind of ghost? Her form rippled and her eyes were beautiful, blank, staring straight through him. Her lips parted. To his own humiliation, he fell to his knees in sheer terror.

Godric was so overwhelmed that he started to sob in joy. Obvious what she was! One of the *Weisse Frauen*, the white ladies: the elf-like beings of the mountains, demi-gods of Alpine legend.

More than that. Surely she was none other than Frau Perchta, the white goddess, consort of Berchtold himself. The Bright One, the Alpine folk called her.

Very slow and cautious, he rose and went towards her. Surely she would retreat or fade – but she stayed where she was, reeling him in with her lovely, glistening, terrifying eyes.

She was real. And she was welcoming him to her world. Telling him without words, *Welcome, Godric. Here I am at your bidding. Soon you will be one with us.*

CHAPTER SIXTEEN

LIKE A SILVER SHADOW

Stefan knew how to throw a party, not least in ensuring that everyone enjoyed themselves without the police being called. As Charlotte and Karl emerged from the Crystal Ring and walked down the footpath from the road, they saw the chalet transformed. Strings of coloured lanterns adorned every balcony and shone in the trees like clouds of fireflies. Even the lake shore beyond was lit up to guide the less sober away from the water's edge. The place looked like a fairytale palace. The front doors were wide open and hired waiters stood ready to take coats and serve champagne as the guests arrived.

Charlotte's heart lifted. For an instant, she felt like a child at Christmas.

"He's made a beautiful display," she said. "I think I might enjoy myself. Is that allowed?"

"It's not why we're here, but I won't try to stop you," Karl said drily. He glanced across at some vehicles parked on the grass to one side. "It looks as if Herr Reiniger and his crew are here already. Your plan worked."

The party was officially Violette's. Persuaded by Charlotte, though reluctant, she had issued the invitations, and no one would refuse the chance to meet her. Not even the haughty Godric Reiniger.

A queue of guests jostled to enter the chalet, all in fashionable finery. Charlotte suspected half of them didn't have invitations. Word of mouth drew them here.

However, Violette had invited no one from the ballet. Instead she'd scheduled a compulsory evening rehearsal.

Her purpose was to keep Emil away from Fadiya.

Heads turned as Charlotte and Karl stepped into the entrance hall. Charlotte loved the feel of her luxurious new dress against her skin, the floaty layers of silk voile in the sunset shades that she loved. Karl had gazed at her for at least five minutes in mute wonder. She'd basked in his appreciation, admiring him in return. In his formal black evening suit he looked utterly breathtaking; now they both stole the breath of the other party-goers. Charlotte found the sensation self-indulgent but very pleasing.

Some might notice the looks they exchanged, the light touches that set off rippling hot waves of magnetism between them. No one would guess the reason for their agonising self-restraint. Exquisite pain.

She could not even feel the corpse-cold presence of the lamia. Had it gone at last? Would it really matter if they gave in to desire later? Karl had been so understanding, so restrained... both pretending that this was not half-killing them.

"My dear friends." Stefan rushed to greet them, Niklas at his shoulder. "Welcome. What did I say about that dress? Charlotte, you look exquisite. *Divine*."

As they exchanged kisses, she whispered, "Who is here?"

"Herr Reiniger and friends – although I've seen no one resembling your Fadiya."

"She's not *my* Fadiya. Violette?"

Stefan rolled his eyes. "Of course not. The guest of honour must be suitably late and make a grand entrance, mustn't she?"

"Naturally. She's making her own way here, so who knows when she'll turn up."

"Well, go in, circulate, enjoy the potential buffet." Stefan winked. "Karl, this is your chance to make peace with Godric Reiniger: either that, or duel to the death in public."

"I'll try not to," said Karl.

"No, be my guest. What's the point of hosting a party unless it's talked about for years to come?"

A babble of accents filled the house; English, American, French, Italian and German. Many were well-off young tourists: Stefan had a knack for seducing the glamorous in-crowd, and no one could resist the lure of meeting Violette. A jazz trio was playing in the big salon upstairs, while the lake room on the lowest floor had a gramophone and soft lighting for those who preferred a more intimate atmosphere.

The night was young and everyone keen to dance. Charlotte found the lower room empty, except for Amy Temple, who was nursing a flute of champagne as she gazed out at the lake. She wore a sequinned sleeveless dress that exposed her upper back; the sight made Charlotte long to taste her lovely peachy skin.

"Hello again," Charlotte said over her shoulder, making her jump. "Sorry, I didn't mean to startle you. Aren't you joining the party?"

"Actually, I'm avoiding my uncle. The more I try to forgive him about that vile Dr Ochsner, the angrier I feel. I realised I *can't* forgive him. Does that make me a bad person?"

"Of course not," said Charlotte.

"I know he adores me, but that makes it worse. His idea of love is to control my every move! I pretend everything's normal, but it isn't. And now Uncle's furious with *me* for going to Paris against his orders."

"Oh. What did he do when he found out? Nothing awful, I hope."

Amy's mouth went thin. "He'd given me a proper acting role in the William Tell film. Now he's withdrawn the offer, as a punishment. It's the nastiest thing he could have done. I'm relegated to costumes and technical duties."

"I'm sorry."

"Don't be." She tried to smile, but Charlotte saw tears welling. "I know his movies are dreadful, but still, it was a proper *part*... but I really don't care. It's his loss. So just now, I don't even want to be in the same room."

"Why come to the party, then?"

"Mainly to irritate him. First he said I couldn't, then he realised he couldn't stop me without locking me up. Then he insisted that *everyone* must come, because Madame Lenoir invited us, and he wants to impress her with numbers. But he has a sour face because she isn't here yet, and he *despises* jazz music." She gave a tight smile.

"I suppose he thought Violette's choice would be classical,"

257

said Charlotte. "Your opinion of your uncle seems a little lower every time I see you."

"I *want* to like him, but he makes it so difficult! Living with him is far from dull, but I hoped he'd be kind and fatherly, not so… full of his own self-importance. Is that a sign of genius?" Amy gave a short laugh. "Everything depends on what mood he's in, and it's hard to tell because he's so wrapped up in his thoughts at home and you don't know if he's going to joke or snarl until he opens his mouth. And his close friends – especially Wolfgang, who's perfectly nice the rest of the time – when they've had a few drinks they start arguing about politics and it's terribly embarrassing. If Uncle Godric doesn't keep them under control tonight, I wouldn't blame Madame Lenoir if she asks them to leave, and then he'll be offended all over again."

"Nothing's happened yet. Perhaps it won't."

"I've been *so* glad of the chance to help you with your project." Amy meant the darkroom that she was helping Karl and Charlotte to construct. Violette wasn't thrilled to have a storeroom full of tanks and equipment, but she'd let them do as they pleased, and even lent a couple of stagehands to aid them. "It helps take my mind off him, which is such a relief."

"And we're extremely grateful for your help," Charlotte said warmly.

"All the same…" She paused, with the charmingly worried look that always sent a pang of blood-thirst through Charlotte. "It may take you months to get professional results, whereas Uncle Godric would make a competent job of filming straight off. He thinks that's why Madame Lenoir's invited him. He's fully expecting a commission."

"I'm afraid he's going to be disappointed. You sound anxious. Do you think he's going to react badly?"

"Well, of course he is!" Amy took a large sip of champagne. "And if he *ever* finds out I've been helping you, he might have me horsewhipped."

"We won't let that happen. I thought you enjoyed defying him?"

"Oh, I do. But sometimes… He scares me. Then I get cold feet and think it's safest to let him have his own way after all. And then I get annoyed with *myself* for giving in. If he was excited about filming the ballet, it would distract him from talking politics, because the *last* thing Madame's party guests need is for him to start haranguing them." Amy winced.

"Don't you share his views?"

She paused, sipping her drink. "He's very sincere and convincing. The Alps are so pure and fresh – green pastures, farmers tending their cattle, the folk music and traditions and festivals – he loves all that. And there's nothing wrong with that, of course. But it's as if he wants to… control it all. He would like to seal this country into a glass sphere and hold it in his hand, like a god. That is not exactly normal, is it? He says he wants the best for Switzerland, which we all do, but…"

"Sometimes people say that, when they actually want what's best for themselves. Power, wealth and adoration."

"I know. I don't think anything less will make him happy." Amy looked uncomfortable. "That's what his movie-making and drawing and writing is all about. He resents not receiving the acclaim he thinks he deserves, but he's not stupid. He knows you don't get anywhere without making a lot of noise and cosying up to influential people. Everything he does is so *important*." She rolled her eyes. "The local dignitaries and clergy love him, because he flatters them and makes films of their activities, and that makes them feel tremendously important too."

Her wryly exasperated tone amused Charlotte.

"That sounds infuriating."

"I let it go over my head." Amy sighed. "Or rather, I try. If I thought too much about it, I'd go mad. But at social events like this, Godric usually manages to offend someone, and it's mortifying. I hope he doesn't ruin the evening."

"I'm sure Stefan won't let that happen."

"Who's Stefan?"

"He owns the house. He organised the party for Violette. You must have seen him – he has an identical twin."

"Oh, the blond angels! Of course. He and his brother are the most handsome pair I've ever seen – even more striking than Emil, I think…" Amy trailed off. "Is Emil here? Uncle Godric even managed to upset *him* the other day."

"How? I didn't know they'd met."

"Fadiya brought him to the house, after we'd come back from Paris."

"Why?"

"She might have been trying to impress Emil by showing him the film studio. Or trying to impress my uncle. Godric might have asked to meet him – after all, who wouldn't want such a gorgeous leading man?"

"In hopes of making his films more successful?" Charlotte wondered if Emil had confessed the encounter to Violette. She doubted it.

"Exactly!"

"Violette won't be at all happy if Emil goes off to be a movie star. But if he did, he'd go to Hollywood, not… to your uncle. Sorry."

"Oh, don't apologise. You've nothing to worry about, in any case. I was eavesdropping. Emil and Godric had a frightful argument and Emil stormed out. I'm not surprised he isn't here."

Charlotte had no intention of explaining that Violette had kept him away on purpose. "I haven't seen Fadiya either. Didn't she come with you?"

Amy shrugged. "She's supposed to be here. All the others – my friends from Paris – they're here, since they'd rather die than miss a party. And my uncle's men-only circle. We don't socialise much with them because they're so serious, until they've had a drink, and then they're obnoxious. But no, I haven't seen Fadiya all evening. Perhaps she'll be along later."

"Fashionably late," Charlotte said, feigning lack of concern.

"Or with Emil," Amy said flatly. "In which case I can imagine what's keeping them. And I'm trying not to."

"Ah," said Charlotte. She frowned. Emil couldn't be with his lover because he was rehearsing, unless he'd disobeyed Violette again, so perhaps Fadiya was out hunting. Charlotte still saw no tell-tale marks on Amy's perfect neck…

But if Fadiya shunned the party, how were Charlotte and Violette to confront her? Did she know they'd found her out?

Amy glanced upwards. The ceiling was shaking to the rhythm of music and dancing feet. "I say, shall we have a dance down here?" Amy said with a grin. "I might as well get squiffy and enjoy myself, instead of moping about Uncle Godric all evening."

"Excellent idea," said Charlotte, squeezing her arm, trying hard to ignore her alluring warm scent. "But why not come upstairs and do that? There's someone I need to find."

Violette made her entrance an hour later.

Meanwhile Charlotte passed the time by dancing with Karl and Stefan, making light-hearted conversation with strangers and observing Godric Reiniger, who was holding court in a corner of the salon. He wore a white evening suit with a red bow tie, treading a fine line between elegance and flamboyance. He seemed less embarrassing than Amy suggested: he certainly talked a lot, provoking debate among his hangers-on. Perhaps that was why they liked his company: the atmosphere sparked around him. He was restless, constantly calling for drinks, passing cigarettes around, encouraging couples to dance even though he did not join in.

Instead he seemed to be watching. His blue eyes glinted behind his spectacle lenses.

"Is he auditioning?" Charlotte whispered to Karl. "He looks as if he's sizing people up for parts in his next movie."

"Or watching them for more sinister reasons," said Karl. "To assess how useful they might be to him."

"Have you noticed how he stares at you, and at Stefan?" she said. "I don't know if it's hatred or lust. Can you smell that bitter sourness in his blood?"

"They all have it," said Karl, "but it's strongest in Godric."

"There's no trace on Amy or her friends, only on the men he keeps around him. Something about him makes my skin crawl – I couldn't take his blood if he prostrated himself on an altar."

Karl gave a thin smile. "The trouble is, once a human has learned to recognise a vampire, they start seeing vampires everywhere. That sends them a little mad."

"I don't think he's mad," she whispered. "Twisted, perhaps. I know how Amy feels: I have a strong desire not to be in the same room as him either."

"Well, I'm going to take him somewhere private quite soon," Karl murmured into her ear.

"Why?" The idea made her anxious.

261

"Unfinished business."

As Karl spoke, Charlotte saw a familiar male among Godric's clique. Shorn red hair, handsome freckled face, serious expression. She froze.

"Karl," she said, nearly losing her voice. "The man who came to the chalet to find the knife…"

"I know." He turned her so they were both facing away. "His name's Wolfgang Notz. He was in the beer hall, the night Emil was attacked. I told you: they are all connected. Just keep away, pretend you don't recognise him."

"Oh, I can do that." She held herself still until the wave of horrific images subsided. Losing her memory had frightened her, but remembering was worse. "I wasn't planning to confront him."

"What about the drunk who stabbed you? Bruno?"

"I can't see him," said Charlotte. "I'm sure he's not here. I'd know."

"Good. Just keep out of their way and enjoy the evening. As I said, I am going to have a word with Herr Reiniger…"

"Be careful," she said sternly.

A ripple of excitement began in the entrance hall and broke across the salon in a wave of sighs and exclamations. Violette walked in. Everyone turned to look, as if a queen had made her entrance. A respectful space opened around her. People bowed. Applause broke out, and Violette took it in good heart, smiling and curtseying as if she were on stage.

She looked like a gleaming ornament: a shimmering silver and amethyst dress, jet beads around her neck, white silk lilies on one hip and in her raven hair. Charlotte's heart filled with a mixture of emotions. Almost every man and probably many of the women would have given anything to take her home… but she was an icon, a faerie queen, too perfect to touch.

Remarkably for her, she was alone. Her usual appearance would be at an after-show party, surrounded by dancers and staff as she held court with her admirers. To see her without an entourage was strange.

"Thank you all so much for coming," she said in her refined English accent, then elaborated the sentiment in German. "*Sie sind herzlich willkommen. Ich bin sehr glücklich.* Don't be afraid to say hello to me. I don't bite."

"Liar," Charlotte murmured beneath the wave of laughter.

Stefan and Niklas guided Violette through the guests, with a couple of waiters following to make sure no one crowded her. The jazz trio played the overture from *Swan Lake* in ragtime, a discordant, jaunty tribute that made her smile.

Then for a long time she was surrounded, as guests swarmed around her and Violette put on her gracious public mask, making small talk.

Her interaction with Godric Reiniger was brief. He made a show of kissing and petting her hand, as if to demonstrate that he was on intimate terms with this goddess – despite having plotted to steal Emil from her? So much for that. Even as she scorned his arrogance, Charlotte had a worrying thought.

"If Godric can perceive vampires, does he know about her?" she asked softly, only to realise Karl was no longer at her side.

She glimpsed him approaching Godric Reiniger on the far end of the salon. People milled around her, blocking her view. For a few moments she had a flashback to her human horror of socialising: the panic of suffocating in a hostile mass of strangers... When the feeling dropped away, Karl and Reiniger had disappeared.

"Charlotte, at last." Violette broke away from the knot of people who'd cornered her, greeted Charlotte with an embrace. "I think the novelty's finally worn off: they might let me alone for a while now."

"What it is to be popular!"

Violette narrowed her eyes. "A good thing Emil's not here. They might have ravished him where he stood. What news?"

"Not promising," said Charlotte. "Fadiya hasn't turned up. Karl and Godric have vanished together. I don't know what that means, but it can't be good. And the man I threw off the balcony, Wolfgang, is here with Godric Reiniger."

"Did he recognise you?"

"I don't know. I'm more concerned about Karl."

"Oh, Karl can look after himself. But – no Fadiya? Are you sure?"

"Amy told me she isn't with them. She also said, er... that Fadiya took Emil to meet Herr Reiniger a few days ago."

"What?" said Violette, as Charlotte related Amy's tale. "Reiniger tried to poach my dancer from me?"

"Without success. Emil has a mind of his own, even under Fadiya's spell."

"He does, but how dare she try to lure him away? Now it's all the more vital that I stop this, so where the hell is she?"

"I keep looking around, but there's no sign of her."

"Damn." Violette's expression went dark. "Well, if she won't come to us, we'll have to find her. Come on, slip away with me."

Fadiya was not hard to find after all. She was in the first place they tried, Hotel Blauensee. Charlotte went in alone and observed her from the foggy veil of the Crystal Ring.

The hotel room was dim, lit by the glow of a bedside lamp. Fadiya was at the window, in a silky slip, as if waiting for her lover to appear on the street below. Then she stretched luxuriously, put on an olive-green dress, shoes and coat, brushed the tangles from her hair. The shiny, wavy bob fell into place without effort.

She was preparing to hunt.

Charlotte watched, hidden in the edge of Raqia, holding herself as rigid as a statue in hope that Fadiya would not sense her presence. Once Fadiya paused and looked around the room, frowning. Charlotte even held her breath, as if that would make any difference, but she returned to brushing her hair.

She was a beauty, with her burnished skin and graceful bearing. Why could she not have been human, and made Emil happy? No – nothing could be that simple.

And vampires tended to attract others, because where one or two vampires were, there was likely to be a pool of luscious humans.

Five years ago, Karl had inadvertently placed Charlotte's family in danger when other vampires followed him. Even Stefan and Niklas, relatively benign, drew trouble after them. Charlotte knew full well why Violette was ever-vigilant about her dancers' safety. Disaster had come close, more than once.

And now an immortal predator had latched on to Emil.

This could not be coincidence.

Fadiya stepped into the Crystal Ring, causing Charlotte to retreat through the ether before she was caught out. Fadiya's human form changed, becoming slim and greenish-black like an exotic sea creature. She melted through the cobwebby hotel walls and emerged in the street outside, human-shaped again, strolling uphill.

Did Reiniger know what she was? How could he not?

All these questions made Charlotte horribly aware that vampires had no divine right to know life's secrets. Layers of events lay around her, impenetrable, like the smoke that rose from a burning letter. Ash and smoke would never reveal that lost knowledge. She shuddered, wondering if Karl felt like this when she'd dragged him to watch horror films.

In a narrow lane – the one where Charlotte had first met Amy – she let herself emerge into the solid world and fell into step beside Fadiya. Fadiya caught her breath and glared at her without breaking her stride.

Then Violette appeared on her other side. Fadiya's face went still but her eyes widened. They walked slightly behind her so she had to keep glancing back at them.

"What's this?" she said, her accented voice soft and nervous. "Hello? Ladies, do I know you?"

"I suspect you do," said Violette. "We know you, Fadiya."

"I'm Charlotte. My friend is Violette. Even if you never attend the ballet, you know of her."

"Yes. You're Madame Lenoir." Fadiya studied the dancer for several strides. "So you're the one… What is this?"

"Can't you guess?" As Charlotte spoke, she had a horrible, familiar feeling of dislocation, as if she'd split in two and was watching herself from a distance. The lamia was there again, not exactly visible but all around her like fog. She felt she was in several places at once, had no idea which was the real Charlotte and which one a mindless replica.

And if the lamia wanted to attack Fadiya, there was nothing she could do to stop it. Charlotte tried to maintain a cool, menacing front while engaged in a frantic private battle to join her two selves together. Impossible.

"We know what you are," Violette said softly, oblivious to Charlotte's plight. "You're like us. You may be older than us, I don't know, but we are stronger. You would not like to find out what I've been known to do to vampires who upset me."

"Oh, but I've heard." Fadiya looked straight ahead. She pulled off her gloves and fidgeted with them, stretching the thin suede between her hands. "Tales of madness and destruction, and heads torn off with your bare hands."

"I'm kinder these days." Violette touched Fadiya's back. She flinched. "But I still have my moments. For example, if any vampire goes near my dancers."

Fadiya said nothing. She seemed vulnerable, Charlotte thought, and easily intimidated. If only she could merge with the lamia, or wish it away... Until then, she was forced to observe the situation as if through frosted glass.

"What do you want with Emil?" said Violette.

Fadiya's lips parted. She twisted the gloves. Finally she said, "I love him."

Violette laughed. The sound was sharp, heartless: Lilith's voice. "Don't be ridiculous. You barely know him. There's only one reason..."

"I don't need his blood. Are you going to tell him? Well, that may work both ways – I can tell him what *you* are. Unless he already knows. Do you know that he's terrified of you? How am I doing him any greater harm than you?"

Violette froze, as if Fadiya's words had pierced their mark.

Charlotte remembered how Emil had fled from her, and how he'd recoiled from Karl, as if he knew exactly what they all were. Why wasn't he equally afraid of Fadiya? If he was in thrall to her, he must not have seen through her facade. She'd soothed him into believing he was safe with her.

"I don't wish to argue with you," said Violette. "I'll try again. What do you want with him?"

"My answer's the same. I love him."

"We will stay at your side until you tell us the truth," said Violette. "You are being watched, my dear. Every moment. Who are you?"

"No one." Fadiya sprang into a sudden run, half in the Crystal Ring. Charlotte watched the lamia spring after her, pinion her arms and bite into her neck, all in one swift motion.

"Charlotte, no!"

Violette seized hold of them both, trying to prise them apart, Fadiya uttering a horrible moan of pain.

With all her will, Charlotte tried to feel the edges of her true self, the membrane that separated her from the false reflection. She *was* the lamia, feeding on Fadiya... and she was two beings at once. If only she could tell which was which, she might be able to shake off the *doppelgänger*, like a snake shedding its skin...

The struggle was inside her, as if she existed in several overlapping realities at the same time. Physical strength was no help. Instead she sought the wispy boundaries of the double in her mind's eye – a task as hopeless as trying to remove a drop of milk from a bowl of water. The spectre slid and billowed through her hands like fog.

There was a trick: stop trying to grasp the spectre. Instead push her away, gently, as if blowing dandelion seeds. *Go,* Charlotte breathed. *Let me see you. From a distance. That's it, further and further away...*

Gradually the lamia separated from her until Charlotte could see it as a whole: her moon-white, mindless reflection. Then, with all her will, she rejected the double – firmly wishing it gone, closing herself to the lamia's smoky, persistent invasion.

And the spectre went. It diminished, clearly and swiftly, like a cloud blown away by a strong wind. Mist, illusion.

At last Charlotte mastered herself. She felt shaken, as if she'd climbed a mountain. The whole battle, apparently endless in her imagination, had only taken three heartbeats.

She recoiled from Fadiya, as if waking in violent horror from a nightmare.

"Don't!" Violette glared at her. "What's got into you? We're seeking the truth, not her blood."

"It's nothing," Fadiya hissed, rubbing her neck, licking her own blood from her fingers. "She only nipped me."

"There, a taste of what may happen if you don't listen to me," said the dancer. As smoothly as Karl might have done, she made it appear that Charlotte's attack was part of their plan. "My friend looks like an angel but I never could control her."

"Will you please leave me alone?" Fadiya said stiffly. "I'm harming no one. I love Emil. That's all there is to know."

"She might be telling the truth," said Charlotte.

Violette gave her a spiky, puzzled stare with a clear meaning:

You attack her one second, then you're the voice of reason again? What...?

"She might, but she's missing the point," said Violette. She held Fadiya facing her, resting her forearms on the woman's shoulders so their faces nearly touched. "If you think I'm letting you loose upon Emil, you're wrong. He's a fine man, but more naïve than he seems. You feed on *someone*, don't you? Herr Reiniger's niece?"

At that, Fadiya's face fell. "No. I haven't touched her."

"But you'd like to," said Charlotte. "She's my friend. I won't let you."

"Hypocrite," Fadiya said under her breath.

"How long can you resist Emil?" said Violette, giving her a little shake. "You may think you're strong enough but one day, believe me, the desire will burn unbearably and you'll succumb. I will *not* lose Emil to you."

"You don't want him!" Tears spilled from her dark-rimmed eyes.

"Is that what he said? It's possible to value people for qualities greater than their desirability as a lover, husband or friend. I need him in a way you can't possibly understand. So you are going to vanish."

"No. I'm not."

"Yes, you are, dear." Violette's mouth was close to Fadiya's, a breath from kissing her. But it was Lilith who held Fadiya now, and she knew. Her face was slack, every angle of her body radiating terror. "Leave, vanish, never return or try to see Emil again."

"Without a word?"

"Exactly."

"That would break his heart."

"How? He doesn't love you."

"All the same, I can't disappear without an explanation."

"Yes you can! Go. He'll get over you. My dancer will be safe and one day, when he's had his fill of all the glory he deserves, he'll fall in love with a sweet human girl who won't tear out his throat and end his life."

"Or is less likely to, at least," Charlotte added softly. Violette smiled, her grin so menacing that Fadiya recoiled.

"Let go of me! I don't wish you any harm. Please, I'll do as you ask."

"I'll let you go, on condition that you go very far from here and never return. Swear?"

"I swear. I'll leave, I promise."

Fadiya ducked out of Violette's hold and backed away looking terrified, furious and helpless. Then she turned and ran, dwindling along the lane with an athlete's speed until she melted into the night.

Violette released a sigh. "I believe she got the message. What a shame."

"What do you mean?" Charlotte took Violette's arm and they began to walk downhill through the lanes and squares of the Aldstadt. She pictured the lamia's departure and wondered, *Has it really gone? Did I imagine it all?*

"Fadiya seemed nice, gentle. Beautiful girl. Someone who might have been our friend and ally, in other circumstances. I was expecting more of a harpy. Someone like Ilona, all claws and cruel mockery. I thought I might have to unleash my full Lilith-self upon her, and even kill her. But... I've severed her from Emil. What a relief."

"Yes." Charlotte was hesitant, unsure what to say. "We still don't know *who* she is, though."

"As long as we never see her again, I don't care. But on that subject, who are you?"

"I beg your pardon?"

"Charlotte, you lunged at her. You simply don't do that sort of thing. Not without extreme provocation, anyway. What got into you?"

"I don't know." Charlotte lowered her head, enduring a wave of shivery dread. "Could you see two of me?"

"No. Just one. Why?"

"Ever since I was stabbed, I have flashbacks... It disturbs me even to tell you this. I keep feeling I've split in two, and can't control the lamia part. It's like a cold, clammy, mindless spectre following me. It's unspeakably frightening. I hardly even dare kiss Karl, in case this thing infects him too."

"Dear, I thought you were better."

"I am... most of the time. But a few weeks ago, I found that I'd actually forgotten about the attack. How on Earth could I *forget* such a thing? Even Karl was shocked, and it takes a lot to shock him. I feel ashamed."

"Whatever for?"

"Because I'm strong. I don't doubt that, especially since the three of us... since we saw through the veil of the dark goddess. So I should be strong enough to dismiss this apparition, but I'm not. Or am I? Just now, I *forced* her away... but has she really gone? Am I going mad?"

"That's how I felt with Lilith, until I learned to accept that side of myself," Violette said gently. She was warm and kind now, nothing like the goddess who'd terrified Fadiya.

"This isn't the same. You're her avatar. This is more like... being deceived or drugged in some way."

"May I...?" Violette's eyes turned sultry. She leaned in and pressed her lips to Charlotte's throat. Charlotte didn't protest, only gave in to her, arching her back, catching her breath with pain and pleasure as Lilith's fangs pierced her. Her head swam and she saw clouds of colour, a thunderstorm raging above her, infinite rows of bone-white figures like skeletons staring at her... A hunched, robed figure with a great skull for a head...

The pain and the visions ceased. Violette rested her cheek in the crook of her shoulder, gasping from the bliss of feeding. Charlotte stroked her hair, careful not to disturb the white silk lily.

"Well?" said the dancer, raising her head. "Did that make any change? Have I scorched the fear out of you and banished the lamia?"

Charlotte exhaled. "I don't think so. As I said, this is different. I saw disturbing images again... but I think that Lilith's bite only works the first time."

The dancer looked sombrely at her. "I suspected as much. It's just as well. I wouldn't want to keep remoulding your mind like a piece of clay every time I tasted your blood, dearest."

"Well... thank you. I'm glad to hear it."

"If you wish to take a sip in return, it's only fair." Violette tipped her head to one side, ran her fingers down the curve of her own neck. Charlotte stared at the enticing skin. She did want to, very much, but she held back, hoping desperately that the lamia's poison had not entered Violette with that mouthful of blood.

"I do, but not now," she said softly. "Did my blood taste wrong? Tainted?"

"No," said Violette. "Perhaps a very faint hint... like pepper. Not unpleasant."

"I tasted that on Fadiya, too. Nowhere near as pungent as Wolfgang's blood, but still there," Charlotte said unhappily.

"Dearest, I'm sure that whatever happened to you is not contagious. Come on. We should go back to the party."

Karl and Godric Reiniger left the salon together and descended to the lake room where several couples were swaying to a romantic song on the gramophone. No one took any notice as they opened the outer door and stepped outside.

"Shall we stroll along the lake shore?" said Reiniger. "I don't wish to be overheard, or observed. And it's a pleasant night, if a touch chilly."

Upstairs, Karl had approached him without a clear idea of what he meant to say. Not to apologise: possibly to make peace in some way, but more importantly, to find out who and what Reiniger really was. The question was how to begin the conversation.

Godric had pre-empted him. "I was unsure if I'd see you again, but I'm pleased. Could we talk in private?"

Now they walked side by side with the water lapping on their left, reflecting the colourful lanterns. Godric Reiniger's shorn head and long face were like a piece of sculpture, not exactly handsome, but striking. Strong nose, high cheekbones jutting over long, hollow cheeks, a firm jaw. The lips were thin but mobile, prone to rare smiles that took people by surprise. If he used this unexpected twinkle to manipulate folk, Karl would not be surprised.

The gold-rimmed spectacles gave him a clinical, intellectual air, at odds with the flamboyance of his white suit. His eyes were hard to read: the distorting effect of the lenses made them appear smaller than they actually were. Once or twice, when he took off his spectacles, the irises were suddenly larger, mesmeric. The frame of pale lashes and brows served to make the blue stare more intense.

Karl noticed his faint yellowish radiance. Not a normal human aura.

After a few yards the lamps ended and they went on in darkness.

"You know what I am, or at least you believe you know," said Karl. "Aren't you afraid of me?"

"Somewhat," said Reiniger. "I'm not complacent. But people who avoid fearful situations never achieve anything."

"And what do you hope to achieve?"

"Well, we have come this far without you tearing out my throat. That's a beginning."

"Or we aren't quite far enough away from the house yet," Karl said without inflection.

Reiniger made a *hmph* noise. "I don't think you wish to harm me."

"How do you know?"

"You could have done so before now. Instead, you came back to *talk* to me. That implies you prefer me alive because... you find me interesting?"

"Yes, I am prone to make that mistake with humans."

"Mistake? You mean you wait to see what they will say and do next, rather than simply kill them? A shame you did not make that 'mistake' with my father."

"Yes, it is," Karl said softly. "I cannot justify what happened."

His simple admission made Godric go quiet. The lake lapped at the bank. The music and noise of the party grew fainter as they walked on. After a while he asked, "Do vampires have a conscience?"

"Some do. Some are tortured by guilt, others survive by becoming ruthless. Most of us tread a middle path. We learn to live with ourselves, or perish."

"You see, this is why I am not *extremely* frightened of you. I sense a mote of humanity. You have an enquiring mind. You seem to prefer words to violence."

"Always."

"As do I."

"And why are you talking to me?" Karl asked. "What do you want?"

"Can't you guess?" Reiniger gave him a sideways look. His eyes gave Karl a chill. They took on a blank, hard quality, like a prison wall. "A friend of mine died recently. A doctor, a hard-working man who was always on hand to help my colleagues with their ailments. Dr Ochsner. Perhaps you heard the news? He was found dead in his office, apparently of a heart attack. Like my father."

"Are you suggesting that I killed him?" The chill intensified, like the unease Karl felt when watching certain films, as if a grey shapeless mass were crawling inside him. The last thing he needed was for this unnerving man to suspect Charlotte.

"I don't suppose you'd admit it if you had. Or would you? You could confess to anything and kill me a moment later, so it wouldn't matter what secrets you revealed. That must be a useful power to possess."

"Not really. Any human can kill another, with a gun or even with their bare hands. I am sorry to hear about your friend, but his death was nothing to do with me."

"Oh, that's a shame."

"I beg your pardon?"

"Because if you were the culprit, I would shake your hand." Reiniger's voice became gruff. "It came to my notice, after he'd died, that he had injured my niece. My housekeeper Gudrun informed me that after visiting Ochsner, my niece collapsed in the street and might have died, had not a kind female stranger brought her home. Amy herself never uttered a word of complaint to me."

Karl was surprised at the outrage in Reiniger's tone. Not wanting to admit he already knew, he said neutrally, "I'd heard rumours that Ochsner was unpopular with female patients. Didn't you know that? Are you sure you didn't *want* her to be hurt for some reason?"

"No! I only wanted to protect her health. Ochsner spoke of 'cleansing'. I didn't know he'd subjected her to a procedure that should properly be done under anaesthetic, nor that he wasn't fully qualified to do so. He might have killed her! I could have killed him myself."

"He sounds a poor excuse for a doctor," said Karl, fascinated that Godric's concern for Amy sounded genuine. But the coldest of men were capable of love, if only a controlling, possessive love.

"He was a great support to me in the past, but I had no more use for him. I know he was not much liked in the town. And I cannot afford to have unpopular people attached to my cause."

"Is your cause more important than your niece?"

"Of course not! But I have to be practical. Whether you caused

Ochsner's death or not – I'm glad he's gone. It's justice. Someone like you could be of great help."

"How?" Karl said, incredulous. "By invisibly killing your enemies?"

"No, no. That is not what I mean. I know you dislike me, Karl, but I am not a fiend."

"I don't dislike you. Nor did I think you were a fiend, until you mentioned it. However, letting your comrades assault Emil, sending your niece to a so-called doctor who deliberately injured her and making the worst films I've ever seen – none of that has endeared you to me."

"You think my films are bad?" Reiniger's face stiffened with indignation. "I assumed you to be a man of taste. Was I wrong? Or is it that you simply don't understand the art of cinema?"

Karl shook his head. "You sound more affronted about that than the death of your father."

"Different matters altogether. I see I shall have to educate you."

"I'm surprised my opinion means anything. After all, I'm not human. You've spent your life drawing pictures of me, as if to keep my face in your memory so you could take revenge if ever you saw me again. And here I am. But have you brought me out here to solicit flattery, or to kill me? I can't fulfil either desire, Godric. I've only given my honest opinion, and if you intend to shoot or stab me – try it. I won't die."

"Ever put that to the test?"

"Oh, yes."

"Indeed?" Reiniger paused to light a cigarette. The match-flare dazzled Karl's sensitive eyes. "Have many people discovered what you are and tried to destroy you?"

"Not many," Karl answered with a faint laugh.

"Good. I didn't think you were the careless type."

"I'm not, but no one's perfect."

"I believe you are as near perfect as makes no difference. Look at you: a fine specimen of male beauty who will never have to work to attract his prey."

"I assure you, I don't use such wiles—" Karl began, but Reiniger spoke across him.

"Eternally in your prime. Impervious to bullets, drowning, or the hangman's rope? Deathless. Able to pass through walls, to sustain yourself on human blood, to bring death without fear of detection or punishment. You sound rather like my ideal human, or the next stage in our evolution. The superior human, who rises above good and evil to dominate the herd. He weeds out all weakness and defects in those around him, and to do this he must act without pity. He engages in epic struggles to become both the supreme warrior and the supreme artist."

"Like Nietzsche's *Übermensch*?" Karl sighed, unimpressed. "I assure you, I'm very far from that."

"He was thinking along the right lines, but my ideas are my own," Godric retorted. "You may have no ambition to reach the ideal, but I have. Why should I not?" He pointed up at the peaks against the night sky. "Folklore tells us that great Swiss heroes sleep in those mountains. I have felt their presence. Why should I not aspire to wake them? To *become* them? Who will do so, if not me?"

Karl tensed inwardly, convinced that Godric was about to attack him out of sheer angry passion. Reiniger sounded mad, but Karl knew he possessed hidden knowledge. He caught a familiar, sour metal stench – the odour of the *sikin* Godric carried. His blood was thick with a similar smell, but there was a subtle distinction. The blade's scent was sharp, almost clinical; the blood gamey and complex, an abattoir smell.

Karl had felt the terrible power emanating from Bergwerkstatt, so forceful he couldn't break through. He'd seen the power leaking upwards through Raqia, like towers of red light.

Perhaps Godric had arranged an ambush: Karl could imagine his brutish comrades crouching in the bushes with daggers, bayonets and meat cleavers, ready to cut him to pieces.

He put out the tendrils of his senses, searching for specks of life. Mice, other night creatures, even fish in the lake were all he could detect. No trace of other humans nearby.

Even if there were, Karl could evade them in a moment by vanishing into the Crystal Ring.

But what if Reiniger had some limited control over Raqia? Karl knew only too well that vampires were not indestructible, nor were all humans powerless against them. *How can I find out, unless he will answer direct questions? Even then, he could lie, and learn more from me than I learn from him.*

Whether Godric was deluded or genuinely dangerous, Karl still could not read him.

"What more can you tell me of your gifts?" Godric asked, startling him. "Strength, speed, intelligence?"

"You seem well informed without my help," said Karl. "I wonder how you know so much, unless you've befriended a vampire, which rarely ends well."

"Oh, the knowledge is there, if you're prepared to dig deep for it." Reiniger sucked on his cigarette. Its red tip flared bright. "My father taught me that."

"Does this talk have any purpose, other than to impress me with your research?" said Karl. "It's natural that you want revenge. You can try. You might even succeed."

"You think I wish to outline how devilish you are before I destroy you?"

"Isn't that what you're doing?"

"It's what I *should* be doing." Reiniger's voice tightened. His breathing grew more rapid and beads of sweat glistened on his forehead. To Karl's keen sight each one reflected the cigarette's glow, like dozens of watery blood drops. "I suppose revenge seems a quite predictable and tiresome motive to an immortal. I understand, because my interest in you greatly outweighs my hatred of you. I think you and I are rather alike."

"Dear God, I hope not," Karl said under his breath.

"You think you're better than me? Think what you like. The point I'm making is that, like you, I can put personal antipathy, brute emotion and morality aside in the service of a higher aim. I wish to become a vampire."

CHAPTER SEVENTEEN

SKIES OF FIRE

Karl stopped in his tracks. Reiniger swung round in front of him, staring hard into his eyes. The force of his ambition was like a hot wind on Karl's skin.

"I want to become immortal. I want the effortless power that you possess. I am asking you to transform me into a vampire."

A dozen responses formed in Karl's mind: shades of dismay, anger, acid mockery. No words came out, because nothing he wanted to say would please Reiniger.

"Well?" Godric prompted, staring eagerly at him. Karl broke the gaze and looked into the distance. "Is my request so preposterous? It happened to you. At least *tell* me how to go about the transformation."

"Why?" Karl said tonelessly.

"Because you owe me that much, at least."

Karl was silent, distancing himself from the desperate heat of Reiniger's hunger. Caught between the urge to vanish into the Crystal Ring, or simply to snap the man's neck, he cursed his own instinct to be courteous in all situations.

Nearly all.

Eventually he said, "I took your father's life. Now you wish me to extend yours in exchange? Is that your idea of a bargain?"

"I wouldn't put it so simplistically, but yes. You can't bring back my father, but you can grant me *some* recompense. Think of it: we could even become colleagues. You made a terrible mistake, but in exchange for this gift, I might find it in my heart to forgive you. We could be equals, Karl. Partners in power!"

Reiniger made the statement as if it were a glorious, irresistible prospect. Karl sighed inwardly. There was nothing to tell him but the truth.

"No," said Karl. "Godric, it's not what you think. After the transformation, you might feel so different that your human ambitions become pointless. The blood-thirst is a curse. In some ways vampires are more vulnerable than you realise, both to each other and to humans. And the prospect of eternal undeath can be more of a nightmare than a dream. Believe me, it is not what you think."

Reiniger's eyes glistened with impatience.

"I'll risk it," he snapped. "What are you doing – warning me, or refusing me?"

"Both."

"Not good enough. You have this – this gift or curse, whatever you call it – but I cannot share it? That seems unreasonable to the point of selfishness."

"Then I'm unreasonable, but I will not create another vampire. I've seen too much suffering. Besides, it's not a straightforward process. It's not a matter of my draining your blood and leaving you to rise from your coffin. I could drain your blood, but you will merely die."

At that, Reiniger stepped back. Karl was glad to see this sign of fear. His sudden pallor indicated that he was not beyond reason after all.

"Not straightforward?" he echoed, his breathing shallow. "What, then? A ceremony of some kind?"

"All your research, and you haven't found the answer for yourself?"

"There are so many different tales. I found references to a ritual requiring three vampires, but there was insufficient detail. The obvious difficulty lies in finding three vampires who will agree to help the human. That seems as likely as a mouse asking a favour of three hungry cats!" Reiniger smirked at his own wit. "And yet, I found you – or rather, you found me. That's a great leap towards achieving my ambition. It's a clear sign this is meant to be. Obviously you know other vampires. I've seen them myself.

Tell me what to do. That's all I ask."

"I'm sorry, but I cannot tell you. I *won't*. Even if your research uncovered exactly what is entailed – well, I can't stop you finding others to help you, but I refuse to be involved. And you're quite right; most other vampires would slaughter you before you uttered a word."

"Indeed." Reiniger moistened his lips. His stare held an ugly mixture of dread and determination.

"Actually, we couldn't even drain you, since you seem to have poisoned your own blood against us. There are other ways, though. Some believe that taking life-energy instead is even worse for the victim."

The blue eyes widened. Eventually he spoke. "I appreciate the warning, but let's put all that aside. I am going to ask again. I wish to become as you are: a vampire. Please will you help me?"

"No," said Karl. His tone was firm: not angry, but stone cold. "You don't know what you're asking. Forget this, Godric. I know you have some kind of occult knowledge and ritual practice. Why shouldn't you? Everyone's entitled to their secrets. Why not be content with that? I've seen evidence that your power is real. You have your art, your film-making and your followers…"

"It's not enough." Again he pointed towards the Alps. "I need to become my country's saviour."

Karl resumed walking, guiding Godric away from the lake shore so they would loop back towards the chalet. He asked, "Is there anyone in the world you put before yourself? Wife, child, sibling?"

Reiniger gave a soft snort. "Not really. I have no wife or child. Only Amy, who brings out what little paternal instinct I possess. I have a soft spot for the girl. Yes, I'd always put her well-being before my own."

"Sending her to Dr Ochsner hardly supports that assertion."

"As I said, I did so with her welfare in mind. Ochsner went too far, *much* too far, and I can't mourn him. But, thank heaven, she recovered."

"Well, imagine this. You are a newly made vampire with bloodlust raging, and your niece comes innocently to you and asks, 'Uncle, is anything wrong?' You would feast on her blood before you even realised who she was."

"No! Not her."

"But you would. And afterwards you'd realise what you'd done and weep, tear your heart to pieces with self-hatred for the rest of your existence. You say you're concerned for her welfare. Do you not realise that there is already a vampire in your house who will happily feed on her, if she hasn't already done so?"

Reiniger went still. A noise came from his throat, a sort of swallowed gasp. "What," he said, "what makes you think such a thing?"

Karl had no intention of naming Fadiya. Knowing that Charlotte and Violette had gone to warn her away, he thought it unlikely she would ever be seen again. Instead he watched the man's reaction. Although startled, he did not seem as shocked as Karl had expected.

He knew, without question.

"Vampires sense others. She has been seen. If you would nonchalantly put Amy and your household in such danger, you do like to play with fire, don't you?"

"She promised..." Reiniger's face was white in the darkness, his teeth bared. "You're right, Karl, I have knowledge. Of course I know what she is. But she has *never* touched any of my people."

"Then why is she working for you?"

Godric's face stiffened into taut lines.

"I cannot tell you," he said thinly. "She's helping me. I'm not entirely unfamiliar with vampires, Karl. I control her. She is not dangerous to me."

Lies, thought Karl, but he let the matter drop for now.

"No vampire can be trusted," he said. "My point is that we all feed on humans whether they're family or strangers, innocent or criminal. Blood is blood. I will not create another vampire. I won't make you into a creature that goes out and destroys lives, as I have for so many years."

"All the more reason, then. Since your kind poses such a great threat to me and my circle, how much safer we'd be if I were also a vampire: ruthless, as strong as a lion hunting down the hyenas."

"But you have your enchanted or cursed knives to use against us. Aren't they enough?"

Reiniger gave him another penetrating, unreadable stare.

"I can't speak about that. And no, they are not enough. Karl, you *must* agree to my demand. One way or another, I will become like you." He edged closer. With his slightly greater height he almost loomed over Karl.

Karl's hand shot out. He wanted to seize Reiniger's neck, but stopped at the last instant and braced his hand against the man's breastbone. He acted to alarm him and to push him away. To repel the pressure of his demands, and the sourness of his blood.

Reiniger radiated a force like electricity or radium, invisible but as tangible as the wind. Karl still couldn't identify the power, but he was convinced it was connected with the *Istilqa* knives that weakened vampires and strengthened humans.

Rarely he'd found an artefact or a place hostile to vampires, but this was different. Reiniger was a blank page, guarding his secrets.

"You're missing the point," said Karl. "I've tried to reason with you but none of my arguments have had the slightest effect, have they? You want what you want."

"As I said, I'll take the risk," Reiniger hissed.

"Then I will repeat my answer, as respectfully and clearly as possible. No. I will not help you become a vampire. My answer to your demand is *no*."

He dropped his hand. Godric stood rubbing his collarbone, swallowing convulsively, his face like limestone in the darkness.

"Very well," he said softly. "You've made your position clear, Karl. I should not have embarrassed you with my unwelcome request. I should have known… better."

"Your friends will be missing you at the party," Karl replied without malice. "Let's go back inside and forget this unfortunate conversation."

"Excellent idea," Reiniger murmured, adding in English, "You cannot blame a fellow for trying."

"My beloved friends," Stefan greeted Charlotte and Violette as they re-entered the salon, arm in arm. "You've been missed. Up to mischief, I hope?"

He and Niklas formed a kind of shield to ward off the admirers who immediately bore down on Violette. The room was chaotic now, the mess outpacing the waiters' attempts to clear away empty glasses and full ashtrays. The band was raucous, guests dancing with abandon. A fug of smoke, alcohol and sweaty perfume filled the air. After the quietness of the night, the noise and bright colours were an assault on Charlotte's senses. As much as she loved Stefan, she wanted to flee.

"There was, um, a situation," she said, kissing his cheek. "All sorted out now."

"I'm glad to hear it. So you found your quarry?"

"Yes, as if she thought not coming to the party would help her." Charlotte smiled. "Violette, please tell me I haven't got my dress dirty. Stefan might kill me."

"You are pristine," Violette replied. "Not a hint of dust... or blood."

"Well, I daren't ask what happened," said Stefan. "If you are going to fight in the street, *please* don't do it wearing an exquisite new gown I've bought you. Come and mingle."

"Just for a little longer," Violette sighed. "I wasn't designed to play the gracious hostess for more than an hour at a time. Besides, familiarity breeds contempt. I have to maintain my mystique, you know." She gave a narrow, self-mocking smile.

"Don't be ridiculous. As if they could ever have enough of you!" Stefan retorted.

"You'd be surprised," she sighed. "Funny, it hasn't changed since I was human; if I talk to anyone for more than a few minutes, they start to think they're my best friend, touching my arm, wanting to exchange addresses... Then, however politely I brush them off, they decide I'm an ice-cold witch." Violette shrugged. "They may well be right, so it's safer to keep them at arm's length before it even starts."

"We'll protect you," said Stefan. He slipped his hand through her other arm. Niklas walked beside him like a cat with knowing, golden eyes.

Charlotte wondered, as she had countless times, what went on in Niklas's head. Sometimes he was an empty shell; at others he seemed fully aware, his lips forever closed on his own mysterious wisdom. Even if he had no true intelligence, he was always serene. And he had Stefan to look after him: there were worse ways to exist.

"Where's Karl?" she said, scanning the room. "He went off with Herr Reiniger. Hasn't he come back yet?"

"I haven't seen either of them," said Stefan. "Do you want to speak to Reiniger about this business of filming the ballet?"

"I can't decide," Violette said darkly. "Half of me says no, not in a thousand years. He's a dangerous egotist. He has a vampire working for him. His followers have attacked both Charlotte and Emil, *and* tried to lure Emil away. Who knows what they were planning? But the other half of me says that if I agree, we could get to know him and find out who he really is."

"And why he's got such an odd weapon as the *Istilqa* knife," added Charlotte. A series of horrible possibilities ran through her mind: Godric drawing a similar knife on Karl, or Wolfgang and the others surrounding him in the dark... "We should have asked Fadiya, while we had her attention."

"She might know something, but it's too late," said Violette. "She's gone."

"*Where* is Karl?" Charlotte repeated, growing more worried.

"I don't know," said Stefan. "Perhaps they're down in the lake room."

As she went on looking around – as if that could make him magically appear – she caught the eye of Wolfgang Notz. For several long seconds they held each other's stare. This time she did not turn away, but glared right into his soul, silently telling him, *Yes, I know who you are and I am not afraid of you. You survived last time, but come after me again...*

He looked younger and more nervous than she remembered. Colour flushed his cheeks. At last he broke the stare and turned away, plainly shaken if not terrified.

Charlotte caught her breath with a sense of satisfaction. Then a voice spoke in her ear, startling her.

"I'm here."

She had sensed Karl's presence only a fraction of a second before he spoke.

"Oh, thank heaven," she said, leaning her head into his shoulder as he embraced her from behind. "I was worried."

"No need."

"Did you find out anything of interest?"

Karl gave a muffled groan into her neck that sent shivers all through her. "I'll tell you later. We should talk somewhere quieter, I think."

"Actually, Karl, I'd like to leave soon," Charlotte said in a low voice. "Violette wants to go, too. No offence, Stefan, but all these people – how do you stand it?"

He grinned, his eyes sultry. "My favourite time is when the crowd starts to thin out and we turn the lights low… Niklas and I always know who our very special guests are by then. Stay."

"Thank you, but I don't think any of us are in the mood for one of your bizarre orgies," said Karl.

"Bizarre? Don't you mean 'beautifully orchestrated'?" Stefan said in mock indignation.

"And don't let anything happen until the Reiniger gang have all gone. We don't want them associating Violette with your nocturnal activities, do we?"

"Very well, I'll hold off the orgy if you'll all stay a while longer. Relax. Perhaps have a drink?" Stefan winked, giving Violette his most charming smile. "Just an hour or so. Madame, it's the perfect chance for you to encourage everyone to come to the new ballet, isn't it? Charm them, promise free tickets. They'll love you forever, believe me."

He kissed her hand, and she relented.

"Emil."

The voice made him jump as he entered his dark bedroom. His eyes began to adjust and he saw Fadiya in silhouette against the window. *What the hell…?* Emil groped for the light switch, and there she stood, blinking in the yellow glow. She clutched her coat around herself, looking upset.

"How the hell did you get in?" he exclaimed.

"Hush, keep your voice down! Shut the door. I'm sorry – I didn't mean to startle you, but I had to see you."

He was halfway across the room as Fadiya rushed to meet him. She put her arms around his neck and pressed herself against him. Her coat fell open, revealing a plain olive-green dress. Her fragrant form against his hot, damp, aching body felt breathtakingly sensual, but he tried to push her away, not wanting to mark her clothes with sweat stains.

"You're like a furnace," she said.

"Yes, I've been rehearsing. Our ballet masters worked us half to death tonight. Fadiya, you can't be here!"

"Don't say that." She hung around his neck, tears welling from her eyes and her expression as intense and serious as he'd ever seen.

"We could have met at the hotel. What's wrong? If you need me to pay the bill…"

"No, I do not need you to *pay* me for anything! How dare you!" She let her arms drop, stepped back and glared. Her mood alarmed him.

"I didn't mean… Good grief, what is this? What's happened?"

"How hard would you find it to live without me? Not hard at all, I suppose. You cannot love me."

"What? That is not fair."

"I'm leaving. I only wondered if you might miss me, even a little."

"*Leaving?*"

Her announcement floored him. He hadn't known her long but he'd grown dependent on her, almost taking her for granted. He could happily work himself to death for Violette, knowing that Fadiya waited for him in all her welcoming sensuality…

"You look shocked," she said softly. "That must mean something."

"But you can't leave. I don't understand. Fadiya?" He made to kiss her but she held him at arm's length.

"Where is Madame Lenoir?"

"She went to a party," Emil said, frowning. "It's not like her to socialise, but she does what she wants, so…"

"Exactly. She went to a party to which *I* was invited, but she made sure you were otherwise occupied. When I was late – I didn't intend to go at all, in fact, because I had no desire to meet her – she came to find me."

"What?"

"Your Madame Lenoir sought me out especially. She said I'm never to see you again. She ordered me to disappear without a word. Threatened me with terrible consequences if I defy her."

"*Threatened* you?" Rage seized him, so intense he couldn't

speak or see clearly. His head throbbed and his vision went nearly black, except for a tunnel along which he saw Fadiya's distraught face. He couldn't find words, couldn't think.

"Yes, commanded me to vanish and never see you again. But I couldn't. Emil? You've turned crimson. Sit down."

"No!" He snarled and lashed out – not at Fadiya, but at a vase on a dressing table. China smashed, shards spinning across the floorboards. She didn't flinch. Her attention on him remained steady. She pressed her hands to his face. They were freezing on his hot skin.

"Violette told you to stop seeing me?" he said, enunciating each word. His mind whirled. He had to control himself, to make sense of what he was hearing.

"Yes. She had a friend with her – as pretty as an angel, but she scared me even more than madame. She tried to attack me. Emil, I'm terrified. I dare not stay in Lucerne."

"Was her name Charlotte?" He spoke raggedly.

"Yes."

"I told you – I'm sure they're not human. Am I going mad, or are they demons of some kind? If they are, that would answer so much... How *dare* she forbid us to see each other?"

"Perhaps *they're* mad, not you." Fadiya stroked his face. "I didn't mean to make you angry."

"I'm not angry with you."

"She's jealous. She doesn't want you, but she won't let you love anyone else. Is this how you want to live – like her slave, her eunuch?"

"Of course not," he growled.

"There isn't much time." Fadiya's soft voice became urgent. "Violette might be back at any moment. If she catches me, I truly believe she'll kill me. Come with me now."

"What? Where?"

"Somewhere safe. I have friends who'll help me."

"I'm not going to Reiniger's mansion again."

"No – I don't mean there. Somewhere far away, warm and beautiful. Either you come with me now, Emil, or you never see me again. I love you. *She* never will."

He stared at her, his breathing high and shallow. What to do? He saw Violette's face in his mind and was flooded with rage – beautiful she might be, but with the arrogance of a snow queen. Was glory on stage worth the price of being crushed as a man? And here was Fadiya in front of him, so lovely, warm and passionate. If love withered when it was ignored, it must flourish where it was nurtured.

"If you don't want me, say so and I'll go." Her eyes brimmed with tears, glistening. "But if you do – throw your clothes in a bag and come with me *now*."

"This minute? I need to bathe…"

"There isn't time," she hissed. "Decide, because I have to go."

"I love you, Fadiya." The words rushed out of him like a thrilling wind. "I'm coming with you."

"Then hurry!" She smiled through her tears, her joyful expression contorted with anxiety. Her panic infected him and he dragged out a canvas bag, threw some trousers and shirts on to the bed, along with his coat and hat, money and personal belongings. Fadiya looked out of the window as if watching for Violette's return.

Then he stopped.

"Wait, I have to…" He fumbled in a drawer for writing paper, pen and ink.

"What are you doing?"

"I can't go without leaving her a note."

"For heaven's sake!" She sounded frantic. "Can you count the minutes until Violette comes back? We need to be long gone from here."

He was already writing, as fast as his hand would move, tears mingling with his sweat so he could barely see. Fadiya moaned in exasperation. "I'll pack your bag while you write your goodbye. Quickly! Is there a secret way out?"

"This place has about twenty staircases. I know the least used. We can escape without anyone seeing us."

"Come on, then." She seized his arm, even as he finished signing his name. Then she paused for long enough to press her mouth to his. So succulent, delicious… For a moment he wished Violette in hell, so he could push Fadiya down on to the bed… but she gripped his hand and dragged him towards the door with astounding strength. "You won't be sorry, darling Emil. She cannot stop us being together, and happy."

* * *

Dawn brushed the mountain peaks, leaving the valleys in blue-green shadow. As the sky began to pale, Violette stepped from the Crystal Ring into her own living room. Her mood was oddly melancholy but calm. She'd done as Stefan asked: danced a brief solo for the guests' enjoyment, announced that the Ballet Lenoir would be delighted to receive them all when the ballet opened, and if they left their names and addresses with Stefan they would all receive complimentary tickets. And she had even enjoyed herself, basking in their pleasure.

Deciding to leave on a high note, she had slipped away, found a victim in the darkness, and then passed into Raqia to rest.

For once, no visions of the giant skull-demon disturbed her.

Karl and Charlotte had been with her for a while, the three of them drifting on the ether in a semi-trance. By the time she revived, she was alone. She travelled straight home through the hidden dimension to ensure that no one would see her arrive. Now she had plenty of time to shed her party dress, bathe and put on her practice clothes while her company rose and ate breakfast.

She let Geli sleep in. If Geli wondered why her mistress required so little attention these days, she was too well-mannered to pry.

Violette combed out her long hair and folded it into a pleat at the nape of her neck. Standing before a mirror to check that she looked presentable, she noticed Charlotte behind her left shoulder. Violette was so startled that she almost leapt into the air.

"Gods, Charlotte, that's the second time – what is it?"

Her friend's face was serene, the amethyst eyes unblinking. She looked... not quite herself, as if she were sleepwalking. Paler than usual, and that strange empty look in her eyes...

Violette finished pinning up her hair and turned. As she did so, someone started thumping on the outer door to her suite.

Charlotte was nowhere to be seen.

"What are you playing at?" she said under her breath. She went to answer the door, calling out, "Yes, one moment!"

Thierry stood there with a piece of paper in his hand. He looked ashen. Grumpy by nature – mainly because he was a perfectionist when it came to the smooth running of the ballet – he deferred to no one but Violette herself. Now he showed no sign of his quick temper, only shock.

"Madame..."

"Come in. What's wrong?"

"Emil was late rising – he didn't come down for breakfast, so I went to see if he was ill. He was not in his room. I'm afraid he appears to have left, and in a hurry. His wardrobe and drawers were half-empty, the room in disarray…"

"*Left?*"

Dumb, Thierry gave her the note. His hand shook. Violette began to read, or tried: Emil had scribbled in Italian and it was all she could do to read his handwriting, let alone translate the meaning. She took a couple of minutes to make sense of it.

My dear Madame Violette,

Forgive me. I did all I could to please you – to please us both. Gave up my longing for you – I admit it was hopeless – and you'll never know what this cost me, but I did so anyway, for your sake. I worked. Your goal and mine were the same: artistic perfection.

And yet! Still not enough for you! I found someone – she was not you, could never be you, but she had that very quality you lack, warmth, warmth and love for me. I see clearly now. If the one you think you love is unreachable, then to find someone new – I thought it impossible but I was wrong! Someone who knows how to love can heal you. And she, Fadiya, knows.

I did all you wanted. Crushed my love for you, found her instead – and because of her I was no longer in despair, I was content and I could work as we both wanted. Tell me, whom were we harming?

And yet you could not even let me have that! You went to her, threatened her. To ask how you dared – how you could be so cruel – I can find no words! Worse than ruthless, I think there is evil in you. You wanted to save our partnership on stage, and yet you have destroyed it.

So you leave me no choice. Glory on stage, or love? Which do you think? I'm going away with Fadiya. Don't try to find us. This is your loss. Yours. At least I shall be happy. Will you? Ever?

Regards, Emil.

Violette stared at the scrawled handwriting until the letters blurred. Rage and dismay paralysed her. There was some truth in his words, but he didn't understand.

"You think you see clearly? I acted to save you, idiot!" she snarled aloud.

Thierry stood paralysed. She stared straight through him, forgetting he was there.

Now Emil would never understand, until Fadiya had drained him to a husk. There would be fever, madness, delirium. Pleasure, too, of course… but then decline – slow or sudden according to Fadiya's whim – and death.

Should I seek him out, she thought, *as I sought out Robyn, and stab my fangs into his neck in order to bring him to his senses? Lilith's bite brings clarity… but Robyn died anyway. Enlightenment is not always enough.*

She sank on to a chair, hands pressed to her forehead, the letter crumpled between them.

"Madame, I'm so sorry," said Thierry. "I should have prevented this!"

"How? You're his assistant, not his nursemaid. Go. Tell everyone – I don't know, tell them he's confined to his room with influenza. Thierry, go!"

Alone, Violette raged inwardly against Emil, and Fadiya, and herself. She allowed herself a few moments of self-indulgent collapse, then she straightened up and put the letter aside, smoothing it flat on a table top.

She had to fetch him back. There was nothing else for it. Even if it meant killing Fadiya and revealing that they were both vampires, even if Emil never forgave her – at least she would have saved his life.

When Charlotte and Karl rested in the Crystal Ring, time itself seemed to stop. They floated hand in hand, as if gliding in nothingness. Around them, the Ring's atmosphere shimmered like liquid in which vast mountains sailed, ever-changing. Below, gilded russet cloud-hills frayed into vapour in the blue void. Earth was down there somewhere, invisible, like the depths of the ocean.

Charlotte often thought that Raqia was composed of layers, like the rings of an onion, each layer floating on the next as oil floated on water. Rippling, ever-changing in its beauty.

And the truth was even stranger, if what she believed was true. Raqia was a ghost-image of Earth and sky, created by the massed dreams of mankind. A tiny mote of light streaking upwards might be a person dying, or one being born. Every change created its own wave. Like a photon or a radio-wave, it travelled onwards and outwards forever.

Raqia was the interference pattern of all those millions of waves. Only vampires perceived it, for they were the manifestation of mortal desires and fears.

Charlotte believed that the recent storms and apparitions were forewarnings of some kind; but the future, all the potential futures, changed constantly and could not be predicted. One of the hardest lessons she'd learned was that vampires were not designed to interfere with human events. They could try, but the Crystal Ring itself would slap them down.

She came abruptly out of her trance, disturbed by a shudder in the air. Although she'd never fully lost consciousness, she felt that several hours had passed between one breath and the next. Karl gripped her hand.

"Time to go back," he said. "It's almost dawn."

"Yes... that's odd, I thought I heard someone calling me."

"Raqia plays tricks on us," said Karl. They met each other's gaze. "I noticed a shockwave, but this realm is always restless. It could have been anything."

"I felt it too," she said. "It was strong, like an icy current in a warm sea. I'm cold."

The healed scar in her abdomen ached.

Like divers they descended towards the ground, ethereal bodies arched, lacy tendrils flowing around them. Gloom swallowed them. They emerged into reality above the ground and fell the last few feet on to grass near the lake – shaken, but suddenly warm again, human-shaped. They'd changed out of their party clothing last night: Karl wore a plain dark suit, Charlotte a simple russet dress. The sky was a wash of pale lemon and lilac behind luminous mountain peaks.

"That was elegant," Charlotte said, laughing. Karl caught her arms and they stood up together. For a few moments they pressed together, his body lithe and hard against hers; and she thought,

Last night I felt the lamia vanish. Perhaps it's gone, perhaps I'm well again and it wouldn't do any harm if we lay down here in this flower meadow by the lake...

It was Karl who ended the embrace, gently putting a forearm's distance between them. She sighed, looking down at the grass full of white and pink flowers. She couldn't look into his eyes.

"At least we didn't land in the water," he said. "We should go home, beloved."

"Look, there's Stefan's chalet," she said. "We're hardly half a mile away, which means we're ten miles from town."

"We can go back into the Ring and take a short cut," said Karl.

"Actually, I'd rather walk. I love walking through the dawn, don't you?"

"Very much. Are you still cold?"

"No." She put her hand through his arm, tipped back her head to breathe the fresh air. "There's still something nagging, like a sound I can't quite hear... Violette was with us in Raqia for a while. I've no idea when she left. Do you think it's her calling us?"

"If so, she'll have to wait," Karl said firmly. "Sunrise and your company are blessings I intend to savour, *liebling*."

These times were her favourite, when she and Karl had nowhere to be and all the time in the world. They walked close together, basking in nature. Imagining there was no cold poison inside her, no spectre haunting her, no wild storms in Raqia. For now, everything was perfect.

"Let's stop and wish Stefan good morning as we pass," Karl said with a smile. "I wonder what time his party finished?"

"It's a good thing he's not human, or he'd be moaning from the after effects of drink, as most of his guests will be," said Charlotte. "Not to mention all the other mischief I'm sure they got up to. I love him, but his idea of entertainment..."

"Actually, I believe he loves to observe how far humans will go with very little encouragement," said Karl. "Perverse, but understandable. Mortals become so very fascinating to us."

"Mm. Don't they," Charlotte murmured. "Well, he swears his gatherings are very rarely fatal to his visitors, so..." She trailed off, remembering her older sister, Fleur. She pushed the thought away. *Her death was not Stefan's fault.*

"Charlotte?" Karl said softly, as if he knew what she was thinking.

"I want to disapprove, I really *should* disapprove, but I can't." She kept her tone light. "He charms his way around everyone, as if an orgy of blood and debauchery is as proper as a vicarage tea party."

They reached the corner of the chalet. The row of windows in the lake room glinted red as the sun rose. Charlotte felt the cold current again. It hit her chest like a kick from a horse.

Inside the house, someone was shouting. A pair of bloodied palms hit the inside of a glass door then slid downwards, leaving trails of gore. Karl was already running up the wooden steps to the veranda, Charlotte a pace behind him, as the door burst open and Stefan fell through, screaming.

He was covered in blood, his clothes torn, his hair matted and his eyes shining white with terror in his blood-spattered face. He stretched out crimson hands towards them.

"Help me," he cried. His voice was hoarse: a desperate, ghastly sound. "Karl, help me. Niklas is dead."

PART TWO

CHAPTER EIGHTEEN

THE DAWN OF SEPARATION

The smell hit Karl like a wall: the dregs of the party, stale smoke and alcohol, the fading mingled body odours of the departed guests. And blood... Vampire blood, subtly different to that of humans, like cognac compared to rich red wine.

Niklas lay on his back in the centre of the wide room. He was naked from the waist up, his chest and torso a red glistening mass of wounds. All around him, the rug was spattered and streaked with blood.

Stefan was wounded too, red flesh showing through the torn remains of his shirt. At least he was alive. Niklas lay like marble. Dropping to his knees beside him, Karl touched his hand, his face. The skin felt like chilled pastry. There was no heartbeat, no breath... and although a vampire could fake death, Niklas had no reason or will to do so. Something more fundamental was missing. Karl sensed no hint of any life force left in him at all.

Meanwhile Stefan's raw voice spilled an incomprehensible stream of panic, misery and grief. Charlotte was trying to soothe him, but he would not be comforted. When she put her arm around his shoulders, he threw her halfway across the room.

"Stefan!" Karl leapt up and tried to hold him still. "For pity's sake, calm down."

"I'm all right," said Charlotte. She rose to a crouch and stared at Niklas. "What happened?"

Stefan didn't answer. He slid out of Karl's grip and collapsed.

His moans faded to a ghastly background noise as he lay on the carpet like a broken doll, hands clawing towards his twin.

Niklas lay with his eyes open: pale yellow glass orbs staring at the ceiling. Karl knelt over him, examining each bloody slash like a policeman with a murder victim. Red gashes disfigured his throat, chest, abdomen – deep cuts that would have killed a human, but should not have killed a vampire.

Charlotte moved to kneel beside Karl at Niklas's side, tears flowing down her face. Karl remained as calm and businesslike as a doctor. Moisture flooded his eyes but he ignored it, only sweeping it away when his vision began to blur.

"Is he really... gone?" Charlotte whispered.

"I think so," Karl replied. His voice was soft and hoarse. "It is so hard to tell with us. We can stop our own hearts. We can enter hibernation in the *Weisskalt*, effectively mummified by the cold, and still recover... but I sense nothing from Niklas, not the merest spark of life."

A muffled noise came from Stefan.

"What did you say?" Charlotte asked gently.

"I said he's gone." Stefan pushed himself up on both hands. His face was ghastly, bloodless, his eyes wild. "He's dead. I feel it here." He struck his breastbone. "Don't you realise we were one being? I was always in his head, and he in mine. He was my other-self. Why is he dead and not me? Why?"

"Because..." Karl tailed off and thought better of attempting to explain. "Stefan, I know this is hard..."

"You have no idea!" He pointed a white, trembling hand at Karl. "You destroyed your own *doppelgänger* with no trace of pity in your heart! How can you understand? Niklas – I loved him, I devoted my life to him even though he never realised, any more than a cat comprehends that his owner would give his life for him – but I did so anyway and I'm sure he knew, *somewhere* deep inside. But you, why would *you* care that Niklas is dead?"

He launched himself at Karl with a roar, wrenched him backwards and pinned him down, hands around his throat, fangs extended – as mindless as Niklas had been. Karl held him away with braced arms, but Stefan was crazed.

"Stefan!" Charlotte seized his shoulders, battling to stop him.

With strength Karl didn't know she possessed, she managed to wrench him loose. Stefan crumpled suddenly and rolled into her legs, taking her down with him. They lay tangled on the floor, until Charlotte sat up with Stefan resting his head like a dead weight in her lap.

He shook with sobs. His blood stained her dress. She stroked his blond hair, whispering nonsense to calm him, as if he were an infant. Her tears dripped on to his face.

Never in his life had Karl seen him like this. He'd often seen people grief-stricken, but no one as demented as Stefan at the loss of his twin.

"You're wounded too," said Charlotte. "Will you let me look?"

Stefan shook his head. "I'll heal. He – he's all that matters."

"Karl?" she said, meeting his eyes. She was ashen-faced. "Is there nothing we can do for Niklas?"

Karl knelt over the corpse again. He pushed a hand through his hair, unconsciously smearing Niklas's blood on to his forehead. "Sometimes lifeless vampires can be brought back by bathing them in fresh blood for days or weeks. We all know that. But the cost! Scores of human lives. Kristian was ruthless enough to do it, but I am not."

"Not even for Niklas?" she asked. Then she flinched, as if she regretted asking.

"It would be for Stefan's sake, not for Niklas himself," Karl answered with a heavy heart. "But no, not even for him."

At that, Stefan lifted his head. "If not for Kristian's ruthlessness, neither you nor I would even be alive now."

"So?" Karl said grimly. "We would have died at our appointed time, as do millions of others. I'm glad to be alive, of course. We're lucky indeed to have experienced all the pleasure and pain and love that we've found during our stolen time. But that doesn't make Kristian's actions any less monstrous."

"But you'd do it for Charlotte."

Karl didn't answer.

Charlotte stroked Stefan's shoulder, as if willing him to stay calm. He went on shuddering, his breath ragged, while she seemed to have stopped breathing altogether.

Karl had learned the macabre truth about Niklas only a few

years ago. He remembered sitting with the twins at a mountainside café, like a trio of tourists, while Stefan explained. A beheaded vampire might regrow their body, if their head were bathed in blood; but the body, too, could also regrow a head.

Later, in different circumstances, Karl had survived a similar horror.

The difference was that Karl had regarded his mindless twin as an abomination to be destroyed. The replica's head, regrown from the body, had no mind: only some remnant of instinct. It was like a moving statue of the original, a revenant. Karl had had no hesitation in destroying his own ghastly double.

Stefan, by contrast, loved Niklas like a true twin. Whether that indicated a generous soul or sheer vanity, Karl was unsure. Both, he suspected. Whatever the case, such love was real and deep enough to tear out Stefan's soul.

"Stop," said Charlotte, jolting him from his thoughts. "Don't start arguing, it's the last thing we need! Please. I shouldn't have mentioned it."

"But we were all thinking it," said Karl. "Stefan, we'll talk of this later, when you're calmer."

"I am never going to be calmer!" His voice was a near-scream.

Karl turned to him and lifted him out of Charlotte's embrace, gripping his shoulders. "Try, at least for as long as it takes to tell us what happened."

A few more groans, then Stefan caught his breath and went still.

"Last night," he said. "The party went on until... three in the morning, I believe. The jazz band and waiters were long gone by then and the rest of us came down into this room. We had a nice time. Some people were wide awake and giggly, others half-comatose. There was some kissing... and yes, Niklas and I indulged our thirst upon a handful of willing souls. Nothing especially outrageous. But by three or so, the last of them had left."

"No one stayed the night?"

Stefan shook his head. "In the past I've found stray guests unconscious in bedrooms but no, last night everyone went home."

"What about Godric Reiniger and his group?"

Stefan began to tremble. Between them, they helped him to a couch and he sat on the edge with his head in his hands. "He and his friends disappeared. I think they went before midnight. I didn't see them leave."

"And then?" Karl asked gently. "You and Niklas were alone?"

"I took him into the Crystal Ring. Just to rest for a while. It was so peaceful... When we came back, it was still dark and we sat looking out at the lake, just the two of us..."

Stefan's mouth formed an oblong of anguish and fresh tears dripped down his face. He went on, "And then... I felt something so strange... can't describe it, except as needles of ice coming at us from all directions. A pressure in the air. I was puzzled, then concerned. I got up but I could hardly move. I walked a few steps, but I couldn't reach the door. It felt as if someone had put an invisible wall all around us, or a wind so strong you can't walk against it. I tried to enter the Ring, but that was blocked too. Felt as if we were trapped inside a cocoon that was squeezing tighter and tighter around us. I wasn't even frightened, just confused, too startled to feel any fear. And then they arrived. Dawn was close – the darkness was more of a grey dusk when they came."

"Who were they?"

"Godric Reiniger and his gang. There were more than twenty of them – I couldn't count. They each had a bone-knife, like the one you left here. They were pointing the knife-tips at us. That's where the power came from. A force that sucked all our strength away."

"Like an electromagnetic field?" Charlotte put in.

"I don't know. You're the scientist. All I know is that they surrounded us and I couldn't move. I've never felt powerless like that – no, that's untrue. Only Kristian ever overpowered me like that before. I had no strength, as if they'd drained my blood and paralysed my nerves. It was vile. I fell to the floor. After that, it's blurred."

"Do your best," said Karl, taking his icy hand.

"I remember being flat on my back with Niklas beside me. They tore our shirts and began cutting us. It seems unreal... as if I wasn't properly conscious, but hallucinating. I don't recall much pain. Do you remember, as a human, if you had a paper-cut? You wouldn't feel it at all for a while, then it would begin to sting like the devil? Like that. All across my chest and abdomen. I was terrified, but I was in a kind of trance, nothing I could do to make it stop. The main thing I remember is the chanting."

Charlotte went to a sideboard and came back with a cotton napkin that she'd dipped into a jug of water. She pressed the cold cloth to Stefan's forehead. Gently she began to clean the blood from his body.

"What kind of chanting?" Karl prompted.

"I don't know, I'm not an expert in chanting styles!" Stefan snapped. "A sort of drone, like monks murmuring a prayer."

"A magic ritual?"

"I thought you didn't believe in magic."

"I don't, but we already know that some humans can perceive and manipulate the Crystal Ring," said Karl. "We know the bone-knives are harmful to us. I don't find the term 'magic' helpful, because it explains nothing, but Reiniger evidently has a stash of these weapons with power over us. What else?"

Stefan dropped his head. He pushed Charlotte's hand away. "I can clean myself. Please, wash Niklas."

She obeyed, fetching the water jug and sponging Niklas's bloodied torso with gentle care.

"I don't know," Stefan went on. "I must have lost consciousness – like Charlotte, the time she was stabbed in the street? Everything was a nightmare of pain and blood and the awful chanting. I don't know if they meant to kill us both. They didn't go so far as to decapitate us, obviously. At one point they seemed to be putting sheets over us, like tiny shrouds – perhaps I dreamed that part. I suddenly came back to myself. They were gone, and I was in this horrible mess, and Niklas – I crawled to his side but I already knew he was dead."

"Were you calling for help?" Charlotte asked.

"Yes! Screaming!"

"We heard you in the Crystal Ring," she said, distressed. "That's what brought us here."

"Too late," Stefan moaned. "Not your fault – I couldn't start shouting until the men had gone. Couldn't make a sound."

Charlotte sat back on her heels. The rag dripped watered blood on to her dress. "Karl? Look at this."

He went to examine Niklas's outstretched, alabaster body. His wounds were red lines on the white flesh from his neck to his groin. Each slash intersected with the next to form a pattern.

Some kind of glyph, with an oval at the centre like a primitive face with closed eyes.

A ritual sigil, with a word carved roughly in Arabic across his heart: the same word as on the bone-knife handle.

Istilqa.

"Dear God," said Karl. "This is my fault."

"What?" Stefan looked stunned. "Your fault, how in hell—?"

"Last night, Reiniger asked me to turn him into a vampire. I refused. This is his revenge."

The men of the *Eidgenossen* sat in the kitchen drinking beer as dawn broke. They were subdued, shocked. Even Wolfgang barely said a word. Their exhilaration and gleeful bloodlust had faded into this dreary aftermath, as if they'd survived a battle and walked away from a field of corpses.

Godric left them to it.

First he went to the meeting chamber, carefully cleaned each *sikin* in turn and put it back in its correct pigeonhole. One was still missing. His own, he kept in his trouser pocket as usual. He locked the cabinet. Stifling, he threw off his jacket and worked in blood-spattered shirt-sleeves. He took the two pieces of blood-imprinted linen to a dais at the far end of the chamber and pegged each one to an art easel.

He moved the two easels until he was satisfied with their position: angled slightly inwards, flanking the place where he usually stood to address the *Eidgenossen*.

Godric felt nothing as he did this. He too was in shock. His own increasing power stunned him. The meeting chamber had no windows, and his nerves were not ready to endure bright electric light, so all he had was a candle. In the near-darkness, a white shape drifted in front of him. The woman made of mist again, his *Weisse Frau*.

Every hair stood up on his neck. She was from the hidden world, a goddess, and the fact he could see her meant that he was moving ever closer to his dream. He put out his hand and she drifted towards him. Her ectoplasmic form enveloped his forearm until he was reaching up to his wrist through her ribcage. It felt like plunging his hand into heavy rain.

He was horrified, but didn't pull back. This was fascinating. There was no emotion in her face, but she fixed him with blank, beautiful eyes and he recognised her.

She looked exactly like Karl's companion from the party. Charlotte.

Wolfgang had whispered urgently in his ear that she was the *strigoi* who had nearly killed him, who'd been stabbed by the unlamented Bruno. Godric had done nothing at the time, apart from telling Wolfgang to ignore her. What was there to do?

He already knew things about her, from Fadiya and others: her name, and that she was the stranger who'd helped Amy home, that she was friendly with Violette Lenoir, and apparently Karl's lover – possibly married to him, if vampires bothered with such human conventions. But Godric had never spoken to her, so why was she here?

Has she come for revenge? he thought.

At the party she'd appeared golden, warm and talkative. Close to Karl, and close to Madame Lenoir... Did Violette know what her friends were? Should he warn her? He hadn't spoken to the ballerina about filming the ballet after all. With all that happened afterwards, it no longer seemed to matter.

Now this Charlotte was more like... what? A spectre? Perhaps she really was from the faerie folk: she could well be both elf and vampire. The very word *Alp* was used for such a demon. Did she mean to harm him? How could you defend yourself against an apparition made of mist? Even his *sikin* would not harm her...

Or would it? She'd been solid when Bruno attacked her. Perhaps she'd even kept the missing knife? Godric was puzzled, terrified, excited.

"Can you speak?" he said, drawing his hand free.

The *Weisse Frau* only stood looking at him, frozen like a single frame of film. His fingers were numb, but he moved closer and cautiously touched her again. His fingertips found her palm. He twisted his hand around, sliding it into the same space as hers, so that her chilly flesh enfolded his like a glove...

Then he understood.

Of course it was not Charlotte. It was an *Alp* that had taken on her likeness. Or – the goddess herself, Frau Perchta, had chosen this disguise. But why? *Unless, unless...* his nervous excitement grew. *I willed her into being with my new powers. I called her to me! This is Perchta herself, submitting entirely to my will!*

Then she vanished.

Godric started, glaring at the empty space where she'd been. His heightened senses told him that she'd disappeared because Fadiya had entered the room, and was standing behind him.

Slowly, calmly he turned to face her.

"Did you see that?" he asked.

"What?"

"Some kind of spectre," he said with a small hint of humour. "Apparently I can see into the otherworld."

"I'm happy for you," she said in her soft, sardonic tone. "You can expect to see all sorts of strange beings."

"You do not seem very interested." Privately he was glad that Fadiya hadn't seen the *Weisse Frau*. The less she knew of his business, the better. He felt the invigorating buzz of the twins' blood sacrifice inside him and thought, *Fadiya is going to tell me nothing but it doesn't matter, I can work all this out for myself now.*

"I don't have time to be interested," she said. "I'm leaving."

He asked why but she gave no answer. Her glance took in his pallid face and blood-spotted shirt, the glyph-patterned linens drying on easels. Her nostrils flared a little, as if she'd noticed the scent of the twins' blood.

Then she raised both hands to his face, placing her fingers lightly on his cheeks. Godric endured her touch, cool against his tingling-hot skin.

"What are you?" she asked. Her eyes paled from brown to green. A small frown dented her serene expression. "I'm seeing... something not human, but not vampire either. What have you done to yourself?"

He looked down at the backs of his own hands, spreading his fingers. They looked translucent. Like a vampire's hands, but with no blood in the veins, only pure energy. No longer could he ask Dr Ochsner, *Are you sure this is not some illness?* All he had left was his own judgement.

"I don't know," he said. "That is what I wish to find out."

She let her arms fall to her sides and stepped back. "I told you the *sakakin* are powerful."

"You did," Godric said, and smiled.

"Be respectful in how you use them. Call on the name—"

"Of Zruvan, Lord of Immortals. Yes. We always do. I have the utmost reverence for them, Frau Fadiya, but perhaps…" He thought better of continuing, *We won't need the knives much longer*, in case she demanded them back immediately.

"If you've something more to tell me, please be brief. I have to go."

"I did something foolish last night." He confessed on impulse because there was no one else he could tell. "I asked Karl to transform me into a vampire."

Her black eyebrows rose. "Why?"

"A moment of weakness. It made sense at the time. I thought that if Karl transformed me, I'd learn the truth, but I don't think he *knows* the truth. That's why he refused. He's afraid. I think I'm already a creature beyond his knowledge, a new being. Does this change mean power or death?"

"You never asked me to transform you," said Fadiya, mock-hurt.

"Would you have done it?"

"No, but that's not the point. Why him and not me?"

"Because Karl is… exceptional. Also, he is male. A female *strigoi's* power might only be a feeble echo. Not good enough."

Fadiya gave him a long, glassy-cold stare. Her irises went nearly white, making her look demonic. She laughed.

"Well, I am sorry I was not good enough for you, Godric. What is it between you and Karl, really? Are you in love with him?"

"No! I hate him!"

The raw words spilled out of him by reflex. He began shaking with rage.

Fadiya only shrugged. "You can hate someone with all your heart and yet still want to bed them."

He drew the *sikin* from its sheath in his pocket and threw it straight at her throat. Didn't stop to think, simply hurled the weapon, lightning-fast and accurate, like a knife-thrower…

Not accurate. Fadiya slipped to one side and the *sikin* hissed through the air, clattered and skidded along the marble floor. They stood wordless. His breath was quick and shallow, her eyes wide.

"Did you just try to kill me?" she said softly. "Is that how you react to truths you don't want to hear? Do not damage the *sakakin*. I still want them back, in time."

"You don't understand." Godric tried to master the shaky growl of his voice. "If Karl transformed me, that would make me his equal. Then the connection between us would enable me to *use* him. To absorb his energy. Ultimately to make him my servant, my abject slave. I grow stronger as he grows weaker, you see. I want him in my power, and powerless. He'd never even know what I planned until it was too late. I would suck all his strength, blood and life force out of him and make it my own, leaving him a corpse, a husk…"

"You've made things very clear," she said, putting up her palms to stop him.

"Good."

"And that is really what you want?"

"Yes," he said thinly. He'd told her too much, but was past caring. "I'll have to find a different way, but my revenge on Karl is also the key to unlocking my plans. A simple equation."

"And I believe you have the strength to do it," said Fadiya, coming too close again, as if he had not just thrown a blade at her. "Don't be angry with me, Godric. I said we would help each other, and we have. I am going to give you Karl."

"How?"

"By taking away everyone who might protect him."

"I don't see how or why…"

She laughed. Her eyes darkened, going brown and soft like a doe's. "You know a vampire when you meet one, don't you? You know about Karl, and his lady friend Charlotte who is not so ladylike, and the blond twins, and me?"

He nodded, mindful of the pale glow around his hands and his strange new hyperawareness of the world. He would soon be able to see into other dimensions, into people's *minds*. Gods and goddesses would come at his bidding.

"But did you notice Violette Lenoir?"

Fadiya's words floored him. Everything changed again.

"*She* is a vampire?"

"She hides it well, doesn't she? But she's no ordinary one, Godric. If you reach your new state of power, she would be the *only* one capable of stopping you, I promise. But she won't be here."

"Why not? Why do you care about this? Why are you so interested in helping me?"

Fadiya looked up at the ceiling and gave a long, quiet sigh.

"I *don't* care, Godric. I could not care less about your life or your plans, nor about Karl or anyone else. But you'll be of great help to me, by keeping Karl occupied."

"I see." He felt a small spark of elation. "You keep Violette away from me, and I keep Karl away from you?"

"Exactly so." She gave a faint smile, as if relieved he'd finally understood. "I wish you luck in your ambitions: use every weapon you find, use everything *as* a weapon. You're ingenious enough. But all I care about... is Violette."

The sea was like blue silk as their ferry left the French coast, sun casting a glorious misty light across the swell. The golden light made Emil nostalgic for his childhood.

Secretly he was terrified of the sea voyage ahead. His fear stemmed from the Atlantic storm, when he'd thought that both he and Violette were going to drown. However, pride would not let him admit his phobia to Fadiya. Instead he pushed all doubt to the back of his mind, not allowing himself to think or feel anything. He trusted his future to her.

The night had been a long ordeal of trains and taxis. He'd slept through part of it, convinced that Fadiya was no longer with him, waking to realise her absence must have been a dream. Now they were sailing towards the North African coast. Too late to turn back.

The voyage would take over a day. In daylight, the sea was calm, idyllic. He basked on deck in the sun, thinking, *I've made the right choice. I can be happy with Fadiya. This is the only thing to do.*

As night fell, the sea grew choppy under the dark arch of the sky. The ship – far smaller than the great liner on which he'd sailed with the Ballet Lenoir – began to rear and buck, plunging like a raging sea serpent. Waves crashed over the prow, flooding the deck, receding like a foaming tide.

Emil had no idea whether he was awake or dreaming. In a trance he struggled across the treacherous deck, desperate to save Violette from the skull-headed sorcerer, Kastchei. Although he was helpless with terror, the stoical part of his mind drove him on. He was doomed to relive this over and over again. This was his fate. There was nothing to do but accept it and fight on.

This time the white gelatinous apparition of the sorcerer vanished into the storm. And the woman he caught in his arms was not Violette, but Fadiya. Her face was expressionless but her eyes were huge with fear, no longer soft brown but white as bone. He seized her as the ship capsized and flung them both into the abyss.

They were sinking through darkness. He was drowning. Falling, falling. Blackness suffocated him... he couldn't breathe yet his consciousness persisted. A succubus held him down, like the hag of death, and he felt the last of his life force concentrated in his groin, in a single blunt point of agonising lust...

Fadiya was on top of him, riding him, gasping her ecstasy. Even as he fell backwards into the chasm, he spilled himself into her, as if dying of pleasure. As if sex and death were natural siblings...

Then she bit his throat.

He fought. He was all blind instinct, with no coherent thoughts left. But she held him down like a dead weight and he felt his blood being sucked into the vacuum of her mouth, blood leaving him with every beat of his heart.

His whole world was hot darkness, roaring with the close sound of his pulse and her heavy animal breathing. The roar of the sea was far away, indistinguishable from the rushing sounds in his ears.

She rose above him. A faint glow outlined her body and he saw her head thrown back, her features distorted with savage, triumphant pleasure. Drops of his own blood fell on to his chest from her lips.

And he *saw*.

She was the same as Violette and Charlotte and Karl. She had the same hypnotically seductive, evil glow. They were vampires, demons... and so was Fadiya. How had she concealed it? And he knew she'd done this before, but his memory had blurred the event so that he rationalised it and then forgot…

"I love you, Emil," she hissed, with blood still trickling from her lips and her eyes glowing a ghastly jade-green in the darkness. "You're mine forever. No going back."

He groaned. Horror suffocated him and he had no breath left to cry for help. He lay paralysed beneath her. He went on falling backwards through the dark waves. Down and down, until sleep or unconsciousness claimed him… a black, watery, smothering world full of writhing serpents.

Stefan's grief was unbearable to witness. When he went quiet, though – that was when Charlotte became gravely concerned.

She took him upstairs and told him to undress and bathe. He did as she asked, to her relief: she had no intention of manhandling him as if he were a recalcitrant child. The old Stefan would have teased her and made off-colour jokes about the situation. The new one was as blank as Niklas. He gazed into the middle distance without blinking.

While he lay silent, up to his chin in warm water, she tore up a sheet to make bandages. In a way she was treating him as she would a distraught, injured human. She had no idea what else to do.

Searching in the wardrobe for a fresh suit, she couldn't tell which clothes were his and which were Niklas's. There was two of everything, identical. She chose a plain outfit: dark-grey suit and waistcoat, white shirt, navy-blue tie.

He didn't stir from the bath until she called him, ten minutes later, and averted her eyes as she held a towel for him. How pointless it seemed to worry about embarrassment at a time like this. She did so anyway, from ingrained instinct.

As the towel touched his flesh, he winced.

Charlotte led him into the nearby bedroom and made him sit on the bed while she looked at the cuts Reiniger's gang had made in his flesh. She flinched to see the horrible pattern of slashed lines, each one made with apparent careless anger, yet forming a symbol. A mark of occult significance, she was certain, or at least a coded message. If nothing else, the rune conveyed utter contempt and menace.

Like the stab wound she'd suffered, his cuts were not healing.

"Darling, sit still. I'm going to bandage you to protect the injuries until they start to knit."

"Do as you wish," he muttered. "I don't care."

"Well, I do."

Carefully she wrapped the cotton strips around his torso. Stefan was like an image of male perfection from a painting: slim, with just enough muscle not to appear boyish. *I'd cheerfully strangle whoever wantonly disfigured such angelic beauty.*

"Who could do such a thing?" she said under her breath. "Someone jealous, perhaps. Or hell-bent on destroying a vampire. But if Reiniger wants to become one of us, that doesn't fit. So, he was taking revenge, as Karl said. Or – by means we don't understand – he was intent on stealing your strength."

"That's four perfectly good reasons." Stefan gave a humourless laugh. "How have I survived this long?"

She knotted the bandage and slipped a clean shirt over his shoulders. "Get dressed," she said.

"What's the point?" His eyes lost focus again. She controlled an urge to shake him.

"The point is…" She sighed. "Stefan, if we were human I would have brought you a cup of tea or some brandy, I would have called the police and the doctor, but I can't do any of that. This is the next best thing. Putting on clean clothes may not help, but neither will staggering around covered in blood!"

"You're right. Nothing will help."

"Just do as I say."

Stefan gave a weak grimace and obeyed. In shirt and trousers, he picked up the tie, only to fling it across the room. He threw it so hard that it caught a candlestick, which fell to the floor with a thud. The tie slithered after it like a snake.

"What—?"

"That's Niklas's tie!" he rasped. "How could you? I cannot wear that, it's *his*! I can't…"

He sat rigid, head bowed, fists pressed to his knees.

"I'm sorry," she said. "Everything looked the same, I couldn't tell the difference."

"Well, I can."

At a loss, Charlotte stood blotting hot tears from her eyes. She groped for the right words, the right gesture to help him... but there was nothing she could say, nothing at all.

She'd thought she knew Stefan. Seeing him now, she realised she did not know him at all.

"I need to be with Niklas," he said dully.

"Come on, then." She held out her hand. "Let's go back down. Stefan, I know what Karl said, but please don't hold him to blame for this."

"Charlotte, I don't blame Karl. But the bastard who killed Niklas – the Devil had better be making a place ready for him in hell."

In the lake room, Karl had covered the body with a white quilt and placed a lit candle on the carpet above the crown of his head. He knelt beside Niklas as if keeping vigil.

Stefan went in slowly and knelt on the other side. He looked stricken.

"I hoped I'd find this had all been a dream," he murmured. "Or a practical joke."

"I'm so sorry," said Karl.

Stefan felt under the quilt and took his brother's hand. "He feels like frozen wax. I think he'd shatter if I struck him. Was he ever truly alive?"

"That's hard to answer," Karl said gently. "I still maintain that what Kristian did was evil, and that the *doppelgängers* he made were a crime against nature. Mine was certainly dangerous. Stefan, I had no choice but to destroy it. But one thing I learned, which you already know, is that because they have no intelligence, they are fragile. Our strength and life force emanates from the mind, not the body. How many times have you fled from danger, in order to protect Niklas?"

Stefan nodded, dropped his head. "Every time."

"He couldn't even feed without your help," Karl went on, his voice kind but firm. "I believe that's why the attack killed him, while you survived. Reiniger probably intended to slaughter you both. I doubt he had any idea that you were so tough and Niklas so delicate. And I suspect that, even if we immersed Niklas in blood for a year, if hundreds of humans perished in that enterprise, it still would not bring him back. Because he is only a copy. He is not *you*."

Stefan collapsed again, clinging to his twin. Charlotte put her arms around his shoulders, kissing his hair – as if that could make the slightest difference. It was all she could offer.

Karl added, "Of course, if you decide to take his body somewhere secret and do exactly that, I can't stop you. But I won't help you."

Very slowly, Stefan extracted himself from Charlotte's embrace and sat cross-legged beside her. He rubbed his tears away, heaved a soul-wrenching sigh.

"I'm not going to do that, Karl. I know you're right. It wouldn't work. Not because you've told me, but because I simply *know* inside that this is the end. Niklas has no life force we can revive, because he had no soul in the first place. Why am I crying? It's as ridiculous as weeping over my reflection in a mirror."

Stefan put his head in his hands. Charlotte watched his shoulders shaking, tears dripping between his fingers, and her heart broke.

"We'll stay with you," said Karl.

"For how long?" Stefan said, his voice savage but muffled. "How do we plan a funeral for a vampire? A vampire who never even existed?"

"We'll stay for as long as it takes," Karl replied.

Charlotte felt a raging thirst for fresh air. The heavy atmosphere of grief and blood was hard to endure. She got up, opened the doors to the veranda and went outside. There she stood gazing across the lake, breathing the sweet air that swept down off the Alpine tundra. Let air into the chalet, until all stale traces of the party were blown away. The bright blue sky and water seemed to mock her.

Nothing would cleanse the scent of Niklas's blood.

Behind her, she heard the occasional muffled moan from Stefan. The noises he emitted were quiet but full of anguish, like an injury so painful he could barely move.

What now?

Neither Karl nor Stefan would rest until Godric Reiniger paid for this. For that matter, neither would she.

And yet... Karl was right. Godric had a power over vampires that they didn't understand. And he had a very particular grudge against Karl. Was it really worth risking their lives to challenge him, when the safest option was simply to vanish?

The air stirred. Violette made a startling appearance on the balcony beside her, as if taking shape from a swirl of frost.

Her long fur-lined coat swung about her like a cloak. Beneath it she was in her practice clothes and her pinned-up hair was coming adrift into a tangle. She swung round to Charlotte and gripped her arms.

"Here you are! Thank goodness – why didn't you come home? Not that it matters, you can go where you like, but I wish I'd found you sooner. Something appalling has happened... Charlotte?"

She stared at Violette, not comprehending why she was so agitated – unless she, too, had heard Stefan's cry of anguish through the ether.

"Yes," Charlotte said faintly, nodding towards the open doorway. "In there."

"Emil is in there?"

Violette's nails dug in, hurting. Charlotte recoiled from her wild expression.

"What? No. It's Niklas... What about Emil?"

CHAPTER NINETEEN

THE LEMON GARDEN

Emil and Fadiya disembarked from the ship in Algiers. The city looked vast, with salt-white buildings curving around the bay and mounting the hills beyond. Boats crowded the harbour. The streets were hectic with tourists, folk in local dress, French soldiers. Motor cars, buses, cranes loading and unloading ships – naively, he hadn't expected the city to be so modern, so frantically busy. Emil shaded his eyes, looking up at huge government buildings, law courts, mosques and hotels, monuments, even a casino.

The air was hot, sunlight turning the streets to a misty golden otherworld. In childhood Emil had enjoyed the hot sun on his back, but years working in France and Switzerland had made him used to a temperate climate. The heat was a physical assault.

He felt weak, confused, as if succumbing to sunstroke. Aware that his mind wasn't functioning normally, he couldn't break out of the hot, dusty fog. His recollection of the voyage was patchy. The little he remembered filled him with dread.

Hallucinations of the ship capsizing, being dragged under the waves. All mixed up with images of entwining with Fadiya, delirious with lust even as he suffocated beneath her. Fangs stabbing into his throat and all his strength leeching away…

She had sucked blood from his veins. Not for the first time. And there was nothing he could do to stop her. He hadn't even tried, as if she'd injected him with some intoxicating, deadly narcotic.

Fadiya *was* the drug. Now he was completely in her power – and worse, he knew it.

She'd stolen his strength and his willpower, left him in a dizzy trance like an opium haze, with no hope of escape. A far part of his mind was screaming for help, but no one could hear. Fadiya was his only anchor in this alien world.

"Please don't pass out," she said sharply. "We mustn't attract attention."

"It's so hot."

"This isn't hot." She laughed. "The *desert* is hot. This is a lovely spring day."

"Where are we going?" he asked as they climbed a tree-lined avenue of French-colonial architecture. She carried his bag. His mouth was so parched, he could barely speak.

"Towards Al Qasbah," she said, smiling benignly. "The old citadel. To my friends. It's not far."

"I need water."

"Just a few minutes more. Their house is cool and they'll give us local clothing so that we blend in. Don't worry, dearest Emil. I know you're tired, but this is our new beginning."

"You drank my blood."

"My dear, you gave it willingly, out of love," she replied warmly. "Don't you remember?"

"You drank my blood!" he rasped. The effort of speaking made his head reel. She caught his arm to steady him.

"I couldn't help it. It's a gesture of love, and you are so beautiful." Her face glowed. The light behind her shone like a bright halo.

"I'm ill. I want to go home."

"You are home, my love," she replied. "Your home is where I am. You're mine and I'm yours. Just a little further and then you can rest."

She led him past mosques and cafés, churches and noisy markets, into labyrinthine lanes where the newer town gave way to the old. A few minutes, she said, but the walk seemed to take hours. As they climbed steep flights of steps, his sight turned black and he resigned himself to collapsing, perhaps dying in the street. He didn't even care…

Eventually she knocked on a door in a blank, high wall that

seemed to extend for miles, like a prison wall. The small carved door swung open.

Soft voices murmured around him in a language he didn't understand. A handful of men and women were welcoming Fadiya and Emil inside. He caught an impression of loose garments in shades of blue, green, rose pink. Smiling faces... all as lovely and as sinister as Fadiya herself. There were men and women, some dark-skinned and others pale. He heard a mixture of languages and accents. Snatches of French, Arabic, Italian, German...

They led him through a shaded ante-room into a courtyard with a fountain at the centre. On all four sides there were walkways lined with pillars and elegant arches shaped to recall minarets, upper galleries with doors to inner rooms, only half-seen through masses of foliage. He glimpsed screens of dark wood pierced with intricate patterns, large filigree lamps in the Moroccan style set with jewel colours, striped cushions and rugs. Every surface was tiled in white and blue, heavy with geometric decoration. Plants spilled from containers, filling the space with greenery and fragrant flowers. The cool air rising from the fountain misted their leaves and petals.

Around this area drifted figures in flowing djellabas.

Someone sat him down on a tiled bench and began to fan him. A glass of liquid was held to his lips: sweet mint tea. He drank it so fast he barely tasted it. A woman in red refilled the glass from an elaborate teapot. A black man, dressed in vibrant sky blue, gave him a tray of fruit, cheese and olives.

Sweet, salty, juicy... the tastes of his childhood home.

Where was Fadiya? After a moment his eyes focused and he saw her, kissing all the strangers in turn as if greeting long-lost relatives. They bowed their heads to her. The interplay of grace and colour was hypnotic. He breathed the scent of jasmine.

Emil had never seen a place so peaceful and beautiful. It was like a small palace built inside out: featureless from the outside, with all the rooms facing inwards around an exquisite garden. A *riad* in the most luxurious Moroccan style. There were lemon trees, fig trees, bushes spilling flowers of white, yellow and pale apricot. Figures moved along the galleries above. He saw a passageway leading through to another courtyard. The filtered golden light was enticing, promising a hidden paradise.

"So this is the creature in question?" the black man said in English.

"This is him, Nabil." Fadiya spoke with pride in her voice. She knelt at Emil's feet, her hands on his knees. "What do you think? Isn't he beautiful?"

"Absolutely magnificent," Nabil replied with a smile. His ebony skin had its own glow, as if brushed with blue iridescence. His eyes shone with powerful serenity, like a painting of a saint looking up to heaven. Like Karl's eyes. And yet... all Emil felt from the inhabitants was menace.

The contrast of tranquil beauty and peril overwhelmed him. He couldn't move. Even if he tried to escape, he knew these people would kill him before he reached the outer doors.

They were all vampires.

"He's famous in the outer world," she said. "He's a great dancer."

"Famous?" Nabil echoed. "Is that not a risk?"

"Yes, but that is the point. Who would care that he's gone, if he were not valuable?"

Valuable?

"Fadiya..." He tried to speak, couldn't form a coherent question. *You brought me here as your lover. Why are you discussing value? Talking as if I were a stranger?*

She ignored his plea. Addressing Nabil, she asked, "Is everything ready?"

"As soon as you are, Fadiya." He gave a small bow. His eyes, when he looked at Emil, gleamed with hunger, or lust. Both. Emil nearly stopped breathing.

"Good. We need to make haste. I posted a letter to her before we left port. When she receives it, she will find us within a day or so. You *must* delay her. Don't underestimate her: she's clever, fast and lethal. She is a goddess."

"Fadiya?" Emil forced the words out, his voice dry as sand. "What the hell is happening? Where are we going?"

"Rest, darling," she murmured as if to a child. "Sleep in the shade while you can. We have another journey to make, but there's nothing to worry about. Rest."

* * *

Violette looked down at Niklas's body, dry-eyed. Although she didn't weep, her shock was palpable. As Charlotte repeated Stefan's story, she stood motionless, a figure carved from quartz.

"This must be connected with Emil," Violette said eventually. She'd given a short account of his disappearance, shown Karl and Charlotte the letter he'd left. "Fadiya worked for Reiniger. According to Karl, he knew she was a vampire, but he couldn't or wouldn't explain why she was with him. Something to do with the *Istilqa* knives? I don't know."

"Your precious Emil!" Stefan, seated beside Niklas, sprang to his feet. "He's run away with his lady friend, that's all. Niklas is the one who's dead! Why try to tangle this with your problems? You think my brother is less important than Emil?"

Karl put a hand on Stefan's arm, but he shook him off.

"Weren't you listening?" Violette's voice was low, shaky. "Emil's lady friend is a vampire."

"And the bastards who sliced Niklas to pieces were human!" Stefan retorted. "So what?"

"Fadiya knows those bastards," Violette said with quiet emphasis. "Stefan, I am sorry about your brother, but he is dead, and Emil is still alive and in danger. I must find him. I came to ask for Charlotte and Karl's help, because I've already spent hours searching. He's gone without trace."

"Perhaps you should not have forbidden them to see each other," Stefan said acidly.

"I may not be free of blame, but I was trying to protect him."

Charlotte parted her lips, hesitating as she wondered what to say first. "We want to help you, of course, but we can't leave Stefan in this state…"

"Did you try Bergwerkstatt?" Karl spoke over the end of her words. "Reiniger might know where she is. She may know about the bone-knives. She might have given them to him, for all we know."

"Why?" said Charlotte.

"If we knew that, we could be halfway to solving this puzzle," said Karl.

"Yes, I tried the house," said Violette, "but only from the

outside. Something stopped me going in: a bad feeling, an aura. I could have burned my way through, but I sensed humans inside and I could tell none was Emil. They wouldn't hide somewhere so obvious, would they? Fadiya didn't live there, anyway. She had the room at Hotel Blauensee – unless that was just somewhere to take victims." Violette sounded contemptuous. "I checked her hotel room, but her belongings had gone. She and Emil are long gone from the town, and probably from Switzerland by now. I couldn't trace his presence *at all*, so she must be shielding him in some way. I sent Thierry and a handful of others I trust to ask around in case anyone saw them leaving, but there's no news, nothing. We've told everyone else that Emil is ill, but I can't keep the truth secret much longer. I appreciate that you can't leave Stefan, but if you three can't help me, who can?"

She went on staring at Niklas's waxen face, as if trying to see inside him. Charlotte knew how fiercely independent Violette was. She never asked for help unless she was desperate.

"Well, isn't this a little hypocritical?" said Stefan. "Charlotte did not *want* to be rescued from Karl. When her brother David tried, the consequences were disastrous, to say the least."

"When Charlotte made off with *me* –" Violette gave her a pointed look "– no one at all came to my rescue. And Stefan, you know the state I was in after the transformation. You were there."

"But you recovered."

"That's one word for it." Violette's eyes were flint, Stefan's like blue fire in the bloodshot whites. "It was a long, horrifying experience that I wouldn't wish on anyone. And I don't trust Fadiya. I don't care what her intentions are. No vampire is ever good for a human."

"Or vice versa," said Stefan. His usually perfect hair was a bird's nest, damp with tears. Charlotte was afraid they might start fighting, from sheer overcharged emotion.

"I must find Emil," Violette repeated. "If none of you can help, I'll go alone."

"We want to help, of course," said Karl, now on his feet. "I don't know whether his disappearance is connected to Reiniger, because he claimed he knew nothing of Fadiya's motives. And he appeared genuinely shocked when I warned him that Amy was in danger."

"Godric could have been lying," said Violette.

"But if he knew, why not ask *her* to help transform him, rather than me?"

"Perhaps she refused, too. Perhaps Godric was angry with her, and that's why she fled with Emil."

"Violette, you know full well that she fled because *we* threatened her," Charlotte put in. "You expected her to obey you when you forbade her to see Emil. She didn't."

"I know," said Violette. "But if Fadiya had an argument with Reiniger, it can't have helped. But why would she, a vampire, fear him?"

Karl spread a hand to indicate Niklas beneath his white shroud. "Because Reiniger has the power to do this. Not all humans are weaker than us. We should know that by now."

The dancer gave a reluctant nod. "They hold power over us in many different ways. Violence is one thing, but love is the most dangerous of all."

Charlotte touched her arm, but Violette, like Stefan, was too brittle to be consoled.

"Dear, you know I want to help," said Charlotte, "but I can't leave Stefan like this. I can't be in two places at once." She thought of her lamia, and shuddered. "Well, sometimes I can, apparently, but the spectral half of me is malevolent, deaf to reason and completely useless."

"I think we should all stay together," said Karl. "If Reiniger and his gang attacked Stefan and Niklas as revenge, there's nothing to stop them coming back and attacking the rest of us. They have weapons and skills we don't understand. We're all in danger."

Charlotte, startled, met his intense amber stare.

"This is a warning. This is just the start," she said. "But – the start of what? Does he think this will persuade us to make him and all his friends into vampires? He must be mad."

"A little knowledge is dangerous," said Karl. "Godric may think it's easy to bully us into creating a small vampire army for him. He wants to be powerful, superior to all the humans around him. He muttered about awakening Woden and all the Swiss heroes of legend. He intends to be godlike: he said as much. However, he doesn't know what happened when that maniac Cesare tried a similar plan. Carnage. He doesn't understand that the Crystal Ring itself may not accept him."

"Well, here's a thought." Stefan's voice was savage. "Let's go up to Bergwerkstatt. Let's pretend we agree to help, begin the transformation and simply kill them all!"

Karl walked to the windows, silent in thought. He folded his arms. "It's a possibility. But, Stefan, I am not taking you near anyone while you're mad with grief."

"Then lock me up, because I can't stop being mad with grief!"

"I will, if I have to," Karl replied. Charlotte saw he was serious. "You realise that Reiniger will be *expecting* us to confront him? He'll be ready. We don't know how many bone-knives he has, but it's obvious he'll lay plans to ambush us. He could torture or kill us all if we try to sabotage his aim. Even if we escape, we'll have made an enemy with terrible, unknown powers. I've no intention of putting you, Charlotte or Violette in such peril."

"I cannot do *nothing*!" Stefan growled. "I've never been one for conflict. But this is different, everything's changed – if I've lost Niklas, I've nothing else to lose. If you won't come with me, I'll go to Reiniger alone and I will drain him to a husk and hear him scream for mercy before he dies."

"Don't," said Karl. "Godric Reiniger has a very particular grudge against *me*. Stefan, don't…"

Stefan ignored him. His eyes were manic. Suddenly animated, he strode to a desk, unlocked a drawer and took out the *Istilqa* knife, wrapped in its black scarf.

Godric was so close to his lost weapon, thought Charlotte, *and didn't know*.

"I'll take my chance," Stefan said, glaring at the others. He had the wild stare of someone in a red mist of rage and anguish, beyond reason. He strode away, half-fading into the Crystal Ring as he went – only to collapse.

He lay face down on the carpet, groaning. Karl and Charlotte rushed to him, but he was barely sensible. Blood seeped through his shirt from the bandages beneath. He moaned in pain, sobbing. Incoherently he raged, his voice barely a whisper.

"Dearest, your wounds," Charlotte said gently. "You're in no state to go anywhere. Hush."

He didn't respond. She looked at Karl's grim face, then at Violette.

"You definitely can't leave him," the dancer said gently. As Karl and Charlotte lifted Stefan on to the couch, she added, "Forgive me, I have to go. First to the academy to see if there's any news – also to create a schedule to keep everyone busy while I'm away. I'll come back later."

Charlotte began wishing her good luck, but Violette was already gone with a silvery shiver of the air.

Stefan lay muttering on the couch, eyes closed. Now and then his back arched in pain. Charlotte fetched a blanket to place over him, but he threw it off. Patiently she covered him again. To see him like this was unbearable.

"What are we going to do?" she asked Karl. "I feel like marching on Reiniger's house, too, but as you say, it would be senseless."

Stefan had dropped the scarf and bone-dagger on the floor. Karl bent to pick it up. He seated himself in an armchair and unwrapped the weapon. Even from feet away, Charlotte felt its unpleasant emanation tingling on her skin. The glow felt cold, disturbing, lethal. It emitted a vibration below the level of hearing that made her dizzy.

Karl handled it with bare hands. She knew how uncomfortable that was. A couple of times he flexed his fingers, as if the haft made them numb.

"What are you doing?" she asked. "God, the smell of that thing, like musty old caves and sour metal – it was on Bruno, and Wolfgang, and all Reiniger's men."

"And strongly on Godric himself," said Karl. "They're using the knives to protect themselves against us. But how? By stabbing the blades into their own veins?"

Charlotte went quiet, caught up in a series of images. A subterranean tunnel, soaked in the ghostly pain of hundreds of murdered souls: the lair of an unknown medieval vampire who'd hoarded their skeletons in a secret crypt. Eventually the raging vacuum created by their deaths had, in turn, drained that vampire's life force.

She recalled the book he'd left behind: a ledger containing all their names and how they had died. The pages were so deeply soaked in death and anguish that the book in itself had become inimical to vampires.

It had held a form of karma, cosmic justice. *Whatever is stolen must be paid back*, Charlotte thought. *When you create a vacuum, you create a fierce power that will eventually suck its lost matter back into itself.*

That was the elusive familiarity that plagued her.

"The Book," she said. "The Ledger of Death."

"What about it?" Karl poised the knife between his forefingers by the tip and the ruby pommel. "I destroyed it."

"Yes, but the knife reminds me of it. The feeling's been nagging me all along. The repellent scent and aura are so similar to the emanations from the Ledger of Death."

Karl was quiet for a moment, then said thoughtfully, "You're right. It's not identical, but close. If the handle is carved from human bone, it must be the bone of a vampire's victim."

"Who would make such a thing?"

Karl didn't answer. He rolled up his left shirt-sleeve and pressed the knife blade to the inside of his forearm.

"Karl, what are you doing?"

He was cutting into his own flesh. She rushed to stop him, not fast enough. In horror she watched the blade slide into the skin, from the elbow towards the wrist, a line of dark red pearls oozing out of the long vertical slit.

"Don't!" she gasped.

He placed the knife on the scarf beside him, and held Charlotte back with his right hand on her shoulder.

"The only way to get inside the knife is to let the blade inside *us*," he said calmly. "You were stabbed. So was Stefan. I need to go wherever it was you went."

She gave a strangled growl. "But I learned nothing! I had nightmares, I thought I'd split in two, I went mad for a few hours and threw Wolfgang through a window. Now Niklas is dead, Stefan delirious – how can this help? Karl, for pity's sake!"

"I don't believe that you learned *nothing*," he replied. "It's a matter of analysing our visions."

"Well?" She was trembling with anxiety. "How does it feel? The wound, I mean?"

Karl flexed his left hand. "Cold," he said. "*Liebling*, hold my hand. You were right, it is really extraordinarily painful."

She took his left hand between both her own. His fingers were icy. His whole hand felt heavy and nerveless, like wax. Then his head tipped back. His eyelids fluttered and came to rest half-open, looking at her – with no sign of awareness.

The first stab went through his ribs.

Karl was on a dark footpath that meandered through the bushes and trees of an unlit wild park. All was black. Even with his night-sensitive vision he could see only greyish shapes and the bright eyes of woodland creatures in the undergrowth. How could the man within his grasp see anything at all in the night? Perhaps he knew this route well enough to walk it in the pitch dark – but that confidence made him easy prey. Karl seized him and fed before the victim even knew he was there. He noted the expensive texture of the man's jacket and felt the rasp of a trimmed beard against his face as he relished the rich delicious blood of this healthy individual...

Then came the poison-cold blade between his ribs.

Karl felt the tip go right into his lung, felt the lung trying to heal itself but failing, as if acid on the blade were eating the tissues before they could mend. He froze in pain and complete astonishment.

No victim had ever retaliated before.

Not like this. Sometimes they struggled. And he'd been injured by other vampires often enough to know that this pain was extraordinary. First there was a flood of glacial cold, then all his strength went, followed by his consciousness...

The next he knew, he was inside a house.

A large room with heavy, traditional furniture pushed back against the walls. There were framed prints hung in neat rows: maps? Several faces stared down at him by the light of oil lamps and candles... five humans, all male, aged between twenty and forty. Each one held a dagger two-handed. Karl was flat on his back on a rug. His chest was bare, his shirt undone.

He couldn't see any chains holding him down and yet his limbs were pinned to the floor as if by huge rocks. He felt terrified but deadly calm.

This was one useful lesson he'd learned from his dread of Kristian: the art of remaining absolutely still and emotionless, despite being scared out of his wits.

In turn each man leaned down and drew a knife-blade across him: down his breastbone, across his chest, slashing diagonals across his abdomen. One cut each. Then they all bent down, each man holding a knife tip in the centre of the wound he'd made. The pain stung and froze and scorched. Karl felt all his power running out through the knives. He saw, or imagined, lines of glowing red mist flowing out of him and into the five men.

Their faces shone. They laughed.

"Stop!" said one, apparently the instigator. Smart suit, cropped dark hair and beard, pocket watch... this was the man he'd encountered in the park, who had stabbed him.

Now he appeared to be taking back the life-energy that Karl had stolen.

This made no sense. He couldn't speak to demand answers, could not even blink. Humans feeding upon vampires?

"Enough," the leader went on. "He's dead. He has nothing left. But you all felt that, didn't you? You all felt the power? Yes?"

Their laughter echoed horribly in Karl's head.

What happened next he couldn't remember.

Long afterwards, he pieced it together. Clearly they hadn't killed him. However, they had weighed him down with stones and dropped him into a lake, because that was where he regained consciousness, deep in obsidian water. Mired in silt, he discarded rocks from what was left of his clothing, crawled his way along the lake bottom and up a turbid rocky slope until he finally reached the shore.

How long did it take him to recover?

No one came to help. He went on all fours until he found a rock-face to support him, and then he walked until the scent of blood and warm, breathing life led him to a drunken man lying unconscious in an Alpine hut.

Weeks of delirium followed. Karl rested and fed when he could. A long time passed before he regained his full strength. The scars took even longer to heal, but at last they vanished and left his skin unblemished. Finally he found himself gasping with relief in a frosty pine forest as he realised he was well again; still not quite in his right mind, but full of controlled, fiery anger.

And that was why he had gone back to the house.

Somehow he'd remembered where it was, recalled the look and the odour of the place. He went back to find the bearded man and to kill him.

Godric Reiniger's father.

"Karl. Karl, beloved, please come back to me…"

Charlotte's voice reached him and he felt his consciousness returning, very slowly, as if he were a human surfacing through a fog of laudanum. He saw her lovely, worried face. He managed to blink – so at least she'd see he was alive – but speaking would take more effort yet.

Had he truly chosen Godric's father at random? The question had plagued him, ever since Reiniger had shown him the crude but horrifying movie scene.

He rarely entered houses. There were folk enough on the street to fulfil his needs. So why had he been inside the Reiniger household at all? Karl's recollection of the past was mostly crystal-sharp, so why had fog obscured those events?

Now he knew.

"Karl!" Charlotte gave him a shake. "Speak to me, you utter… *idiot*!"

He swallowed, managed to sit up in the chair. The room came into focus: outside, the sky was darkening to deep blue and lilac over the lake. Stefan curled on his side on the couch, clawing at thin air.

"I was unconscious," said Karl.

"I know! I've spent two hours trying to wake you."

"But we don't sleep. Not as humans do. How is it possible?"

"An effect of the bone-knife," she said, sitting back on her heels. "It happened to me, too, although I didn't realise until I woke up. You will need to feed. That might help Stefan, too, although I'm afraid he might be uncontrollable."

"Perhaps we could bring one of his friends to him." Karl sat forward, resting his elbows on his knees. He examined the cut he'd made. The bleeding had long stopped and the wound was clean. Apparently Charlotte had licked the blood away. The edges showed signs of healing, sensation was returning to his left hand.

"Karl, how do you feel?" She reached up and stroked his hair. "Was your experiment worth it?"

"I'm sorry, dearest. To do such a thing in front of you was not the brightest idea I've ever had, but it was an impulse. If I'd waited, I might never have dared try."

"Better than doing so in secret. I might have found you like Niklas." Her face lost colour. "You didn't throw anyone off a balcony, at least. Visions?"

He nodded. "Oh, yes. Better still: answers."

Pressing her hands between his, he told her everything he'd seen in his trance state. "What happened to Stefan – the symbol carved in his chest – the same thing was done to me, all those years ago. But I *forgot*. I knew I hadn't killed Reiniger's father for no reason. I went back to his house – I hesitate to say for revenge, though I must have been angry – to stop him doing the same to any other vampire. When I saw the boy watching me – Godric – I fled. So I didn't find out as much as I would have wished. However, I remember something about bone-knives in a sack, and maps framed on the walls... The details aren't clear. If his father was an explorer who unearthed the knives, that would explain how Reiniger came into possession of them. However, we still don't know where, or why."

"More questions than answers, then," said Charlotte.

"True. But I cannot believe I forgot the entire episode. I had no memory of it at all, until Reiniger himself reminded me. How could I have forgotten?"

"I forgot, too," said Charlotte. "The effect seems to wear off. I haven't forgotten a second time, but it's frightening. Weapons that can manipulate our consciousness, memory, strength, almost everything about us...?"

"In the hands of an egomaniac like Godric Reiniger."

"What are we going to do?"

"Just give in and do as he asks," Karl said flatly. "That is one option."

"I beg your pardon?" Charlotte glared, so indignant that he

almost laughed. "Give in and make him a vampire? Has the knife scrambled your mind as well as your memory? My Karl would never dream of giving in."

He smiled. "That's not strictly true. I'd do anything to protect you. Herr Reiniger does seem to have a particular fixation with me, for which I don't blame him."

"Nor do I. It's hardly modest of you to say so, but it is true."

"I meant a fixation because he saw me kill his father!" Karl shook his head at her. "Not what you seem to be suggesting."

"Oh." Her eyebrows rose. "Are you *sure*?"

"Completely."

"I'm not joking. Or only joking a little, but… well, you know him better than I do."

"And that's why I should be the one to deal with him. Since he's obsessed with me, my task is to keep his focus upon *me*, his enemy, and away from anyone else."

"You're not thinking of confronting him alone?"

"Yes. I have to. If I take anyone with me, they may get hurt."

Charlotte went quiet, biting her lower lip.

"I know you want to argue with me," he said.

"Of course I do, but it's pointless! I can't let you go on your own, but I can't dissuade you, can I? You know, perhaps all those other vampires were right: Cesare, Simon, even Kristian. We need a leader. To play devil's advocate for a moment: Karl, if you'd consented to lead them, you could have had a formidable army of supporters by now. Godric's gang would not stand a chance."

"Engaging in a bloody battle – how would that help? You know it's not in my nature. I've always fought for the right to a quiet life and privacy. Otherwise known as freedom. That will never change, beloved."

Preying on humans to live, he thought. *Such a way of life requires adjustments that not all vampires can make.* Compelling thirst for blood overrode conscience, but the changes in the psyche were more subtle. Some vampires shed their guilt completely. Others experienced blood-thirst as intense passion, affection, even love. The hunger had many tricks.

Karl had learned long ago to accept what he was, to take blood without guilt. Without violence or sadism, but also without mercy.

The transformative effect of Lilith's bite had made him less puritanical, more relaxed about choosing his prey. That didn't mean he would ever be a hedonist like Stefan, nor a gleeful predator like Pierre or Ilona. Certainly he would never be a tyrant like Kristian.

"If we have a leader at all, it's Violette," he said softly. "That's why she will always have enemies."

Charlotte began to say something about Reiniger. Her words were lost beneath Stefan's scream.

It was the most horrifying raw noise Karl had ever heard. Charlotte blanched. Stefan writhed on the couch, waking from his stupor and seeing Niklas laid out under a white shroud, his face exposed, a candle burning at his head. He groped towards his twin – emerging from a well of amnesia, seeing the horror as if for the first time, and remembering, an agonising moment later, what had happened.

"Niklas," he moaned, falling to the floor and crawling towards the corpse. "No. *No.*"

Charlotte gripped Karl's hand so hard he flinched. Stefan's rasps of anguish were low, even more chilling than his scream.

After a time he went quiet, and lay down with one arm over his twin's corpse. Karl observed that Niklas's face was already beginning to deteriorate: not decaying, exactly, but turning grey and collapsing inwards like melting wax. He remembered, with a shudder, how easily his own *doppelgänger* had disintegrated when attacked.

They weren't true entities, only walking imitations, as fragile as unfired clay. And yet Niklas had been everything to Stefan. Brother, companion… perhaps lover, too, although Karl had never dreamed of asking. Some things were better left unspoken.

"Stefan is notorious for vanishing when situations become dangerous," said Karl. "But – as annoying as he could be – I understood his need to protect Niklas."

"They got away with anything, through pure charm," said Charlotte. "And to be fair, they always helped me when I asked. Rather, Stefan did, but Niklas was always with him. I can't imagine one without the other."

Karl pulled down his shirt-sleeve and put on a jacket. He was steeling himself to confront Godric, but Charlotte's gaze became urgent.

"Wait, before you go – I've an idea. A way to protect you. Insurance, if you like."

She explained her plan and Karl could produce no objection. It only meant he must wait with Stefan while Charlotte went to find Amy.

Then Charlotte said, "Where's Stefan?"

Karl, who'd been entirely focused on her, looked up. Niklas's waxen remains lay in the flickering candlelight. Stefan had vanished.

They jumped to their feet and went through every room of the chalet, calling him, but they already knew he wasn't there. There was no trace of his presence.

"He shouldn't be able to enter the Crystal Ring," said Karl. "I thought he was too weak."

"Despair can give you strength to do anything," said Charlotte.

"He must have gone to Reiniger's mansion," Karl said in dismay. "Of all the reckless..."

"But he doesn't care what happens to him." Charlotte was wide-eyed with alarm. "He doesn't care if he dies!"

"Well, I do," Karl said grimly. "I'm going after him. Do what you have to, dearest – with the greatest of care."

Another letter had arrived for Violette, apparently written before Emil vanished, but timed to arrive after he'd left the country. That meant there had been forward planning on Fadiya's part.

Violette stood holding the paper with its two neat creases, her hand shaking. Not Emil's writing this time. Instead, it was typed, and the scrawled signature was illegible. It did not look like "Fadiya" or any name she knew. A small hand-drawn map showed a square with four roads leading into it: she could barely decipher the place names.

Madame Lenoir,

If you want to see Emil Fiorani alive again, please follow these instructions. Come to us. Come to this square in Algiers at four o'clock on the afternoon of the 18th, and a man named Nabil will greet you there with the word "Istilqa". He will be your guide. Come alone, and surrender yourself. Do this, and Emil will live. Fail, and he will be tortured day and night until you arrive, or until he dies: whichever falls the sooner.

Come to us and submit. This letter is written and signed on behalf of our gracious lord and protector...

The rest was handwritten. Violette stared until she managed to decipher the words: *The great Soul of the Universe, Zruvan, Lord of Immortals, the god who came before all other gods, the great void before space and time.*

She laughed at the pomposity of the title, its matter-of-fact arrogance. Dizzy horror filled her as she tried to take in the truth, the surreal manifestation of her worst fears.

CHAPTER TWENTY

THE COMPANY OF VAMPIRES

Charlotte found Amy in her favourite place; at Hotel Blauensee's café overlooking the lake. How strange, she observed, that the outside world went on as if nothing were happening. Tourists sipped hot chocolate, pleasure steamers chugged across the water. Amy's expression was pensive and far from happy.

Thank heaven she's here, Charlotte thought with a rush of relief. If she'd happened to be at home with her uncle, this scheme would have been dust – or at least far harder to achieve. She'd considered ways to lure Amy out of the house without anyone noticing. Now, thank goodness, subterfuge wasn't needed.

She hoped.

She sat down beside the girl, who gave an exaggerated start and clutched a gloved hand to her chest.

"You always startle me! How do you appear out of nowhere like that?"

"Forgive me." Charlotte didn't even attempt a smile. "Did you enjoy the party last night?"

"Yes, thank you – at least the parts I can remember. I still have the most dreadful morning head, now an afternoon head, for which I can only blame myself."

"Do you remember going home?"

Amy shrugged. "Barely. Obviously I did. Hardly anyone was up this morning, so I dread to think what time they went to bed. No one's seen Fadiya at all. I'm a little worried, to be honest. I do hope my uncle hasn't dismissed her. He's been so grumpy lately, I don't know what's wrong with him."

"Truly, you don't?"

"It might be to do with Madame Lenoir's rejection: if they made peace last night, I haven't heard anything. That and the bad reception of *The Lion Arises*. He *hates* being criticised. If *Triumph in the Mountains* doesn't do better, I think he might explode."

Charlotte interrupted. "Did you happen to notice if he went out in the early hours of the morning?"

"No. I didn't wake up until ten. Why would he come home and go out again?"

"Because your uncle and his followers killed one of my friends last night," said Charlotte.

Amy went pale. Neither spoke for a while as Charlotte let her words sink in. It might not be wise to tell the blunt truth, but it was the quickest way to get a reaction. Then Amy said shakily, "I don't believe you. That's impossible! Who?"

"Stefan's twin brother, Niklas."

"That sweet... blond... lovely young man who couldn't speak? *No.*"

Charlotte leaned forward, touching Amy's arm and looking straight into her eyes. "Would you do me a favour? I don't think you know what kind of man your uncle really is. If you come with me, I'll tell you what happened. I promise you won't be harmed."

"Why would I be harmed?"

"You won't be. Please?"

Amy hesitated, confused. "I've many reasons to be angry with him, but the idea that he'd *kill* someone...?"

"I know it's a shock. Come, and I'll explain."

Trembling, Amy gave a stiff nod. "All right, but... why me?"

"It's an acting role, in a way. We need you to pretend that you've been kidnapped."

Karl struggled to enter Raqia. The knife wound and hallucinatory sleep had weakened him. He pushed into the grey-violet layers of the hidden realm, but the ether was like quicksand and spat him out before he could gain any height or momentum. He gave up in frustration, and seized the second fastest option: a blue Citroen Cloverleaf, several years old and starting to show its age, parked outside the chalet. He wasn't even sure it belonged to Stefan, didn't care.

It was a devil to start, and he suspected it lacked the traction for the steep roads up to Reiniger's house. Still, it would have to do.

Charlotte had already fled through the Crystal Ring towards town. Karl hoped she would find Godric's niece. Grimly he willed Amy to walk into Charlotte's path, as if will alone could change anything.

Sometimes it can, he thought. *Every thought we have changes something, both in Raqia and the real world.*

All the time Karl was urging the vehicle up winding roads towards the hills, he projected his senses out through Raqia, trying to pick up Stefan's trail. A herd of cows, being moved up towards the high Alpine meadows, held him up for ten minutes. Cattle could not be rushed, and the cowherds were in no hurry.

At last he caught a vision, a scene faintly overlaid on the reality of woodland and meadow.

He saw Stefan entering the Bergwerkstatt; taking shape in the hall and pausing there, like a wounded wolf scenting its prey. A woman appeared – not Amy, but an older female with brown plaited hair, brown clothes. The housekeeper, Gudrun. She questioned Stefan with some force, but he shouldered her aside and began to mount the sweeping marble staircase. He went slowly, as if walking against the wind. *Why?* Karl wondered. Was his own weakness holding him back, or Godric Reiniger's power?

Karl had tasted that power. It was a real force, like air or gravity.

The car's engine began to grumble as the slope grew too steep. Karl abandoned the struggling vehicle five hundred yards from the mansion and ran the last stretch on foot. He needed blood, but there was no time to feed. His head swam with double vision – the tree-shaded lane in front of him and his inner vision of Stefan, now moving towards a grand set of double doors on the upper storey…

The snowy walls of the house towered above Karl. He took the front steps in a single leap, found the front door locked, simply kicked it open. Inside the hall, Gudrun stood gaping at him, furious as a Valkyrie.

"Sir, you cannot— *Herr Reiniger!*"

Karl ignored her. He raced, virtually flew up the staircase. An invisible, muscular force opposed him but this time, from urgent force of will, he forced his way through.

Not fast enough. He saw the tall doors opening as Stefan walked inside.

The chamber was a grand meeting room with lofty ceilings and lit alcoves, designed to impress. Karl took in the scene over Stefan's shoulder. Godric Reiniger was on a dais at the far end of the room. Twenty-eight men gathered before him, standing in a loose group. They all wore blue cloaks: typical ritual dressing up to add a sense of occasion.

Godric stood between two art easels, each displaying an oblong of rough white linen clipped to a board. Both pieces of cloth were marked with messy red sigils the size of a human torso...

Just like the designs carved into the flesh of Niklas and Stefan. Karl noted this with rising fury.

Had Reiniger taken *prints* of their wounds, treating their bodies like inked lino cuts?

"And as we can take pride in the triumph of our earlier operation..." the leader was saying as Stefan entered.

Godric Reiniger stopped in mid-sentence. Silence fell. Every head turned to stare at the intruders. Karl recognised faces from *The Lion Arises*, from the gang who'd beaten up Emil behind the beer hall, and from the party. Each man held a bone-handled knife in a slashing or stabbing grip. The ruby cabochons shone like blood clots.

So they were expecting us, thought Karl. *As I warned Stefan they would be.*

How could Godric look so poised and fresh, as if he had not spent half the night carving Stefan and Niklas to shreds? His aura was stronger than ever to Karl's eyes, like crackling white flames, so strong that even his human acolytes must see it. *Life-energy stolen from Niklas,* he thought.

Karl made to hold back his friend, but Stefan evaded him. Instead, with a throat-tearing cry, he ran straight at Godric Reiniger.

The hall was some forty feet long. Stefan covered the distance in three seconds, dodged through the audience as if they were hardly there and sprang at his prey – but those seconds were enough for three of Reiniger's men to form a wall in front of their master.

Stefan grunted with pain as their blades pierced him. He got one of them around the neck, bit savagely into the man's throat and began to feed.

The man collapsed. Stefan spat out the blood – that foul taste – and flung him at his comrades, his weight taking them down. The ejected blood spattered them, rained on to the floor.

Others piled in, ready to drive their blades into Stefan, and still he managed to reach Reiniger. His hands clawed towards the leader's neck.

Karl saw Stefan's face in profile, unrecognisable – his angelic, amiable features transformed to those of a raging demon – and for one pleasing instant, he saw outrage, shock and complete terror on Godric Reiniger's face.

All this happened in half a second. Time ran slow to Karl's vampiric senses, enabling him to register every detail as he raced the last stretch of polished marble and flung himself between Stefan and Reiniger's gang.

Several knife points entered Karl's shoulders through his jacket as he grabbed Stefan from behind. The pain made him gasp and a familiar, unpleasant drowsiness began... This time he fought the feeling. He must stay conscious, at all costs.

Stefan struggled furiously. He didn't seem to know it was Karl who held him, or didn't care.

"It's me," Karl said into his ear. "Stop!"

But Stefan went on clawing towards his target. Reiniger stepped backwards, out of reach, weaving his own dagger in front of Stefan. Its movement left trails of light, glyphs pulsating with silver fire. A shield.

Karl managed to get Stefan's arms behind his back. Stefan kicked at him, then tried to rush head first at Godric, his neck twisted upwards and fangs bared. He uttered a piercing shriek that made the group members step back, flinching and pressing their hands over their ears. His momentum took both him and Karl off balance and they stumbled without grace to the floor, legs tangled.

Karl pinned him down. Stefan writhed beneath him like an enraged cat.

"Don't!" said Karl.

"Why not, why the hell not?" Stefan growled.

"Because they were expecting this! If you attack them, they'll kill you."

"Do you think I care? Get the hell off me!"

"*I* care," said Karl. "There's no use in you dying unless you take them with you, and you can't."

Reiniger's voice rang out. "Remain on the floor, both of you. We hold the power here and you know it. You've seen proof. You feel it, don't you?"

Karl bowed under the increasing air pressure. The weight was so intense it made his ears ring. He glanced around and saw the gang now in a tight double circle, surrounding them. Sky-blue cloaks, pale savage faces, shining blades. They held their daggers aloft as if they were about to start a crazed knife-throwing act.

Such weapons could land hilt-deep in the flesh. How many wounds could he and Stefan endure, Karl wondered, before they actually died as Niklas had?

Killing us should be easy, he thought. *They only need to pin us here long enough to hack off our heads. However limited Godric's knowledge, he must know that much. If in doubt, they'll cut us up and burn the remains.*

With Karl and Stefan immobile, Godric Reiniger appeared confident enough to approach them. He straightened his cloak and stalked forward with his *sikin* held casually in his right hand.

"Perhaps now you realise I am deadly serious, von Wultendorf." He raised his chin, glaring down his nose at them. "*No one* says no to me. When I asked you to transform me, it was not a suggestion."

Karl managed to disentangle himself from Stefan and crouched beside him, one hand keeping him quiescent. The massed vibration of the knives made him dizzy. He met Godric's haughty eyes.

"And when I told you I can't, I was not making excuses. I will not create more vampires. Even if we tried, there is a high chance that the change would kill you."

He felt Stefan jerk beneath his hand. This exchange had confirmed that his twin's death was an act of revenge. Karl thought, *Stefan, with all my heart, I am sorry. Perhaps we should have done as Godric asked: transformed him but let him perish. What's wrong with me, that I can't harm this petty tyrant?*

"Separate them," Reiniger snapped, gesturing to his henchmen. Karl and Stefan were dragged to their feet, held with knife-points digging into their necks and six feet of space between them. "I may require you to kill the blond one – the head needs to be severed. The dark one – Karl, I would talk to you again. If you refuse, your blond friend will die."

"Let him go, and I'll talk to you," Karl said simply.

"Not possible. He's like a spitting wild cat. I can't let such a dangerous beast go free."

Karl felt the heat of Stefan's gaze on him. From long years of habit he composed himself and made his face expressionless.

"Herr Reiniger," he said, "when did you last see your niece?"

"I beg your pardon?" Godric came closer to Karl, stone-faced.

"Think when you last saw her."

Godric paused, eyes narrowing.

"Last night."

"We have Amy in our custody," said Karl. Inwardly he prayed that Charlotte had found her and that his statement was not an empty bluff.

"What?" Godric was speechless for long seconds, to Karl's satisfaction. A shifting restlessness built among his followers. "Where is she?"

"In the company of vampires," Karl said softly. He let his true nature shine through; his pallid dangerous beauty, his eyes unhuman like an angel's. This hadn't impressed Godric much before, but was always worth a try.

"You're lying!" His breathing quickened. He half-raised the knife, hand trembling.

"Try finding her, then. Are you willing to gamble her life? You've protected yourselves, but not her. Let Stefan go, and you'll get Amy back. Let him go, and I'll talk to you willingly."

Seething, Reiniger turned away. He took Wolfgang and six others away from the main group, whispering urgently to them.

"Karl, why do you want to *talk* with this monster?" Stefan demanded. "After what he's done to Niklas, to us?"

The Stefan of old would have delighted in the irony of a vampire calling a human a monster. The new, red-raw Stefan was deadly serious. Karl understood, but a horrible chill spread through him; the old, wickedly charming Stefan might be gone forever.

"Because I created this monster," Karl answered softly. "My actions in the past are at least partly to blame for what he's become. Everything we do casts a long shadow."

"Don't get philosophical with me," said Stefan. "Just kill him!"

"Will you trust me and do as I ask? Be calm. Or at least pretend to be calm."

"If you have my niece, prove it!" Reiniger spoke over them, loud and furious.

"I can, but that may take an hour or so," Karl answered. "If Stefan has not been released by then, it may be too late for her."

Blood crept into Reiniger's ashen complexion. Karl added, "You can afford to let Stefan go. You still have me."

"I don't want to be released!" Stefan retorted. "Give me ten minutes with these pigs – if I make them suffer a tenth of what Niklas went through, I won't perish in vain."

Karl took a breath, close to anger and wondering what would force Stefan to leave. He said quietly, "You realise *who* went to capture Herr Reiniger's niece?"

"Wait a minute," said Stefan, his eyes suddenly blazing into Karl's. "Who is with Niklas?"

"No one," Karl said steadily.

At that, Stefan shook as if he would combust with emotion, a column of white-blue flame. "You left Niklas on his own? How could you? I'll never forgive you for this."

"I had no choice," Karl said steadily. "I followed you here. Violette had to leave, as did Charlotte. Niklas is dead. He won't know."

"You bastard! That's not the point! *I* know!"

Stefan struggled and hissed in his captors' grip. His face was chalk white, ghastly.

"In which case, why don't you go to him?" said Karl. "If he needs anyone, Stefan, it's you."

That persuaded Stefan at last. He threw a look of pure hatred at Karl – but he shook off the human hands and strode out. Karl closed his eyes in pain, wondering if Stefan would ever recover. *He'll never be the same again,* he thought. *Never.*

When he opened his eyes, Godric Reiniger was standing in front of him. His expression was alarmingly intense and eager.

"Well, Karl? Shall we go somewhere more private to talk?"

Emil woke in the soft half-light of a bedroom. Fadiya was asleep beside him.

Asleep.

He realised that he had never seen her sleeping before. On the bedside table beside her lay a small dagger, hardly more than a letter-opener, with a ruby set in the pommel.

He got up and looked out through the filigree screen across the window. Below lay the courtyard garden. His gaze drifted around, taking in the hazy beauty of flowers and fountains and blue sky. Light-headed, almost too lazy to move, he wondered if they'd drugged him. This place was so beautiful, with its falling water and shaded galleries.

"They're all vampires, aren't they?" he said as Fadiya rose from the bed and drifted to join him. "Every single one. Once you've seen, you can't *unsee*. What is this place?"

"A safe house, dearest," she said, placing her hand on his arm. "Our secret dwelling, Bayt-al-Zuhur. House of Flowers."

"If I go outside and tell the authorities, it won't be a secret, will it?"

"Now, why would you do that?" Her smile and her seductive eyes worked their usual dark magic on him. Whatever she was, he still wanted her desperately. "Or rather, how? You can't escape. I know how high you can leap, but even you can't clear these walls. And if you could, and soldiers came to break down the doors, we'd simply vanish."

"They might come with guns. Hand grenades. Bombs. Turn your palace into rubble."

She gave a slight shrug, indifferent. "We'd find somewhere else to live. It's only a house. But isn't it beautiful? Why would you want to destroy such a splendid *riad*?"

Emil couldn't form a sensible answer. How weird, to feel so terrified and yet numb, as if his fear were miles away. *I am mad, or drugged,* he thought. *If I know, why can't I fight it off? What's happening to me?* Every minute he sat there, he felt his fitness fading, his blood-starved muscles turning soft like overcooked spaghetti...

"What are you doing?" Fadiya asked as he straightened up and placed a hand on the wall.

"I need to practise. Violette will be furious if I lose condition," he said.

The room tilted. He staggered, catching himself with one hand as Fadiya helped him back to the bed. She murmured something strange. Surely he'd misheard.

"Let me worry about Violette's fury."

"What did you say?"

"Bathe and get dressed. You can eat breakfast in the garden. We have to leave soon."

"Leave? I don't understand."

She would not answer his questions, so he did as she asked, then went outside and sat on a bench in the shade, trying and failing to shake off his dream-state. He was afraid, but his mind's warnings would not connect with his body to force him into action.

A commotion pierced his trance; a rumbling engine, clouds of orange dust, voices. It was coming from somewhere beyond the walls but sounded alarmingly close.

A man said, "We're ready."

"Coming, Nabil," said Fadiya.

Three pairs of hands, as strong as steel cable, seized Emil. He tried to ask what was happening, tried to resist, but he couldn't make his limbs or tongue work. He uttered a faint laugh, only to choke on exhaust fumes and sand. This was ridiculous, couldn't be happening. Not to Emil Fiorani, the greatest male dancer of his time—

"Not yet, you aren't," said Mikhail in his mind.

I should not be here, he thought as graceful, pitiless demons bore him away.

He was stuffed into the back of a truck with a canvas roof. His legs and wrists were bound with rope, and a rag tied around his mouth – when had they done that to him? He felt the truck's grumbling vibration, breathed in a nauseating combination of fuel and hot metal and a ripe farmyard smell, as if the vehicle's usual cargo was goats.

"And you know where to wait?" Fadiya was speaking in

French to someone outside the truck. "We should have over a day's head start. And make sure you explain fast, Nabil; it's said she is quicker to kill than to talk."

Reiniger brought Karl to his private cinema again. The room was bright, illuminated by modern chandeliers made of black struts. Black velvet curtains hung closed across the screen. Karl hoped there were to be no more movies, but Godric only sat on the arm of the nearest back-row seat. It occurred to Karl that this was somewhere Reiniger felt comfortable, safe. Like the meeting chamber, there were no windows.

He sensed men guarding the doors, but no one came in with them. The energy that radiated from the bone-knives still tingled painfully on his skin. Immunity might develop eventually, but he guessed the process would take more time than he had.

Part of the reason he'd cut himself was to see if exposure would lessen the dagger's effect. He had a brief flashback to the musty cellar where Charlotte's father had his laboratory. Karl had endured considerable pain as he sought chemicals to destroy vampire flesh. He'd never been afraid to experiment on himself.

"Well, now," said Godric, drawing on a cigarette. "If anything happens to Amy, you've seen what I'm capable of in return. None of your friends are safe from me. Especially not your lady friend – your wife? – Charlotte. Doesn't that merciless streak make me a perfect vampire candidate? I'm giving you a chance to reconsider."

Karl suppressed his reaction. He couldn't let fear distract him.

"Why would you wish to be a vampire, when you have all this? Weapons to paralyse us, followers who share your dreams – what more do you need?"

"Because…" Reiniger took a deep drag and blew out an acrid cloud. He sat with his legs crossed at the knee, all poised arrogance except for the raised foot tapping at the air. "It's all external, isn't it? The *sakakin*, the bone-knives, aren't part of me. Any of my followers could betray me. It's the difference between being a mouse with a matchstick sword and being a lion."

"There's probably a fairy tale about that," said Karl. "The mouse always wins."

"And by using its wits, of course, not fangs and claws." Godric drew back his chin in a subtle sneer. "But your kind has intelligence as well as strength. Why can't the two coexist? I need to become more than I am. I know I have the potential. Why should you keep this gift to yourself? Jealousy?"

"Believe me, it is not jealousy. I told you before that this existence is not what you think."

Reiniger gave a soundless laugh. "How do you know what I think?"

"Actually, I'm interested in what everyone thinks," Karl said softly. "That is why I spend too much time listening to the ramblings of an egomaniac, rather than breaking your spine. I learn a lot. I cannot resist waiting to hear what comes out of your mouth next."

"What?"

"You strike me as a man who loves to talk but never listens. You are so wrapped up in your own ideas and plans, you close your ears to other voices except those that agree with you. It must have stung to hear the audience laughing at your film. You think that if you become an immortal predator, you can force people to recognise your genius. If your group seizes power, you could pass a law."

Reiniger's cigarette broke between his teeth. He spat out the stub.

"Amusing, Karl. And partly true. All great men are obsessive. Yes, I have an appetite for power. Mainly for the good of my country, but also to open people's eyes."

"To make them pay attention to you?"

"I seem to have *your* attention. And you're correct: I don't care for your opinion. However, I still believe we could be comrades, Karl. And there's a vacancy in my circle. I'm missing a knife and I suspect you can locate it. Bring it to me, and join us."

Karl half-smiled in surprise at this offer.

"But I killed your father."

"You did. But I was standing there, and I failed to save him. *There*, probably, is the reason that I loathe feeling powerless."

"That would make sense. You were only ten years old, yet you think you should have saved him." Karl moved away and down the steps, looking at framed artwork on the walls. Each was a piece of stretched white linen showing a similar rune roughly drawn in brown paint.

Not paint. Dried blood.

"Don't open their eyes too wide," said Karl.

"What do you mean?"

"Let us say you got into government. You don't want the populace knowing about *this*, do you? Your occult activities. Carving patterns on to the bodies of living people and taking a print, as if their blood is ink. Do such symbols have actual power?"

"Oh, yes." Reiniger came slowly down the steps after him, lighting a fresh cigarette. "Blood is life, and intention is energy. Everyone who joins my circle undergoes this initiation. It isn't fatal – unless we cut too deep – but the ritual adds power to the group, and brands each member as one of us. These are not mere abstract paintings, but records of sacrifice, pain and blood initiation. A seal of each man's dedication. When we're ready to make our move, the Swiss government will not withstand us. Alliances and federations make the nation weak: I intend to make us strong. We'll all possess your gifts: charisma, persuasion, hypnotic power, physical invulnerability. Karl, I hope you're beginning to see that you'd be wiser to join us than oppose us."

"I'm seeing something," Karl murmured. He wondered just how much power Reiniger's group had drained from Stefan and Niklas. Although he believed that "magic" meant no more than "lack of explanation", he knew the universe could behave in enigmatic ways. He touched the textured surface of a canvas with blobs and smears of blood so fresh they still gave off an odour. He saw a name written small in one corner. *Bruno Glor.*

He suspected that Bruno had not survived.

"I don't oppose you," he added. "Your politics don't concern me, but your attack on my friends does, very much. Where did you get the bone-knives?"

"From my father," said Reiniger.

"And how did he acquire them?" Karl didn't expect a straight answer, but he suspected that Reiniger was talking openly in order to win him over, or at least to impress him.

Godric needs my approval, Karl thought, puzzled. *Everything he's done has been to seize my attention: an unpalatable mixture of ruthless brutality and mysticism. Is he really prepared to forgive me, just because I might be useful to him?*

"He was an archaeologist," said Godric. "He unearthed them on the northern edge of the Sahara Desert, along with scrolls he estimated to be at least four hundred years old."

"From a grave?"

"He didn't believe so. They were simply buried, like hidden treasure. His painstaking translation revealed what seemed to be description of creatures that lived on blood and never died. As for the rune ritual, he derived that from what he read. Each knife is a channel that takes energy from the victim to the attacker."

"Ah," Karl said softly. "So if humans stab a vampire, it creates a kind of vampirism in reverse?"

Godric gave a snakelike smile. "We've had precious few vampires to experiment on. It works on humans, too." He rolled up his shirt-sleeve and gave Karl a glimpse of silver-pink scars along his arms. "Self-inflicted cuts draw power from the *sikin*. Cutting others invokes a surge of energy that everyone present can absorb. But I suspect vampires yield the best results of all."

"Have you tried this on Fadiya?"

"No, not her."

"Tell me about her," said Karl. "How did you meet?"

Reiniger hissed smoke through his teeth. "A few weeks ago, she appeared inside the house and yes, I knew at once what she was. We had an argument, a stand-off, you might say. She had fangs, I had my *sikin*: fighting was pointless. She claimed that my hoard of *sakakin* were originally hers. However, she couldn't take them by force. Nor could I make her leave."

"How did she know they were here?"

Godric shrugged.

"They're artefacts of power. They give off a powerful emanation which she claimed to sense from a distance. I've experienced such phenomena, so I've no reason to doubt her."

"Yet she let you keep them?"

"She had no choice. It was rather as if she tried to demand a gun from me while I was pointing it at her."

Godric's gaze fixed on Karl, cool and unwavering through his spectacle lenses. The look was unnerving. Not hostile, but knowing, yearning... infuriatingly enigmatic.

"Do you know anything else about her?"

"Almost nothing," he said abruptly. "I'm not interested, to be frank. I asked her to leave, but she refused. In the end we reached a sort of truce: she would let me keep the *sakakin* if I let her stay. To be fair, she's kept her word not to feed on anyone, and she gave me advice that made our rituals stronger."

"Advice?"

"Yes, to call on the name of Zruvan, some long-forgotten deity. I was reluctant, but I can't deny that it works."

"Why would Fadiya want to help you?"

"H'm, that's the question. She seems to approve of our using the *sakakin* to evoke power. When I asked about this Zruvan, she replied, 'He's more than a god. He is a force beyond your comprehension. Honour him, and he'll open his secrets to you.' I was sceptical. I'm not a religious man in the conventional sense, but... this 'incomprehensible force' speaks to my soul. It is beyond good and evil."

Godric nodded to himself.

"What did she want in return?" Karl asked.

"That I employ her, giving her a reason to stay in Lucerne."

"I'm sure she could have done that without help," Karl said thoughtfully. "Unless she wasn't here for her sacred knives, but for another reason. Looking for someone? Perhaps what she actually wanted was to meet Emil."

"I don't care," Godric said, irritated. Karl sensed a wall going up. "Her business is her own. We had a simple agreement: to help each other without asking questions. In any case, she's gone. No longer relevant."

"That must be a relief," said Karl. "Her presence must have been frustrating for a man who likes to control everything."

"You're wrong about me," Reiniger said brusquely. "I don't gather followers by controlling them. They're men who share my vision." He waved at the blood prints. "I can't create these glyphs without the participants' consent. It takes courage to tolerate blades slicing into your skin. I need men of courage around me, not weaklings."

"Charlotte did not consent, when she was stabbed in the street."

"That was a mistake. The perpetrator was punished."

"Bruno?" No reply. "Stefan and Niklas most certainly did not consent."

"That was a warning," Reiniger said acidly.

"Incidentally, did you know that your father tried the ritual on me?"

His words threw Godric. "My father's been dead for thirty years."

"And it happened thirty years ago." Karl turned to him. Godric, who was standing close behind, took a step back.

"My father?"

"And four of his friends. They had me on my back, in the dark, just as you had Niklas."

"Show me the scars!"

"There are none. They fade, albeit more slowly than normal wounds. I don't know what they gained from the experiment, but I do know that when I came round, I was underwater, weighed down in the bottom of a deep lake."

Reiniger looked stunned. "I know he invented the ritual, of course – I learned it from him, or rather from the papers he left. I refined it. But I had no idea that he'd tried it upon you."

"He did. He used the *sakakin* to overpower me, he dragged me back to his house, and afterwards tried to conceal what he thought was my corpse. And that is why I went back to his house and killed him."

Godric Reiniger's jaw worked. A grey pallor added years to his face. "Revenge?"

"No. I wasn't even angry. However, I was extremely disturbed. I intended to stop whatever he was doing, to me or to anyone else. That's all. I would have taken the bone-knives and his papers, too, if I'd had the chance, but you interrupted me."

"You fled from a ten-year-old?"

"A child in the doorway, staring while his father's life ended at my hands? Yes, I was horrified, and I left. And then I forgot those events entirely, because of the narcotic effect of the blades."

"But this means you and I are more deeply connected than I dreamed." Godric's breathing quickened. He moved restlessly down the steps, paced in front of the curtained screen. Waves of agitation, distress and excitement pulsed from him. "This means something – if I can put aside my father's death, and you put aside your friend's – if we can rise above weak human emotion – isn't this what being the highest form of predator means? We're like gods. Tell me, do you know what the *sakakin* are?"

"Too dangerous for human hands," Karl replied. "They should be destroyed."

"I thought you, of all people, would see the beauty of creating art from pain and blood! The sword, the gun, the mortar shell should also be destroyed – but never will be, because they're too useful. I won't give up a cache of weapons that protects us from vampires – particularly when there's one standing in front of me. But when I become immortal, I won't need them any more. I may still amuse myself with them, but I won't *need* them."

Karl was on the lowest step, a few feet from the screen and as far as he could be from the doors. He saw no side exits. Against the black curtains, Godric's aura shone like a halo of cold flame, a fierce white fire radiating from him. Karl felt its chill from a distance. As he walked carefully towards Godric the power grew, pushing against him like a snowstorm. He felt his own strength fading.

The lights seemed to dim. His ears rang with the awful pressure he'd felt in the meeting chamber, as if an engine was rolling on its way to crush him.

Godric knew, and yet *didn't* know, just how unhuman he already was. And the change was happening fast. Even as Karl watched his aura grew wilder, writhing and flashing with energy. Godric appeared to gain height, his flesh turning pale and hard like marble.

If only Godric Reiniger had been a crazed fantasist. Instead he was metamorphosing into a creature that didn't know its own strength, but when he realised...

Karl saw that there was nothing to do except to stop him. And the simplest answer was usually the best.

Karl braced himself against the wintry power. He reached Godric and looked into his unblinking, triumphant eyes.

"Your father's death was not revenge," said Karl. "*This* is revenge."

He seized Godric's upper arms, held him rigid and sank his fangs into his neck. The blood was foul with the metallic taint of the knives, but Karl overcame his revulsion. If he couldn't swallow the blood, he could still bite through the windpipe, through arteries and nerves—

Reiniger seemed to crumble like chalk in his hands. Dissolved, vanished.

Karl heard a commotion at the top of the room as men burst in to defend their leader. He stood heedless of his own safety – empty-handed. Where his victim had stood there was a shimmer of frost and air. Nothing.

Godric Reiniger had fled as only a vampire could: into the Crystal Ring.

CHAPTER TWENTY-ONE

BLOOD-RED SUNSET

Charlotte left Amy in the Ballet Lenoir's auditorium. She seemed happy to stand in the wings, fascinated by the set-builders at work and the musicians rehearsing.

They were preparing to stage Violette's current ballets – *Swan Lake* on some nights, *The Firebird* paired with *Witch and Maiden* on others – oblivious to the fact that the whole project was in jeopardy. *But there must be rumours,* thought Charlotte. The ballet, like any organisation, teemed with gossip. Even the boy who swept the floors must have heard whispers that Violette and Emil were nowhere to be found.

Presently Amy came to Charlotte's side in the stalls and asked if she could fetch the Bolex cine-camera and do some filming.

"Yes, that's a wonderful idea," said Charlotte, distracted. "I'm sure Violette won't mind. It's in our rooms, but I'm not sure where Karl left it and he's not here. Come on, I'll go with you."

The activity would help take Amy's mind off her uncle. Charlotte couldn't forget so easily. With every breath, she saw renewed images of Niklas lying dead, Stefan shaking in wordless grief, Karl drawing the blade down his own arm.

She led Amy from the theatre into the academy next door, wondering if Karl and Violette were safe and if she should try to find them.

Which of them is in greater danger? And would my presence actually help, or make things worse?

Upstairs, at the far end of a corridor, she saw the door to their suite of rooms standing open. Karl was just inside the entrance. Charlotte saw him as if from a great distance, the passageway distorted like a scene from a horror film, the angles of the walls all wrong.

Her brief flash of relief at seeing him evaporated.

Karl was leaning back against the open door, and in his arms was another woman. She had creamy-pale clothes like gossamer, and was pressing the length of her body into him. Her lips touched his, and his arms clasped her back with affection…

Behind her, Amy gave a muted gasp.

Charlotte's head swam. She couldn't see properly. The woman moved away from Karl and walked deeper into the apartment, giving his arm an affectionate touch as she went. Just as Charlotte herself might.

"Stay here a moment," she said to Amy, who obediently remained in the corridor, wide-eyed.

When Charlotte reached him, he was standing in the doorway alone.

They stared at each other.

Karl was so practised at appearing calm in most situations that she rarely saw him surprised by anything. Now he looked astonished. Thirty seconds passed like an hour, then he broke the silence.

"How did you do that?"

"What?" she said, confused. "I didn't think you'd be home yet. Amy wants to film, so we came for the camera… and I find you being terribly friendly with someone else. Who is she?"

"Charlotte," Karl said helplessly, "she was *you*."

"How?" A mass of questions rose inside her, then all her emotions went as still as winter. "I'm here now. I was not here a few moments ago."

"But you were. I was embracing *you*, not someone else. I thought you'd slipped into Raqia and gone in a circle, for some inexplicable reason…"

"I assure you, I didn't. What did 'I' say?"

Karl's gaze drifted over her shoulder. His expression went dark. "I don't remember. Just endearments."

"So I didn't mention Amy, or anything else? I didn't ask if you found Stefan with Herr Reiniger, or ask if you were hurt?"

He shook his head. "I'm not sure you said anything at all, in fact."

"Don't you think it odd that I wouldn't mention *any* of our concerns?"

"Strange in the extreme," he said quietly. He looked towards the bedroom. "There was quite a scene at Reiniger's house. I persuaded Stefan to leave. When I left, a short time later, I caught up with Stefan and brought him here... And I have just watched you walk into that room after him."

"I saw her too. But that was not me. God, Karl..." Her voice went faint. "I tried to drive the lamia away, but I knew she hadn't really gone."

Karl and Charlotte hurried into the bedroom, a spacious room with a big double bed. Her breath stopped as she took in an appalling sight: Niklas's body was on one side of the bed, a white sheet covering him to his chin. Stefan lay beside him, eyes closed, holding Niklas's hand. He, too, looked dead – except for the occasional shallow breath or faint moan.

Of the "other" Charlotte, there was no sign.

"We both saw her come in here," said Karl.

"Perhaps she went into Raqia." A horrible feeling cascaded through Charlotte, like melting ice. "That knife wound really did split me in two. She isn't me, she's a living ghost, like part of my soul, and she has no mind, any more than Niklas did... yet you mistook her for the real me?"

"She felt solid," Karl murmured. "I couldn't tell you apart... except..."

"Except that she said nothing rational to you? Wasn't that a telling sign? If it wasn't, I'm insulted."

Stefan sat up, making her start. "What are you two muttering about? No one came in here."

Godric came back to the real world and to his human form in a meadow, high above Bergwerkstatt. Rather, he crash-landed: flew through a mad world of cloud and flame and ice-crystals, knowing with the irrational, sure knowledge of a dream that he'd become something more than human... then he plunged down, skidding along the grass like a grounded kite. Tall pine trees rustled around him. Clouds fleeted across the bright blue sky. Everything seemed too fast, too vivid.

He pulled himself into a sitting position and stayed there, gripping his knees, until his shock faded. Then the clarity of his thoughts astonished him. Obvious, *obvious* what had happened.

"I do not need Karl to transform me," he said to the sky. "It's happened. I've transformed myself."

He sat there for at least an hour. The only sounds were of a stream gushing downhill and the distant music of cowbells. Presently he saw a figure toiling up the green hillside towards him. Wolfgang Notz.

Only when he saw Wolfgang did he remember Karl's threat to his niece.

"Godric, Christ, there you are!" Wolfgang pushed a hand over his shorn hair and caught his breath. "We've been looking everywhere – we thought—"

"That the *strigoi* had killed me?"

"Well... yes! You both vanished from the screening room..."

"He tried," Godric said off-handedly. "But he can't. I have become impervious to death."

Wolfgang stared as if he'd gone mad. "You've... what?"

"Is anyone looking for Amy?"

"Yes, of course, but... It's no good panicking, because she'll be no use as a hostage if they harm her, and they must know that."

"When do I ever panic?" Godric rose smoothly to his feet. His spectacles were askew. He straightened them, wondering if his metamorphosis would include perfect eyesight. "Where did Karl go?"

"Don't know. As I said, vanished. We were more concerned about you, sir. What happened? You're covered in blood and grass stains."

"Don't look at me like that, Wolf." He raised a hand palm upwards, fingers curled as if gripping a ball. "You still feel this intense power from the sacrifice of Bruno, the ritual with the vampire twins, from every single *Eidgenossen* gathering we've ever held?"

"Yes."

"Then you know it's real. I haven't lost my mind. Wolf, I *went into another world* – how else do you think I got here? I'm changing. We all are, and I'm taking you with me, but only one of us can become the ultimate leader. It's happening to me, Wolfgang. It's wonderful."

His deputy took a step back, his expression turning hard and wary. Not the expression of awe that Godric expected to see. "And how many more of us are you going to sacrifice to complete this process?"

"As many as necessary. Are you wavering?"

"No, but what we did to Bruno…"

"The men loved it," Godric said with a smile. "You felt their excitement, their blood-lust. *You* loved it."

"I'm not especially proud of that."

"Embrace it, Wolf, unless you want to *be* the next sacrifice. It's simple psychology. Fear keeps the men loyal. And as long as they stay loyal, their reward is to be part of the inner circle with a share of this astonishing power. It's an easy choice, isn't it?"

Wolfgang paused a little too long. That hard gleam of doubt was still in his eyes. "Not that easy. I believe in a strong nation. I believe in you – but I did not sign up to murdering our own comrades, nor to our becoming vampires. What, you want us to turn into the very monsters you despise?"

Godric thrust out his hand, seized Wolfgang by the shirt collar and twisted, almost lifting him off the ground. His strength shocked them both. Wolfgang's freckly face went crimson.

"How dare you question me? I can destroy you at a stroke, Wolf. You know that. *Are you with me or against me?*"

"With you," Wolf gasped, choking.

"I can't hear you. State yourself clearly. Are you still loyal?"

"Yes, I'm loyal. I'm with you, sir."

Godric dropped him and Wolfgang stumbled on to his knees, spit flying from his mouth as he coughed and cursed. When he straightened up, the two men stood glaring at each other – Reiniger ice cool, Wolfgang red-faced and gasping.

"We are not turning into vampires," Godric stated. "We shan't do anything as crude as drinking blood – unless we want to. No, we're becoming strong in a nobler way. That's my father's legacy to us, through the *sakakin*…"

"All the same, I thought we'd win people through a sound

mixture of reason and appealing to Swiss German hearts through your films. This business with the blood rituals has never felt clean, or honest, or right."

Godric was suddenly tired. The flesh Karl had bitten was beginning to burn. He rubbed the wound, exhaled.

"I am deeply sorry to hear that," he said, layering his voice with all the disappointment and irritated condescension he felt. "If you wish to withdraw your support, go – and see what happens."

"I've said what I think." Wolfgang stared into the middle distance, like a soldier at attention. "I won't mention it again. You have my loyal devotion."

"Excellent." He pointed a finger at Wolfgang. "Everything goes ahead as we planned: the release of *Triumph in the Mountains*, the filming of *Three Tells*. Everything. But I need you to do one essential thing for me. *Find Amy and bring her home safely*."

Wolfgang's face still had a stubborn look that made Godric want to strike him.

"If we knew where to search… Would they take her to the ballet academy?"

"Keep a hostage somewhere so public, and obvious? No. They will have taken her back to that mountain chalet."

Godric read his reluctance in his expression – *The place where the madwoman nearly killed me?* – but, to his credit, Wolf only swallowed and said, "Yes, sir."

"I believe you'll find everything there: Amy, and the missing *sikin*. It's obvious. But don't put her life at risk. Take all the men you need, take weapons, but don't do anything rash. Remember, we are stronger than vampires now. Find my niece, and we'll forget this difference of opinion."

"Difference?" Wolfgang said under his breath as he turned and started down the hillside. He broke into a run.

Godric watched him through slitted eyes, then looked up at the drifting sky. He felt exhausted but invincible. He tried to keep his thoughts on Amy but she seemed remote; all he could see was Karl. That haughty, captivating face, the demonic eyes and razor-sharp teeth, the fire-tinged black shadow-cloud of his hair in a mess from their fight…

He thought about Fadiya, helpfully luring Violette away, leaving his way clear. He pictured the *Weisse Frau*, the woman of mist who would answer his call and take any shape he commanded...

There could be no clearer confirmation of divine approval than Frau Perchta's blessing.

He knew exactly what to do. He felt for the bone-knife, drew it from its sheath and opened his own shirt, breaking off buttons in his haste. Closing his eyes and opening his whole self to the power of the otherworld, he began to cut a new symbol over his heart. A rune, symbolising two creatures bound together. A call, a summoning, a command. Light shone from the slits he'd made.

Immediately he sensed the *Weisse Frau* taking shape and drifting towards him.

As little time as he had for females, he had to admit they had their own particular value. He made a mental note to honour them, when his new nation took shape. Fresh-faced maidens in traditional costume, raising their sweet voices in song. Jazz, flapper dresses, dancing and nightclubs – he would ban all such depravity. His heart lifted at the thought.

But that was for the future. First he had a dark journey to complete.

Karl, he thought. *I still need your life force, and I'm going to take it. If it transpires that I only want rather than need, I'll steal it anyway. Just as I told Fadiya. Oh, I am strong enough to take you now. Be in no doubt.*

Out loud he said, "Wherever I am going, Karl von Wultendorf, you are coming with me."

"She came drifting towards me," Karl said, "just as you did, the second time."

"There was no second time." Charlotte sat upright on a couch, tense, her hands braced on her knees. "I arrived home *once*. What came before me, I don't know."

They had given Amy the camera and tripod, everything she needed, and – smiling, pretending nothing was wrong – sent her back to the auditorium. Now Karl sat with Charlotte and Stefan in the living room, in a dappled bower of evening light filtering through lace curtains.

He kept turning over in his mind how she'd approached him, how he hadn't questioned for a moment that she was Charlotte... until the real Charlotte appeared, and the first one vanished.

"Nor do I," he said. "She was luminous, smiling and near-silent... and I was taken in. I don't believe in spells, but she cast one anyway. It felt like a dream in which there's no need to question anything."

"We've all been cut by Herr Reiniger's knives. Am I the only one to be shadowed by a ghost of myself? Why?"

"It appears to affect everyone differently," said Karl. "We all had a period of madness afterwards..."

Charlotte glared. "Do you think I'm still mad?"

"That is not what I meant."

"Now you're staring at me," she said. "Do you think *I* am the impostor?"

"No, *liebchen*, I don't. I cannot be sure – but I hardly think your spectral lamia would be so argumentative."

Charlotte threw a cushion at him. He fielded it with a raised forearm. She'd thrown it quite hard.

"Whatever she is, I must lay her to rest."

"Now you know how I felt when I destroyed the double that Kristian made of me," Karl replied.

Stefan cleared his throat. He, too, looked like a ghost of his true self; his face gaunt and bloodless, his eyes hollow caves.

"Stefan, forgive me," said Karl. "That was tactless. The circumstances were different."

"Niklas is rotting in there," Stefan said hoarsely. "I can see him fading before my eyes, and there's nothing I can do, is there? You would not let me destroy Reiniger!"

"Because you could not. I tried, and I couldn't either."

"Karl, what happened?" Charlotte asked. "All this diverted me from my utter relief at finding you safe. I suppose you thought it natural that I'd throw myself on you without saying a word, because that's what I would have done. Kissed you first, and asked questions second."

He described how he'd pursued Stefan to the house, fended off Reiniger's gang and persuaded Stefan to leave. Then he related his talk with Godric Reiniger in the screening room. Charlotte and

Stefan sat riveted as he spoke of Fadiya, of Reiniger's past and his bizarre ideas.

Not so bizarre, Karl thought, *considering that his powers are tangible.*

"I decided to kill him," Karl said simply. "I could see no other way to stop the danger he presents, his threats. But he escaped. He went into the Crystal Ring."

Charlotte and Stefan exchanged a baffled look.

"How?" said Charlotte. "Has he become a vampire? If so, why is he still pestering you about it?"

Karl shook his head. "He still seemed human, or nearly so, but he has a form of power I've never encountered before. A very strange aura. When I attacked him, his men came rushing in – as I knew they would – but he vanished in my hands. I followed him, or tried. I had only enough strength to enter the Crystal Ring very briefly. Just enough to escape through the house walls and to see a shape streaking away like a comet."

He paused, recalling the sight. Shadows and mist, like a monochrome film. Reiniger, a pale smudge arcing towards the higher regions that Karl could not reach. He still couldn't comprehend what he'd seen.

"I had the presence of mind to flee the house. Then I found Stefan's motor car, drove back to his chalet, put him in the front and Niklas in the back seat, and brought them here. It's as safe as anywhere, and best that we're all together."

"So Reiniger's men saw you both disappear?" asked Charlotte.

"Yes. I wonder what they made of that? I don't know how much their leader has told them. They might know everything or nothing. He may not have explained what his blood-rituals are for, apart from the obvious: sealing the oath between them."

"They must know something," said Stefan. "What does he say to them? 'Here, have a magical cursed knife. Stab yourself freely and often. Why? Oh, just for the hell of it!' They *must* know, unless he only recruits idiots."

"I wouldn't underestimate them," said Karl. "Reiniger might feel threatened by anyone cleverer than him, but he has the sense to know he needs strong supporters, not weak ones. And he's both intelligent and obsessive. I've often wondered if a human who could enter Raqia by their own willpower would be more dangerous than any vampire. Reiniger's using the bone-knives to siphon off our powers, but he's still not satisfied. Why become a mere vampire, if he can become something even more dangerous?"

"I don't care what he is," said Stefan. "For what he's done to Niklas, I will not rest until I've destroyed him."

"Dear, have you fed?" Charlotte asked gently, leaning over to touch Stefan's hand.

"How can I?"

"You should. You look terrible. You'll need your strength."

"I'll go with you," said Karl.

"I'm not a child," Stefan growled.

"That's debatable." Karl spoke patiently, giving him a firm look. "But you are our friend."

Stefan rose. "All right. But let me sit with Niklas for a few more minutes. I want to look at him while he's still here."

He returned to the bedroom. Charlotte leaned back and put her hand to her forehead. "He's not going to get over this, is he?" she said.

Karl moved beside her and drew her on to his knee. Her body felt warm and real, her lips silky against his temple, but he still had a lingering sense of nightmare: the same feeling that silent films woke in him. Unreality. What if a *third* Charlotte entered…?

Niklas and Stefan had always been a shimmering presence in his life, even when he was at odds with them. Now they were two corpses: one decaying, the other still a moving, talking shell.

"None of us will," he whispered.

He took in Charlotte's lovely scent, the texture of her skin, the light in her eyes: everything about her. Tried to recall what was different about the spectre… Nothing at first, then details began to emerge. He recalled the apparition having no warmth or scent, soulless eyes, a smile that looked genuine – if it hadn't been so inappropriate in their harrowing situation…

"I'm real," she said, as if reading his thoughts. "But perhaps the other one thinks she's real, too. There could be half a dozen of me walking around. I might have to share you with five other Charlottes! Or twenty-five."

"I'm glad you can joke about this."

"And I hope I'm joking."

"*Liebling*, I thought I was embracing you. You walked away, then reappeared from the opposite direction... but I've heard of this happening. Folk tales, anecdotes that send icy winds down the spine if they're to be believed. You see a loved one in the room. You even speak to each other. Then the loved one goes on their way – let's say they go upstairs. And you immediately meet the person again, in a different room, somewhere they could not possibly be unless the first encounter was an illusion. And they deny that they've seen or spoken to you until this moment. They're as puzzled as you are."

She shuddered. "Isn't seeing a *doppelgänger* a forewarning of death?"

"Superstition," said Karl. "I think it's a trick the universe plays upon our minds, with no explanation, no purpose but to remind us there are things we can never understand."

"You had a double that was real," said Charlotte. "So had Stefan."

"Dearest, that was Kristian's doing."

"I know. I've never had my head severed, nor have I been regrown in duplicate in a blood-filled sarcophagus... I think I would have noticed, don't you?" She gave a nervous smile. "But... I forced the double away because I truly had no idea which of us was real. And still she keeps coming back. I am the lamia who entrances humans and drinks their blood without conscience. I'm Charlotte, who has good intentions but often does rash, mad things she shouldn't."

He wrapped his arms around her waist and held her firmly against him.

"You feel real to me."

She sighed into his hair. "But you thought that about the other one, didn't you?"

"At the time, yes. Her presence lulled the suspicions I should have had."

"So she enchanted you? Cast a veil over your senses. Does the apparition have the power to control our minds?"

"To a limited extent, it seems." He spoke quietly, not knowing what to say. He didn't want to alarm her, but he couldn't offer false reassurance. "I'm as puzzled as you."

His lips touched her neck. He felt her stiffen, preparing to pull out of his arms and distance herself. A shiver went through her, but he held firmly on to her, this time not letting her out of his embrace.

"Charlotte, don't push me away. I won't let you. If the bone-knife poisoned you in some way, I am equally poisoned, and so is Stefan. We can't possibly harm each other. So what are you afraid of, really?"

She stopped struggling and let her arms tighten around his waist and shoulders. "I think" – her voice was low, painfully hesitant – "rejecting her was the worst thing I could have done. She started as no more than a looking-glass reflection, but now I've no control over her at all. I'm terrified that as she grows stronger, I'll grow weaker until I disappear. A different Charlotte will take my place… Still me, but not me at all."

"My God," he whispered. A subtle but intense current wave of horror drove through him. Even if she was wrong, her terror was enough to unsettle him to the core of his soul.

"What am I going to do? What if she – it – comes again and you can't tell which of us is real?"

He had no words. Instead he bit gently into her throat, took three small, deliberate swallows of her blood. She gave a faint moan, but didn't try to stop him.

There *was* a different taste to her blood, but only a remnant of the *sikin* attack: a peppery taste, not unpleasant at all.

"There," he said softly against her skin. "Now you're inside me, poisoned or not, and your blood tastes as divine as ever." He loosened his collar, baring his neck to her. "Take mine in return."

Her beautifully shaped lips parted, glistening plum-red. Her eyes were sultry, smoky. He saw the tip of her tongue and her shining white teeth. She paused a moment then struck, groaning as if she couldn't hold back any longer. Three times he felt her mouth pulling on his vessels, a burning yet delicious pain. He felt her tears drip on to his throat as her fangs retracted.

"The blood exchange," said Karl, caressing her cheek, her hair. They were both breathing deeply, hot, clinging hard enough to melt into each other. "As if we need reminding, beloved – we're part of each other, for good or ill. So don't be afraid. I will always know my true Charlotte – just as you knew that my *doppelgänger* was not me. I love you. No more fear."

"None." She licked clean the wound she'd made. The puncture marks would soon vanish. "I wish we could stay like this forever, but there's too much to worry about."

"I know." Karl kissed her, tasting his own blood on her mouth. It had that same spicy-bitter hint. "Godric Reiniger will not go away, to my regret."

"And Amy – we *can't* send her back to her uncle after what you've told me. And poor Stefan. And where have Violette and Emil got to?"

"Violette can look after herself, at least."

"That doesn't stop me worrying." Charlotte sat up straight on his knees, her hands braced on his shoulders. "Karl, do you think that Amy could capture the lamia on film? If it comes back again?"

"I don't know. It would be an interesting experiment. We know that physical vampires show up on film..."

"But ghostly vampires? It might be a way to... contain the spectre, or dismiss it by proving it doesn't exist. Actually, I don't know what it might prove. But I'm going to ask her."

"All right." Karl was pleased to feel her sudden renewed energy, transmitted to his hands through the warm curves of her body. "But that may mean we have to tell her too much."

"I rather think she knows too much already," Charlotte said ruefully.

Hours spent jolting on the truck bed left Emil nauseated, exhausted. Night fell; the strips of sky he could see through gaps in the canvas turned black. His world became a lightless box, like a tiny ship rolling on a stormy sea. Nightmares again...

Cold air bathed his face as he was dragged out by his feet and held upright. He heard Fadiya murmuring in an unknown language... then they carried him a short distance and flung him down on a hard stone floor.

He slept.

Some time later he woke with a cry. Where was he? Eyes shone in the darkness. Fadiya was bending down to him, holding a cup to his lips. The water, icy cold and tasting of minerals, flowed deliciously over his parched tongue.

Behind her stood two dark figures. Guards. Also vampires. He'd learned to recognise them, as easily as he could tell a tiger from a cat.

"I am sorry, dearest," she whispered as he gulped the water. "No harm will come to you, as long as *she* comes after you."

"She?" he rasped.

"Your mistress. Violette."

"What?" Then he understood, and fell back on to the hard floor, cursing himself. "You captured me – to bring *her* here? Why?"

Fadiya did not answer. She refilled his cup.

"What am I to you? A hostage? Bait?"

"Bait," Fadiya said under her breath. "That is a good word."

"She won't come," said Emil. He flung the cup away, heard it break. "You think she has nothing better to do than come looking for me? She won't even notice I've gone, you idiots!"

"You're wrong. You had better be wrong. Don't try to escape. Lie on the palm fronds I brought: you'll be more comfortable. We'll look after you, but if you flee, you'll die within a day. There is nothing around us but desert."

Then Fadiya rose without sound and left.

Presently light slid into his prison and he saw they'd put him into a cave, a small stone cavern of a dull orange hue like the patch of rock-strewn sand he could see outside. There was nothing in here but a metal bucket and a pile of dried palm fronds for a bed.

No gate on the narrow entrance, but there were guards. Emil saw the dark shapes of men – vampires – wrapped head to foot in Bedouin-style robes. As the hours dragged on, two or three of them were always there. Sometimes he heard voices murmuring as different figures came to take their place. Usually they stood like statues. In the darkness, he could not even tell which way they were facing. He imagined each one with two faces, looking both inwards and outwards, like two-headed gods of the underworld.

Now he had nothing left. Not even sanity. He was almost too weak to stand, let alone to attempt escape. He could sense vampires everywhere, like dozens of spectres thirsting for him. He was aware of the immensity of the desert beyond the fortress.

Fadiya was right. Even if he escaped, where would he go? There was nothing for miles but sand and rock. He might be crazed, but hadn't entirely lost his common sense.

I do not want to die, he thought. *Violette, I am so sorry.*

When the sun rose, a cloth-veiled figure would bring him a bowl of water to wash in, mint tea to drink, fresh dates and mushy spiced couscous. The same repast was brought again when the sun was high, and when it set. Or flat bread, goat's cheese and figs. How did they know what to feed humans, unless they'd been human once? He would see vampire eyes shining down at him with interest, hunger, lust. He noticed their long slim fingers – graceful yet taut, as if longing to seize him... but they did not.

Not yet.

Nothing to do but watch the changing light on the cave walls: from a dull peach as dawn came, to a flaming golden-red glow as sunlight crept into his prison, back to beige and then darkness as the sun passed on.

Oddly, he could smell horses: a gentle, earthy ripeness that reminded him of his family farm. A comforting smell, for all the unhappiness he'd felt there. His past misery seemed trivial now, caused only by his rebellion against his father's expectations. But the death of his brother Alfonso meant he could never go back. Never. His father would find a way to blame him...

Sometimes he heard the horses snort or whicker. The sounds echoed, as if they were in caves nearby.

He scented a wet chill in the air, like an underground river beneath the caves. That would make sense, because people settled where they could drill wells. Vampires might not need water, but horses did... and so did human captives.

Are there any humans here? Sometimes he lay awake at night listening for the cries of other prisoners in distress. Nothing.

Violette came to him in his dreams. He saw her far away on a stage, dancing without him. Twice he woke with Fadiya leaning over him, her eyes gleaming, even tearful... She was so beautiful and so horrifying.

"I'm sorry, my beloved Emil. So sorry."

She stroked his cheek – but when he woke properly, she was gone.

I'm alone. The knowledge circled endlessly around his mind, an obsession. *I am the only human creature for hundreds of miles in any direction.*

After the first two days, he forced himself to his feet one

afternoon and drilled his body through his regular routine of stretching and strengthening exercises. His head whirled and he thought the effort would kill him, yet he forced himself halfway through before collapsing.

Tomorrow he would try again. It was all he had left of who he used to be.

"May I go yet?" Amy asked worriedly as Charlotte approached her. Most of the theatre staff had gone, and she was sitting in the front row, turning her cloche hat around in her hands. The cine-camera stood on its tripod beside her. "Everyone was such a good sport for the camera. I've had a fascinating time – I've met so many wonderful people that I wish I'd gone into ballet instead of acting – but I don't know what to do now. I am rather tired, and hungry. Are we still playing hostages?"

"Yes and no." Charlotte sat beside her. The stage lay in darkness. "We got our friend back from Bergwerkstatt, but he's not well, and your uncle…"

"What about him?"

"He's angry. He might come here looking for you, and it's not safe for you to go back to him."

"I wasn't planning to go home." Amy's tone darkened. She looked so alone that Charlotte longed to comfort her… but embracing humans led to dangerous temptation. "I'll never forget that he sent me to Dr Ochsner. He doesn't care about *me*, only about how I behave."

"Where would you go?"

"I don't know. A hotel, I suppose, while I decide what to do. Oh, I will so miss Mariette, Peter and the others…" She looked down at her hands. "But go back to my uncle, the murderer, and let him choose a husband for me? No."

"That's his plan for you?"

"Oh, yes. He would have to be the *perfect* Swiss hero, so that I can produce a new race of superior humans!" She laughed bitterly. "That's what women are for, in Uncle Godric's new world."

"Breeding stock?"

"I think he had some idea of pairing me with Emil, but that's a non-starter. Fadiya's in the way, and Emil's too… Italian. However princely he looks, he's not of the right blood."

"Good lord. Amy, you really must leave."

"I have no choice, after all the things I've seen and heard…"

"Go on," said Charlotte. "You can tell me anything."

"Blackmail," Amy whispered. "People wonder where Uncle Godric gets the money to employ his crew and live in such a grand house and make his films. Donations from his supporters aren't enough. Sometimes he twists their arms."

"In what way?"

"He's in a dilemma. He wants strong heroic types around him, but men like that can be terribly competitive. He's always looking over his shoulder to see if someone else is more popular than him. They might be a threat. They might even oust him and take over. So he has everyone spying on everyone else. He finds out their weakness and uses it against them. It's dreadfully poisonous."

"What sort of weaknesses?" Charlotte was fascinated: she'd had the notion that Reiniger's followers supported him without question.

"All sorts of things. Having an affair. Stealing from work." Amy's voice dropped to the faintest whisper. "Being homosexual."

"Is that such a difficulty? I didn't think it was regarded as any great crime here."

"Well, it's legal in certain cantons, so I'm told. In the rest of the country, if there's enough evidence, you can get several years in jail. No one wants that sort of thing made public: the disapproval from all quarters would be unbearable. And my uncle takes a very strong stand. His ideology decrees that it's wrong, wrong, wrong. I've heard him boast that if ever he got into political office, he'd put all homosexuals into prison camps, along with his opponents, foreigners and other undesirables. He wants Switzerland to be *just so* and perfect."

"You mean some of his followers aren't as perfect as they should be? They want power, but they can't all live up to his standards?"

Amy nodded. Her expression was unhappy but quietly, immovably defiant.

"That's how it seems to work. They're all frightened of him, Charlotte. He turns a blind eye and treats everyone as his best friend – until he wants something, then he holds vicious threats of scandal, disgrace and prison over them. You say he killed your friend. I don't think it's the first time he's murdered someone."

Charlotte lived among vampires, but even so, Amy's statement shocked her.

"Who?"

"One of his close circle, Bruno, has just… disappeared. I can't be certain… Their shiftiness whenever his name is mentioned speaks volumes."

"Amy, it doesn't matter in the slightest how fond of you he claims to be. He's evil."

"The trouble is, I don't know what he might do when I leave. If he comes after me…"

She fell quiet, and Charlotte wondered what else to say. Where was best to take the girl? Not to her own rooms, because Stefan and Niklas were there. Violette's apartment, then? At least kind-hearted Geli would look after her.

"Well, you're safe here for now. Bear with us a while. Please come upstairs. You can spend the night here. I'll make sure you have supper, and a bed. You look so cold and pale – I'm sorry, I should have looked after you better. Let me carry the camera."

"It's all right, it doesn't weigh too much. I'll take it to the darkroom – I'm eager to process the film, actually."

"Can't that wait until tomorrow? It'll be something to keep you busy."

"You're right. I am rather tired."

Charlotte put her fingers on the back of Amy's hand. She flinched, very slightly. "Amy, one thing. This must all seem very strange, and I don't know how to explain, but… You saw the woman upstairs, who looked like me?"

Amy nodded, wordless.

"I know this sounds preposterous, but she's a kind of… phantom. She's been bothering us quite a lot. We wondered, if she appears again, if you might try to film her?"

The young woman went so pale that Charlotte thought she would pass out.

"I didn't mean to frighten you. Think of it as a scientific experiment."

"No, I'm not frightened," Amy said at last. "Well, only a bit. It's just that... I think I have filmed her already."

"When?"

"No more than half an hour ago. I had the viewfinder trained on the stage. I was about to stop, because people were leaving and the stage was empty. Then you walked on from the wings – at least I thought she was you. No one else seemed to notice. You – she came right to the front of the stage. I waved and called out, but she took no notice."

"It wasn't me," Charlotte whispered.

"She looked just like you, a shade paler perhaps, but it was the way she moved – very slow, gliding more than walking – that was so eerie. I kept filming until the film ran out. It was only a few seconds."

"Where did she go?"

"I don't know." Amy pointed vaguely to the left. "She seemed to slide down into the orchestra pit and then fade away. She was gone before she reached the wall."

"And you stayed here? You're a brave soul, aren't you?"

"Not really. There didn't seem anything to run away from. It was just so *odd*."

"Odd things do happen here," Charlotte said gently. "I can't explain properly, but if you will carry on being brave and helping us, we'll protect you."

Amy gave a wan smile. "It seems that everywhere I go is haunted and full of peculiar things happening. It's no worse here than at Bergwerkstatt. I'm almost used to it."

Charlotte enclosed her hand between both her own.

"What do you mean, no worse?"

"Charlotte... I've seen the ghost who looks like you in my uncle's house, as well."

Geli appeared startled when Charlotte asked her to look after Amy, but she didn't question her story that Amy was a friend of Madame Lenoir, to be treated as her honoured guest.

"No, I haven't seen Madame all day," Geli replied to Charlotte's question.

Having settled her in, Charlotte made her way back to her own suite, eager to tell Karl and Stefan what had happened.

Halfway along the passage, she walked into Violette.

The dancer looked wild: no coat, her silver-grey dress dusty, her hair an untamed straggle. Her face was bone-white, her eyes wide and glistening – she hadn't looked like this since her early days as a vampire, when she had turned into Lilith and run wild.

"Where the hell have you been?" Violette demanded. Her fangs were extended, gleaming in the half light.

"Me?" Charlotte held her at arm's length. "You're the one who's been gone for hours on end. What's happened to you?"

"For heaven's sake, drop your hand. I'm not going to attack you. I've been trying to find Emil."

"No luck, I take it."

"It's worse than you think." Violette pushed a letter at Charlotte. "Read this. I was frantic because he'd run away with a vampire. Now they've sent me a ransom note!"

"Who?"

Charlotte read the typed letter, deciphered the scrawl at the end, noted the day and time they demanded Violette meet her contact. Tomorrow, late afternoon.

"Algiers?" said Charlotte, her voice weak with disbelief. "Is this a joke?"

"I've already been there." Violette mimed flight with her hand. "Through the Crystal Ring, obviously. I searched all day, but the place is a tangle and there was no hint of his presence. Hopeless. Now all I can do is meet this go-between, Nabil – whoever he is – and put myself at his mercy."

"This is preposterous," said Charlotte. "I'm sorry, that was an appalling understatement, but I don't know what to say. Who would do this?"

Violette was motionless, like an image of herself frozen on the air. "I don't know, but I believe it's connected to the skull-creature who's been watching me for weeks. Fadiya must be working for him, her, or it – I don't know what this means, but *they* knew the perfect way to lure me to them: take Emil! Apparently they want *me* in exchange for him. 'Furious' doesn't begin to describe what I feel."

"But you're going anyway?"

"I must."

"You'd walk into a trap set by strangers? For Emil?"

"Darling, I'd do the same for any of my dancers. I'd do it for the boy who washes the pots."

"Of course," Charlotte said softly. Violette had once run into a burning building to save her dancers.

"No one harms my company. That is my weak spot, I know, but that's the way of things. Will you come with me?"

"You don't think I'd let you go alone?"

As soon as she'd uttered the words, Charlotte remembered all the complications. Stefan. Reiniger. Amy.

"What?" said Violette, eyes narrowing. "You're hesitating. I need you to bring Emil safely home, because I may not be able to."

"I'm afraid to leave Stefan, and…"

"Surely Karl can look after him?"

"It's not that simple. Godric Reiniger might be connected with this, and there's a chance he's become a monster of some kind – not a vampire, but worse – and his niece is in your apartment…"

"I do not have time for this! Charlotte, if you won't come with me, that's your decision. I'll go alone. I'd love to know every detail, as much as I'd love to know why you were in my room staring over my shoulder, moments before this letter arrived, but it will have to wait."

"I wasn't in your room," Charlotte answered. *Not again,* she thought in dismay. *Violette's seeing my lamia, too?*

"Then I was imagining things. Never mind. I am going to feed upon some poor soul and then, once my strength is renewed, I'm going to this rendezvous with 'Nabil'. Wish me luck."

Her voice was very calm and low.

"No need," said Charlotte. "I'll be with you. As I said, I can't let you go alone."

CHAPTER TWENTY-TWO

A TIMELESS SEARCH

The heat and the blinding force of the sun overwhelmed Charlotte. She blinked at dazzling white buildings rising from the port. Algiers was brighter and livelier than anything she'd imagined. Thrilling, in all its exotic commotion.

Vampires could tolerate daylight, but for the first time she feared she might actually go up in flames.

So busy, thronging with Berbers and Arabs and tourists and workers... In their salt-white pomposity, the great buildings were overwhelming, too much for their setting and almost ugly. She wanted to see the real Algeria, the ancient city hidden behind the new.

"Come on," said Violette, "We have nearly two hours. We'll go to market and buy some local clothing – I bought a djellaba yesterday, and left it behind when I went home – but it will be easy enough to retrieve it. I made friends with a stallholder who couldn't have been more obliging. The only difficulty is escaping, because he loves to talk and talk. Just be your charming self while I make the deal. Then we'll be ready. And when this Nabil appears to meet me, you must hang back and conceal yourself, since I'm supposed to meet him alone."

"I'll follow you," said Charlotte, trying to smile in hopes of feeling braver. "Your invisible bodyguard, dearest."

They made their way uphill through the bustling streets, half in the Crystal Ring to avoid curious stares. Their trip through Raqia had been the wildest Charlotte had ever known. Violette, holding her hand, had dragged her through the firmament at breath-taking speed as they arced over the Mediterranean towards the North African coast. Charlotte hadn't yet shaken off the mix of exhilaration and horror. She had felt like a leaf carried on a hurricane.

The souk was thick with people, both locals and tourists. Animal smells, perfumes, vegetables, spices, the stink of cured leather – a multitude of odours engulfed her and she wanted to stop in her tracks, close her eyes and take in everything, identifying each scent, savouring the heat of blood that lay beneath everything else... to select the perfect victim. A young woman caught her eye, as lovely as Fadiya, carrying a basket full of fruit and herbs. A brown-skinned boy, lithe as a gazelle. An English visitor, lobster-red from the sun, haggling in a loud slow voice as if shouting would help the trader to understand his language...

"Charlotte," whispered Violette, pulling her inside a clothes stall, a small forest of coloured fabrics. "Concentrate! If you're thirsty, there will be time later."

"No, I'm not. But there's so much to see..."

The stallholder – a lanky man with leather-brown skin and lively, kind eyes – flattered them with attention, plainly thrilled to see Violette again and eager to provide perfect outfits. When he named a price, Violette casually paid him double: the opposite of his usual expectations, judging by his wide smile.

It would have been easy to sneak some blood from his veins, but Charlotte resisted.

Soon they were covered in long, layered creamy robes, with head cloths to veil their hair, tough sandals for treading the sandy ground.

"Now we separate," Violette said softly as they walked out into the white-hot street. "Can you sense any vampires nearby?"

"No one," said Charlotte. "That doesn't mean there aren't any."

"I know. I'm worried that someone's already watching us, but we have to take the chance. You know where we're going? Stay behind me, at least two hundred yards back."

"Don't worry," Charlotte answered. "You won't see me, but I'll be there."

Karl hadn't been happy at her going with Violette, but he had understood. Charlotte was always grateful for his common sense. However much he might wish to protect her, he knew she was strong, and that he could not always keep her out of danger.

They could have swapped places, but that would have meant Charlotte staying with Stefan and Amy, and facing a potential visit from the unpredictable Godric Reiniger. And Karl hadn't regained enough strength to enter Raqia, let alone make the long, breakneck journey with Violette.

After a discussion – *not an argument, never that*, she thought with a private smile – she and Karl had reached the most practical decision.

At times like this, she wished they had more friends – but even those closest to them, such as Pierre and Ilona, were hardly the most reliable allies.

Some distance ahead, Violette walked into a public square: a white and golden space, with a charming fountain and palm trees grouped on the far side. In the shade of their fanned leaves, a man stood waiting. He was all in blue, no flesh visible except around his eyes. His skin was like ebony.

Charlotte hung back, hoping he hadn't seen her. More importantly, that he could not *sense* her. She heard their voices, far off but clear.

"*Istilqa?*" said Violette.

"*Istilqa*," he echoed. "I am Nabil. I will take you to Emil."

"Where's Fadiya?"

"With him."

"Can you show any proof that you have him?"

Nabil looked irritated that she asked, but produced a white shirt from the folds of his robe. Charlotte watched with her heart in her throat as Violette lifted the garment to her nose. She would distinguish his scent as keenly as a hound. The man gave her something else, too: a small gold item. A cufflink?

Violette had given all her male dancers cufflinks inscribed with *Ballet Lenoir* as gifts last Christmas. Her face, in profile, turned to limestone as Charlotte saw the reality of the situation hit her. Fury and fear.

"Is he here in the town?"

Nabil shook his head. "Out in the desert, beyond Djelfa. We'll go through the Crystal Ring."

"Wait. Do you swear that you'll release him in exchange for me?"

"That is the promise made by Zruvan, Lord of Immortals. Yes, he will keep his word."

"He had better," Violette said with soft menace. "If he does not, this 'Lord' of yours will be sorrier than he can imagine."

Nabil stayed impassive. "Come with me." He paused: for a frightening moment, Charlotte thought he'd seen her, but he seemed to be checking for danger without actually noticing her.

There were people around, but no one saw Nabil and Violette vanish into Raqia. Charlotte gave them two seconds: she daren't wait longer, in case she lost them. Then she followed. The world changed, becoming a dim and eerie version of itself. Humans turned into fireflies, only their auras visible. All normal sound stopped. As Charlotte began to climb through the ether, a low, hissing moan filled her ears, like the wind moving over desert sands.

Violette and her companion travelled miles to the south, a journey that would have taken many hours in a motor vehicle. They flew low. Distorted through the medium of the ether, she saw the extraordinary landscape below: sandstone mountains shaped like fantastical pillars and spires, dyed purple and red by the sinking sun. There were deep violet chasms. Salt flats. Stretches of sand marked by giant black circles: the remains of spent volcanoes.

Violette caught a clear view of their destination only when they dropped out of the Crystal Ring. They were in the open desert, a sweep of orange rock and sand that spread to the horizon in every direction.

A thrill went through her. She'd always felt drawn to desert places. This was the clean wilderness where she could be free... a memory from Lilith's past, not her own, but still powerful. Her soul was entwined with that of Lilith, a wild spirit who had fled to the desert rather than submit to the will of men or God.

She saw a ruined fortress, worn away by sandstorms for hundreds of years. The shell of jagged walls was sinking back into the desert, all features worn away, nothing inside but swirling sand. Curving around the ruins were rock walls striped with red and gold layers, glowing as the sun set. The rock faces were pocked with caves.

All this she took in as they glided in from above and landed on the sand, light-footed as birds.

"Where are we?"

"We call it Al Bir," said Nabil. "It no longer appears on any map."

"And is there water here? I mean for Emil. Humans can't survive on air alone."

He pointed at the ground. "A river runs deep below. There are wells. We are looking after Emil; we don't wish him to die."

"I want to see him."

Nabil led her towards the ruin, through a rock arch into a kind of courtyard with the crumbling fortress walls in front and the caves to their right. "It is not permitted until you have surrendered yourself to our Lord Zruvan."

Violette held back a flare of rage. A voice roared in her mind, *How dare you do this? Who do you think you are?* She knew that if she unleashed her anger, the Lilith part of her wouldn't hesitate to tear off Nabil's head, or that of anyone who tried to stop her.

She kept her fury down, well aware that if she lost control, Emil would certainly die.

"What does your Lord Zruvan want with me?"

"That is for him to tell you."

"He's had every chance," Violette said tightly. She stopped, forcing Nabil to turn and face her. "Wait a moment, and tell me the truth. A huge figure in dark-brown robes, with a skull-mask covering his head and a staff glowing in his hands: wasn't that your Lord Zruvan, stalking me through the Crystal Ring? If he could keep following me and finding me there, why couldn't he speak to me?"

"His ways are mysterious," said Nabil. She knew by now he wouldn't give a clear answer. "But he never leaves his dwelling. He cannot. That's why he instructed us to bring you here."

"He can't leave his dwelling," she echoed. "So what did I see?"

"The power of his will."

"You mean a thought-form. A kind of astral projection. That's what I thought. He's very good."

"Good? He is a great deity, beyond your comprehension." Nabil turned and began walking again. She fell in beside him.

"And yet he can't physically go out?"

She was goading him, trying to get at the truth, but Nabil

would not play. She saw a glitter of anger in his eyes. His reply was low and abrupt. "You cannot understand."

Cannot, she thought. *That's rather more judgemental than, "You do not..."*

"I fear that once I go to him, I may not come out again." She tried to hide the genuine fear in her voice. "What proof will I have that Emil is safe and free?"

"I am sorry, my lady." Nabil bowed, inviting her forward with an open hand. "I like this no more than you. But I ask respectfully that you follow me."

His deference surprised her – but she was a goddess, after all. And, however reluctant he was to acknowledge it, he knew.

Charlotte's journey through the Crystal Ring was one of the hardest she'd ever made. The layered robes weighed her down, as they would in water. The weight sapped her energy. From Raqia, the vista of sand and mountains seemed to boil. Keeping sight of Violette and Nabil, while staying far enough behind to avoid notice, was nearly impossible. Her mouth was dry, every bone aching with effort.

Finally she lost them.

Panic rose, but she controlled her anxiety. *Karl would not panic,* she scolded herself. *Violette most definitely would not. Stay on course. Observe.*

Minutes later she sensed specks of warmth, far below her on the veiled surface of the Sahara where mountains gave way to the desert. Human? Certainly not vampire. Animal, perhaps.

She dropped lower in her flight. The Crystal Ring's glow above her faded. She was dangerously close to the ground now. Huge cliffs thrust out of the land, tiered around what appeared to be an oblong ruin. The heat-motes grew stronger. Just as she made to step from the firmament into the solid world, she saw Violette and Nabil together on the sand.

Charlotte veered away, willing herself invisible. High up on a wall of rock, concealed by sandstone outcrops, she re-entered reality and crouched there to watch.

The last of sunset turned the world to a flood of red and bronze.

The two robed figures talked for a while – even her acute ears couldn't discern their words – then they walked away, vanishing inside the ruins.

Dread washed over her. Where was Nabil taking Violette? She might as well be walking into the underworld, like Demeter trying to rescue Persephone. The dancer was the toughest, most wilful woman Charlotte had ever met – yet she meekly gave herself up to unknown danger in the narrow hope of saving Emil? Charlotte thought, *Does she know something I don't?*

What if I never see her again?

Utter silence lay across the wilderness. Darkness came swiftly, and the stars blazed as thickly as falling snow. Charlotte began to make her way down the rugged slope, focusing hard on the dust-motes of warmth she could feel. They grew more vivid, like fingertips pressing her forehead.

The rock wall was full of caves. She imagined people living here, in aeons past. Now there was only emptiness... with three specks of life. A familiar, animal scent emanated from a cave mouth at ground level. Horses?

And from another cave, a few yards away, came the rank scent of human sweat, dehydration, illness. From her vantage point, directly above the entrance, she leaned out and saw two heavily robed figures standing guard. They might have been rock pillars: shapeless, motionless, emitting no blood-warmth.

Vampires.

The last thing she wanted was to reveal her presence and start a fight. Her only way into the cave was to go back into the Crystal Ring and force her way through the rock.

She hated doing this. When she'd feigned her own "death", some perverse impulse had made her endure the entire funeral: being sealed in the coffin, the burial, then clawing her way up through clay soil to escape afterwards. It was a kind of self-punishment for her family's grief. Even when she could avoid such horrors, she would make herself go straight through the heart of them instead.

But the feeling of being trapped, suffocating, swimming through rock or earth as if it were quicksand, always brought dread. Now she floundered through viscous slabs of stone, breath held even though she didn't need oxygen, praying she had the energy to stay in Raqia. If she slipped back into the real world now – she would be entombed in rock forever.

Thin air. She fell a few feet, then let herself back into reality, drawing deep breaths as if she'd nearly drowned. Darkness lay around her, but she could see well enough. Starglow filtered in to illuminate the rough walls of a cave. A cell, in effect.

Emil lay on a bed of palm leaves. It looked uncomfortable, but he was in a deep sleep of total exhaustion. They'd put him into a djellaba, but she saw his trouser hems and plain black shoes jutting below the hem of the garment. He looked dirty, his hair an unwashed mess, sand stuck to his face and hands. Tragic, to see his muscular dancer's body limp and helpless.

Charlotte looked down at him with mixed emotions. *Thank goodness, he really is here!* Then, *Poor lad, he doesn't deserve this. His misfortune was to fall for one vampire, and then to be seduced by another. This could have been me – in fact it* was *me, until Ilona rescued me from Kristian. Humans tangle with vampires and this is the result: ruin.*

She wondered how to get him out of the cave. She couldn't escape the way she'd arrived, since it was impossible to take a human through the Crystal Ring. Even if she confronted the guards, there would be a hellish fight, and they were bound to have comrades. And even if she won – how to take Emil across hundreds of miles of desert and mountain? He'd never survive.

If she tried, the repercussion for Violette, too, might be instant death.

Charlotte sat beside Emil, her arms wrapped around her bent knees. She watched him, aware that, if he woke, her priority was to stop him crying out. Would he realise she was here as a friend?

He'd already run from her in terror. More than once, she'd seen him recoil from her. He knew she was a vampire. Such knowledge could unhinge human minds.

Something moved in the gloom. Charlotte jumped to her feet and found herself looking straight into Fadiya's dark, gleaming eyes.

* * *

Violette followed Nabil into a narrow fissure and down through a winding fault in the rock structure; tight passages, with twists and drops that no human could have negotiated. She'd thrown off her robes and djellaba at the entrance, realising they would be a hindrance. All she kept on was the grey silk dress that she'd travelled in from home. Now she was glad of her dancer's training, as well as her vampiric sinuosity.

At first there was no light. Even her sensitive sight perceived nothing in the pitch blackness. She followed Nabil by touch and sound as well as the higher senses that helped her locate him in the convolutions of the tunnel. Presently a dim glow appeared, gleaming sand-red on the narrow rock walls. The temperature grew warmer.

She'd expected chilliness down here, and instead felt she was walking towards a fire.

They entered a larger tunnel that seemed to be floored with cobblestones and sand brushed into the seams. Here there was room to stand up straight. The passageway stretched for an indefinable length – at least three hundred yards – straight and purposeful like the entrance to a tomb. At the far end she saw the red glow. A furnace mouth?

Then Violette went hot and cold with dread. Had these unknown vampires lured her here to burn her to ashes?

What is this place? she asked silently. *If extreme cold can finish us, why not extreme heat? I understand why they might want to kill me, and they're not the first, but who are they?*

"Would you answer some questions?" she asked. It was the first time either of them had spoken since entering the warren.

"It's not my place to do so," said Nabil. "My duty was to bring you here, that's all."

The walls vibrated with unpleasant energy, a prickling static that numbed her hand whenever she touched them. Her feet hurt as if she were walking on knives. Something of Raqia penetrated the space: a clamour of dream-energies, the massed thoughts of humanity. Or nightmares, she guessed from the hostile atmosphere. Voices whispered. Thousands of voices.

Then she knew that this was an in-between place, lying both in the Earth and the Crystal Ring at the same time. The further they went, the more fiercely the unseen energies assaulted her, an invisible sandstorm. She tasted the bitter acridity of the bone-knives, and of Lord Zruvan's staff.

"How do you bear this place?" she asked.

"We learn to endure," said Nabil.

"Do you mean that you *have* to, as a form of penance?"

"You could say so."

"Self-punishment – for being a vampire?"

"No more questions, my lady goddess."

"That's unfair. I've been forced to come here, I have done everything you asked, but you will explain nothing in return."

He stopped and turned to her. "I apologise, my lady, but you are about to meet Zruvan, Lord of Immortals. He will choose whether or not to answer your questions."

"Very well." She kept her expression calm, but the growing heat was uncomfortable. She envisioned the goddess part of her psyche, Lilith, a desert dweller, writhing in a mad dance of ecstasy and pain as she died in flames. She tried not to wonder how agonising it would be. Nor would she think about escape, because she was not a prisoner. She'd come here voluntarily... not that she'd had much choice, since she could not leave Emil to perish.

"I won't ask any more," she said. "I know you are only a servant."

Nabil glowered at her.

"A servant who is honoured to serve Zruvan, and who thanks you for your cooperation. You may go on alone from here. Lord Zruvan waits for you in the Bone Well. Follow the light."

Is Zruvan even real? She caught a dry, hot breath. *Perhaps he perished in the inferno and they worship his ghost? And if I'm to be a sacrifice to him, that makes some kind of perverse sense.*

If only they'd tell me who they are before it ends.

As a human, and as a vampire, Violette had endured fear, oppression, even persecution simply for being what she was: gifted, beautiful, powerful, disobedient and female. *But every time,* she thought, now walking steadily towards the hell-mouth, *every damned time, instead of walking away I throw myself into danger. Lilith's rage helped me in the past, but her anger has mellowed now. Too much. Perhaps fighting her, instead of accepting her, was what made me strong. I may have no defence at all against what waits for me in the fire.*

The hall grew broader as she walked steadily along its length. Here it had obviously been carved out by hand, the last stretch forming a grand, intimidating antechamber to Zruvan's lair. There were patterns in the walls. She recognised the sigil from the knife handle: a labyrinth enclosing a crude skull with its impossible closed eyes. The whole underground kingdom was the same dull ochre colour of sand and ancient bones, oppressive with sullen, fiery power.

The patterns were made of femurs, tibias and ribs inlaid into the rock. She realised that the "cobblestones" beneath her feet were also bones: ball joints from the hips and shoulders of countless individuals.

Human, of course. They were the source of the prickling, hostile energy. She saw, like a film projected across her imagination, tribal wars raging on the deserts above. People dying of natural causes. People dying from the bite of hidden vampires.

Vampires emerging from the sand at night, like camel spiders, to take their prey and vanish again...

Any human venturing down here would suffocate in the heat. Most vampires would collapse, all their strength sucked out by the mass hunger of endless dead souls. What madman would create such a terrible place? Violette pulled her own aura close for protection. She looked all around her as she went, at thousands of yellow bones forming the walls and curving up into the domed roof, far above her head. Even the sand infilling the floor, she realised, was crushed bone.

Violette reached the entrance to the chamber Nabil had called the Bone Well: a plain arch, eight feet high. She stopped on the threshold. The glow from the interior was dazzling. She looked inside and saw a circular space, forty feet across, rising to a great height and narrowing as it rose, like the inside of an enormous curved bottle. A kiln.

She could make out only the edges through the glare that came from the heart of the space. Not an actual fire, but an oval of painfully brilliant light. The heat pounded in from outside, as if this were an oven suspended within a volcano.

Walls and floor were layered with human bones in a crude mosaic. Leg and arm bones, spines and pelvises, spindly hands protruding as if in supplication. And skulls. They'd been placed in a pattern: a grid, one skull every few feet, row upon row until they dwindled from sight into the narrow chimney above.

Violette took this in as her eyes adjusted to the red-orange blaze. The light emanated from the figure that stood waiting for her at the centre of the chamber.

Gradually the glare dimmed to a bearable level, and there he stood: her self-appointed nemesis, towering over her, attired like Kastchei the Immortal in heavy robes the brown-red of dried blood. He held a staff, ten feet high, that shone with its own sickly light and – she knew – would paralyse her with pain if she touched it. A huge skull-face stared down at her.

Zruvan, Lord of Immortals, Soul of the Universe.

Karl watched attentively as Amy threaded the film into the projector, using one wall of the living room as a screen. He'd also watched as she went through the stages of processing the film: hand-dipping the negative – wrapped around a frame – through different baths, constantly checking the time and temperature, hanging the fifty-foot long ribbon to dry, then making the print and going through it all again.

He'd sensed her shaking with nerves when they were in the dark laboratory together, so he kept a careful distance and asked questions only about the chemistry. Charlotte had been like this with him, a long time ago. However diligently he maintained a courteous human mask, it was as if all humans *knew*, at a deep primordial level, what he was.

The sensitive ones, at least.

He couldn't force her to relax without deliberately hypnotising her. Instead he let her calm down in her own time as she worked. Let her trust him.

He wasn't especially comfortable at being alone with any human. However good his self-control, the temptation of blood was always under the surface. So he kept as far as possible from her, addressed her as Miss Temple, and was careful never to catch her gaze. In response she was equally polite and impersonal. By the time the film was ready, night had fallen again and they were as comfortable as they could hope to be, like work colleagues.

Now she asked him to switch off all the living-room lights, and set the projector in motion. As she did so, Karl saw Stefan watching from the bedroom. The door was barely cracked open and the interior was dark: Stefan was no more than a glistening pair of eyes. Amy, concentrating on her task, did not notice him.

Blurred grey images danced on the wall. She adjusted the focus, and there was the inside of the auditorium: stagehands waving at the camera, the corps de ballet running jerkily through some steps on stage while a lad in overalls painted a wooden tree behind them.

"It's good," said Karl, genuinely surprised. Despite the inevitable flicker, the scene was bright and lifelike. He almost felt he could step into it.

"It's only a test," she said. "To see how the lighting is. The whole reel only lasts three minutes, if that – you'll need to buy a much bigger camera, preferably two, if you're going to film entire ballets without missing anything."

She stopped, moistened her lips.

"Here comes the important part. Just after the dancers leave the stage... and the set-painter moves out of the frame... Now."

Feeling a sudden chill, Karl stared at the empty stage. Unoccupied, it became meaningless, sinister.

The film ended in a flurry of blank frames.

"Oh," Amy sighed. "I'm so sorry. There's nothing there. I really did see the spectre, I promise. I wouldn't make things up."

"I know that. Can you run it again? Just the last part?"

"Of course... give me a moment..." Amy switched off the projector lamp, turned on a room light and fiddled with the mechanism, muttering under her breath. "*One* day they'll make projectors that don't jam or unthread themselves or ignite the film. There. Ready."

She flicked off the light and the six-second shot of an empty stage ran again. This time Karl was sure he saw the faintest wisp of silver drifting across the boards and fading away to the left. Perhaps it was wishful thinking. Just variations in the grain.

"No, nothing," said Amy, resigned. "I saw her as large as life, but why should we expect ghosts to show up on film?"

Karl turned on some lights, but the unsettling atmosphere lingered. Amy shivered. He noted that the bedroom door was closed, but Stefan was no doubt listening to their conversation.

"It's getting late, and dark," said Karl. "Won't you sit down and have a drink to warm you?"

"I don't know. I feel strange without Charlotte here. I wonder what my uncle is doing or thinking? He might have called the police by now. How long can we keep the charade going?" She laughed shakily. "Unless you really *have* kidnapped me, of course."

"I promise we haven't." Karl moved to face her, keeping six feet of space between them. For the first time he held her gaze, firm and serious. "However, I'm sure your uncle will come looking for you eventually. Or for me."

"But... What if he does? I don't want the two of you fighting. If he brings his men with him, he could be really dangerous. I'll do my best to calm him down, but I don't know whether I can."

"Miss Temple," Karl said, "If he comes, I won't let him near you. We know he's dangerous, but I can defend myself." He tried to sound more confident than he felt. In truth, Karl didn't know the limits of Godric's strength.

"I'm not afraid." Amy paced to the window and back. "Actually, that's a lie. I am fairly terrified, but it doesn't matter. Sometimes I remember how kind Uncle was, when I first arrived, and I feel terrible about all this. But then I think of what he's done – not least to your poor friends – and I'm not sorry at all. I don't want to hurt him, but I do want him stopped."

Karl saw the fire in her eyes. Amy Temple's sweet, compliant demeanour masked her deeper self: slow to anger but ferocious once aroused.

"We're truly sorry to have involved you in this, but we very much appreciate your help," he said. "Do you need to rest? Geli will take care of you, as she did last night."

She shook her head. "I'm not tired. Herr Alexander... Karl?" She folded her arms, held his gaze. "I know that you're not human. I hear the word 'vampire' whispered. I don't pretend to understand exactly what you and your friends are, but I do know that my uncle believes in what he calls the *strigoi*, and I've seen so many strange things lately that I'm almost used to it. So I promise not to run away screaming at any point. I know Charlotte's something *other*, and I can't pretend that she doesn't make me nervous, but I trust her. I no longer trust my uncle, but I do trust her."

"I hope you'll learn to trust me too," said Karl. His response to her admission was guarded. "We've told you far more than we'd usually confide in any human."

"And trust goes both ways, so... thank you." She gave a faint smile. "This is all so dreadfully strange, but a little bit thrilling, too. I can't possibly sleep. I need to do something practical."

"As do I," said Karl. "I think we should bring the cine-camera up here, loaded with fresh film."

"That's easy enough. I brought plenty of spare reels. Are you thinking that if the lamia reappears, we'll try to catch her on film again?"

"Exactly," said Karl. "I don't give up at the first attempt."

"Nor me. Yes, let's get everything set up." She came to life, bright-eyed. "Perhaps the lighting was wrong."

"And if your uncle or his men break in, their activities will be recorded, too."

Amy's expression darkened. She seemed to have a question on her tongue, but said nothing.

"Agreed?" Karl asked.

"We need a plan of action, then," she said quietly. "A way to alert each other if someone or something appears. Where to place the camera. Which of us is going to film, depending on what happens. A plan, Herr Alexander."

"What in the devil's name are you doing here?" Fadiya hissed.

Emil groaned and writhed, but did not wake.

"Violette is here, as instructed," Charlotte answered coldly.

"She was told to come alone."

"And she did. No one told me not to follow her. I'm frightened for her, and I don't trust you; what did you expect? Emil was supposed to be released in exchange for her arrival. She cares more for him than for her own safety! I'm here to make sure that he *is* released."

Fadiya was quiet. Her face was hostile, unreadable. She said, "It's not that simple."

"What is it, then?"

"Violette has been summoned to meet Lord Zruvan. He means to interrogate her. Emil can't be released until Zruvan is satisfied and calls an end to the encounter."

"What does that mean?" Charlotte bit back a host of angry questions and watched every nuance of Fadiya's face. Not unreadable after all: there were quick glances at Emil, small movements of her lips and tongue that suggested nervousness. Conflict.

"I cannot answer your questions."

"Try one, at least. How long will it take?"

"As long as it takes. Days, perhaps."

"Emil may not survive that long. What will happen to him if Zruvan is not happy with the meeting?"

"If Violette…" Fadiya's languid blinking grew more rapid. "If she does not survive, Emil will still be released. But if he dies afterwards, that is not our responsibility."

"What do you mean, if *Violette* does not survive?"

Charlotte stood there with fear swarming through her, her thoughts a flood of denial. *No, that wasn't the bargain, how dare they threaten her! Would they really kill her? Yes of course they would, just as Lilith's enemies have always wanted to destroy her.*

"I can't let your Lord Zruvan harm her," she said, her voice small but steel-hard.

"You can't stop him, if he makes that decision. Understand, Charlotte: this is Zruvan's domain. There is nothing either of you can do."

"Well, you don't know her," said Charlotte. "Fools rush in, as they say. She's the bravest person I know, but sometimes a little unhinged. Fadiya, did you hope she would not arrive so that you could keep Emil to yourself?"

Fadiya started to look angry. "There is no point in us arguing. We cannot let Emil go until Zruvan gives the word. We wait."

Charlotte would not give in. Fadiya was a deceiver: when they'd confronted her on the night of Stefan's party, she'd fled, pretending to be much more frightened than she actually was. Now she put on a mask of heartlessness, but Charlotte saw it was full of flaws.

"So you pretended to love Emil, solely to lure him here?"

"I was not pretending," Fadiya whispered, gazing down at Emil's sleeping face. "I do love him."

The admission startled Charlotte. The guards were distant shadows in the entrance: she couldn't tell if they were eavesdropping or oblivious.

"Our kind of love is lethal to humans," Charlotte said at last. "Loving them does not stop us tearing their lives to shreds. I understand the paradox that you can love him, and yet lure him to an unspeakable fate. Your duty is to your master Zruvan, isn't it? Whoever he is."

"Don't speak to me with such contempt." Fadiya's tone was low with menace. "You don't know him. He has his reasons. Good ones. All he thinks of is the good of our kind. His whole life is a sacrifice to our well-being!"

"I've known vampires like that," Charlotte said flatly. "They have all ended up dead, so far."

"He's not a vampire, he's a god. More, in fact. You don't understand."

"That's true, I don't." She glanced down at Emil. "I'm thirsty, may I...?"

She moved only inches towards him, as if preparing to drink – then Fadiya's hands gripped her shoulder and flung her into the farthest wall.

The rock slammed into her back. Charlotte was too shocked to breathe. Eventually she swayed upright, rubbing her shoulders where she'd taken the impact.

"I wanted to see how you'd react if I threatened Emil," she said. "If Zruvan is displeased with Violette, if he destroys her and 'releases' Emil to the mercy of his guards, will you fight them all off with such vigour?"

Fadiya glared. Her hands, hanging at her sides, made fists and then stretched flat like blades.

"Perhaps you really do love him," Charlotte said gently. She tugged Fadiya's sleeve, drawing her into a curved side wall so the guards wouldn't see them if they turned round. "To me, this is simple. I couldn't stop Violette coming here – I can't stop her doing anything – and I have no control over what happens between her and this more-than-a-god. All I can do is what I promised – to take Emil home. But I need your help. If Zruvan sets Violette free, you do realise that she'll kill *you* before she goes? But if she never reappears – do you truly want to give up Emil to such a horrible fate? Do you want to risk waiting for Zruvan's decision? I don't. Violette's fulfilled her part of the bargain, just by coming here. Now I will do this one last thing for Violette, and take him home."

Charlotte felt a tear run down her cheek. Inside, she wanted to rip out Fadiya's throat, slay the guards, confront Zruvan in his lair and rescue Violette. The more rational part of her mind knew that acting as an army of one would be disastrous.

"I'll help you," Fadiya murmured into her ear. "I wish this had never happened, but you're wrong about me. You don't understand..." Her dark eyes went pale green, making her look sinister, torn and distressed, all at once. "I'm not evil. I do love Emil, with all my foolish heart. I love Zruvan too, but that does not stop me loving Emil."

"Do you have transport?"

Fadiya nodded. "The truck went back to town, but I have two horses."

"We can take on the guards, one each..."

"No need," said Fadiya. Her sorrowful eyes took on a spark of fire. "They'll do whatever I tell them to do, because I command Bayt-al-Zuhur. I am Zruvan's wife."

Lord Zruvan, Soul of the Universe, appeared to be alone in the Bone Well. He might have guards hidden in the blurred edges of Raqia, but Violette perceived nothing. Even her guide Nabil had gone. There was only Zruvan.

He did not move. Was he real? He might be a giant statue, for all she knew. She probed him with her senses, like a butterfly tasting a flower with its tongue. She knew now that his appearances in Raqia – even when he'd tried to attack her – had been astral projections, an energy-form so strong that it could seem solid even though it was not really there.

Here was its originator. An authentic, physical being.

Nabil said that he never left his bizarre temple. She wondered, *How long has he been here?* He'd pursued her by the power of his mind alone. But that had not been enough for him. He wanted her here in person.

Wanted her because she was the avatar of Lilith: a rival deity.

The kiln-heat was extreme. A deep, continual roar made the air shudder. The walls glowed fiercely and the ground trembled.

"Well, you got your way," she said. "Here I am."

"Here you are," echoed the skull. "At last."

CHAPTER TWENTY-THREE

THE BREATH OF HEAVEN

The horses were beautiful. Charlotte could hardly believe her eyes as Fadiya led them out of the cave: two dancing creatures so lovely she could only stare in wonder, forgetting everything else. One was chestnut, like a burnished copper coin, with a flaxen mane and tail and long white stockings flashing on its hind legs. The other was dapple-grey, the colour of a cloudy sky. They had compact bodies, arched necks, exquisite chiselled heads, legs that appeared too fine to bear any weight. Huge dark eyes, full of kind intelligence. Both animals pranced, full of fire, their tails held high.

"Can you ride?" Fadiya asked brusquely as she slid saddles of soft, decorated fabric on to their backs. The saddles and plaited bridles were bright with embroidery and adorned with rows of coloured tassels.

"Yes."

"You're staring as if you've never seen an Arabian horse before."

"I haven't," said Charlotte. "I mean, I've seen them in photographs. Never in the flesh. They are so beautiful."

"Aren't they?" Fadiya's expression softened and she smiled. "They're mine. Both mares. The chestnut is called Ghazale and the grey is Dabab. Gazelle and mist."

"Yours?" She was startled that Fadiya should do anything as human as own horses. True, vampires enjoyed all manner of worldly activities, but glimpsing a new side to this stranger threw Charlotte. Above, the night sky was bright with countless stars, dwarfing these wondrous creatures that appeared to have dropped from heaven. Everything about them mesmerised her: their tapered, flickering ears, the flare of their nostrils. They carried their tails like banners.

"Emil?" said Charlotte. "Have you ridden before?"

No answer. The dancer leaned back against the rock face, silent and ashen-faced. He hadn't said a word since they brought him out of the cave.

"Don't worry," said Fadiya. "He'll sit behind me. These desert-bred horses are far tougher than they look. The Bedouins rode mares like these into war. They're forged in fire. They can bear great weight and run like the wind for hours."

She spoke with tender reverence, her gaze a thousand miles away. She sounded nothing like the treacherous vampire Charlotte knew.

Mounted on Dabab, Charlotte felt secure and balanced, as comfortable as if she were seated on a cushion, even though the mare felt like a ball of lightning beneath her. Both mares danced, joyously eager to gallop. A word from Fadiya, and they were racing into the night.

Emil sat behind Fadiya on the chestnut Ghazale, his arms tight around her waist and his head slumped on her shoulder. The mares ran with long fluid strides like a flash flood across the sand. They – and Fadiya – knew exactly where they were going. Without her guidance, Charlotte knew this journey would have been infinitely more difficult.

The sun rose, a great red sphere trailing a plume of light, casting a rosy light over the plains of sand and rock. Fadiya led the party down into the shade of overhanging rocks, to a narrow archway that couldn't be seen unless you already knew it was there. She dismounted, pushed Emil into the gap in front of her, and signalled Charlotte to follow.

The mares only just fitted through the entrance, but they went in willingly as if they'd entered this place a dozen times before. The narrow ingress curved into a small, intricate cavern, all pillars and arches of glowing orange rock.

A small pool of water welled from below ground to fill a central dip in the floor. The mares went straight to drink. Emil fell to his knees beside them and dipped his whole head under the surface.

"We'll rest here until sunset," said Fadiya. "Give Emil some food, while I see to the girls."

Emil sat with his back against a pillar, wordless. Water streamed from his drenched hair. His eyes were open but dull. Charlotte wondered what, if anything, was going on in his mind. If this ordeal had broken him beyond repair – she pushed the potential tragedy out of her mind. She already had too much to think about, not least what might be happening to Violette... and to Karl.

Charlotte held a flask of water to his lips and tried to ignore her own thirst, no matter how tempting the throb of blood vessels in his throat... A human, alone with two vampires in the wilderness, was hardly in the safest of hands. But duty came before thirst.

He turned his head away when she offered him flatbread, even refused a sweet raw date. Charlotte watched Fadiya tending the mares at the edge of the pool, removing their saddles, rubbing their backs and checking their hooves.

"She loves her horses, doesn't she? She can't be all bad."

Emil said nothing.

"Dear, we'll get you home safely."

"Vampires. Witches." His voice was a dry, cracked hiss. "You bring me to this and expect gratitude for not killing me after all? I'd rather be dead."

"Drink some more water, then try to sleep," said Charlotte.

Nothing she said would soothe Emil, or repair his crushed spirit. She longed for dusk, when they could travel again. The day was going to be baking hot, endless.

The voice inside the skull sounded light and mellow. Not a voice to wake terror, but its smooth quality disturbed Violette in a less definable way.

"What language do you prefer to converse in?" she asked.

"English will suffice."

"I've come for Emil," she said calmly.

"I know."

"Then you understand that I am not here for your benefit. I'm here to take my dancer home. I don't want to hurt anyone, but if any harm comes to *him*..." Violette paused as all her emotions went still. She became icily focused and ruthless, with Lilith coiled under her heart ready to strike. She'd seen vampires and humans alike flee from her arctic stare.

The intelligence behind the skull remained impassive.

"We have heard about you, Lilith, Queen of Demons. Come closer."

He towered over her, wrapped in robes the colour of the desert; russet and purplish red. His head, concealed by the huge skull helmet, looked grotesquely out of proportion with his slim figure. The staff he held was taller than him and shone like white-hot metal. It was a weapon, she was certain, that could kill her with ease.

A weapon to destroy a goddess.

Violette had expected to find this creature seated on a throne. A grand chair constructed of bones would have looked fitting. Some vampires liked displays of pomp, but Zruvan had none. He only stood there as if imprisoned in an oubliette, like a martyred saint.

She saw *Istilqa* knives lying in neat rows around the circumference of the cave. Dozens of them. Carving tools, also. A hammer and small anvil to shape metal, small heaps of rubies... some in the rough, some polished. Perhaps he supervised craftsmen, but she suspected that he made the daggers himself.

Apparently he had to control every tiny detail... just as she did.

"I was told you never leave here," she said. "Is that true?"

"I used to, long ago. Not now."

"But what do you live on?"

"My attendants bring me sustenance."

He glanced up, where the ceiling attenuated to a narrow pipe. Violette imagined humans being forced down that chimney, falling in terror.

"And leave the bones here? You do know – you must know, since I'm sure you're a wise man – that vampires shouldn't remain too close to their victims? Hoarding their corpses around you will bring disaster. Eventually they start to suck back their stolen life. Friends of mine have witnessed it."

"Of course we know," he said patiently. "That's *why* we hoard the dead. That is why I bear the agony and guilt for all those like me. I always have and always will."

"You live here in suffering, like a... a scapegoat?"

"It's my duty."

"This is unhealthy," said Violette. "To keep the bones of your victims around you and wallow in their pain is ridiculous. Dangerous."

"Unhealthy? But to do otherwise – is that not denial of our guilt? It's part of our nature to live with what we have done."

"That's true," Violette said softly. "You have a point."

"Sit with me," said Zruvan.

"I assume you lured me here to kill me," she said. "Or at least to try. What is the point of us sitting down?"

"I want to talk. I tried to talk with you many times, but I could not."

"Because you weren't really there," she said. "What I saw was only projection of you."

"Yes. That is why I had to bring you here. So indulge me, please."

She hesitated. "I don't want to fight with you, but I do want Emil back."

"Sit," he repeated.

He planted his staff in a cleft in the floor and sat cross-legged, his rusty robes falling in folds over his knees. Cautiously Violette knelt before him, like a disciple before a guru. The idea of such a role made her bristle. It was not who she was. Roaring heat oppressed her. She felt she was melting like wax while whispering spectres clawed at her skin, taking her apart cell by cell.

He means to destroy me, she thought, glancing up into the apex of the cone. *I won't escape alive. Charlotte, you had better get Emil home or I'll come back from hell and haunt you!*

"May I ask questions?" she said.

The huge skull-head nodded. "You must have many."

"Why were you following me? What do you want?"

"We know that you are Lilith. A wild and destructive spirit. The hag of the night wind."

"How did you find out?"

"Rumours come to us, even here. We have spies in the outer world."

"Fadiya?"

"Not only her. You have been watched since the moment of your creation."

"Even when I was human." She remembered three figures that had haunted her childhood. Angels, they called themselves, claiming to be sent by God to tame the disobedient Lilith. Now she believed they were actually sentient fragments of Raqia, products of the vast sea of dreams and myths formed by mankind.

Still real enough to cause her torment and peril for years.

"Did the angels warn you?" she said. "Self-styled angels. Senoy, Sansenoy and Semangelof…"

"I am older than such myths. But yes, we were warned." A noncommittal reply. So, he meant to learn about her while giving away nothing in return.

But he's afraid of me, she thought. *Why else did he lure me here?*

"You think I'm a threat to the very existence of vampires, don't you? Humans reviled Lilith. They saw her as an enraged demon who was out to drain men's life force and murder their infants. Vampires fear me too, because they can't control me. Is that it? You feel you have a duty to destroy me."

The skull went silent, pondering.

"It's my duty to find out what you are," he said. "To protect my flock. My beloved friends."

He has friends? she thought. *Fadiya, Nabil and the others I've sensed around here… how many more?*

"It's polite of you to ask, rather than just hacking off my head," said Violette. "But it's none of your business. I don't mean to insult you, Lord Zruvan, but I don't know who you are. My life and affairs are no one's concern but mine. I'm not obliged to explain my existence to you. I have had enough of paranoid would-be tyrants persecuting me like a witch. Truly, you are *very* late to this game. It is already over."

She heard him release a heavy breath inside the mask.

"Lilith is a disruptive force, causing storms in the Crystal Ring that have made my friends wary of going there."

"The Crystal Ring is always stormy," she replied.

"It has grown worse since your reincarnation. When we try to create new vampires, most die."

"Hasn't that always been the case? Those storms are not my fault."

"Are they not?"

"No. I might lay claim to *some* of the disturbance…"

Months ago a concretion had appeared in Raqia like a fortress of coal floating in the void: a manifestation of her soul that was also a house in the real world, just as Zruvan's cave sat in both realms at once. One of Raqia's many mysteries.

"There was something," she went on, "but whatever disturbs the Ring now is not due to me. You must realise that *every* thought we have, human or vampire, makes ripples in the Crystal Ring. Some are more powerful than others. Your own psychic journeys, pursuing me, caused worse storms than I ever have! Now there are tempests emanating from the human world. Political upheaval. It's always been so. Your spies should have told you that."

"The human world is of little interest to me. It's simply there, like an anthill."

"Then we're the anteaters! We couldn't exist without it."

"Still, my concern is to protect my own circle. They've had little rest of late."

"Why? Do you mean they daren't enter the Crystal Ring to rest?"

"They dare, but it has never been safe. I won't tolerate it growing worse. I swore to find the source of disruption and end it."

"What are they afraid of?"

She wished she could see his face. Was he angry at her questions? She could read nothing from his level tone.

"You know the dangers," he said. "Vampires have been lost there, or they grow too cold and drift into oblivion. My friends are creatures of warmth and peace who take badly to change. That's why, centuries ago, we discovered a safer way to take our rest."

He picked up one of the bone-knives from the floor. It lay across his gloved palm like a living thing, blade and haft and ruby all shimmering with reflected heat. "These bring the most precious gift: sleep."

"*Istilqa*," said Violette, understanding. "Like a drug? If we surround ourselves with too much human death, it drags us down with it. But a tiny amount makes vampires... sleep?"

"I did not expect you to understand, but yes, you are right."

"The daggers also cause horrific nightmares and hallucinations."

"That happens with inexperienced use of the *sakakin*. In the hands of those who don't know what they're doing, yes, the blades can be deadly."

The eerie resonance of his voice and the thrumming, fierce heat were making her weak and disorientated. Zruvan's apparent politeness did not make him less dangerous. She was trapped and more certain by the moment that she might well die here. Perhaps Lilith would survive and fly free, but she wouldn't be Violette any more.

She closed her mind to those thoughts and wondered if he knew that Godric Reiniger had a stash of bone-knives. She thought, *He must know. Fadiya must have seen that Godric had the knives – perhaps she even supplied them to him, God knows why – but surely he must know. Is he angry that a human has them? Perhaps he doesn't even care, since he has so many others. If I have one last wish, it's to know what Zruvan is before I expire in this oven.*

"Tell me your thoughts," he said, sounding a touch anxious.

"Can't you read my mind?"

"I wish that I could, but no."

"Very well. I was thinking that using the *Istilqa* knives is not wise. The Crystal Ring is there for us to rest and replenish our powers. We are not human. We need to be alert and we're designed to stay awake always: it's part of our nature. Vampires should not be stabbing their veins with the equivalent of… opium or morphine."

Zruvan exhaled. His breath reverberated within the mask like the sigh of a bear.

"You seem to be suggesting that it's a weakness," he said.

"Exactly so. A very human weakness."

She wanted to ask if they could leave this terrible furnace of death and talk elsewhere. She was almost ready to beg, but – no. She wouldn't let him see she was struggling. She detached herself from her physical discomfort and concentrated on what he was saying.

"We are not weak," Zruvan retorted. "However, there is a problem. We have used the knives in a sparing manner for hundreds of years. But because the Crystal Ring is so wild these days, my beloved friends are resorting more and more to the *sakakin*. And the more they use them, the less effect the blades have. For that reason, we need Raqia's storms to cease. We need the vampire realm under our command. You are no ordinary vampire, Lilith. I still believe that *you* are the stone thrown into the pond. Some ripples flow outwards, becoming tidal waves."

"Perhaps once, but not now," she said sharply. "No one commands Raqia! It's a law unto itself, and you can't change that. I am no threat to your circle of followers. I'm only dangerous to those who threaten me and my loved ones. It sounds as if you and I are not so different."

"We are entirely different," said Zruvan.

With that cool, dismissive remark she knew he'd made up his mind to kill her. Better safe than sorry.

Besides, it was beneath her dignity to justify her existence to him. She thought with horrible certainty, *Even if we sit debating for a thousand years he will not change his mind.*

"I don't care about your *Istilqa* knives. Leave me alone, and I'll leave you in peace. I came to you of my own free will for one reason only – to release Emil. What must I do to make you fulfil the bargain?"

Zruvan did not reply. He went as still as a statue again, making her wonder if he'd left his body and drifted into Raqia again. Heat shimmered around his motionless red form as if he were on fire. The air scorched her throat.

Violette looked around warily, wondering if there was any possible escape. Flight up the narrow throat of the chimney, or back the way she'd come, or even through the walls of stone and bone? But it was no good. This couldn't end until she understood *what* Zruvan was.

The skull turned to face the burning white staff. He touched it with his gloved fingers, then looked up at the spot of sky far above.

Then, very slowly, he turned the death-mask to face her. Bone-rimmed black pits for eyes, teeth clenched in a malevolent grin. She felt a shudder of dread building in the pit of her stomach, rising into her throat. Regardless of the fierce heat, her skin became a tingling sheet of ice.

"Emil has gone," he whispered. *Now* he sounded angry.

"Are you sure?"

"Yes. Fadiya and your friend have taken him, against my command."

"Thank goodness." Her relief was immediately swamped by anxiety. His tone was ominous, a loud whisper echoing from inside the unmoving jaw.

"This means you have broken our agreement."

"Does it matter?" She couldn't keep her feelings out of her voice. "I'm here, am I not? I came in exchange for him. You have what you want, so let him go!"

Zruvan unfolded from his seated position, towering over her. For a second she was like a tiny child staring up at him. Then she sprang to her feet and backed away. No longer the quiet-voiced guru, he transformed back into the terrifying figure who'd first menaced her onboard ship.

Fire scorched her. Stinging liquid ran into her eyes and she realised she was perspiring. She felt her dress clinging to her clammy body, looked down and saw that she was sweating her own blood. Her clothing and her whole body was slicked in pink fluid. The Bone Well trembled.

"My decision whether or not to let you go was in the balance," he said. "But the facts remain. I have been here since before the beginning of time. I gave birth to space and time. Everything in the universe proceeded from me."

"What?" Violette laughed from shock. "You *gave birth to space and time*?"

"Don't mock me."

"I'm not mocking, just… Are you claiming to be a god? Now I've heard everything. Angels, sorcerers, gods – the Crystal Ring sends us all mad!"

Lord Zruvan did not appreciate being laughed at. He grabbed the staff and stamped its heel on the floor, like a furious wizard.

"No. I am greater than any god. I came *before*. I am space and time itself. I am the void from which all gods proceed."

His words sounded ridiculous, but the deadly serious timbre of his voice and his overwhelming presence chilled her to the marrow. Even in the kiln-heat, she convulsed with a fever-chill. What lay under his costume? Black nothingness, an abyss for which there were no words, not even "god"?

"That is how I know who you are," he said quietly. "I came before the beginning. That's why I endure this existence of pain so that my beloved friends may live in peace. I know the order of the universe: I, then the gods, then the dominion of the sun over the moon, then vampires over mortals, then male over female, and mankind over the beasts. Any other way is chaos. Lilith is the female beast, the very embodiment of disorder and turmoil. If I allow you to continue, chaos will tear the Crystal Ring apart. But if you cease to exist, order will return. Those who stood against you in the past were not strong enough, but I am."

Violette felt her strength draining away, her own blood dripping out of her pores to water the bones of the dead. She looked up into the dwindling chimney high above. She smiled.

"I never expected my life to end like this. However, we did make a bargain. As long as Emil is safe, I am in your hands. But do you know there is a saying among the wise?"

"What saying?"

"That the suppression of Lilith brings destruction? Slay me, and I'll take you and everything around you with me. Heed this folk tale. Once upon a time, a terrible she-demon took the shape of an owl and made her nest in a barn. Nothing, nothing would evict the owl from its lair until they burned down the very barn itself. The owl was gone, but not until their livestock and grain and everything they needed to survive lay in ashes."

"Empty threats."

"It's not a threat. It's the way things are. You can ignore the female beast, but she's always there in the shadows. Lash her, and she lashes back with tenfold fury."

The terrible, skeletal creature loomed over her – not Kastchei the Immortal, not a vampire, not even a god or a devil but a being so far beyond her understanding that his judgement was worse than death itself. He would not simply kill Violette, but destroy Lilith, destroy all that she had ever been, even the memories and myths. Annihilate her completely.

And because he feared her, destroying her was his only choice.

She knew, yet she still couldn't bring herself to escape.

Zruvan raised his staff and set the heel against her chest. He pushed her, gently but firmly, back against the wall and held her there. Its painful electric energy made her limbs twitch and turn to string. She felt the bones in the wall digging painfully into her back. First her dress then her skin itself was burning, blistering.

She endured this with patience. She wondered why she wasn't afraid any more, then realised that she was, but the fear was far away, drowned by the horrific sensation of burning and melting, healing, blistering again.

How long would this cycle last before the fire overwhelmed her self-healing ability?

Not long.

Tears and blood-sweat streamed down her. She was drowned by a strange ecstatic relief that it was almost over.

"Keep still," he said. "You will soon fade. This is not suppression but cleansing."

"Lord Zruvan?" she said, looking straight into the eye-holes of his mask. "Would you take off your mask and robes for me?"

"No, I will not. Why?"

"I would like to see your face before I die. Your skin. Is anything human left under there, or only the void that came before the universe?"

No answer, but the pressure on her breastbone increased. Her vision went black for a moment. She thought about Robyn, her lost love, and wondered if there was an afterlife where kind faces waited...

"Lord Zruvan, I know what's happened to you," she said, surprised at the steadiness of her voice. "The same thing happened to me. I am not really Lilith. *You are not really Zruvan.*"

"Your words make no sense. Be still now, and silent."

"No. As long as I can speak, I have to tell you the truth. There are thousands of thought-forms floating in Raqia, and sometimes they're so strong that they attach themselves to us. Perhaps we attract them. I always felt like an outcast, so when I became a vampire, my natural inclinations made me become Lilith. And you: you are not primordial. You were human once."

"The human shell is long gone. I stretch infinitely back and forward in time, I transcend time."

"No, it's an illusion. When you transformed, an archetype from the Crystal Ring fused with you and made you believe you are Zruvan. It's real, but only as an idea. It's not all you are. Think about it. If you were not Zruvan, who *would* you be?"

That brought a growl of rage, echoing horribly inside the skull. He thrust the staff so hard she felt her breastbone crack. The greedy thirst of a hundred thousand dead humans began sucking out her life. She was molten hot and freezing cold, her very cells coming apart, yet her consciousness persisted.

She had a flashback to a time when Karl's friend Pierre had done this to her. His spear, seized from a fortress wall, had no occult power, but it had pierced her to the spine.

Things had not ended well for him, either.

"This isn't working," she said. "I'm still not dead. And you are not really Zruvan. What was your name in life? Where were you born? Algeria, Egypt, Persia? You were a little boy once, before the vampires came…"

He snatched back the staff and aimed it straight at her mouth.

That might have worked. Severed her brain stem, silenced her forever. But she dodged and fell to the floor. The surface was red hot, searing her palms.

From her position – crouching on all fours like a wounded wolf – she looked up at Zruvan.

He was struggling to pull the staff free from the wall. It must have lodged deep. Bones and sand crumbled from the hole and pattered down like rain. No longer statuesque and forbidding, he was agitated now, desperate to retrieve the weapon so he could attack her again. If anything, the wall seemed to pull the staff deeper into itself.

His sleeves rode up as he struggled and she saw, in the gap between robe and gloved hands, the bare dark skin of his forearms.

Not nothingness, not bones, but flesh.

Violette gathered herself to spring. She aimed for his lower legs, leapt like a pouncing cat, felt his knees buckle as she struck in exactly the right place. His legs folded and he lost his balance, lost hold of the staff, collapsed on top of her like a felled tree.

Then the world was pure chaos. The inferno heat roared. Voices muttered and screamed. She could barely think for the noise, let alone fight, and the hot red light dazzled her. Her fingers found the edge of the skull-helmet and she began to work at it, trying with the little energy she had left to push it off his head. Irrational but deep instinct told her, *Take off his mask and you take away his power.*

He resisted, but their twisted position meant his hands could not gain a purchase on hers.

The Bone Well began to tremble. She didn't know what started the quake – his staff piercing the wall, their struggle, her challenge to what he believed himself to be… all of it, perhaps. The chamber shuddered violently, the floor bucked beneath them. They lay entangled and powerless against the onslaught.

Bones rained down from the chimney. A few at first, delicate finger-bones and toes. Then more. Femurs and skulls, shoulder-blades. Whole skeletons.

The entire structure of the Bone Well was collapsing.

The tremor released a massive landslide from the walls. The deluge of dry hail became an avalanche of bone and stone that swiftly covered the bottom of the well and began to rise up the sides, burying them both. The crushing weight increased by the moment as the whole chamber above them filled up with the rubble of centuries, of a hundred thousand deaths and ancient bones.

Zruvan's exquisitely constructed vessel of hell was no more.

With the mares dozing, Emil, Charlotte and Fadiya sat in the cavern, waiting. No one stated the obvious, that without a human in tow they could have been back in Algiers by now, or even back in Europe… Charlotte thought of cool, rainy streets by night, and imagined a victim wilting in her arms, with all the passion of a human dying of thirst in the desert.

At least Fadiya was not a grumbler. She could think of one or two vampires who would have made this journey insufferable.

"Charlotte?" said Fadiya, interrupting her reverie. "Make a little cut near your wrist."

She looked down in dismay to see that Fadiya was offering her an *Istilqa* knife. The patterns carved on the handle seemed to move and whisper.

"What for?"

"It will make you sleep."

"Like a human?"

"Yes. Isn't it the worst thing about our lives, that we never sleep? This will help you."

"When someone used one of those blades on me, I went mad for several hours. I haven't been the same since. They're evil.

Worse than poison, they cut right into our souls and there's no telling what damage they do."

"Only if you've never used one before, or if the wound goes too deep. You need to build a tolerance. That's why I suggest a small cut."

But Charlotte stared at the blade, hesitating. Tempted. Just a nick, and she would sink into a beautiful deep sleep... Almost the only human pleasure she missed. What bliss, to escape the pain of thirst and anxiety, to stop thinking, just to rest in the lovely soft blackness for a while.

And only once? she thought. *If it's as blissful as I imagine, shall I want to do the same every day?*

Charlotte gently pushed away Fadiya's hand.

"No. Thank you. I prefer to stay awake."

"As you will."

Fadiya drew back the sleeve of her own robe and brought the *sikin* towards her skin.

"Wait," said Charlotte. "You're not going to sleep now, are you, while we're in the middle of nowhere? Shouldn't we stay alert, at least for Emil's sake?"

Fadiya shrugged, rearranged her sleeve and put the knife away in a pouch in the folds of her robe. "I suppose you're right, although this cave is well hidden and there's no one for miles around us." She held Charlotte's gaze and added, "You look at me as if I'm nothing, or an object of pity, but what do you know about me?"

"That's not fair." She frowned, but knew Fadiya had a point. "You kidnapped Emil. And I *don't* know you at all. But if you think I'm judging you, I apologise."

"Think what you like," Fadiya said coolly, looking away.

One thing was clear: the nervous Fadiya who'd fled from her and Violette on the night of Stefan's party was not the real Fadiya.

"I don't understand why you would damage yourself with such dangerous weapons."

"But they're not dangerous unless they're misused. They bring pleasant oblivion, that's all. They're made from the ivory of the Bone Well, where Zruvan lives. You won't understand. You come from a different civilisation, where all the old mysteries have been lost."

"Not all of them." Charlotte lowered her voice, as Emil seemed to be asleep. "In England, I once found a place – a subterranean lair – where a vampire had hoarded his victims. The very walls were soaked with their agony. The emptiness they left, the bitter cold, was so intense that it almost killed us. The bone-knives are the same, aren't they? I do understand. Too much exposure brings us the suffering we've dealt to humans, madness, weakness, even death. But a tiny dose makes you unconscious for a while. Am I right?"

"I had not seen it like that, but yes."

"I think each *sikin* holds the power of all the bones," said Charlotte. "The macrocosm within the microcosm. That was one of my father's favourite sayings."

"What?" Fadiya frowned.

"Does your Lord Zruvan make the knives?"

"He invented them. He is older than time. Before him there was no one and nothing."

Charlotte mouthed a silent *Oh* of surprise. She wondered how to respond. "So you are married to a god? Does he mind you taking human lovers?"

"No one can explain or describe Zruvan," said Fadiya. She rose on her haunches and whispered, "Come with me."

Bent nearly double, they went to a narrow, odd-shaped cavern behind the main one. The light here was dim red, the floor a churned-up mess of rock and sand, the air thick and hot. On a smooth curve of wall, at eye-level as they crouched, Charlotte saw handprints on the rock. No, not prints, but negatives: shapes outlined by a blackish mist, as if several folk had placed their hands on the rock like stencils and blown pigment over them.

There were drawings of animals, too, depicted in simple rust-red brushstrokes, crude but full of life and movement.

"People lived here," she murmured, knowing with a flash of insight that these marks were ancient.

"Who knows how many thousands of years ago?" said Fadiya. "Zruvan says the desert was a green plain, long ago. I didn't believe him, but how else could such animals have lived here? Look…" she bent to the floor and swirled her hand through the loose stones. "This is where I buried a sack of *Istilqa* knives, four hundred years ago. I've buried others in many places, for safekeeping. They are for vampires who are travelling, or stranded. I even wrote an explanation, for those who did not understand. And if anything happened to our supply, or to Zruvan, we would always have these in reserve."

Like someone hiding weapons, or treasure… or opium, thought Charlotte.

"You really can't live without them?"

"We could, but it's our way," said Fadiya. "Your disapproval won't change our traditions."

"I'm not trying to. I'm curious, that's all."

"One day, nearly forty years ago, I came here to find the ground dug up and the *sakakin* gone. Some cursed archaeologist from Europe! He didn't even know what he'd found."

"Is that why you went to Godric Reiniger, to get them back?"

Fadiya sat back on her heels and gave a chilling smile. "No. I was in Lucerne looking for Violette. I happened to discover that Herr Reiniger had the knives. We argued a little, but I let him keep them in the end because, by using them, he was honouring Zruvan without even realising it. Rather, I tried to *tell* him, even knowing he didn't care or understand. I want them back, of course, but I didn't make too great an issue of it because Violette was my priority."

"Zruvan sent you to find her?"

"Yes. I'm his agent in the world. I do what he cannot."

"But you dared not approach her directly," said Charlotte.

"Of course not. It would have been impossibly dangerous. I'm not a fool."

"No, you aren't. To take Emil instead was a master-stroke."

Fadiya sat back against the cave wall with a sigh. Her eyes were brown again, not the jade green of danger. "I never meant him any harm. I was entirely focused upon what Zruvan commanded, because… you can't understand."

"He's your master, so you do what he says?"

"No." She spoke with fervour. "Because he sacrifices every moment of his existence to keep me safe, to keep all our loved ones safe. To keep safe every single vampire who comes to us. That's why."

"You say he's your husband?" Charlotte said after a few

moments. "It can't be easy, being married to a god who never shows his face."

Fadiya said nothing.

"What happened to your other husband?"

"My…?"

"I heard you were a widow. You were married to a French soldier who died."

"Oh." Fadiya laughed. "I made that up. The tale elicits sympathy, and it is a reason for me to be in Europe, all alone."

"I see. And are you going to explain *that* to Emil?"

"As if it matters. You're so human, Charlotte."

"You must be too, a little, or you wouldn't have agreed to help him escape."

She thought Fadiya was ignoring the remark, but after a while she said very softly, "It was nice to be with him. To see his face and touch his skin… I have only once seen Zruvan's face – to be truthful, I didn't see it clearly, but I did feel his mouth… I cannot talk about him."

"Never mind him. I'm more interested in you. What is your story, Fadiya?"

Charlotte expected more stubborn silence, but Fadiya began to speak, her voice tranquil and languid, like honey.

Six hundred years before, her father and brothers dead in a tribal battle, Fadiya and her mother had taken precarious refuge in a cave, hiding from enemy tribes and foreign invaders. But her mother was ill and someone had to fetch water so Fadiya went alone, barefoot across the sand, walking tall and straight so that the jug would not spill its contents. The wind made her robes flutter around her ankles and perhaps that was why the bandit decided to attack – to throw her down, to violate and strangle her before she knew what was happening. The jar fell, the water surged out in a dark stain, wasted. She only saw a silhouette as he rose and staggered backwards, gasping. His clothing was alien; he was a warrior from a hostile tribe. Some brute who didn't care that she was ruined, her honour destroyed.

She lay and stared up at the new moon. The white sliver kept fading to blackness with her vision and she knew she was dying… but that was for the best. Then the stink of his body would be gone, along with the inner contamination that would never wash away. The only balm for dishonour was death. She thought of her mother, and wondered who would fetch the water instead and who would warn them of the danger before...

But someone else was there. A shadow – silent and odourless, unlike the sweating, heavy-breathing stranger. This shadow seized her attacker from behind and snapped his neck between hands and mouth. He fell like a rock. Then the demon bent over her and she felt two sharp pains pierce her throbbing, bruised throat. Her last impression was of blood everywhere, blood flowing from the dead rapist to pool around him... her own blood on the demon's mouth as it raised its head. She could see no detail, only its eyes in the darkness and her blood shining on its lips, dripping on to her face.

She closed her eyes and prayed to the new moon.

"I woke beneath a lemon tree," she told Charlotte. "I knew... The lemon tree is sacred, you see. It was a sign that I was safe."

Charlotte nodded to show she understood that this was important.

"I was in a blue, dusky place, a courtyard. The light was beautiful and I could smell jasmine." Fadiya gave a half-smile. "I thought I was in Paradise and couldn't understand how I deserved to be there. But I felt a very long time had passed, so perhaps I'd been forgiven."

"The attack wasn't your fault!" said Charlotte. "Ask Violette: she'll tell you exactly the same. No man has the power to dishonour you."

Fadiya only smiled. "I know that now. The point is that I knew I had *died*. I was strangled and left for dead. The shadow that came was a vampire who killed my attacker as a boy kills a fly. Then she fed on me. She saw I could not live, and she could simply have finished what she started – yet she saved me. I woke in a world where everything was different: light and colour and sound. Tiled mosaics like a palace, a fountain in a courtyard, strange beautiful creatures around me like none I'd ever seen before. I thought they were *djenoun*. Demons."

"And it was Zruvan who saved you?" Charlotte was confused. Fadiya had always called Zruvan "he" before. But he had companions, of course.

"Saved me and damned me. I cast aside all my old beliefs and gave myself to him instead."

"You called the vampire 'she'."

"Did I? In the darkness I thought the vampire was female. The mouth and skin were so soft... but I never again saw Zruvan without his priestly garments. No one ever sees his face."

She sounded sad. Emil stirred, coughed.

"Even though he became your husband?"

"I cannot explain the feeling – that I felt my heart would explode with love for him. Not for his looks or wealth, which did not exist, but for his gentleness. Everything is different, outside the human world. I am his devoted wife, but more – I'm his representative in the world. While he exists in seclusion, I have to be."

Charlotte wondered what strange kind of marriage they had. She thought of a nun, "married" to Christ... but that comparison did not fit, either.

"Without him, the safe house of Bayt-al-Zuhur would not exist," Fadiya went on. "His eternal sacrifice gives us our freedom. Of course we all do his bidding – do you think he's a monster? He loves us, and we love him. One day he took my hand and declared me the best beloved of all, his wife in the eyes of the cosmos. That was in the days before..."

"What?"

"He used to emerge from the Bone Well and come to us, once or twice a year. Gradually he came less and less. Now he stays there always."

"Is he afraid to come out?"

She expected indignant denial, but Fadiya paused. "He is afraid that if he ceases his eternal vigilance, evil will befall us. It's a sacred calling. He is more than a god and we do all we can to serve him. If it means spying for him, finding enemies such as Lilith, using Emil to lure her to him – I am sorry for the suffering caused. But to aid Zruvan, I will do anything."

"Only now you've disobeyed him and run off with Emil," said Charlotte.

Fadiya didn't answer. She got up and wound her way across the cavern where Emil and the mares dozed, and through the hidden archway to the outside. Charlotte followed and stood beside her, watching until the sun dropped at last, turning the sky into a glorious ocean and flooding the desert with blood-red flame.

"We can go on now," said Fadiya. "Make Emil eat and drink, while I saddle the mares."

Karl watched Amy wandering around the living room, unable to settle. Another day had passed and nothing had happened: there had been no sign of Godric or the lamia, no word from Charlotte. Geli reported that the girl was barely eating.

She was growing agitated, and Karl didn't blame her. With no news of Reiniger's whereabouts – or what he'd become – the atmosphere grew tense and oppressive. Ballet rehearsals continued, but the mood was changing. Everyone knew that Violette and Emil were absent without explanation: questions were being asked that no one could answer. Unease filled the whole building, like spectral fog.

He'd brought Amy to his rooms again for company, and because he dared not leave her alone. Stefan stood leaning in the doorway to the bedroom, also watching her without expression.

She was unaware that Niklas's corpse lay on the bed inside, decaying.

If Stefan had some mad plan to show her the remains – to share his suffering, and turn her polite smile to horror – Karl was ready to stop him.

"I don't think my uncle's coming," she said. "Either he thinks I'm somewhere else entirely, or he just doesn't care. He's arranged a private showing of his new movie in a few days' time. Getting ready for that is obviously more important to him than looking for me."

"I can only apologise, again, for this situation," said Karl. "I still believe he hasn't finished with me, and I don't know where to send you that's safe."

"I don't know what to think, Karl. Truly, if nothing's happened by tomorrow, I am going to go back to Bergwerkstatt and pretend all innocence."

"But what would you tell him?"

"That I was invited to stay for a couple of days by one of the dancers. 'What kidnap, Uncle? I don't understand. I was staying with a friend who wanted to show me the academy.' He'd have to believe me. *Then* I can make my escape without arousing his suspicions." Amy made a small, sour grimace. "Where's Charlotte? I hoped she'd be back by now. Part of me keeps hoping this will all turn out to be some ghastly misunderstanding."

Stefan, usually the first to charm and soothe a human guest, remained in the doorway, staring from bruised eyes.

"There was no misunderstanding, believe me," he said. "I was there when he killed my Niklas and tried to kill me too. When his men attacked both Karl and me. Karl saw him change into something... not what you would call fully human. Do you want to see my wounds?"

"Stefan," Karl said.

"What? Why shouldn't she know the truth?"

"I think she knows quite enough already."

Amy swallowed. "Stefan, there's no need. I've spent hours and days trying to accept that you and Charlotte and Karl are... something other. I won't pretend you don't all give me cold shivers sometimes, but then I remind myself that my uncle is hell-bent on turning into something even worse. So I'm stuck. I've made a vow that if Uncle turns up, whatever happens, I'll help Karl and you against him."

Her reply appeared to surprise Stefan. "Well, you're a spirited young thing," he said. "Braver than me."

She raised her chin. "It's actually a bit thrilling, being this scared. Part of me hopes he'll stay away, but part of me just wants it to be over. Come on, Uncle. Make a move."

The lights flickered. Karl felt the air stir, moving with shadows he couldn't quite see. A chill went over his neck.

"This waiting is ridiculous," Stefan muttered. "Nothing's coming."

"Believe me, it is," said Karl. He looked into Stefan's wild, red-rimmed eyes. Wisps of the Crystal Ring swirled between them, tuning the air cold like a snow-flurry. Distant but clear, he sensed a speck of energy moving towards them. He couldn't tell what it was, but his deeper senses told him that it was hunting him, locked on to him like an arrow in flight.

Stefan's face dropped. He looked waxen with shock.

"You sense it?" Karl said quietly. "We've nothing to use against it but the camera."

"Miss Temple, I suggest you run for your life," Stefan said, still staring into Karl's eyes. "Go."

"Then, if it pursues her, we can't protect her."

"I'm not leaving," Amy spoke briskly. "If something's going to happen, do you think I want to be outside on my own? Told you, I'm staying." She put on a sweater that she'd left over the back of a chair. "It's gone awfully cold. Switch more lights on."

She went to the far window, where her cine-camera stood on its tripod, hidden behind the heavy curtains.

"You do know that no phantom ever makes an appearance when the lights are on?" Stefan exclaimed.

"But if we're going to film anything, we need as much light as possible." She bent to look through the viewfinder. "This covers most of the room, but I can hand-hold it if necessary. Oh, *please* let something happen!"

"Be careful what you wish for," said Stefan.

"But if it's my uncle, won't he knock on the front door? What will you do, just... let him in?"

Karl didn't answer. The amorphous shape that drew gradually closer in his mind's eye would not need to knock. No barrier would stop it.

"You know the camera makes quite a noise? Uncle will hear it. The curtains might muffle it a bit."

"I'll put on a gramophone record," said Stefan. "Let's have the jolliest song I can find, just to brighten the mood a little."

"Will one of you *please* put the main light on?" Her voice trembled.

Karl flicked a switch to illuminate the central electric chandelier that they rarely used. The room stayed unnaturally gloomy and the air shivered. Again the Crystal Ring intruded into the room, strongly this time, like a column of whirling ice feathers hardly three feet from him.

It left behind a solid figure.

Not Godric Reiniger, but Charlotte.

She stood caught in the halo of dissipating ice-flakes as if veiled in light. So beautiful, but so pallid, like an ethereal spirit of winter. Again Karl had to study her carefully to be sure. This time he took only a moment to see the truth.

Charlotte's cold *doppelgänger* slid her hands up on to his shoulders and tilted her mouth towards his.

"Karl, I'm back. Aren't you going to warm me?"

CHAPTER TWENTY-FOUR

MASTER OF MANY, SAVIOUR TO NONE

Karl heard the camera begin to roll, a steady whirr in the background. Amy was hidden behind the curtains and Stefan had retreated to the bedroom: heaven knew how they'd moved so fast. Dance music played on the gramophone, jaunty and incongruous.

He was effectively alone with the ghost-Charlotte, who had so completely fooled him the first time. As she touched him, her skin and gorgeous amethyst eyes and full, rosy mouth seemed a perfect imitation. The silk of her dress, the firmness of her body felt real enough... but he caught the tell-tale cold vapour rising from her, the faint metallic smell that warned of danger.

"I've waited so long for this," she murmured.

She kissed him. He wanted to push her away but instead he let her, giving himself time.

A dozen thoughts whirled through his mind, all holding different shades of horror. If this being truly believed she *was* Charlotte, how could he reject her? If she were some mockery, a spectral echo conjured by the Crystal Ring – she was still too much like the real woman for him to contemplate destroying her. In any case, how could you destroy a spirit? And if he succeeded – he might be destroying an actual aspect of Charlotte, temporarily divided. If he did so, he might kill *her*.

But something was different. Before, her double's aura had struck him as chilly but soft, like rain. Now it felt heavy, focused, intense... A horrible possibility formed in his mind. He had no way to be certain. And he had only two more minutes before Amy's film reel ran out.

"You could show more enthusiasm." She pulled back, smiling. "I have waited so long for this, beautiful Karl..."

Then he knew.

When she leaned in again, he returned her kiss with enthusiasm, feigning passion as best he could. He shut his eyes, shut his mind. She pushed him back into the wall, solid, heavy, almost muscular. Even her breath was tainted with bitterness.

Still he forced himself to continue. Her hands went everywhere, down his back, between his thighs. Oh, very different. He pulled her away from the wall and edged her towards the middle of the room. He groaned, to cover the whirr of the camera rolling.

"That's better," the *doppelgänger* gasped into his neck. Its breath was heavy and fast, its groin pressing hard into his. "I think we need fewer clothes, don't you?"

"Oh, yes," said Karl. He drew back, holding her at arm's length. He held her with his eyes, pouring all the supernatural glamour he possessed into her. "One moment."

He set the gramophone playing again – Schumann, this time – and went into the bedroom. Beneath the chandelier's glow, the double began to remove her clothing. Dress, slip, everything. She turned her head a little, as if she heard something behind the curtains, only to dismiss it. Too eager for what was to come.

"What's happening?" Stefan whispered urgently, his eyes gleaming in the darkness.

"It's not Charlotte. I cannot do this," said Karl. He caught his breath, rubbed his temple with the heel of one hand. They spoke rapidly, voices very low. "Truly, I cannot follow this to the end."

By now the first reel must have run its course. He knew Amy had mastered the art of loading a new one very fast. Karl hoped he was giving her enough time to do so, that her presence would not be discovered.

"And this apparition wants the pleasure of your body?" Stefan's voice was full of savage amusement. "But if that gains us what we need? It's not like you to shirk from anything."

"Danger is one thing. This is entirely different."

"If it's only a shade of Charlotte, so what? No harm done. But if..."

"It's not her. It's far worse. As bad as it could be."

"Are you sure?"

"It's someone else... I believe it's *him*. And I have no time to wonder *how* he has done this."

"But this is exactly what we need." Stefan's blue eyes shone with fire: mischief, twisted into ravenous insanity. "This is even better than we imagined! Give the apparition what it wants. Just get it over with."

"I swear, I cannot."

Stefan grabbed Karl by the wrists. "Oh, but I can. Continue the performance, get the creature in here, and I'll take over. Amy might need to move the camera a little way, that's all. It will be my pleasure."

"Karl?" said the false Charlotte, so near the door she made him start. She was naked now, shimmering like a goddess. Over her shoulder he saw Amy edge into view, now holding the camera in both hands. "What are you doing?"

"Preparing the bedroom. We'll be more comfortable in here."

He flung off his tie and collar, unfastened his shirt, seized her, let his mouth travel hungrily all over her jaw and neck and shoulders. He bit her without drawing blood, making her gasp. Her flesh was cold and sour. All the time he held her in full view of the camera's glinting lens.

Dreading to think what Amy was seeing or thinking.

Never mind that.

He steered the lamia towards the bed.

"If an intruder appears, no matter who or what it is, we'll film everything." That was the plan they'd made. *"Whatever happens, keep filming."*

"Yes, you have waited so long," Karl breathed into her ear. "Look, our friend is here. He wants you too. Both of us, is that not everything you desire?"

"Oh God, yes." The creature ground itself against his leg, all too hard and solid. Its hands reached into his trousers and began to undo buttons. "There is not an inch of you I won't explore with my tongue. You *and* Stefan, how wonderful."

Inside the room, lights flared as Karl flicked switches. As he released the *doppelgänger*, Stefan took over, pushing her on to the bed, covering the pale wide-eyed face with kisses.

Stefan would go through with this, Karl knew.

Karl was fastidious: Stefan most decidedly was not. He would cheerfully ravish this individual senseless. Ghost, demon, impostor: whatever it was, he didn't care. Karl saw the camera lens just beyond the door frame. Amy was intent on capturing everything. Regardless of her feelings about the scene before her, she didn't flinch. He checked again that the false Charlotte had not noticed the camera.

But the lamia was on her back, her view obscured by Stefan, apparently too enraptured to notice. Karl still couldn't grasp the discord between the spectre's appearance and how it behaved and tasted and felt to the touch... He couldn't accept the impossible truth.

"Karl," said the apparition, reaching past Stefan's shoulder and clutching thin air. "Join us."

"Would you like to play the man?" said Stefan, breathless. "Go on, get on top! You can do anything, everything you want. Perhaps you'd like my brother to join in, too..."

With that, Stefan rolled, lifting the naked double on top of him. He did so with some force, and the false Charlotte overbalanced, collapsing on to the other side of the bed.

Straight on to the remains of Niklas's corpse.

Then the Charlotte-illusion collapsed, evaporating. In its place, Godric Reiniger's downy, naked form crouched inelegantly, motionless, staring into the sunken face of Niklas. Abruptly he began to scrabble in horror like an animal trying to escape a trap. He uttered a deep, blood-chilling scream. Then slipped down on to the floor on the far side of the bed, and vanished.

Violette struggled upwards. Her awkward scramble through the debris was closer to swimming than climbing. She made painfully slow progress as she writhed her way through the mass of rubble, rising as smaller particles shifted and settled beneath her. Bone and rock and dust. With every few feet she gained, the heap would shift and threaten to bury her again.

With her left hand she dragged Zruvan upwards with her.

He did nothing to help himself. His weight wasn't as great as his height would suggest, but enough to make her escape nearly impossible. She clung to his arm through his sleeve and hauled. Scrabble upwards, haul, slip back. Over and over again. Stones and sand rained on her head.

She reached out for Raqia but the two realms were already entwined. She had nowhere else to go. There was a dot of light above and she saw heads in silhouette staring down into the well. Zruvan's guards.

At last Violette reached the top of the pile. The entrance to the well was still far above her head. The Bone Well's heat rushed upwards around her like a hot wind escaping through the narrow flue.

She and Zruvan both lay sprawled on top of the heap, exhausted, spreadeagled as if on quicksand. His staff was lost, robes torn, skull helmet askew. She saw glimpses of smooth brown flesh.

Looking up, she thought that if she could reach the narrower part of the chimney, she could brace herself with hands and feet and climb to the top...

Zruvan groaned.

"May I?" she asked. When he didn't object, she began to work again at the gigantic skull-faced helmet. This time it slid easily off his head.

The face beneath was astonishingly young. She'd been prepared for monstrosity, and instead saw a boy of no more than eighteen. His face was all straight lines, a neat oblong with a flat mouth, long straight nose, elongated black eyes. Almost feminine. His hair, raven silk, fell to his shoulders. The body beneath the torn robes was brown and as slender as that of any of her ballet students.

He was barely six feet in height. No giant. Perhaps he'd worn built-up shoes beneath his garments. After all, he was a creature fabricated of illusions.

"Why did you drag me out?" he asked in a raw voice. "You could have left me there."

"Because I want to talk to you. And I'm not entirely heartless."

"I too wanted to talk." He looked and sounded dazed.

"But only on your terms. And you did not like what I was saying, so you tried to silence me, but..."

"How did this happen?"

"I warned you: you can't destroy Lilith without destroying everything around her. I'm going to climb out now. Once I reach the top, I'll drop a rope, or knotted robes, and haul you up after me."

"No." He scrubbed his forehead with dusty fingers. "I die here. I should have perished with the Bone Well. I cannot let those above see me... exposed."

"Then I'll send them away. Don't argue with me. You are not dying."

"I thought you spared no one."

"You know nothing about me," she retorted.

Violette began to climb, finding precarious hand and footholds in the steep, inward-curved wall and clinging to them like an insect. When she reached the place where the chimney narrowed, she gained a firm purchase across its width. Slowly she edged upwards, one hand, one foot at a time. Blood-red sweat oozed from her.

At the top, the round ingress was tiny, barely the width of her body. The edges crumbled under her fingers.

Fresh desert air hit her skin like an icy stream. Three vampires in dark robes stood there, staring. One of them was Nabil. She expected them to seize her in rage, but they seemed too shocked to do anything.

"Help me get your master to safety," she snapped. "Avert your eyes! Give me a robe for him. And as soon as he's above ground, leave us!"

Her demeanour was intimidating enough to command their obedience. She wondered how she looked to them: white as the moon with witch-black hair, as terrifying as a hunting owl appeared to a shrew?

That was all the power she needed.

Presently Zruvan lay like a corpse on the rocks beside her. He'd almost become wedged in the narrow gullet of the well, and the effort to haul him out tore the last scraps of clothing from him. Now he lay naked, face down, as silky-brown as a nut. No monster at all beneath the costume.

She draped the garment they'd brought over him. It was the djellaba she'd discarded when she had entered the underworld.

Two of the vampires left quickly, as she'd asked, but Nabil hung back, glaring at her. She expected violent rage. Instead he looked confused. His eyes – all she could see of his face – shone with pain.

"We always wanted to release him," Nabil whispered. "Not like this – I didn't expect this. He was the one who insisted on remaining in the Bone Well. Only an entity of equal power could prise him out... but now what? I did not think he would lose all his strength like this. What has happened? What will become of him?"

"I can't answer your questions," she said.

"Please do not harm him."

"I won't." She put one hand between Zruvan's shoulder-blades, unconsciously protective. "Even though he tried to kill me down there, I won't. It was *because* he attacked me that this happened. Let me talk to him. Later, he may need you to look after him."

"I will be waiting," said Nabil. He walked away into the night, but his expression of shock and stoical patience stayed with her.

"Zruvan?" she said softly. "I sent your guards away. I think they were more frightened than you and me. What's your real name?"

"Zruvan is my real name."

"Your birth name, then."

"Don't." His breath chattered. "It's freezing out here!"

"Yes. It will be, if you're used to living inside an oven. Welcome to the cold world of reality."

He pushed himself up and sat with his thin arms wrapped around his chest, knees bent up, the djellaba loose on his shoulders. How young he looked, only just on the edge of adulthood. More like some elf that had crawled up from the roots of a tree than a fiery god of death.

"What have you done?" he said.

"I don't know." Violette spoke gently. "I did tell you that the violent suppression of Lilith always brings disaster. Didn't I warn you?"

"Yes, you did."

"I destroy something else, too: self-delusion."

Zruvan rested his forehead on his knees, ebony hair draping over him. He remained like that for a long time.

She saw – with a strange witch-sight that went directly into her mind – his slow mental and physical collapse. She *felt* it. For centuries he'd believed himself to be a primordial entity. Now those beliefs dissolved and streamed away, as if he'd woken from a dream.

The experience was not painful, but horribly strange, indefinable. Yes, very like waking from a nightmare, struggling to accept the reality you'd forgotten…

She let him sit in silence for an hour, while the stars turned above them and the wind snaked across the sand. Eventually she spoke.

"So you are still alive, but you are not what you believed yourself to be. Won't you talk to me?"

"I have nothing to say."

"I've met others like you. So afraid of God's wrath that they live in a well of misery and guilt until it destroys them. Or they convince themselves they're doing God's work by punishing the sins of mankind. Is that who you are?"

"There are no others like me," he retorted, raising his head. "I told you, I don't fear any god. I came before all gods. I am the black void of space and time that existed before creation…"

"But you know that's not true."

She saw his face freeze into a stricken expression, felt his waves of denial as he tried to reweave the strands of himself. It was too late. "Zruvan" was gone, the wisps melting between his fingers.

"*No one* is that," she went on. "Or perhaps you were for a time, and will be again, but you're also a human: rather, a creature that used to be, and knows perfectly well what it is to be mortal. That's why you were so angry with me. The truth does tend to upset people. Like me, you're a victim of the Crystal Ring, an unwilling avatar. We're not enemies. You can still feel Zruvan within you, as long as you understand that he is an *idea*, not objective reality."

"I don't understand."

"Yes, you do. I am the same, a paradox. I know I'm not really Lilith, but in spite of that, sometimes I *am* her. And for as long as I feel I'm her, it's real. The difference is, I never lost my true identity. Well… I did for a time, but I found it again. And so can you."

"What makes you think I want to? I knew you were a force for chaos."

"Then you shouldn't have brought me here."

"I did so to protect…" His fierce voice trailed to nothing. His head dropped on to his knees again.

"Your loved ones, I know."

"More than that. Our very survival."

"Do you still want to destroy me?" No answer. "I believe your motives were noble. But vampires who wallow in a mass grave of their own victims will have their own life force stolen back. They perish. Many would say that's a well-deserved punishment. And you did so consciously, trying to take on the guilt of all your followers, didn't you? You even made the *Istilqa* knives to help them. That is impressive alchemy. But the weapons are toxic. They're part of the Bone Well, full of anger, grief, madness. They try to steal back what they've lost, like a vampiric force in their own right."

"I know. I have endured it for centuries."

Violette looked more carefully at him. He might have alien ideas, but that did not make him wrong. He was intelligent. If he'd set himself in the Bone Well to protect other vampires from their victims' revenge... He might be misguided, she thought, but without question, he was exceptionally brave.

"I suppose you know that a mortal has some of your knives."

"Fadiya told me."

"Did you never think that mortals might use your *sakakin* to create occult powers of their own?"

He looked up. She could just see his eyes shining through skeins of hair.

"Never. I rarely think of humans. Fadiya will bring them back, but it was more important that she brought *you* to me first."

"You think I'm more dangerous than a human experimenting with your sacred daggers?"

"That was my judgement, yes."

"You were wrong. I am no threat to your followers, but the *Istilqa* knives are lethal. No one wants their weapons falling into the wrong hands, do they? Yet it always happens."

"They are not weapons." His voice was weak with exhaustion. "I made them to protect my flock, not to cause harm. To bring sleep, so we needn't enter the Crystal Ring unless it's essential. And to strengthen us against the very dangers you were talking about! Like... I don't know the word."

"I think you mean inoculation," said Violette. "I see why it seemed a good idea, but vampires don't need such help. Will the knives lose their power without the Bone Well?"

After a long pause, Zruvan answered, "I don't think so. All the victims are still there. New Bone Wells can be built."

"That wouldn't be a good idea. Let it end now."

"But it is our way. My flock will always want the *Istilqa* knives. I've no wish to stop them."

"Nor have I." Violette was suddenly weary from the hours of heat and struggle. "I don't think your traditions are necessary, but I don't seek to change them. Your flock will live as they please."

"How, without Zruvan's protection?"

"They'll survive, believe me. Now you've tasted fresh air and seen the stars again, you don't want to go back to" – she pointed at the tiny hole in the rock – "to that, surely?"

He closed his eyes and shook his head in pain. "No. Even if I wanted to, I cannot. You have stripped my vital nature from me."

"And I'm sorry, but I think you're better without it. I am not your enemy. You could have talked to me as yourself, without the death-mask, instead of sending Fadiya."

"I had no choice. And I don't believe you would have listened."

"That's true," she sighed. "I have little patience with most other vampires. The only way to catch my attention was to do exactly what you did, but that hasn't turned out well for anyone. Or has it?"

Zruvan went quiet, looking up at the stars: a snowstorm, lighting the heavens.

"It's so long since I saw the sky!" he said. "How magnificent. I feel as if the creature I was, who immersed himself in the Bone Well and was hell-bent on confronting Lilith, was someone else. It wasn't me. And yet it was."

"We need not be enemies," she said again. "Those who fight me always regret it. But let me alone, and we'll live in peace. If you open your mind, you'll see something in the darkness you've never seen before. The wisdom of the crone. The Black Madonna. Cybele. Sophia, goddess of wisdom."

"I know nothing of this."

"So learn!" Violette paused, scolding herself. *Exasperation*, she thought, *is not much of a divine quality.* "I know how it feels to be several different beings at once. It's horrifying. It takes a long while to understand. I don't have time to hold your hand through it, but Nabil is waiting, and Fadiya. They'll help you."

"Fadiya is with your friend, taking Emil home," he said, his voice very low.

"But she'll come back, won't she?"

"I don't know. I can't go to Bayt-al-Zuhur. If I'm not Zruvan, they won't accept me. I belong nowhere now."

"Then why does Fadiya work for you? Is it because you're a dreadful tyrant, or because she's devoted to you? Tell me. I don't know."

He only sighed, pushed back his hair, and lay down on the rock with one knee raised. "Soon it will be dawn. I have not seen the sun rise for so many years."

"The dawns and sunsets here are beautiful. I'll wait with you. It's all right, Zruvan."

She saw tears spill out of his eyes, making a track down each temple.

"Kurgara," he said.

"What?"

"Kurgara. That was what they called me. I know I was human once. But I..."

"Go on." Violette waited, willing him to tell the truth.

"I was born neither male nor female. Or both. That's what *kurgara* means: man-woman. I don't know if they thought me a god or a demon, but they were afraid. My mother tried to keep me, but I was cast into the desert to die."

"How long ago?" Again Violette's view of him changed. Her impatience softened to curiosity.

"A thousand years? I don't know. A group of vampires took me in – I didn't know what they were at first. When I reached adulthood, they transformed me. It was then I became Zruvan. A revelation."

"Yes," said Violette, clasping his right hand. "You were an empty vessel. The Crystal Ring filled you with the archetype that best fitted you, for good or ill."

"I forgot my human life entirely... but it's still there in my mind, after all."

Kurgara put his left forearm over his eyes briefly, let his raised knee fall to the side, long enough for Violette to see an unusual set of genitals: a small phallus, protruding from a hood of skin that folded down into a swollen vulva, as if testicles had partly transmuted from female *labia majora*. She saw purplish folded flesh, curly black hair. Different, intriguing.

She felt unexpected warmth pooling inside her. A sensation she hadn't felt for a long time. She moistened her lips, caught a quick deep breath.

He needed to feed. So did she.

"This is why I had to hide, and change," he said. "I am neither and both. Outcast."

Violette was more than startled. She couldn't gather words to express her reaction; mainly a sense of wonder, fascination. In the surface world, such anomalies were never discussed, except between doctors. Then her deeper wisdom kicked in, running a score of ancient tales through her mind.

"Both male and female," she said at last. "Why not? Do not tell me you are *nothing*."

"What am I, then? What does your black crone goddess say about this?"

"She tells me that people are always terrified of anything unusual. They blame it on devils or gods. However, nature knows better. Just because something is rare, that does not make it unnatural. Don't you have the best of both worlds?"

"I hardly think so."

"But you could. You're a vampire, not bound by human conventions. I see how the archetype of Zruvan would fit you – the primordial void that came before male and female?"

"Yes. No place for gender at all."

"But ancient myths are full of androgynes. Adam and Eve, Lilith and Samael... there are stories of androgynous creatures being split into male and female by the gods, or of male and female fusing back into one, perfect being. Long ago, hermaphrodites, or those who changed their sex or had no clear gender at all, were treated as sacred. They were priests. Magical beings."

"Then I was born too late."

"Perhaps you were. But you didn't come into the world without precedent."

Now she saw Zruvan-Kurgara differently; not a young male, but man and woman in perfect balance. The moment imprinted on her mind, transcendent: the vast dome of the Milky Way and billions of stars above them, the wind moaning across the sculpted infinity of the desert, and this exquisite, slender boy-girl lying before her, head tilted back as he-she revealed mysteries.

"So I'm not unique? Not the first?"

"And far from the last. It's a quality of the angels, to be both female and male. Rare, but no cause for shame. And think: as a vampire, an immortal, you can be anything you wish. Human prejudice has no power over you."

"Humans don't concern me. But my followers do. If I am no longer their protector, but a being they don't even recognise... What am I? Even Fadiya will spurn me. She was my dearest companion, but I could never be a true husband to her. She even chose your dancer above me, and I do not blame her."

"I can't fault her devotion to you." Violette was bemused to think of Kurgara and Fadiya as husband and wife. How could they be, while he secluded himself in that terrible pit? Little wonder that Fadiya might turn to Emil in sheer sorrow and loneliness.

"I kissed her once, when I found her near death in the desert. After, she only ever saw the death-headed monster. She loved me anyway... *because* she never saw what lay beneath."

"Exchange blood with me," said Violette. "Only a sip. Everything will be clearer then."

The youth looked uncertain, but did not try to fight as she leaned in, put her arms around the slim shoulders and took a sip from the tender neck. The fluid tasted appalling, like hot metal and ashes, but she forced herself to swallow.

Whatever poison his blood contained, she was strong enough to tolerate it. She must.

She thought she might even develop a taste for it.

The warmth inside her grew more insistent, a distinct stirring of desire. Kurgara was beautiful, and female enough to snare her interest... but so young, at least in appearance. So naïve, with all the trappings of Zruvan stripped away.

Violette pulled her blood-sodden dress and undergarments off, relieved to be free of the damp clinging fabric. Naked, she lay down on the smooth rock beside Kurgara.

She never did things like this. True, she'd had her moments with Charlotte, with Robyn – even with Karl, in bizarre circumstances

– but her nature was solitary and reticent. She could not be free and easy with her passions like Stefan, or Ilona, and did not even envy their lack of inhibition. Solitude suited her. Ah, but sometimes she longed…

Very gently she laid her hands on him: one on his shoulder, one on his chest. She felt the slight swell of breasts, which she'd taken for muscle. And she felt the slim ribcage, motionless and unbreathing, expand with a sudden breath.

"Take my blood," she said.

"I don't know that I can. It is so long since anyone touched me…"

"Is my touch unpleasant?"

"No." The slender back arched upwards a little. "Your hands feel like heaven."

"You needn't live any longer without being touched." She pushed her hair back to expose her throat. "Don't be afraid."

"You are covered in blood!"

"I know… So hot down there, it streamed out of me."

Kurgara put his face into her neck, but did not bite. Instead she felt firm lips, and then the tip of his tongue, licking… Moving over her neck and face, all down her body, licking the blood away, cleaning every inch of her skin that he could reach.

He, or she, was lovely: female enough for her. Female enough for this moment, at least. That mysterious in-between state entranced her: the genitals were like a folded purple orchid. She flung her arms over her head. Her whole self shimmered with pleasure. At last she felt the tongue-tip exploring tentatively between her thighs. An instant, uncontrollable explosion of pleasure convulsed her. The universe turned red and golden. Then Kurgara was sliding upwards and she felt his thin sharp fangs slip into her throat…

He gasped, drinking more that she'd meant him to – she knew she would be weak afterwards, but now she didn't care. Her fingers found the velvet petals, probed and explored as the elfin creature rocked against her hand.

They entwined their arms around each other, found each other's lips. The taste of her own blood, like sharp autumn fruits, washed away the bitterness of his. They pressed close, thighs interwoven so tightly they were almost inside each other. Entering that striving, mindless state of bliss that no power in the universe could stop.

She felt the small hard stamen throb powerfully against her as he came. Kurgara made no sound, but his whole body stiffened in a seizure of pleasure. Violette's back arched with a second, overwhelming orgasm – for those long seconds they were nothing but two hot, swollen orchids fused together, pulsating like a heartbeat.

They lay side by side on their backs, holding hands as the sky began to pale.

"When the sun rises," she said, "it will warm the rock and we'll lie here like two basking lizards."

He didn't answer at once. Sunlight touched them, crimson and gold. Eventually he said, "I had forgotten so much about the world. The colours of the sand... But to enjoy this, I have abandoned my duty."

"Don't you think that a thousand years of hell is enough? It's over. You have no reason to feel guilty."

"I would like to believe you, sweet Lilith."

"Violette."

"Violette," he echoed. "You are persuasive."

She sat up, leaning on one elbow.

"Fadiya wants this with you," she said. "Why would she not? Don't lock yourself away in a temple like some mad, untouchable god. She wants your skin against hers. She wants the sharing of blood. I am not telling you to be 'human' again, because we can never be that, but... try being part of the physical world, where there is touch and sensation and scent and pleasure, the delight of love or of simple conversation..."

Violette didn't know whether she was talking to Kurgara or to herself.

She offered him her wrist, felt the warm lips and the slender fangs piercing like needles. He took several long draughts, as if starving, and would have gone on if Violette had not pulled free.

"Enough," she said softly. "We are inside each other now. This will help us both to understand. We ought to leave. You need to feed properly, and so do I. You'll soon remember how to hunt for yourself: the instinct never fades."

As she passed him the djellaba, and put on her own disgusting, ruined dress, he said, "I do not know where to begin. I'm lost."

"May I suggest you come out of your hole and study some

books?" she replied bluntly. "Or go into the desert and meditate. You don't have to live with illusions. If you still feel that part of you is Zruvan, accept it, but understand that it's only a thought-form. He or she is not your master. Why not go to your flock and explain what's happened?"

He rose, and she had her last glimpse of his body as the djellaba covered him from neck to toe. "They'll scorn me!"

"No, they won't. They'll welcome you. Tell them you've had a revelation! Or say nothing at all. You don't even have to tell them who you are."

"No, I owe them the truth."

"Good," she said. "It's time to understand that you are a vampire, like them. I was going to say an 'ordinary' vampire, but none of us is ever quite that. You can learn to live as yourself, instead of hiding behind costumes and illusions. Not that I'm anyone to talk. I hide behind characters all the time, but I don't believe I really am Odile or Giselle."

"Who are they?"

"Come and ask your friends." She made to walk away, then hesitated, turning to look back at Zruvan-Kurgara reborn: no monster, but brown and slender as a dryad from the deep forest, cloaked in black hair. As fragile as a moth, newly emerged from the thick crust of its cocoon.

"You're beautiful, Kurgara. Your true spirit is gentle, and one day you'll be strong again. They'll adore you. Whether you choose to be male or female or both – that's up to you, but what a wondrous choice to have."

"I want to see Fadiya," he said.

She'd planned to leave him to fend for himself, but changed her mind and held out her hand. "Come on. I'm taking you to Bayt-al-Zuhur, with Nabil's guidance. No argument. You should have learned not to argue with me by now."

"We don't need Nabil," he said. "I know the way."

Fadiya brought Charlotte and Emil inside a wondrous garden enclosed on all sides by the balconies and rooms of the house. Glorious decoration, fountains, sunlit foliage and passages to further courtyards captivated her.

Vampires shrouded in colourful robes came to greet them. Their reverence and love as they bowed to Fadiya was clear. Charlotte felt decidedly humbled.

"This is the Lemon Garden," said Fadiya. "There are other gardens beyond. Our friends here built this place like a *riad*, closed away and secret."

"It's beautiful." That was all Charlotte could say.

"I know," said Fadiya with the hint of a smile.

They dismounted from the mares as two male vampires closed the small side-gate behind them. Between them they helped the wilting Emil from Ghazale's back. Charlotte was sad to think of parting company with Dabab.

"I'll stable the mares, if you show me where," she said. "You take care of Emil."

He was exhausted, hardly able to keep his feet. Fadiya passed him into the hands of three others, the two dark men and a Nordic-blond female.

"You trust them?" Charlotte said, wary. She and Fadiya led the mares along a cloister and into a warm, dusty stable with four stalls.

"Yes. They won't touch him; he's an honoured guest. We are not beasts, any more than you are."

"I know, but we all have moments we regret…"

"He's safe. He stayed here before, on our outward journey. No one touched him."

"Except you."

Fadiya blinked. "He needs rest, that's all."

In the stall, once Dabab was watered, fed and groomed, she rested her muzzle on Charlotte's shoulder and breathed a long, hot sigh down her neck. Charlotte felt no desire for animal blood and never had: it wasn't the same. These horses had no conception of vampires, but they knew predators, and knew they were in no danger from Fadiya or Charlotte. The mare's affectionate trust made her tearful.

"I'll miss you, too," she whispered.

Outside in the Lemon Garden, Charlotte admired the *riad* with its tiers of galleries, ornately carved doors and arches, foliage heavy with blossom. The light was hazy, beautiful. There was a sense of peace here that made her want to stay.

"So this is Bayt-al-Zuhur. Your safe house."

"You've never heard of it?" said Fadiya.

"Never. Karl would have told me if he'd known. He's often said there must be other, secret groups of vampires somewhere. Perhaps everywhere."

"And here is ours," Fadiya said with a smile. "You will always be welcome."

"Do you mean it? Why? We haven't exactly been friends."

"But I hope we're not enemies any longer."

Fadiya fetched a basket and began to pluck olives and dates.

"For Emil," she said. "What a waste that we can't eat them ourselves."

"At least we can enjoy the flowers. The colours and scents. So lovely." Charlotte looked around at the profusion of trees, vines, yellow and violet and blue flowers. She sensed vampire presences in the shaded rooms that led off the galleries. Here and there she saw them relaxing on benches in the shade. Some appeared to be dozing. They had bone-handled *Istilqa* knives stuck in the belts, or even loose on the bench beside them.

How eerie, to be among vampires who were passive and sleepy. It felt soothing, but so *wrong*.

"Everyone here is a vampire," she said. She couldn't make an accurate count – some auras were faint, like Fadiya's – but she estimated at least thirty.

"We live a pleasant enough life," said Fadiya. "The *sakakin* help us rest during the day. At night we hunt and feed, we make music and play our games of love beneath the stars. But Lord Zruvan protects us, our divine guardian. His sacrifice, dwelling in the Bone Well, makes our existence possible."

Charlotte thought about Violette. Fresh fear hit her like an ocean wave. The desert journey and the heat had lulled her into torpor, as if getting Emil here was all that mattered. Now she was suddenly on full alert, alarmed but ready to fight.

I have to go back for her – if I'm strong enough to enter Raqia. If not, I'll ride back.

"What's wrong?" said Fadiya. "You look as if you're about to murder me."

"What about Violette? Will he harm her? Zruvan, I mean?"

Fadiya drew Charlotte to a fountain. They sat on the tiled rim with water misting over them.

"He'll do what he has to. There's nothing you can do, and you know it. It's too late."

Charlotte swallowed what she longed to say. *If she doesn't come back, this will never be forgiven. I don't want to destroy your paradise, but oh – once we gather those who love Lilith, even though we're only a few – you'll learn all about revenge, Fadiya. You'll regret the day you came spying on us.*

"What are you thinking?" said Fadiya. "Sometimes we've had to battle other groups who were jealous and wanted to destroy us. Zruvan is our protector."

"This is only my opinion," Charlotte said carefully, "but I think the Bone Well is an appalling idea. Vampires who hoard their victims around them come to a sorry end. And the *Istilqa* knives are extremely dangerous. Why create daggers that can kill vampires but give humans power against us?"

"That isn't their purpose."

"But that's what they are. My father devoted his life to exploring the inside of atoms – a perfectly noble study, yet I've had nightmare premonitions about where his research might lead one day. The best of intentions may have appalling results."

"The same is true of everything," said Fadiya. The vulnerable, confiding Fadiya of the cavern was gone. Her shutters were closed again. "You are in no position to judge us."

"Granted, but I still think the knives are a mistake. You use them as humans use laudanum. The Crystal Ring's there for us to rest in, but you're afraid of the very realm that created you."

"So? Humans fear the desert and the sea, especially during storms."

"I'd like to know why Zruvan focused this fear on Violette."

"He wants the truth, that's all." Fadiya's voice tightened. "If you disapprove of us, that's unfortunate, but this is how we live. Don't come here, with no understanding, and tell us to stop."

"It's only my impression," Charlotte repeated. She looked up at the blue square of the sky. "Everything feeds in a circle. I believe humans like Godric Reiniger are *causing* the Crystal Ring's moods. Not Violette. She doesn't deserve this."

"I can only do what Zruvan asks."

"You're not the cold-hearted predatory vampire I thought you were. I know you're not. But you deliberately seduced Emil to ensnare *her*."

"As you said, plans don't always have the expected outcome," Fadiya said softly. "I fell in love with Emil. I helped you free him because I couldn't risk Zruvan letting him die. I do love him, Charlotte. I do."

Charlotte believed her. She smiled with bitter-sweet sadness.

"Then I feel sorry for you. We fall for the wrong people and end up tearing lives apart all around us. If I can't help Violette, my duty is to get Emil back to Switzerland. What will you do, Fadiya?"

Emil slept for hours – too long, he thought. The nightmarish trance of shock he'd entered when they first threw him into the truck had softened to a mellow state of languor. He remembered speeding across the desert on horseback, his mind screaming while his body felt like a sack of coal. Now he saw he was back in Fadiya's courtyard palace again.

He felt a surge of anger. A sign he was coming back to life.

He washed in a bowl of rose-scented water they'd left for him and dressed. Between a choice of colourful robes and a plain suit, he chose the suit.

When he came out from behind the screen, Fadiya was sitting on his bed.

The room had a soothing brownish light, dappled with fretwork patterns of daylight falling through the windows. A ceiling fan stirred the torpid air.

Fadiya beckoned, and he reluctantly sat beside her. She took his hand. She still had her lovely scent of flowers and spices. She'd bathed, changed, perfumed herself: there was no whiff of horse left on her. He thought of her skin sliding against his, her hair brushing his chest... turned his head away in pain.

"Darling, I am so sorry," she began.

He gave a short laugh. "Why? You used me!"

"Yes, I deceived you, but I didn't know I would fall in love with you."

"Please. I'm not a fool – well, plainly I am, but not stupid enough to be taken in twice. When I was held prisoner, didn't I hear you say you lied about being a widow, that you were married to someone else?"

"Zruvan. Yes, but not in the sense you'd understand. And I've betrayed him to save you."

"Betrayal should be your middle name."

"Forgive me. The love I feel for you is real. Vampires and humans can love each other…"

"Not according to Violette. I've tasted your love. It consisted of you sucking out my strength and replacing it with mad nightmares."

"Ask Charlotte, then. She was human when she met Karl."

"I do not care to ask Charlotte. I don't care about your reasons. You used me to lure Violette to your – your husband, whatever he is – and to her death?" He stood up, fists clenched at his sides. "This is your fault. And mine. After this, I have no future, nowhere to go, nothing to be…"

"Then stay here with me," she murmured, rising and sliding around to face him. Then she kissed him and he couldn't resist the warmth of her mouth, the slender warm body against his and the feel of her hair between his fingers. He groaned.

"I love you, Emil. We could start again. You loved me too, didn't you, just a little?"

"I could have loved you. Fadiya, Fadiya…"

"Please forgive me. I'll explain and make up for everything."

"Too late."

He pushed her away. Her beautiful, tormented face quested towards his, her eyes glistening with tears, and he believed she was sincere. To his own dismay, he felt pain pushing up at his heart like a boulder. His throat ached – *Damn it,* he thought, *why am I in tears?*

But it was too late.

"After what we've done to Violette, you and I? If she's dead – I don't even want to know. But this is over, Fadiya." He opened his hands. "Go on, drink my blood and kill me if you want – I can't stop you. Whatever you decide, I never want to see you again."

She stared at him, tears streaming down her face. Then she was gone – simply vanished into the air – the sound of her departure not retreating footsteps, but the sifting of sand.

The best time to escape from vampires was in the day. That was obvious, Emil thought after he'd watched the courtyard for another hour. No one came near him. After all, who was interested except Fadiya, who was now gone for good?

They were sluggish in the heat, active at night. His only chance was to go now, while no one was paying attention. There must be a discreet way to the outside, and if the gates were locked he'd climb over a wall, like the athlete he was.

He quickly rifled through the bag he'd brought. He had his money and documents still. That was all he needed.

Now that he had no future, there was only one thing left for him to do.

CHAPTER TWENTY-FIVE

THE WILD HUNT

Concealed in the darkened projection booth, Karl was amazed by the size of the audience settling in Godric's private cinema. He'd expected this to be a small private showing for his supporters only. Instead he counted forty men, twenty women. Crew and cast sat at the back, and the front rows were full of local dignitaries and business owners. Karl understood: if Godric presented their town, and Switzerland, in a flattering light, support and money would flow his way. His political group would become a real force. He could make all the melodramatic propaganda films he wanted. After all, his aim was to glorify his home country: who would object to that?

Reiniger himself was the last to arrive, resplendent in white tie and tails. He strutted down the steps to a round of applause.

Karl was astonished that – after the events of a few nights ago – Godric was going ahead with his movie launch as if nothing out of the ordinary had happened.

He had to admire the man's aplomb.

Reiniger raised one hand, nodding his appreciation. He cleared his throat and spoke in a clear, piercing voice that conveyed a blend of pride and humility.

"Welcome, my friends, to Bergwerkstatt: my home and workplace. If you wonder what Reiniger Studios has been doing over the spring, the answer is this: editing together our hard work in what I hope will come to be regarded as a masterwork of the project. Reiniger Studios is proud to present a drama set in our beloved home country!"

He took a seat in the front row. His second-in-command, Wolfgang, sat to his right and Amy on his left.

She'd insisted on returning to him, even after the bedroom incident. She had done what she told Karl she planned to do: walked back in, let the fuss die down and insisted that she had never been kidnapped. She'd simply been a guest of the Ballet Lenoir for a few days. If his enemies had said otherwise, they'd lied.

"He mustn't find out I helped you," she'd said to Karl. "And don't worry about me. This will be the biggest acting performance of my life."

Her uncle must have swallowed the story – after all, it was more or less true. Karl was certain Reiniger had no idea she'd been present that night – too wrapped up in his own activities even to suspect.

He certainly wouldn't have confessed his exploits to anyone. A facade of normality must be maintained. Now Amy sat beside him as if in total innocence, more calculating than her ingénue manner would suggest.

The lights went down, the curtains slid back from the screen and Stefan began to crank the projector. There were twin projectors, the second poised to take over as soon as the first reel ran out. Karl had had to learn fast, and he knew they had little time before Reiniger began to suspect that his experienced projectionist was drunk, or battling with technical difficulties. Stefan struggled to run the film at the precise speed: slightly too fast, then slightly too slow, as words lit up the screen:

Reiniger Studios presents... TRIUMPH IN THE MOUNTAINS.

Karl and Stefan exchanged a look. The grey and silver images began. A breath-taking Alpine panorama blended into a scene of foreign soldiers pouring down a mountain pass. The usual message, Karl noted. Switzerland in danger from every direction. A pure Swiss maiden – played by Mariette in a blond, plaited wig – was captured and tormented by bearded Slavic brigands. Much overacting ensued.

"He does like to linger on his torment scenes, doesn't he?" said Stefan, as the villains took a whip to the brave but wilting heroine.

"Oh, he enjoys a little torture," Karl said softly. "The technical quality is actually not bad, but always the same story…"

"With practice," Stefan said mordantly, "he will get better until one day he tells the *perfect* story, the one that fires everyone's heart with crusading fervour and, who knows, starts the next world war."

"With practice, could you try to find a consistent speed?" said Karl.

"I thought these damned things would have electric motors by now," Stefan retorted. "Do *you* know what you are doing?"

In the corner of the booth, the official projectionist lay unconscious. Stefan's fangs had taken him down – he wasn't one of the inner circle, so his blood was untainted – but they'd tied and gagged him to make sure.

Stefan ran the movie for as long as it took Karl to unload the reel from the second projector and replace with a different one. The process of threading the film into place took concentration: it hadn't seemed this difficult when Amy had tutored him.

"It's done," Karl said at last. "I'm ready."

Stefan stopped turning the handle of the first projector, with the result that the frame caught in the lamp's heat and melted. The picture on screen flared to white. The audience uttered a groan.

Reiniger turned in his chair and glared up at the projection booth.

"Turn off the lamp!" Karl exclaimed.

"Well, turn yours on. You said you were ready!"

Karl thought of rousing the projectionist and making him take over before Reiniger stormed up there to see what was happening. Surely they could perform the task more smoothly than this…

"Bolt the door," said Karl. "At least stop anyone coming in here."

"For God's sake, hurry."

Herr Reiniger was actually out of his seat, glowering, when Karl got the new reel running. Amy sat motionless, eyes fixed forward.

Cut from the terrified maiden to her brave peasant fiancé weeping over her body. He shook his fist at the heavens and – in captions – swore to join the Swiss army and avenge this dastardly deed.

The audience settled again. The film ran on for a minute or three, long enough to lull them into the story…

Then it cut to a new scene. Dark and grainy, it sat out of context and seemed to be from a different movie entirely. The lighting was poor. No captions flagged the sudden change of mood. There was a room, full of ornate curtains and furnishings, mostly in shadow. In the doorway, two people were kissing. Two men.

A suppressed gasp went up from the audience.

Both men's faces were plainly discernible. One was Karl, who was known to barely anyone here. The other, however, was unmistakable as Godric Reiniger.

Utter silence fell as they wrestled in the doorway with apparent feverish lust, Godric thrusting Karl back into the wall. Then Karl moved away, and Godric went into the centre of the room and stripped naked. The audience murmured with confusion and blank shock.

"Not bad for his age," Stefan whispered. "He'll run to fat if he's not careful, though."

The images jumped forward a little: that was where Amy had spliced the first reel to the second. Then the action continued.

No sign of the ghostly Charlotte whose shape he'd borrowed. Only Reiniger, unclothed and faintly ridiculous.

There were sniggers in the audience. A couple of women and a priest marched for the exit, their faces pictures of outrage. Everyone else stayed riveted in their seats. Even Reiniger appeared paralysed. Karl saw the muscles in his neck stand out, his shoulders rising as he gripped the seat arms.

There was some jerkiness as the camera operator moved towards the bedroom door. Now there was a narrow view of Karl just inside the room, his shirt undone, while Reiniger grappled with another man on the bed. He rose above Stefan, poising himself with clear intent –

Karl had cut the film there, just before he fell on to Niklas's body and vanished, screaming.

Stefan had added some captions.

"Herr Reiniger demonstrates the vices... That we shall obliterate from the glorious Motherland!" Another in smaller letters, "The rest of this scene was deemed too obscene for those of a sensitive disposition..." And a final frame, "Private viewings on request. Worth every franc!"

"We should have left Niklas in," whispered Stefan. "See, even in death he helps us. Reiniger's screaming was hilarious."

The film ended there. Karl turned off the projector, flicked on the house lights and waited for the storm.

"He demonstrates those vices with great enthusiasm, doesn't he?" someone called laconically from the audience.

The murmur grew towards uproar, an awful brew of mockery and outrage. Another man in the front row leapt to his feet and snarled at Godric. "You dared to blackmail *me*?"

It was Wolfgang. Amy shrank in her seat, like a schoolgirl trying hard not be noticed.

"He did what?" said someone else.

Wolfgang Notz turned to face the crowd, waving one hand at the blank screen. He was shaking with anger. "Godric blackmailed me for years over these so-called vices, and there he is – you saw him – doing the same and worse!"

Reiniger was on his feet, red-faced and yelling.

"Fakery! Lies! This is a prank designed to humiliate—" All the time he glared up at the projection booth, trying to discern who'd betrayed him.

No one was listening. Over the noise, a second man stood up and called out, "He's coerced me, too."

"And me."

"Oh, let's talk about bribery! Attack Wolfgang and you attack us all!"

Another five men were on their feet – all members of the inner circle, Karl saw – declaring solidarity with Wolfgang Notz.

Deathly silence fell and lasted a full five seconds before more voices rose, hurling questions and accusations.

Some of the town officials were sitting very still, saying nothing at all.

Reiniger barked at them, "Where do you think the money comes from to finance this enterprise, and your jobs, our party, your role in my plans, our very future?"

He continued haranguing them, but Wolfgang stood with his feet braced, an expression of profound disgust on his face.

"Now the truth's out," he said. "Now you all know! I am no saint – Reiniger threatened me with public disgrace and jail, if I did not nearly bankrupt my family to keep funding him – but look, how is he any better than me? Than any of us?"

"This is all trickery and lies!" cried Reiniger.

Wolfgang looked stoical in the face of injustice, while Godric appeared to verge on hysteria. Amy had told Karl that Godric's followers trusted Wolfgang, making him a threat to her uncle's leadership. People could overlook sexual proclivities more easily than they could forgive hypocrisy, it seemed. Extorting money from the most popular member of their clique went beyond the pale.

"I have no answer to this, except to leave," Wolfgang said calmly. "If you support Godric Reiniger, stay. If you don't, you're free to leave with me."

There was a shuffling sound of feet moving towards the exit. Dignitaries first, then Godric's supporters, employees and his entire household followed Wolfgang Notz out of the cinema. Amy came last, casting Karl and Stefan a quick glance as she passed. Her expression was like stone.

Godric stood furious and bewildered as he watched everyone abandon him.

Stefan unlocked the booth door. Karl untied the dazed projectionist and pushed him out after the others. Then he and Stefan descended the shallow steps to the front of the theatre, guided Reiniger back to his seat and sat down on either side of him.

Reiniger produced an *Istilqa* knife from his pocket, twirled it between his hands then stabbed it into the velvet arm of his seat. He seemed to realise the weapon would not help him. Stefan and Karl had both suffered enough wounds to withstand the worst of its power.

"I hope you are pleased with this day's work," said Reiniger.

"You were the star of your own movie," said Stefan. "What's to complain about?"

"How did you do it?" His gaze was fixed on the blank screen, his fingers drumming the knife handle.

"We purchased a camera," said Karl, bending the truth for Amy's sake. "We bought the equipment and chemicals and we learned how to use them. It was not especially difficult. I'm sure it's hard to make a *good* movie, but not to make one so basic."

"That is not what I meant."

Godric stopped. Karl hoped he wouldn't ask who was operating the camera, but he seemed to have something more complex on his mind.

"Are you referring to the fact that we knew it was you in the guise of my wife?" Karl asked coolly. When Godric didn't answer, he went on, "Did you think your illusion would fool me? It did not. Nor did it fool the camera."

"Much to our delight," Stefan put in.

"How did *you* do it?" said Karl. "That's the real question. How have you acquired the power to enter the Crystal Ring? We expected you to appear at some point – that's why the camera was ready – but as yourself, not in disguise. How did you gain the skill to take on someone else's shape? That is a form of magic, and I don't even believe in magic."

"You have been the bane of my life, Karl," said Godric.

"Are you going to answer?"

"You're the curse of my life, not least in killing my father, but in this damned... *obsession* you woke in me. Isn't that the very essence of a vampire? You're not content with taking the blood and energy of the living – you have to hold us in thrall, too. You make humans fall in love with you because you have to possess *everything*, even our beating hearts. I swear to God, I never felt a moment of lust towards another male until I saw you."

"Oh, come off it," Stefan said with vicious scorn. "You needn't lie to us. You do understand the reason they all walked out, don't you? Aside from the fact that you showed them an embarrassingly obscene film starring your good self? Some might be scandalised by your sexual preferences, but far worse than those are your double standards. *Don't* tell me you have never looked at or touched another man but Karl. Pretending to be Charlotte while you accosted him is one of the worst displays of cowardice and duplicity I've ever witnessed. And for *me* to say that is quite something."

"Shut up," Godric growled, "you filthy little male whore."

"Don't talk to me like that," Stefan replied with terrifying sweetness. "You tried to deceive Karl in order to molest him. Your actions were a shade away from rape, weren't they? You molested me quite thoroughly, come to that. And my brother. Shall we add necrophilia to your list of interests?"

"*Shut up.*" He sounded on the verge of exploding. "It was

Karl's power I wanted. Nothing else. His power."

"You liar."

"Godric, I am sorry," Karl said, raising a hand to quiet Stefan. "I wish my path had never crossed yours or your father's. What you say about vampires is true. That's why I try to keep out of human sight, to avoid such complications. I never set out with the intention of making you hate or desire me. If you've suffered those feelings, I am truly sorry. But Stefan's right – your actions are your own responsibility. So I ask again, have you become a vampire? If not, what are you?"

"I thought you had the answer to everything, you creatures of the supernatural realm."

"We don't."

He lit a cigarette and puffed on it as if it were oxygen to save his life.

"I've already told you. The *sakakin* cuts let in the light and energy of another realm, a little at a time. I thought the only way to enter the... the 'Crystal Ring' was to become one of your kind. But after you rejected me, I thought... Why should not a man enter the higher realm of his own will? And I did it. I'm not even sure how. I was angry. I cut the necessary patterns in my own flesh, I felt the realm reaching into me, and I *willed* myself to enter."

"As simple as that?" Stefan said in a small, sardonic voice.

"Not simple. It's taken years. But I had support and encouragement from the higher world."

"What about the need for blood?" Karl asked. He was mystified. He knew of humans who'd tried to enter Raqia without help. He'd never heard of anyone succeeding so consummately.

"I have no need for blood," Reiniger snapped. "I achieved what you told me was impossible. I have all a vampire's powers with none of its unfortunate habits. Strength, access to the other realm, higher perceptions. I have become, in effect, the first perfect, superior human. A springboard towards something immense..."

"Not quite perfect, since you've just lost all your followers," Karl interrupted.

"I don't care," Reiniger said through his teeth. "I'll find new and better ones."

"I rather think you do care," said Karl. "Who will follow you now? Everyone knows that you don't practise what you preach. For your sake I hope no one calls the police."

"D'you think they'll try to prosecute me for blackmail, or obscenity? Let them try! Humans cannot touch me now. Charlotte? I put her on like a coat."

His sneering remark made Karl freeze with anger.

"What do you mean?"

"I kept seeing her, like a ghost haunting me. I realised she was from the hidden world, a *Weisse Frau* as they're called in folklore. Perhaps even Perchta herself, a goddess – and here she was, submitting herself to *my* needs by taking the shape of your lady friend. It was a clear sign. So I summoned the *Weisse Frau* and used her form to cloak mine."

"Summoned her, how?"

"Beckoned her to me. Used the force of my resolve. She was a *very* willing collaborator indeed. She displayed no mind or intention of her own, any more than an image on film has a mind. Perfect." Godric smirked. "I stepped inside her shape, as I said, as if putting on a coat. It was easy. Her shape did exactly what I willed it to do. And I almost fooled you, did I not?"

Malign energy radiated from him: a blend of anger, frustration, arrogance, and the deadly chill of the *Istilqa* knives.

He is not bluffing, thought Karl. *Whatever he has become, it's dangerous. An entity that might wish to annihilate vampires, as well as dominate mortals.*

"'Almost' was not nearly close enough," said Karl. "As Stefan said, trying to mislead me by impersonating Charlotte was a singularly vile act of deceit."

"But Karl, the point is that I've learned what needs to be done with you," said Reiniger. "Obsession is a form of weakness. Anything that wakes lust or infatuation must be crushed. It's nothing but a distraction, an obstacle to enlightenment. Therefore desire can *only* be used as a pathway to domination. The object must be used, violated, destroyed. Like a tumour, it must be cut out."

On the last word, he seized the dagger and plunged it at Karl's throat.

By reflex, Karl caught Reiniger's wrist with the blade-tip just grazing his throat. The next Karl knew, they were in the Crystal

Ring together – Reiniger following as Karl tried to slip free. Gripping each other's arms with hands like vulture claws they struggled, fighting as he and Kristian had fought in the old days.

Karl propelled himself upwards, through the cobwebby ceilings until he soared above the house and into the higher layers. Cobalt-blue light shone between storm clouds edged with white fire. As always, he became a dark, lacy demon, but Reiniger changed too.

The change was subtle at first. Godric glowed. He became a manic waxwork replica of himself.

At least he did not look like Charlotte.

He had dropped the knife. Instead he fought and moved with all the agile power of a vampire, his hands like shackles on Karl's arms. He showed no sign of fear. Clearly he was already an adept in this realm. Terrifyingly strong, even without the ability to drink Karl's blood.

"I will have your power, Karl," Godric rasped in his ear. "I'll feast on you in every possible way."

Karl grew cold as they rose. His attacker was stealing power, not from his veins, but directly from the aura of his life force. Reiniger's body began to increase in size: muscles thickening, marble-white head lengthening.

"I have become the first perfect, superior human," he had said. "A springboard to something immense."

"What are you?" Karl whispered.

A huge hand closed on his neck and began to squeeze. The face staring into his was now twice its human size. Tangled white hair emerged from Godric's skull and began to writhe and tumble towards his shoulders.

"I am Berchtold, Lord of the Wild Hunt," came the voice, a distorted roar. "I am Woden, god of the mountains. I am here to protect and save my land, destroy all our enemies. I *am* the land, and no demonic *strigoi* feet shall tread here."

"You are insane," Karl tried to say; he couldn't force out the words. The only hope left to him was his greater knowledge of the Crystal Ring.

They rose towards the higher layers of ether. Karl moved into the stream of a powerful current that carried both him and Reiniger upwards like a pair of life-sized dolls. Chasm walls rose high above them, then swiftly dwindled away below. Karl saw the curve of the Earth and the glittering ceiling that was the *Weisskalt* above him. Cold vapours poured down. Reiniger began to shiver, but didn't loosen his grip.

He was still changing. Nubs of bone appeared on his forehead and began to push outwards, becoming two devil-horns. Karl heard the ghastly creaking sound as they continued to grow.

He felt tiny in the grasp of Berchtold-Woden, but he hung on tenaciously, like a small but ruthless scorpion.

The god that had been Reiniger made incomprehensible growling noises, more animal than human. Was he trying to speak? Karl was past caring what he had to say. There was only one chance, and that was to carry him up to the *Weisskalt* where the sub-zero temperature would claim them both.

I've already defeated him in the mortal world, Karl thought. *His public humiliation was the end for him. This – this is revenge. But I did not anticipate it and I should have done.*

A bitter, glacial wind full of ice needles showered down from the blinding white light above. Leaving his enemy to hibernate in the *Weisskalt* made him no better than Kristian.

Karl, however, was beyond caring whether he was more moral than Kristian.

For all the harm Godric's done, he thought, *for his malevolent plans, and to avenge Niklas and Stefan, he has to die.*

"And especially to spare us any more of your appalling films." Forming the words was a struggle, but the Woden-Godric entity heard him and emitted a blood-chilling moan.

As they gained altitude, their speed slowed. Karl struggled to make progress, but the giant in his arms was a dead weight. The closer they drew to the *Weisskalt*, the heavier Reiniger became, until Karl could go no higher. They hung together in the upper atmosphere with the exosphere still some miles above: stranded there, as if treading water on the surface of the Antarctic Ocean.

Stalemate.

And still Reiniger went on changing horribly, the horns thickening and spiralling into a corkscrew shape. His visage narrowed, cheeks becoming gaunt as the face pushed forward. A beard sprouted from the chin like matted grey horse hair. His eyes were entirely blood-red. There was nothing human left of him. Karl glanced from his hideous aspect to the infinite void below them and his heart stopped.

Options raced through his mind without words.

Until this moment, Karl had never let himself admit that Reiniger might win.

Godric's flight through the Crystal Ring was ecstatic. Although his transformation was painful and horrific, it was also the most wondrous thing any human had ever experienced. Sublime exhilaration.

His dream was complete.

"I have become Berchtold, Lord of the Wild Hunt. I have become Woden, god of the mountains."

He had stolen Karl's energy and used it to complete his metamorphosis.

I am Woden, he tried to say. He could no longer form clear words. *I am the sleeping hero, William Tell, reincarnated to save his land. I am the god of the mountains, the god to whom all others bow down...*

Unintelligible sounds rumbled from his throat as he tried to voice his triumph.

The chill at this height was excruciating, but he was stoical enough to bear it. He would have to be, for long enough to suck out the dregs of Karl's energy. The vampire was already an empty husk but still clinging on, like a dead spider entangled in Woden's great fur cloak.

But something was amiss. The metamorphosis should have stopped when it reached perfection. Instead it continued.

Pain racked his huge body. He heard his own bones cracking as his skull changed shape. He felt that the weight of his new, spiralling horns would pull him downwards, out of this fantastical realm before he was ready.

Clenching his jaw – his teeth felt enormous, with lightning-bolts of pain shooting through them from the ice-cold air – he made a determined effort to end Karl's life. His fist tightened, muscular enough to compress the spine and rip off the head as if the vampire were made of clay. *To kill that which he had desired.* Strong enough to fling the remains into the void…

Instead, Karl remained in one piece and stubbornly alive.

"Sometimes the Crystal Ring gives you what you need," said Karl. His voice was raw with agony but the words were clear. "And sometimes it gives you what you deserve."

Suspended in the void, Karl watched Godric changing. Grotesque ever-growing horns, sunken face, horrible staring eyes and all that thick, tangled, filthy grey hair.

He had become more goat than god.

He looked exactly like the demon whose face had loomed out of the screen in *The Lion Arises*. A gargoyle in shades of silver-grey.

A man in costume at last year's *Fasnacht* festival.

"*Krampus*," Karl whispered.

Godric grunted, as if asking, "What?"

"*Schmutzli*," said Karl. "That's all you are, Godric Reiniger. You're not a god. You're nothing but a fiend to frighten naughty children. A man in costume with a goat's head."

With speed that Reiniger couldn't match, Karl wrenched the strangling hand off his throat. He broke the hold so abruptly that he felt the wrist fracture, heard it like a gunshot. Then he lunged for Reiniger's throat.

One thing his enemy could not do was drink blood.

He seized his chance, bit into the saggy grey flesh of Reiniger's neck. A repellent taint infused his blood – the anguish of long-dead human souls tasted like death to vampires – but Karl forced himself to drink. This time he managed to endure the taste, locked on despite Godric's desperate writhing. This was the only way to take back his strength.

Locked together, they began to fall. The intense cold was too much for them both. Something else, too: because Godric was not a true vampire, perhaps the Crystal Ring had decided to expel him by force.

Reiniger screamed.

All though their long, long fall towards Earth, Reiniger screamed. His form shrank until he was the same size as Karl again, but he stayed in his grotesque *Schmutzli* shape and would not die. Perhaps he'd truly made himself indestructible. He didn't need to be Woden. A grisly, unkillable, vengeful *Alp* would cause chaos enough.

I can't let him back to Earth like this, thought Karl, *but how to deal with him?*

Karl ached all over from frostbite, exertion and the sour venom of Godric's veins. He felt suddenly that it would be easiest just to fall asleep and let all this go...

"I will be the master of my own fate," Reiniger's words were distorted but intelligible. His voice shook Karl back to alertness. "Torment me all you like. You cannot control me, Karl, short of killing me. You may have won this time, but – I had you all dancing like rats on a hotplate, and I shall again."

"I don't think so," Karl said under his breath.

He thought of Niklas lying dead and Stefan howling in pain. Emil bruised and sobbing in an alleyway, and Charlotte pushing him away with dread in her eyes because a cold knife had cut her in two.

Karl turned Godric around and clamped his arms behind his back. He changed direction, arcing downwards, leaving behind the fierce currents and curving towards the south... out across the Mediterranean, down towards the North African coast and the bleak otherworldly beauty of the Sahara.

Coast, towns, mountain ranges and wilderness flashed beneath. Gripping his enemy, he dropped out of Raqia and hit the ground.

Blessed warmth enveloped him, and turned all too swiftly to roasting heat. Godric writhed in his arms, groaning with pain like a human.

Karl dumped him on the edge of the desert where rocks jutted from the sandy hills. Still in gargoyle form, Godric crouched on the ground, cradling his broken wrist, hardly able to raise his head for the weight of the immense twisted horns.

Karl felt a small pang of pity. The thing that had been Godric was unlikely to force its way back into Raqia. Without the metabolism to live on blood, how would he get his strength back?

Then the horns tipped back and Godric glared up at him with such blazing hatred that the pang of sympathy died.

"You can't leave me here!" Godric rasped.

The sun scorched the blue sky, and there was nothing but sand

and rock all the way to the perfect circle of the horizon. Was this more cruel than the *Weisskalt*? Perhaps, but Karl was not in a merciful mood.

"We're on the northern edge of the Sahara. You told me that this is where your father found the *Istilqa* knives."

Reiniger stared at him. Some hint of his human self flickered inside the scarlet eyes. He stood up unaided, swaying, so deep in trauma and rage that, Karl guessed, he would either perish or transform into something worse.

But their fight was over. Karl saw no way to end his life, and didn't want to. His desire to kill was entirely gone. All he could hope was that Godric Reiniger would wander into the desert and lose himself forever.

"Don't come back to Switzerland," Karl said, catching a breath. Now he was in human shape again the hot air hurt his lungs. He felt a shadow stir in the back of his mind, a presence that might be close or a hundred miles away. "I do not ever want to see you again."

"Not over," said Reiniger, pointing a clawed hand at him.

"Perhaps you should see what else you can unearth. Follow your father's lead and search for more ancient mysteries."

"Don't mock me." The voice was thick and hoarse. "My father will guide me to secrets, and you will regret this day bitterly. *Not over.*"

Godric turned and began to walk into the wilderness, staggering as he went. He was in shock, but that didn't make him less dangerous. Karl thought, *He might yet be capable of recovery and heaven alone knows what else.*

Karl pushed a hand through his hair and folded his arms. He watched the gargoyle figure with its ridiculous horns for a minute, feeling strangely helpless. *I don't want to follow him but how can I let him wander off in this state? What if I cannot go back into Raqia? Curse the day I ever met his damned father!*

Again he sensed someone else nearby. The feeling was more insistent this time. Someone was coming towards him... someone he knew? They were walking towards him, and straight towards Reiniger, too.

Karl started forward and saw Godric making his unsteady way along a sandy path between two low ridges of rock. Sunlight dazzled him and the distant sand rippled like water, a mirage. Against the glare two figures appeared, hand in hand.

Violette?

His shock passed quickly. Of course it was Violette. Her signature was subtle but unmistakable: a unique black-white-violet aura scented with lilies. *She* was the reason he'd landed in exactly this place. He'd been drawn to her without even knowing.

She walked proudly upright, barefoot, her hair and clothes a ragged mess. At her side was a slender stranger: male or female, Karl could not tell. Brown skin, silky black hair, also barefoot beneath the striped robe. The aura he projected was faint and rust-red. Definitely not human. Karl made a brief scan of the stranger, then focused his attention on Violette.

She's alive. Thank all that's sacred. He started towards her.

Seeing the bizarre figure of Godric approaching her, Violette and her companion stopped. Did she recognise him? He looked very different, but her higher senses were sharp. She might well see straight through his distorted appearance. Karl saw her eyes widen...

Godric Reiniger put back his head, went into attack posture like a stalking cat. He swung his head side to side, and Karl could see his mouth opening to reveal huge, dripping teeth and a red tongue.

Karl began to run after him.

Reiniger uttered a dreadful noise, a tearing roar full of squealing harmonics that tortured the ears, as if he were venting all his accumulated fury at the world. White light crackled around him.

His power was returning, as if from nowhere.

No, thought Karl in dismay. *He's drawing it straight from the Crystal Ring.*

Then he sprang at Violette and her companion. Claws and teeth and blazing, mindless rage.

Karl caught him, one second before he reached his target.

In a single, fluid strike, he grabbed the neck from behind and jerked the grotesque creature backwards off his feet. Its entire body went limp, as if every bone had shattered.

What lay on the ochre sand at his feet was... fur and horns. A costume. Nothing inside. A demonic-looking *Krampus* or *Schmutzli* costume, empty.

A lizard skittered from under Karl's heel as he took a step back.

Stunned, he pushed at the ashen fur heap with his shoe. It appeared the Crystal Ring itself had transformed Godric's clothing into a kind of disguise that he'd shed like a skin. But real fur, leather and bone? Had Reiniger discarded a layer of *himself*?

He'd never seen anything like it before. Godric was simply... gone.

"Karl?" Violette ran to his side. "What was that? What in hell was that?"

CHAPTER TWENTY-SIX

HOUSE OF FLOWERS

Two days later, Karl and Violette and Kurgara found their way to Bayt-al-Zuhur.

Too exhausted to enter the Crystal Ring – and too wary of using the bone-knives to rest – they'd simply walked.

Violette told him that she and her companion had travelled all the way from the Bone Well on foot. She said very little about what had happened there, and Kurgara had barely spoken at all. In turn, Karl had no energy to explain about Godric Reiniger. They simply trekked in weary, comfortable silence until they reached their destination.

He came to love the mesmeric allure of the mountainous desert with its ever-changing palette of light and colour. Crimson and amber melted to plum and violet. There was not another soul for miles... Even his blood-thirst subsided, at least for this dream-like journey.

The house of vampires, Bayt-al-Zuhur, broke his trance-state with a burst of colour and light.

The high featureless walls that surrounded the *riad* gave nothing away. A small side-gate swung open to admit them and Karl found himself in another world, a glorious courtyard garden with foliage veiling the galleries and shuttered rooms beyond. Everything seemed veiled and secret. Fountains cooled the air.

Violette greeted a robed man, addressing him as Nabil, and a mild argument ensued. Karl gathered that Nabil had gone ahead through the Crystal Ring and offered to drive back in a truck to collect them. He was unhappy that she and Kurgara had turned down the offer.

They had actually *wanted* to make the slow journey alone and on foot. It was the start of Kurgara's healing, Violette insisted.

Later, Karl came to understand what she meant, but now he barely registered their exchange. As soon as he stepped inside, the presence of at least thirty vampires shivered through the ether. Some were bright and vivid, others muted. What was the mood here?

He sensed passion, jealousy, blood-hunger, satiation, calm content... all those emotions leapt out at him, a shocking cacophony after hours of silence. The *collective* mood was a different matter. It was subdued. Soporific, calm... drugged, almost, as if they were humans dreaming in an opium den.

So many vampires, all living in secret here? They pierced themselves with *Istilqa* knives to evade the torment of being always awake... but how would they react if the blades lost their potency? That might not happen for many years, but eventually it would.

They will have to adapt. During their trek, he'd heard Violette say the same to Kurgara, more than once.

Vampires gathered around the new arrivals. Some were in simple robes, others in more elaborate garb, dripping with gold and beads and amulets. Karl sensed no hostility, only confusion. No one seemed to understand what was happening, and they were making quite a clamour about it.

But where was Charlotte?

"Don't crowd him," said Violette, keeping a protective hand on Kurgara's arm. He looked uneasy: his feminine face was blank but his dark eyes gleamed with alarm. "Everything will be explained. Please, allow him some space! Nabil, is there somewhere we can take him, a room where he'll have peace and quiet? Where's Fadiya?"

Karl stepped away from the tumult.

The sinking sun gleamed through leaves and flowers. The garden around him was breath-taking, almost too lush. The scents alone seduced him. Jasmine and citrus and spice, sandalwood and resin... he blocked out all distractions, searching for the only presence that mattered.

"Oh!" Charlotte ran straight into him as he turned round. "How did you—?"

He wrapped his arms around her, felt the heat of her body, kissed her rosy cheeks and lips. Her hair tumbled over his hands. Her gorgeous sun-warmed scent was unique. How could he possibly have mistaken an impostor for her real self, for even a second?

Silently he cursed Reiniger's deceit. There was only one Charlotte, as wild as a gypsy, all sweet bronze and golden warmth.

"It really is you," he murmured against her throat. "God, Charlotte..."

"Yes, it's me. What's happened? Karl, are you all right?"

"I will be. I think we both have stories to tell. Now we're both full of so much *Istilqa* poison that we can't possibly harm each other. And we'll cleanse it away with pure blood. It doesn't matter any more. We'll live."

"I can hardly smell or taste it now," she said, caught between smiling and sobbing. "Or it's no worse than hot pepper. As with humans: if *everyone* eats garlic, no one notices. And we'll drink sweet fresh blood, and be ourselves again. Karl, thank God, I daren't think about it but I really thought I might never see you again."

"I'm here." They stood there entwined hard against each other, exchanging kisses, lost in sheer relief.

"I must speak to Violette," Charlotte said at last. "I've been so afraid for her, I was on the point of going back to that awful place. How did you find her?"

He explained, as briefly as he could.

"Her appearance is shocking, but she survived," said Karl. "She'll recover. You can talk to her later."

"No, it's got to be now." Charlotte drew back, her hands resting on his upper arms. She looked sombre and worried. "I've some dreadful news and I'd rather she heard it from me. Emil's gone missing."

Violette had finally extricated herself from the throng. They found her alone, seated in the shadows of a pillared walkway that edged the Lemon Garden. Her silver-grey silk dress was torn, patched with sand and apparently soaked through with watery blood, now dry. Blood and sand plastered her bare arms and face, and her hair hung like tangled string.

Charlotte wanted to embrace her, but she held back. It wasn't easy, after all, just to blurt out the news that Emil had run away. She felt she'd let Violette down.

Violette greeted her and Karl with the merest tilt of her head. She appeared composed but utterly weary. They sat down on either side of her.

"Why are you covered in blood?" asked Charlotte.

She plucked at the pinkish, ruined fabric. "This is what happens when you enter a furnace so hot that you sweat your own blood. Think of the underground lair you found at Parkland Hall, where the ghosts were so hungry they could freeze a vampire to death. It was like that, but with fire instead of ice."

"Dear, is there anything we can do?"

"Oh, I'll be well again soon. I survived. Thank you, but I'm just... shaken."

"What happened?"

"I met myself." She smiled. "Not literally. I mean I met another vampire who'd absorbed an archetype from Raqia and lived it to the extreme. And I don't know if I've saved or destroyed him. Lord Zruvan: he was a youth beneath the terrifying disguise, an innocent. His other name is Kurgara, an individual who is both male and female. He can't or won't tell me his birth name. The community here lives under his protection, but he has no idea if they'll still accept him now he's not Zruvan any longer. That's why I asked Nabil to take him somewhere quiet. He needs solitude, and time to reflect, rather than dozens of people clamouring around him. I understand that need."

Karl began to ask a question, but she raised a hand to stop him. "I'll tell you later. You can tell me about Godric Reiniger, too. I'm tired enough to avail myself of a long *Istilqa* sleep."

"No," Charlotte said firmly. "We need blood, not narcotics."

"I was joking. A very poor joke, admittedly. Is Fadiya here?"

"Ah... yes."

Charlotte was hesitant, trying to break the news gently, but Violette sat bolt upright. "What? Something's happened. Tell me!"

Violette leaned forward on the stone seat and pressed her fingertips into the edge as Charlotte did her best to explain.

"I truly didn't think he'd have the energy to leave after what he's been through. We arrived three nights ago – I don't know what Fadiya said to Emil, but he simply disappeared."

"How long was he gone before anyone noticed?"

"Hours. I went to his room to make sure he'd settled in…" Charlotte waved vaguely at one of the upper galleries. "He told me to leave him alone, so I did. Later, Fadiya went to see him – she said that he threw her out, too. So we left him in peace. We thought he was sleeping. I went out to hunt – I was so close to coming back to find you—"

"That wasn't what I asked you to do." Violette dug her nails into Charlotte's forearm.

"I know, which is why I stayed here. I planned to take him on the ferry to France and back to Lucerne. But when Fadiya took his breakfast to his room… He'd gone."

"How did he escape with no one noticing?" Violette's eyes were wide and stone cold.

"This isn't a prison. The outer doors are locked, but they have keys on the inside. And I… I didn't think there was any need to watch him. I'm so sorry. It was my misjudgement."

"Then why didn't you try to find him?"

"We did! There were rumours he'd headed down to the port to sail back to Europe. Fadiya and I searched the town without luck. We think he took a ferry within an hour of leaving, and that's nearly three days ago."

"And you didn't try to follow through the Crystal Ring?"

"I couldn't," Charlotte said, her tone hardening. "I had to make a choice and, to be frank, I was more concerned about your welfare than Emil's. *You* were the one in greater danger."

"But I asked you to look after *him*."

They glared into each other's eyes.

"Arguing isn't going to help," Karl put in. "Do you really blame Emil for wanting to escape, after what he's been through? Here he was, surrounded by vampires, no doubt frightened for his life. It would be more surprising if he *hadn't* fled."

Violette broke her death-stare with Charlotte and rested back against the tiled wall. "You have a point. He's not a vampire, but he's not a child, either. He's a man with his own stubborn ideas and I should have anticipated this." She groaned. "All this effort to rescue him – and where's he gone? Back to the family farm? Idiot!"

"He must have had his reasons," Karl said calmly. "You know the effect we have on humans. An unholy assault of terror and madness. Think how afraid he must have been. Shell-shocked, if you like. His instinct to escape to the human world is natural."

Violette took a slow breath in and out. "How was his state of mind?"

"Not good," said Charlotte. "He barely spoke on the journey back. He called Fadiya and me 'witches' even while we were rescuing him."

"Do you think he might harm himself?"

"Attempt suicide, you mean?"

"Yes, that's exactly what I mean," Violette said thinly.

"He could have done that here, without bothering to board ship."

"But he may have planned to throw himself *off* the ship," Violette retorted. "Vanishing at sea? A perfect way to end his torment and punish us."

"And pure speculation," said Karl. "He's three days ahead of us. He may well be in France or Italy by now."

"So rather than think the worst, we'll start looking for him," said Charlotte. "Now."

"I wish you had started sooner, and tried harder," said Violette.

"And leave here, not knowing if you were alive or dead?" Charlotte turned fiercely on her. "Force me to make a choice and I will always choose *you*. And if you say one more word to me about Emil, I'll find him for certain. I'll drain every last drop out of his veins!"

Violette was taken aback. She sighed.

"Charlotte, forgive me. I deserve your harsh words, I know, but *please*. We have to find him before he does something even more insane than running away with Fadiya."

"We'll all go," said Charlotte. "But Violette, please change out of that dress, or at least put a robe over it."

"I don't care how I look. I only care about Emil. We'll split up, agreed? Better chance of finding him that way. You two go ahead. I need to speak with Fadiya, then I'll follow. Hunt and regain your strength to enter the Crystal Ring, but *go*."

With that, Violette rose and strode to the stairs that led to the upper level.

"I expect he headed for Tuscany," said Charlotte, alone with Karl. "It would make sense for him to go home, to see his family before... No, I refuse to entertain the idea that he would kill himself. Before he decides what to do next."

"I'm worried about Stefan too," Karl said, stroking her shoulder. "One of us should go straight back to Lucerne. He shouldn't be left on his own."

"Well, I care more about Stefan than I do about Emil," she said. "But I let Emil vanish, so I feel responsible..."

"We *both* care more about Stefan," said Karl.

"That's true, but Emil still matters. You go back, I'll search."

"No, I don't want to abandon you to the task," said Karl. "We should both go home, then look for Emil later."

"It may be too late by then."

"Haven't you already done enough for him and Violette?"

"No, I can't place a limit on it. We're helping no one by arguing." She took both his hands. "A compromise? I'll go straight to Stefan, on condition that you make a thorough search for Emil. Agreed?"

Karl nodded, looking grim. "And I'll find the wretch before the night's out, believe me."

Nabil and another vampire were guarding the door to Kurgara's room. Fadiya stood further along the gallery, leaning against the rail and staring at a shuttered window as if there were a dangerous animal inside.

"Why don't you go in?" said Violette.

"I don't know him." Fadiya, dressed in a clean djellaba, folded her arms and refused to meet her eyes. "You say this is Lord Zruvan, but this Kurgara... I can't believe they are the same person."

"By your own admission, you've never seen his face before today."

"I still haven't seen him. When you arrived, I didn't look at him. It's wrong. This cannot be him."

"It is him," said Violette. "And you know it, if you have any vampire instincts at all. Can't you sense that he's the same? Would you recognise the softness of his lips, at least? Are you afraid of what you'll find?"

Fadiya's mouth tightened. She said nothing.

"Fadiya, I have to leave now. As you've managed to lose Emil, it's vital I find him before gets into any more trouble. I can't bring myself to *thank* you for not killing him, but... thank you, anyway, for sparing him. Now, just go in and speak with Kurgara. Please."

At that, Fadiya turned on her. Her eyes blazed pale jade with anger.

"You have to control everyone, *own* everyone. I could not kill Emil, or let anyone else hurt him, because I loved him. You think I'm heartless, but you know nothing about me. I knew that bringing you here would end in disaster. Everyone prostrates themselves before you, Madame Violette-Lilith – even Zruvan!"

"Well, blame your husband for that. *He* wanted me here. You were only doing his bidding, weren't you?"

"He's as much a fool as Emil," Fadiya spat. "You don't care that you've destroyed them both. You care about no one, as long as you get your own way."

"Are you any different?" Violette said, very low. "We have to take what we can. When women seize power of any kind, however small, it is soon snatched back. When we achieve anything, in art or science or any other field, it is buried and forgotten as swiftly as possible. Every time we emerge from the kitchen, powers arise that push us back."

"You're talking like a human."

"It's not long since I was human. You are much older than me: this wisdom is inside you already, if you'd only look for it. Perhaps you've forgotten, but I remember all too vividly what it's like to live under the pressure of a great lie: that we are less than men. But in the outside world, that lie remains everyday reality. It will stay so for decades, perhaps forever. And not only for women, but for anyone who deviates from society's rules, even by thinking the wrong thoughts. I've seen terrible visions, Fadiya."

The woman's eyes began to darken, glistening. "So have I, but visions can deceive."

"I know. I don't believe the future's set in stone, but it pays to be watchful. As vampires we stand outside all that, but that doesn't mean we can disengage. Some vampires choose to do so, but the world is still there and we have to exist in it. I believe that we can immerse ourselves in human life without drowning. We can work from the shadows."

"At what?" There was a catch in Fadiya's voice. "Helping humans? Helping our *prey*?"

"Yes," said Violette. "Because we need them, and a few of them may join us one day. So let's not engage in a personal feud. We should work as friends, not enemies."

Violette watched Fadiya's expression turn calmer and more serious.

"Friends, I'm not sure. Allies, perhaps."

"Everything changes, even Bayt-al-Zuhur. You'll learn to adapt, because you must. You see this as a disaster, but is it? Would you force Kurgara back into the Bone Well?"

"No," Fadiya whispered. "Never."

"You don't need an eternal martyr to protect you. You'll find another way. Become joint leaders and protectors of your flock, or live with them as equals. If they can't accept you, just walk away. The point is that you're free. And he can probably hear everything we're saying. I hope he can. May I say goodbye to him?"

Fadiya looked startled. "Ah... yes, of course."

Violette turned, but Fadiya took her elbow, stopping her. "I am not a very effective enemy, madame. I treated Emil badly, but when I say I loved him, it's the truth. He was so beautiful. He rejected me and I don't blame him: he made the right decision. I knew we couldn't be together but still, it hurt. We hurt each other."

"I'm afraid I can't find much sympathy. What about Zruvan-Kurgara? Do you still love him? Can you?"

"Of course. Always. It's possible to love more than one person, isn't it?"

"That's true."

"I've always loved Zruvan and always will, but... I don't know who he is now. Yes, I am afraid."

Violette leaned in and kissed Fadiya on the cheek. The kiss lingered, warm and forgiving. She took Fadiya's hand. "Come in with me. Are you ready?"

"Yes," said Fadiya. "I'm ready."

Nabil and his comrade stood aside, bowing to them both. Fadiya knocked. No protest came from inside, so they opened the door and went in.

Inside, the bedroom was cool and dim, with a tiled floor, carved furniture, dappled light falling through the fretwork shutters and jewels of colour from the Moroccan-style lamps. There were carpets and cushions woven of thick wool. An inviting, exotic bower.

Kurgara sat in the centre of a large bed. He was crossed-legged in loose white trousers, his chest bare except for the thick ebony fall of his hair.

Fadiya looked away. Violette waited, catching his glance with a slight but meaningful smile. Eventually Fadiya raised her head and looked straight into his eyes.

They held the look.

How could she not find him beautiful, in soul as much as in body? He or she... Fadiya claimed they were husband and wife, yet they'd barely ever touched each other. Violette felt mildly envious that they had so much still to discover.

Fadiya wants this with you, she had told Kurgara as they lay skin to skin.

To step out of the red-hot madness of imprisonment and back into the real world of touch and scent and cool air on the face, conversation and affection, the richness of human blood taken under the stars... Neither could turn away from that gift.

"I must go," she said. She kissed Kurgara on the forehead and stood back.

He rose from the bed. He and Fadiya trod cautiously towards each other, their gazes locked together, captivated.

Violette was reminded of birds who paired for life. No one else existed for them. She had wanted to say something severe about the fact that they'd abducted Emil and it would take time for the matter to be forgotten, let alone forgiven... but there was no point. They were no longer the people they had been when they conspired against her.

Softly she said, "Fadiya, meet your husband. Kurgara, meet your wife. May the blessings of all the gods, goddesses and angels of the Crystal Ring fall upon you."

Kurgara raised one hand to touch Fadiya's cheek. She sighed, resting into his palm. The first touch in hundreds of years, the first time they'd freely pressed their lips to each other's faces and hands and throats. So tender, yet insatiable.

Violette doubted that they'd heard her. When she left, they didn't notice.

Any of them might have located Emil, but – since Violette had stayed behind for a short time, and Charlotte had hurried on to Lucerne – Karl happened to reach him first. He spent the whole day searching: a new morning dawned before he finally he caught Emil's distinctive red-gold aura among thousands of other humans.

As predicted, he was in Italy, but nowhere near the family farm.

Karl located him in Rome, weaving through the edge of a crowd that had gathered to watch a military parade.

The ground shook in time to the rhythm of tramping boots. Onlookers crowded forward to watch the procession pass. Rank upon rank of soldiers, motorcycles, flags snapping. And at the centre was a stocky figure standing proudly in his grand limousine: their leader, Il Duce, Benito Mussolini.

Karl looked on this display of human pomp with a sense of dismay. The taste of dust and diesel fumes was bitter on his tongue. Sunlight reflected off the buildings, and the crowd's excitement overwhelmed all his senses. Somewhere, in this immense swarm of people, was Emil.

This is the past and the future, he thought. *Arrogant displays of might, which grow ever grander and more intimidating. When I was a young mortal, the troops had horses. Now there are motor vehicles and tanks, leviathans of war. Who can stand against this? The Great War was not enough. They still want more.*

Karl identified Emil's aura – a speck among thousands – and began to push his way through the crowd. Not far, a few hundred yards...

Mussolini's vehicle trundled towards the place where Emil waited. Karl caught a clear view of the dictator's face: fleshy, pompous, self-satisfied.

He thought, *This is what Reiniger wanted.*

Karl was running now. He wove and pushed his way through

the barrier of humans, ignoring their curses in his wake. He saw Emil, his golden hair distinctive, standing in a grassed area lined with trees. He stood slightly apart, behind the densest part of the crowd, hands deep in the pockets of a long dark coat.

As Karl struggled to reach him, he saw Emil's right hand beginning to emerge from the pocket, and the dark shape of a pistol rising to point at Mussolini's heart...

Karl barged into him from the side. He caught the wrist that held the gun, shielding it from the view of anyone around them. Emil fought him. His strength was extraordinary, his eyes glazed.

If the gun went off, even if the bullet hit no one, the game would be over. The crowd around Emil would lynch him.

As they had his brother.

Karl struggled to wrench the weapon out of his hand, at the same time forcibly edging him backwards, away from the horde edging the road. He tried to make the struggle discreet – an argument between friends – so as to draw as little attention as possible.

Emil fought, his face red and distorted with effort. His trigger finger contracted and the gun went off.

The bullet ploughed into the earth between his feet and Karl's. The retort was drowned by the crowd's roar and the noise of the cavalcade passing them. Then Mussolini was gone, his entourage sweeping onwards into the distance as Karl forced Emil backwards through the trees. His hand, still gripping the pistol, went white under the pressure of Karl's grip.

Emil stood gasping, red-eyed.

"Why the hell did you stop me?"

"What did you think you were doing?"

"Finishing what Alfonso started!"

"By taking a pot-shot at your leader? You know you would have been seized and hanged from the nearest tree?"

"Yes!" Emil snarled. "But if I killed that monster, it would have been worth it. How *dare* you stop me? This is none of your concern!"

"I disagree. Do you not understand that Violette offered her life to save yours? How do you imagine she'd react, to learn that you showed your gratitude by throwing yourself away in a rash political gesture? Or that I failed to stop you? You waste your life,

I fail Violette... No, Emil. The consequences don't bear thinking about. I couldn't let it happen."

Emil dropped the pistol. Karl quickly took it and removed the bullets, vowing to dispose of the weapon at the first opportunity.

"I have no future," Emil said bleakly.

Karl put an arm around his shoulders and guided him firmly away. "Why do you say that?"

"I am a born fool. Violette rejects me. Fadiya renders me a gibbering wreck, so weak and befuddled that I almost lose my life and have to be rescued by *women*."

"No shame in that. I suggest you swallow your pride and acknowledge the magnificence of the women who risked themselves to save you."

"All I had left was to die fulfilling my brother's brave quest. That's all. And you took it from me."

"Or I've given you a second chance. No one need know about any of this. How do you wish to be remembered, Emil?"

"What?"

"As a failed performer who was hanged or thrown in prison for a crazed assassination attempt? Or as one of the greatest male dancers in history? You can't save the world – none of us can – but you can give inspiration to thousands with your talent. I'd choose the latter above anything."

Emil was quiet for a long time. They walked until the sun began to set. Karl noticed that broad roads were being driven through places where Roman remains had stood only a few years before. In almost every street he saw evidence of Il Duce's attempts to use art and film, the press, sport, everything to promote his cause. The sights made him depressed.

Emil rubbed his face, scraped his fingers through his hair. Eventually he spoke.

"Is Violette safe?"

"Yes, she's safe. Still worried to death about you, but otherwise well."

"What happened? I remember boarding a ship with Fadiya. It seemed a wonderful idea at the time, but after that... I can't claim it's a blur, because I remember everything, but it's all in jagged fragments."

"Violette can explain better than me what happened, but we need you to come home to Lucerne."

"Home?" He laughed.

"I'm under strict instructions," said Karl. "Violette wants you where you belong, at the ballet, working with her."

Emil gave a disbelieving gasp. "After all this? I don't know how. It's impossible."

"Why?"

Another long silence. With darkness falling, Karl thought he should take Emil to a café and feed him before he collapsed.

"You and Charlotte and Violette, Fadiya and all those people in the Algiers house," Emil murmured. "All vampires. How am I supposed to live with this knowledge?"

"With complete discretion," Karl said drily. "Pretend you don't know. Tell no one."

"And the other members of the Ballet Lenoir? Do they know?"

"Not to my knowledge. Most humans are easily deceived. However, there are a few rare sensitive ones, like you, who see what we are. Can you cope with knowing?"

"I haven't coped well so far."

"You can learn. Violette has gone to great lengths to keep you, Emil. Do you think you're in danger from us?"

"Aren't I? I'd be a fool to think I'm not, after all that's happened to me, and I still know almost nothing about you or what sort of monsters you really are. Nothing, except that you drink blood and drain our energy and send us mad."

Karl noted his bitterness.

"I can't deny that," said Karl. "I can't force you to come home. Well, I could, but I won't. Believe me, though, when I say you're in no danger from us. Violette would kill anyone who threatened you."

"Yes, I think she would. But what are you, when you're not drinking human blood? I simply don't know. Does anything human matter to you at all?"

"Many things. You know how passionate Violette is about her ballet. Yes, we have human interests. We feel love and jealousy…"

"But what do you *believe* in? You, Karl, in particular? God, Satan, what?"

Karl smiled. "I believe in a quiet life."

"You? A quiet life?"

"And you've seen how hard it is for us to attain that – but yes, the more others try to take our freedom, the harder we fight. The more precious it is."

"I need a drink."

Light and voices spilled out of a nearby restaurant. Emil stopped and stared longingly in through the window. Standing out here in the dark with a vampire, gazing in at the vibrant mortal world...

"And food," said Karl, feeling a tinge of regret that he couldn't share the long-lost pleasure of eating. "Forgive me, I should have thought of this earlier."

"I need a glass of wine. Or a bottle," said Emil. "And everything on the menu."

"Whatever you desire." Karl steered him to the door with a light hand on his back. If they looked too travel-worn to be let in, he was ready to cast his ruthless glamour over the maître d'.

"What about you? You don't... eat, do you?"

"I'll order something and you can have that too."

"I will, believe me. I'll be able to think clearly once I've eaten. No dancer can give his best without fuel."

"Perfect wisdom."

"Plain old peasant wisdom," said Emil.

"So, will you come back to Violette?" Karl repeated.

"Ask me again," said Emil, "when I've had that bottle of wine."

The restaurant let Karl use their telephone while Emil was eating. He gave them no choice, since he was not in the mood for arguments and used all the polite sinister charm it took to deflect their protests. He tried several times before he finally got through and – after a frustrating chorus of buzzing and clicking on the line – Thierry answered and managed to connect him to Charlotte.

He heard her voice on the other end, tinny and far away. "Karl?"

"Beloved, he's with me. We're in Rome. We'll take the first train we can and we should be back tomorrow, I hope by the afternoon..."

"Travel safely." She sounded exhausted, wrung out by anxiety, not herself. "And come back quickly, Karl. I'm with Stefan. He's… I'm here with him, but please come home as fast as you can."

CHAPTER TWENTY-SEVEN

UNDEAD

Stefan lay on the double bed beside what was left of Niklas, naked except for a corner of the sheet across his hips.

Charlotte was already there, sitting with him, when Karl arrived. A long train journey had delivered him and Emil back to Lucerne: he'd left Thierry to settle Emil in his room and come straight to the bedroom to find her keeping vigil, grief-stricken and desperate.

"I found him like this," she said. "You were right, we shouldn't have left him. Not for a moment."

"You did what you had to," Stefan rasped with all that was left of his voice. "And so have I."

He had made cuts all over his own body. Across his windpipe, giving his throat a ghastly red smile. Straight into his own heart. Slashes across his abdomen, long cuts down the inside of his forearms, even into the deep arteries of his thighs.

The bone-handled *Istilqa* knife he'd used lay on the bedside table, smeared from hilt to tip with blood. Karl realised, from the way Stefan's right hand lay curled, wet and red, that Charlotte herself had taken the knife from him. She'd put it out of his reach, and he was too weak to seize it again.

But his vampire blood oozed too slowly to let him bleed to death: it was more a ruby gel than a liquid. The red slashes were vivid against his blue-white skin. And still he breathed, eyes open, left fist tight on Niklas's arm.

"Stefan," said Karl. Tears burned his eyes. "What have you done? We took our revenge on Reiniger. You enjoyed it. Why would you want to leave such pleasures behind?"

Stefan spoke in a bubbling whisper. "Without Niklas, it's meaningless."

"We need you," said Charlotte. "What about us? Darling, please don't leave us."

He gripped her hand. "Charlotte, I'm so sorry, my sweet friend. It's harder to die than I expected. If you would find a sword or axe to sever my head, it would be quicker. Please."

Charlotte and Karl exchanged a look of despair. Stefan was right. If he was determined to die, their intervention would be a mercy. He was in agony. It would not be the first time Karl had struck the head from a suffering vampire.

But they weren't in the habit of keeping weapons nearby. Where would he find an axe or a sword here? There would only be theatrical props...

"No," said Charlotte. "Look, there is a line between grief and self-pity. You've made your point, but it's time to stop." Then, "Stefan?"

He was no longer responding. His face was bloodless, like a carcass hung up and drained in a butcher's shop. No breath. Karl leaned down and detected no heartbeat, either. And yet... he hung there, suspended between life and death.

Undead.

Karl made an instant decision: went into the Crystal Ring, straight through a dozen walls and floors to the kitchens and seized the heftiest implement he could find. A butcher's cleaver.

He couldn't carry such a heavy object through Raqia so he returned on foot, sprinting along corridors and up flights of stairs to the bedroom. A walk that would take ten minutes, there and back, took thirty seconds.

Nothing had changed. Karl glanced over the ghastly scene in the gloom – Niklas a pallid husk, Stefan like a fresh corpse beside him – then he sealed all emotion away in a casket of ice.

Charlotte rose to her feet, blocking Karl's path to him. "Don't you dare," she said. Her eyes were wild. There were imprints of Stefan's blood all over her dress.

"Charlotte, we can't leave him like this. If he wants to die, what right have we to keep him alive and suffering? He could stay like this for weeks, months. Forever."

"Don't touch him." Her eyes grew even wider, ringed with white.

"Wouldn't you extend this mercy to *me*?" said Karl. "He's nearly gone. It will be quick. Take the pillow from under his head."

In response, Charlotte lifted one arm to form a protective barrier over Stefan's supine form. She was like a marble wall blocking his way and Karl knew, with dismay, that she was not going to move.

Karl felt that he'd gone mad. The room was full of ghosts. He saw Kristian and Katerina, Robyn, Fyodor, Simon and Rasmila, Niklas... Even the false Charlotte and Godric Reiniger himself, still in his *Schmutzli* shape. They all looked like smoke. A single blow of the cleaver and Stefan would join them...

"Beloved, we have no choice," he said softly. "Leave the room. I'll tell you when it's over."

She raised her other hand and pointed her forefinger at his heart as if aiming a pistol.

"Karl, I swear to God, if you touch Stefan, I will kill you."

They stood frozen as Karl heard ten seconds tick by on the clock. He counted them. How long did they seem to Stefan as he lay there undying?

Then he stepped back and put down the cleaver on a chair, facing Charlotte again with open palms to show he was empty-handed. "If not now, we'll have to do it later," he said. "Every moment we hesitate, Stefan is in hell."

She glared back like the Medusa. "I will not give up on him. I'm going to fetch Violette. On second thoughts, *you* fetch her. I don't trust you alone with Stefan."

"You don't trust me?" Karl paused, wondering if Charlotte had finally lost her mind. If she had, he didn't blame her. He too felt unhinged, like Stefan, like Emil and Violette... Was there anyone sane left?

"Stefan's the one who matters, not us," she said. "So the faster you find her, the better."

"Very well, but Violette won't hesitate to end his misery."

"She'll do as I ask. Just bring her."

"Why?"

"Because I refuse to let him go. If it takes three to initiate a vampire, why not three to reinitiate?"

Charlotte's voice was level, measured and ruthless.

"I don't believe it's ever been tried." Karl spoke quietly, caught between the urge to dissuade her and the knowledge that her instincts, however wayward, were usually sound. The spectres faded, except for one smoky shape that stayed in the corner, watching.

"We are going to be the first to try, then."

Stefan fought them, rousing from his coma as he realised what they were trying to do. He fought as violently as Violette herself had struggled against her own transformation.

He truly doesn't want this, Charlotte thought in horror. *Wouldn't it be kinder after all to let him go, as he wished, to join Niklas?*

It took all three of them carry him into the living room, where there was more space. And more light, although the room seemed dim and foggy despite every light being on. Between them they held his inert body upright.

Karl was the first to sink his fangs into the torn column of his neck. Then Violette, supporting Stefan from behind, drank from the other side. At that, Stefan went rigid, his whole body a taut bow of pain, his expression wide and blank with inexpressible agony.

Charlotte stared at the scene of Karl and Violette with their dark heads bent as they fed, Stefan stretched like a martyred saint between them. *No one has ever tried to re-transform a dying vampire before,* she thought. *To kill them again, to fill them with Raqia's energy again. Is it possible, or are we just prolonging unspeakable suffering? Stefan, I'm so sorry. Perhaps Karl's right – he's always right – but I had to try.*

Then Karl caught her wrist and pulled her in to take his place. She found the holes his fangs had made in their friend's neck and drank.

She realised how little blood Stefan had left. She sucked hard to draw the last drops. The *Istilqa* taste was barely there. His blood was like slushy ice, but still delicious, like a strange cocktail of caramel and salt and cognac, yet none of those. She convulsed against him, her appetite on fire, desperate for more – but Stefan had nothing left. Pleasure and misery left her weak-kneed.

Was this even possible?

Karl drew her away and she tasted the salt of her own tears.

"Quickly," he said.

They formed the circle of transformation, all joining hands with Charlotte and Karl on either side of Stefan, Violette facing him. Together, the three shifted into the Crystal Ring, hauling Stefan with them.

The world changed. They ascended through layers of purplish fog, upwards into sky until they floated on the rich blue ether. Sunset-golden hills rolled below them. Charlotte saw Karl and Violette altering in form, turning to ebony and lace. She saw her own body change, but Stefan remained the same, his hand skeleton-white in hers. He hung between them like a drowned, floating corpse.

As hard as she pushed away her rising anxiety, it persisted in the back of her mind, pale and terrifying like her lamia. The process wasn't working. How could it? The Crystal Ring itself wanted no new vampires... or only a tiny, select few.

"No vampire has ever been reinitiated," Karl had said. And Stefan himself did not want this. Like Robyn, Violette's lost love, he preferred death.

Energy danced around them, tangible like clouds of fireflies. Charlotte felt electricity flowing from Karl to Violette and then through her own hand to Stefan. There it stopped, where their palms joined, creating a burning build-up of force. Charlotte flinched with pain. The power threatened to push her hand and Stefan's apart. Her instinct was to recoil and let go, to make the pain stop – but she held on.

Then a storm hit them.

A small tornado spun them round and round in space. They managed to hang on to each other, fingertips painfully interlaced. If they broke the circle, Stefan would die. Or worse... not die. Charlotte had a horrific vision of him floating helpless forever.

As they whirled, a shape rose up into the middle of the circle, a grey comet made of smoke and ice...

It resolved into a clearer form: Charlotte saw a large bony

head with a bizarre face, like a medieval image of the devil staring back at her. A long grey face, with tangled white hair and huge spiralling horns. Eyes like bubbles of blood.

The horns and head rose into the space between them and the red eyes burned into Charlotte's.

"It's Reiniger." Karl's voice was faint and distorted by Raqia's wild air currents.

"I know," said Violette. "Determined, isn't he?"

"Let's gain height." Charlotte's hair – dark tendrils, not her natural hair – whipped across her eyes as she spoke. "Ignore him. Don't let go."

She felt Violette's hand working around hers until they got a firm hold on each other's wrists. A cloud funnel spun around them, pulsing with red and silver lightning. The demon dropped away as they rose upwards, clear of the storm. Glancing down, Charlotte could no longer see him – but it was hard to see anything in the clouds that boiled beneath them. They rose into the blue void. The storm sank, taking Godric with it.

All she saw, between skeins of hair, was a charcoal blur, as if Reiniger had torn a hole in the Ring as he escaped. Cold shivery dread went into her bones. Again she wondered if this was a mistake, if she should have let Karl grant Stefan his wish after all.

Too late. They were suspended in a broth of crazed human dreams. Godric had not even touched them, but she couldn't shake off the image of the devil head rising between them, staring, falling away again.

Ever since the night she'd been stabbed, Godric Reiniger had been channelling the deadly power of the Bone Well into all of them.

She tried to speak out loud, but the words were only in her mind. Stefan's hand stayed dead and cold in hers. The indigo void spun slowly around them.

"Charlotte," said Karl. She met his serious, worried gaze. "This isn't working."

"Keep trying," she said. Then, "Stefan, let us in. We're here with you."

Karl and Violette did as she asked – as much for her as for Stefan. They made sure the circle was firm. Then they tried again, letting their little remaining energy spill from one to another.

Violette's silver-white fire, Karl's dark red strength and Charlotte's autumnal golden glow twined like a plaited, rippling thread. When the current stopped at Stefan's palm, Charlotte used her will like a needle to force it through the flesh barrier.

A trickle of energy went into him. She felt and saw it: a strand of spider-silk covered in dew. And then a fine necklace of diamonds... swelling into a rush of fire. Like crackling electricity the current went surging around the four of them, building until she thought its sheer force would hurl them all apart and carry her away.

Still she hung on, eyes squeezed shut against the pain. *Stefan, come back...*

How long did the process last? Seconds, minutes.

Without warning they fell. The world shuddered, and they were abruptly back in their living room again. They broke apart, all finding their feet except Stefan, who slumped on to his side on the carpet.

Although the lights were on, they gave no more illumination than small dim moons seen through smog. *Was it dark when we left?* Charlotte thought. Even her sensitive sight could find no colour or detail in the shadows. Everything felt wrong. The room was like a poorly-shot film, grainy and ill-defined, full of flickering shadows.

Godric Reiniger was sitting in an armchair, luminous in the gloom. He was still in his ridiculous but terrifying gargoyle form, all matted ash-grey fur and twisted horns.

"I thought you'd killed him," Violette whispered.

"I couldn't be sure," said Karl. "He vanished back into Raqia. I told you, he's changed."

"Into something that keeps shedding its skin and slithering away every time we attack it, then coming back?"

"I have never seen this before," Karl whispered.

Violette faced the apparition and said, "Get out of my house."

Reiniger did not speak or move, but he wasn't inactive. His presence was a weight on the atmosphere, like a mass deforming space itself. He seemed to be drawing all the worst energies of Raqia into the room, all the grim malevolence he'd absorbed from his bone-knife rituals.

Trying to disregard him, Karl and Charlotte knelt down on either side of Stefan.

He'd curled in a foetal position, eyes shut. Every now and then he drew a ragged breath. His wounds, Charlotte saw, had stopped bleeding. He was heavy, pliable and colourless, like a veal carcass. Dead flesh. Was he aware of anything?

"Stefan," she whispered. "Can you hear me?"

No response. Her heart sank even lower. The whole room was flickering in black and white, as if they were trapped inside one of Godric's films.

"Your friend is beyond hope." Reiniger's goatish mouth did not move, but his voice echoed all around them. "You are all beyond hope."

Charlotte saw Karl start to get up and then freeze, like a jammed film.

Time moved one frame at a time. Paralysed, Charlotte could do nothing but hold Stefan's stone-cold hand. She sensed Reiniger generating a sort of bull-like anger, sucking all the energy from the room, projecting it back at them in shuddering waves. She felt the temperature drop. Her head buzzed.

She felt as a human would when a vampire stole their blood. Shivery, faint. Consciousness slipping away.

All she could hear was Godric Reiniger's voice, crackling like a gramophone record but painfully clear and loud.

"They all haunt you, don't they, Karl? All your victims. All the loved ones you've lost. Everyone you have ever killed, friend or enemy. Well, count me among them. I am part of the Crystal Ring now, and what did you say to me? 'Sometimes the Crystal Ring gives you what you need, and sometimes it gives you what you deserve.' The rule applies equally to you. *You* have made me into this wretched creature, this demon – and what is a demon but the sheer torture of your own conscience?"

Charlotte had one hand on Stefan, the other reaching out blindly for Karl, trying and failing to touch him before she blacked out altogether. It was like trying to move through the densest of Raqia's fogs, through clay or concrete.

Her fingers found something – Violette's hand. Charlotte began trying to push away the heavy grey fog and draw in brighter energies. Violette was helping her. Perhaps it was only happening in her imagination, but it was all they had left.

"Who told you I had a conscience?" Karl said softly. "I hoped you had died in the desert."

"No, Karl. I died in my cinema. I died when you pulled that fatal trick on me in front of my audience."

And then the "film" jumped.

Karl was gone. Charlotte thought he'd entered Raqia, but a second later he was back again – of course he was back, he would never flee and leave her – and he was moving in slow motion, carrying the meat cleaver he'd left in the bedroom. Holding the cleaver two-handed like an axe, he swung it straight at Reiniger's neck.

Charlotte heard the sickening noise of contact, blade severing bone. She saw the head part from the body. For a surreal moment, it floated. There was no blood.

Instead, the thing that had been Godric Reiniger vanished – crumbled to ash and dust, swirled away as if through a portal into Raqia.

The cleaver wedged deep in the chair back, still vibrating from the impact.

"*Now* it's over," said Karl.

The lights came up at once. Colour returned to the scene and feeling crept into her limbs in a mass of tingling pain. Like floodwater receding, slow and thick with silt, Raqia melted away and the world returned to normal.

If anything could ever be normal in their world. For now, this was enough.

"Charlotte." Karl's voice was rough with exhaustion. "Stay with Stefan. I'll be back as quickly as I can."

"Don't go after him!" she cried. "He *must* be dead now. Reiniger, I mean."

"I am not going after him," he answered. "Just stay here. Violette?"

"Yes, I'm coming with you."

Charlotte was too dazed to understand what they were doing. Alone with Stefan, she could only gather her sanity and keep him in the living world. She kissed his cold cheeks and stroked the matted blond hair. She couldn't find the emotion to weep. Ten, fifteen minutes crawled by...

He opened his eyes and said, "Where have I been?"

"Sweetheart, I'm here with you. Take a sip of blood from me. I haven't much left, but it's yours."

He closed his lips, silently refusing.

Now we'll know, Charlotte thought, watching every small movement, trying to read his state of mind. *If Stefan means to die, he'll refuse to feed. He might even tear off our heads, if he finds the strength and he's still angry enough... unless we destroy him first to protect ourselves. Then all our efforts will have been for nothing.*

Presently she heard voices murmuring in the corridor outside. Karl and Violette ushered in three humans, one woman and two young men. Charlotte recognised them all. One was Leni, who'd helped revive her after the knife attack. It seemed so long ago. They were all friends of Stefan, who knew what he was and loved him enough to give their blood freely. An unhealthy love, perhaps, but at this moment – vital.

Seeing Stefan, Leni made an inarticulate noise and began to weep.

Karl and Charlotte helped him to sit up as Leni offered her wrist. Stefan groaned. He turned his head away, resisting. Then he released a long breath.

Tenderly he took her slender pink arm, bit down, and began to drink.

CHAPTER TWENTY-EIGHT

THE GHOST WHO LOOKS LIKE YOU

"Here we are again," said Charlotte. "How are you?"

Amy Temple was at her favourite table overlooking the lake, absently stirring a cup of hot chocolate. She attempted a smile. "Hello. I'm well, thank you. Rather shaken up, but it will pass. Eventually."

"Your uncle…" Charlotte sat beside her, trying to open the subject as delicately as she could.

Two nights ago, Karl had destroyed an entity that was determined to finish them: a vampire that fed on vampires. At least, they hoped he had. Reiniger had become so different, so elusive that no one knew whether anything *could* kill him.

"When did you last see him?"

"What do you mean?" Amy gasped.

"We went up to Bergwerkstatt yesterday. Twice, in fact. There was no one there. I was worried about you."

"No, I… I was at the hospital, and then I stayed in a hotel with Gudrun." Amy had turned white. "You know that he's dead, don't you? Perhaps the news didn't reach you. My uncle's dead."

"Are you sure?"

Charlotte wasn't exactly shocked, but she was startled and confused. Surely Amy would only believe him to be missing. She couldn't know more than that.

"Of course I'm sure. I found him."

"*Found* him, where?"

"Lying in bed." Amy shook her head, wide-eyed. "I didn't even know he was home at the time – he'd vanished for hours and we didn't hear him come back. I still can't believe it. Whatever his faults, part of me loved him and I can't simply stop."

"I know. I'm sorry, but what happened?"

Karl's attack in the desert didn't kill him, she thought. *Godric escaped into Raqia and went straight back to Bergwerkstatt. He must have been weak.* She pictured him, materialising naked in his bedroom and crawling between the sheets. *He couldn't face his humiliation and killed himself?*

"I found him and called Gudrun. Everyone else had deserted him by then – we saw them all go." She paled. "My poor uncle – he looked dreadful when we found him, so swollen and covered in a livid blood-red rash. The doctors believe it was septicaemia. Blood poisoning. They said that the infection can overwhelm the body and cause death within hours. They took him to hospital, but it was already too late."

"My God, that must have been terrible." Charlotte hardly knew how to react.

"There were little cuts all over his arms and chest, like patterns. Strange, I don't know why he would do that. The freshest ones were very infected." Amy indicated her own breastbone. "He'd cut a sort of symbol over his heart that was inflamed and weeping... horrible." Her shoulders drooped. "But he didn't tell us he was ill! Apparently he must have gone to bed with a fever, and he didn't wake up." Amy gave a single, choking sob. "I wanted him humiliated. Not dead."

"I'm so very sorry." Charlotte meant it. She was sorry, not for Godric's death, but for Amy's grief.

"The doctors think he had an underlying illness, possibly the onset of tuberculosis. If so, he hid it well. I thought he had a smoker's cough... but he never looked properly well, and he had this feverish energy..."

"All symptoms?" said Charlotte, thinking that the *Istilqa* knives' power must have masked his illness.

"I think his energy came from using something to keep going. Cocaine? I don't know. But that *useless* Dr Ochsner kept telling him he was fine, when he wasn't. So when the sepsis took hold, he wasn't strong enough to fight it."

"Amy, when did this happen? Two nights ago?"

"What? No, days ago. The morning after the debacle with the film."

Days ago, thought Charlotte. *I've lost track of time. So that means he died at least three days* before *the crisis with Stefan.*

"Charlotte, are you all right? I feel so odd about the whole thing. Part of me wants to mourn, but then I keep thinking of the vile things he did, and how I betrayed him."

"For filming him in, er, a compromising situation?"

"Partly that, but…" Amy flushed.

"Don't be embarrassed. Karl told me what happened."

"It was so bizarre." Amy spoke in a rush, as if relieved to spill her feelings. "The apparition looked like you, which was bad enough, but when she, or he, turned into my *uncle…* I'm still having nightmares. I never expected to find myself filming some weird kind of pornography, but the real betrayal was that I processed the film and spliced it all together and let Karl *screen* it, while I sat next to my uncle, pretending innocence, as all the important people in town sat there with their mouths open."

Charlotte grinned. "Oh, I would love to have seen their faces."

A giggle burst from Amy. She put her fingers to her mouth. "I shouldn't laugh. It was ghastly. But it would have been hilarious, if it hadn't been so… mortifying."

"I can imagine."

"I never meant to do such a thing to my uncle, but…"

"He did rather bring it on himself."

"I dread to think what he would have done if he'd found out that I helped, but he never even guessed. And now he's gone, and I don't know what to do. I miss Mariette and the others. I even miss Fadiya."

"What will happen to his house? His studio?"

"I don't know. It depends what's in his will. He spoke of setting up something called 'The Reiniger Foundation' to continue his work in perpetuity." Her voice went tight, sardonic. "Perhaps when the scandal's died down, someone will take on Bergwerkstatt and make movies about what a wonderful, forgotten hero he was. But after I've packed my belongings, I shall never set foot there again. The place feels… haunted."

Charlotte touched her gloved hand. "Karl and I never wanted

to involve you in this sordid matter. I can't apologise enough, nor ask for forgiveness, but you were more helpful than you know. Can you go out into the world and pretend you never saw a thing, that you don't know we exist?"

Amy's eyes glazed for a few seconds.

"I'll have to try, or everyone will think I'm mad. Oh, the things I've seen, Charlotte. *I* would think I needed locking up, if I didn't know it was all real." Her expression turned pensive. "I know Uncle Godric could be difficult, and cruel, but I miss him, in an odd way. Now I've no one to kick against! He could have been a good man…"

"If only he hadn't been a sadistic megalomaniac?" said Charlotte. "If he hadn't carved people up for the thrill of it, sent you to a butcher for medical treatment, planned to marry you off as if sending a cow to a prize bull?" Amy didn't reply. Her gaze fell.

"What about Wolfgang Notz?" said Charlotte.

"I won't be marrying him," she said with a thin laugh.

"I didn't mean that. Won't he want to lead your uncle's organisation?"

"There is no organisation any more. It's true people liked Wolfgang – that's why they were so horrified about the blackmail – but now it's all out in the open, I don't think they can run a political movement that preaches one thing and does the exact opposite in private."

"Ah, that's the thing," said Charlotte. "Not to get found out. My aunt's philosophy."

"She sounds like a wise woman," Amy said wryly.

"A difficult woman, but I learned a lot from her. Amy, I must go. I hope you'll remember us with a touch of fondness, not horror. It's time to think of your own future now." She pressed a thick roll of British notes and American dollars into Amy's hand. The girl looked astonished.

"I don't want money from you! Take it back!"

In response, Charlotte snapped open Amy's purse and pushed the notes inside. "Please don't refuse. Violette would like you to film the ballet."

"Really?" Amy frowned, uncertain.

"Yes. Will you? Treat this as an advance payment. I don't want you to think we're paying you out of guilt. Well, maybe a little –

but mainly because we want to help. It's enough for you to travel to Hollywood."

"Oh, that's just a dream. My name's tainted, thanks to my uncle's appalling movies."

"Nonsense. I doubt they've even heard of you." Charlotte spoke teasingly, but it was the plain truth.

Amy laughed. "I'm not going to make it in the movies. I won't become a film star, the next 'It girl'. It's a ridiculous idea."

"Seriously, you can change your name and be anyone you want. You are an actress, after all."

"A very bad one."

"Well, even if you fail, at least you won't look back and regret that you never tried."

"Actually, I do enjoy working behind the camera. Perhaps I should do that instead. Would-be actresses are ten a penny, but female movie-makers aren't."

"Then you should become a director. And if anyone tries to stop you, which they will, get angry and let it make you even more determined."

Amy's eyes lit up. Suddenly she was rosy-cheeked, coming back to life again.

"You have just offered me an assignment, haven't you?"

"Well, Violette has, but yes."

"A proper job. What am I thinking? Of course I'll do it." Her posture straightened, her eyes shone. "This is enough money for Mariette to come to America, too..."

"Then take her with you. You want to do this, don't you? Work for Violette, then go on your travels?"

"And start my own film company? Oh, more than anything."

"Well, now you can," said Charlotte. "But watch out for the vampires."

You could not go searching for a *doppelgänger*, Charlotte knew. You had to wait until it came to you. She sat in the dark bedroom, reading by candlelight, calm and composed – as calm as anyone could be while waiting for a ghost.

Niklas's remains had been carefully collected from the bed – he was not much more than dust and crumbling bone by then – and placed into an urn. Sheets, pillows, quilts, everything had been replaced. All the same, Charlotte could not look at the bed without seeing his pitiful pale body lying there, and Stefan beside him...

She was glad she did not have to sleep on that mattress. Whether she and Karl could ever make love there again was another matter.

When she looked up, her other-self was floating in front of her: a figure in a loose ivory dress, her innocent face haloed by a shimmer of spun-gold hair. The second Charlotte looked like a reflection, with no mirror between them.

She started, as she'd known she would. However hard she schooled herself not to react, she couldn't help it. She hoped the double would not notice her fear...

If the ghost was aware of anything at all.

"I've been waiting for you," said Charlotte. No answer. She put her book aside, went slowly to the lamia and put her arms around her.

The creature had substance, but she was cold, and gave off a light, chilly scent like the smell of snow. This was the apparition that Godric had boasted of putting on like a coat. Charlotte was furious that he'd used her image in an attempt to seduce Karl, and equally in awe that he'd had the arcane skill and cunning to do such a thing.

But Godric had not created the lamia. If he thought she was a *Weisse Frau* showing him favour, he was simply mistaken. He'd used her as a disguise, but she existed in her own right. Now he was dead, but the spectre was still here, mindlessly yearning... unable to express what she wanted.

Charlotte embraced her in love, not fear.

"Stay with me," she murmured into the sea-cold whorl of her ear. "You are not separate. You are only a shell, an illusion. An impostor. I have not split in two. I was always whole. If you are a projection of my guilt and my fear, I salute you, because I don't want to lose my human emotions entirely. If I did, what sort of fiend would I be? But you forget, or rather, we both forget: I've been touched by the dark goddess, Lilith. She opened my inner eyes. I even once *became* a goddess, if only for a short time. You cannot fool me forever."

The spectre was motionless in her arms, waxen and weightless as Niklas had been.

"If you are the half of myself that I sometimes want to disown – the vampire half, who is all appetite and no compassion – that won't work, either. I accepted what I am when I decided to go with Karl and gave up my human life. We are monstrous, I know, but that's not *all* we are. And if you simply want to terrify me – well done, my dear. You succeeded."

She kissed the other Charlotte on the cheek. It was like kissing frost. Her lips burned, and the spectre's flesh began to dissolve. Where Charlotte's mouth had touched, a lip-shaped hole appeared and began to spread.

The pale figure smiled. It turned away, and went to look out of the window, apparently gazing at the moon over the mountains. Now Charlotte could see right through her double, as if it were made of glass, or melting ice. After a few moments it dissolved altogether. Charlotte was the one standing at the window... and only the mountains remained, white and ghostly against the night.

"Natural causes?" said Karl.

"Exactly," Charlotte replied. What a pleasure to be alone in their rooms at last. They stood together at the open window, talking by the glow of a single lamp. A sharp breeze stirred the curtains. She felt the need for fresh air to blow away the remnants of Reiniger and all the spectral silt that had pooled in the darkness. "He fell ill and died, as people do."

"But several nights *before* we saw him here?"

"Apparently."

"So what was it that came to us?" Karl asked softly. "Whose head did I sever?"

He held her gaze as he spoke. The shocked look in his eyes, amber-golden and too bright, disturbed her. Aroused her, too, as he always had. His expression was dark and chilly and fervent all at once, sending thrills through her: hot, cold, hot again.

"I don't know. I'm sure it was him, but..."

"A revenant," said Karl. "Something more solid than a ghost. He said that he was part of the Crystal Ring now. And if he still exists in some form, that means we can never be rid of him."

"Perhaps he is part of the Ring, but not in a coherent form." Charlotte pressed closer to Karl. She let her hands stray on to him, caressing his shoulders and his beautiful beloved face. "You banished him. He became part of the ether."

"Oh, I hope so." He slid a finger between the back of her dress and her skin, stroking her neck. "I think he knew. That's why he spoke of himself as a metaphorical demon, hoping to torment my conscience forever. It was all he had left."

"But you mustn't let him."

"I doubt I can exorcise him entirely. We influence the Crystal Ring. In turn, it penetrates us."

"I think that the Crystal Ring is completely insane!" Charlotte said fiercely.

"How so?" His breath was warm on her neck. He drew her hair aside and kissed her there, making her nearly collapse with desire. It was so long since they'd touched each other freely...

"It's like the mind of a lunatic," she said. "A brew of human and unhuman thoughts, simmering with ambition and malevolence and passion, governed by no logic whatsoever – what else could it be? A man like Godric Reiniger, trying to tap its powers, was bound to come to grief. No wonder we're all half-mad, too."

"I played my part in how his life shaped him."

"But you didn't start it."

"In a sense, I did, when I fed on his father."

"His father was only prey in the dark. You couldn't know where it would lead."

"True. Just prey in the dark. We never know where chance encounters will lead, do we? I think he meant it when he said he died in his cinema. Humiliation can be worse than death."

"I never knew you had such a devious side," she said. "Filming him *in flagrante*? How absolutely perverse."

"I always told you I have no morals, beloved," Karl said with a smile. "That said, we had no idea what he planned to do."

"Stealing my double to use as a disguise?" she said with a flash of anger. "How dare he? That went far beyond immorality to outright violation. Of *her*, as much as us."

"Yes. One more reason to destroy him. If only I'd done so sooner, but..."

"You found him a little fascinating, didn't you?" She narrowed her eyes. "Admit it."

"In a way," he said with half a shrug. "Yes, certain humans... We all have a weakness for them. I'm not immune. And he was a remarkable specimen. They say the desert is like an alchemist's crucible: it will burn you up or transmute you. I took him there with some idea that he could be redeemed, but it was too late."

"He was irredeemable," she said. "I could never forgive him for what he did to Stefan, or Amy, or you. The harm he did all of us."

"Well, Godric had his revenge on me. I took my revenge on him. I think all things were equal in the end."

Karl's hands slid firmly and slowly all the way down her back. Now she couldn't catch her breath at all. She nipped the skin of his throat between her teeth. He lifted her chin and kissed her, pushing his fingers into her hair. His mouth was so warm, familiar... she opened her lips to him, thirsting, tasting him as if she were a bee starved of nectar.

Almost unconsciously their fingers began to work at each other's clothes. It seemed forever since they had lain naked together, entwined. This was the first time since the night of the cold knife that she'd felt free to love Karl without harming him.

Logic suggested that the danger had been all in her mind, but she knew – her deep, subconscious instinct knew – that it had been real.

The dread had lifted only when Reiniger vanished for the last time. To think he'd exerted sinister control over everything, and they hadn't even known until it was over – she couldn't think about that. Nothing mattered now but Karl and this rising, uncontrollable thirst, the bliss of complete abandonment.

His ardent response told her without words that he knew the lamia was gone. He didn't need to ask, and she was glad. They were as healthy as vampires could ever be, or as contagious as each other: whatever the case, they were equal. Inside each other, sharing blood, sharing pain, pleasure, everything.

Later she would tell him, *Yes, the lamia's gone – because she's part of me again. She's me and I am her. One being. And I know what she wanted after all.*

She wanted to come home.

* * *

A final dress rehearsal was not the best time for Fadiya to reappear. Violette completed her solo and ran into the wings – resplendent in her 'dark temptress' costume from *Witch and Maiden* – straight into a figure camouflaged in olive green.

Fadiya's eyes widened. Violette realised she'd never seen her in stage costume before, now looking every inch the glamorous witch in black and purple tulle.

"Fadiya," said Violette without inflexion. "I didn't expect to see you again."

"I'd love to see the ballet," said Fadiya. "You look... astonishing. I did not know so much work went into it: all these musicians, wonderful scenery... I would like to see Emil dance, just once."

"Well, I'll leave you a complimentary ticket at the box office," Violette answered mildly, "as long as you keep away from him. Why are you here?"

Fadiya held up a plain rucksack. "I came to take back the *sakakin* to Bayt-al-Zuhur. I have all thirty now; Stefan gave up the last one without argument. I'll take them home, as Kurgara asked, away from covetous human eyes."

"Thank you. It's for the best. Their potency may take a long time to fade."

"I know you disapprove," said Fadiya, "but the vampires of Bayt-al-Zuhur will not give up their *Istilqa* without a struggle. Kurgara won't let them make a new bone well, so we'll have to find a different way in the end... but not yet."

"How is he?"

"Recovering," said Fadiya with a smile. Her manner was dignified, even friendly. "We told everyone what happened, and they have accepted him for who he is. They still revere us as their protectors. It will take time to adjust, but we won't abandon them."

"I'm pleased to hear it. I can't be sorry that I shattered your way of life, because living on illusions is good for no one."

"At times I hated you," said Fadiya. "Now, though, I'm glad it's over. You set him free. We walk together under the stars every night. They say that the desert is a good place to strip back the soul to its essence."

Fadiya was silent then because Emil appeared on stage, dancing his own magnificent solo as the hero, torn between his virtuous wife and his dark lover. She watched with such blatant rapture that Violette felt a touch of sympathy. She thought, *You claim that you loved him. Now do you see the person whom you betrayed and so nearly destroyed?*

"Would you pass on my apologies?" Fadiya murmured. "I hope in time he'll remember the blissful times we had, and not the bad."

Emil finished his scene and leapt into the wings: radiating exuberance. Seeing Fadiya, his energy vanished like a doused fire.

She was already turning to walk away, giving one brief glance over her shoulder as she dissolved into the Crystal Ring.

Emil stared into the shadows after her, transfixed.

"What did she want?" he asked.

"She came to fetch something, that's all," said Violette. "She asked me to say that she's sorry and hopes you'll remember her more kindly one day."

Emil took a couple of steps away. Violette left him to compose himself. She saw him push back his hair and blot his eyelashes, smudging his stage make-up.

"I want to forgive her," he said, "but I can't."

"Emil, I'm to blame for all this; I attract trouble. You became a pawn in the middle, regardless of my efforts to keep you safe. You know the truth now. I am a vampire. So are Karl and Charlotte, Stefan and Fadiya. Can you still work with me, knowing this? After what you've been through?"

"I had this conversation with Karl," he said. "I think it's best not to talk of it any more."

"You certainly won't *mention* it to anyone else. But I'd like to talk, just this once. Can you live with what you know, and keep it secret?"

"I intend to try, madame." He folded his arms, looking everywhere but into her eyes.

"When humans see through the veil, they lose their grip on sanity. They are never the same again."

"I know. But I'm learning to live with it. As long as I'm not slain in my bed for knowing too much about the hidden world, I will cope."

"You have a brave spirit." She stopped, waiting patiently until he finally met her gaze. "Emil, you know we were all human once. I've never suggested this to any dancer before, but has it crossed your mind how it would feel to be one of us? Changeless, virtually immortal? Your youth and talents would never fade. It is a great risk… but if you wanted this, I can arrange it."

He let his hands drop to his sides and stared at her as if his eyes would catch fire.

"No!" he said fiercely. "No, madame. I've achieved my skill through human hard work, not supernatural intervention. I'm proud of that. What, you're suggesting I become a blood-drinking demon like Fadiya? It's not a price worth paying!"

"You seem to have rather a low opinion of vampires." Violette smiled coolly.

"Not you. You're different."

"No, I'm not. We are far from perfect, but we're not all bad."

"I appreciate that, but still – to survive by drinking blood? Unthinkable. I'd rather achieve all I can by my own efforts and grow old with grace."

"Thank you for your candid answer." She went on probing him with her higher senses. Of course he was full of conflict. How could he not be? "I'm relieved, to be honest. The transformation is not easy, and I would hate to take such a risk with your life. In a few years, though, you might feel differently."

"I've seen through the veil, seen things no human should see," he said softly. "I can't contemplate becoming what you are. But in twenty years?"

He fell quiet, his face tightening into severe lines. She asked, "What?"

"Mikhail. I found him drowning his sorrows at turning forty. When my strength starts to fail, when I look in the mirror and find grey hairs, while you remain the same, still gazing at me with those glorious eyes, eternally beautiful like a painting? I don't know how I'll feel then. Perhaps I'll go mad. Again."

"It's not an easy choice," she said. "If you do change your mind, what will be at stake? Your principles, your pride?"

"And my very life."

"Mm. Well, there's no hurry to decide. Today, and for a long time yet, we can go on as we are. But can you bear to stay with me, knowing the truth? Do you feel the same magic when we dance?"

"Yes. More than ever. You have no idea how determined I am."

"Oh, I'm seeing more of that every day. I want you as my partner, always."

His posture relaxed. He dipped his head, almost in a bow.

"That's all I want in the world, madame. And I give you my word, on my brother's life, that I will respect your rules. And it won't be difficult."

"No?"

"No, because it's easier to accept that you and I will never be lovers than it would be to lose our partnership. There are nobler goals in this world than taking a lover, seducing your heart's desire or even marrying her. Given a choice between my hopeless yearning for you, Madame Violette, and my passion for eternal fame – I chose fame."

His sincere tone, spiced with self-mockery, made her laugh out loud.

"Profound, Emil," she said. "Welcome back."

By sheer hard work with a good dash of panic, Violette's new theatre opened on time. This was not the first time she'd performed these ballets, but the first time in her own domain was magical.

Taking her curtain calls to a storm of applause and bouquets afterwards, it struck her that this was the happiest night of her life. That she was actually *happy*.

Emil had been astonishing. No one outside their circle would begin to guess what had happened to them. He was the gleaming golden prince again, the perfect foil to her ineffably beautiful ice maiden. And he, too, was back in his true element.

Long may this last, she thought, her hand resting on his as if they were a king and queen before their court. Somewhere in the darkness, Amy Temple and Karl were capturing everything on film.

A hundred years from now, people may look at our efforts and smile, she thought. *I only hope they smile in pleasure, not disdain.*

Backstage, amid the bustle of post-performance activity, Violette was amused to see Emil leaning against a wall near his dressing room, a towel slung around his neck, cheerfully shaking his head as Stefan made a blatant attempt to flirt with him. As an excuse to listen, she paused by a hamper and rested each foot in turn on the lid to untie her pointe shoes.

"Are you absolutely *sure* you only like women? Couldn't you be persuaded to be a little more… adventurous?"

"I really think not," Emil said with good humour. "To be frank, my friend, I have decided to put my art before all other… distractions. There are things in life greater than mere love and desire. That's the path I've chosen."

Violette smiled to herself. She doubted his vow of celibacy would last long. She felt sorry for those women whose hearts he would break along the way, but as long as she had her ideal partner once more, she was content.

"What a shame," said Stefan. His blue eyes were alight with mischief. "If you change your mind…"

"Stefan, leave him alone," said Charlotte. She slid up to him and put her hand through his arm, ushering him away. "You're outrageous. Emil, he's only teasing."

"I know," said Emil, giving a haughty smirk as he stepped into his dressing room and shut the door.

Despite Charlotte's scolding tone, Violette met her gaze and they shared a moment of amusement. Stefan was as roguish as ever. Perhaps his eyes were a little too bright. He wore a silk scarf, she knew, to conceal the bright red scar across his throat. The wounds were slow to heal.

"Believe me, I meant it," Stefan told Charlotte, looking at the closed door. "He's a challenge. And I think he likes me."

"Everyone likes you," said Charlotte. "That's why you get away with anything. But *no feasting on Violette's dancers*, or there'll be hell to pay."

"I wouldn't dream of it!"

Violette smiled pointedly at him as she walked past, a look that said, *No, you had better not*. In the doorway to her dressing room, she turned to look back at them with affection.

"Good," Charlotte said gently, "I can't tell you how happy I am to see you coming back to life, my dear friend."

Stefan kissed her cheek. "You endured my selfishness, my

tantrums, my self-centred death wish, everything. I can't express how much I regret my behaviour, or how deeply I value your patience. I love you, Charlotte."

"You are insufferably annoying at times. That's true. But you were grieving. All the thanks we want is for you to live."

"I wasn't sure I could," Stefan said quietly into the middle distance. "Was Karl actually going to hack off my head, or did I dream it?"

"Um," Charlotte said faintly. "Those bone-knives bring terrible dreams..."

"Oh, the *Istilqa* sleep was blissful," said Stefan. "Each time I woke, I cut myself again to return to that oblivion... hoping it would last forever. Don't frown at me: I've no desire ever to try again. I see how addictive it could be."

"A false comfort."

"Yes. Really, there is no comfort. It's so strange. I keep looking around for Niklas at my elbow, but there's no one there."

"You're not alone. We're here, all your friends."

"I must admit, it was fun helping Karl with that movie scene," said Stefan. "Plotting together. I thought the one thing I needed was revenge on Reiniger, and then I could die. But you wouldn't let me. When I came back to myself, I realised... that perhaps I can survive after all. If my friends would go to such lengths to save me, who am I to argue?"

In the main auditorium, in an alcove high up in one wall, there sat an urn containing Niklas's remains.

Violette had been most unhappy that Stefan had brought the body into her house. Initially, she'd feared he was unhinged enough to carry his twin around forever, like some ghastly decomposing doll. But once the corpse had shrunk and crumbled, Stefan quietly surrendered Niklas to the urn.

Violette had offered to display the vessel in pride of place, hoping to discourage any urge he had to take it everywhere. To her surprise, he'd readily agreed. That was a good sign. It meant he knew he must let his brother go.

She felt a touch ashamed, now, for crediting Stefan with so little wisdom.

494

Anyone looking up from their theatre seat might notice a large porcelain jar of blue and gilt in the Sèvres style. If they used opera glasses to look more closely, they would see that the vessel was hand-decorated with a portrait of a smiling young man, an angel in blue satin and white lace.

Violette would never explain to anyone why it was there. For as long as the Ballet Lenoir remained in Lucerne, people would look, and wonder.

Long after the ballet and the after-show party were over, Karl and Charlotte walked alone along the snowline where the steep meadows met the Alps. A crescent moon hung above the peaks. Karl tasted the blood of a recent hunt on his tongue, felt Charlotte's affectionate presence close by his side, and was content.

"You've often told me there must be unknown circles of vampires, hidden from us," she said. "And we found one. Or rather, they found us, which is disturbing."

"I'm sure there are others," said Karl. "There must be. If Ilona and Pierre don't return from their travels before the year's end, I may start to worry."

"I'd be more concerned for the vampires they meet," she said with a soft laugh.

They walked in easy silence for a while.

"Karl?" she asked at last. "You never answered Stefan's question. If I were *fully* dead, whatever that means for us – let's say beheaded – would you react like Kristian and slaughter scores of humans to bring me back?"

Karl looked up at the stars: delaying tactics to put off the impossible question. "I think that I probably would. Only for you."

"Well, don't," she said softly. "I release you from the obligation to do so. If I did such a horrific thing, you wouldn't thank me, would you? You'd rather stay dead? Well, so would I."

"Charlotte, dearest." He slid his arms around her in a strong embrace. "If you died, I wouldn't want to exist without you. Will you please desist from being so morbid?"

"We're vampires. We're allowed to be morbid. I'll desist when you answer me."

"All right. I would hold your lifeless corpse against me, like this, and take us both up into the *Weisskalt* where we could sleep forever."

"You mean it?" She drew back her head to meet his gaze. "That's the most weirdly comforting thought… as comforting as anything could be when we're talking of dying and freezing for eternity."

He smiled. "It's the best answer I have. Not to be parted, in life or in death."

"And if things were the other way round, I would do the same."

"Ah, love, no. You'd survive without me."

"You should know better by now than to argue with me about matters of life and death." Charlotte gave him a long solemn look. "My heart still stops, every time I see you. I've tried living without you, and once was enough. We'll do this for each other. Promise me."

They promised each other.

"An easy vow to make, while we're still full of passion for life," he murmured, "but I don't make it lightly, beloved. We may have a hundred years left, a thousand, or a single day. What a blessing that we don't know."

"Well, one day or centuries: we've made a binding pact," she answered.

Fresh air scented with melting snow blew into their faces as they turned and began to stroll arm in arm towards the town.

Talk of death made them hungry for life.

Now they lay together in a bath tub filled with steaming, rose-perfumed water. Karl was underneath, Charlotte lying back in his arms with her hair spread out and drifting on the water. Candlelight shimmered around them. There was no sweeter distraction than Karl's fingers stroking her, his lips moving over her shoulders. His hands left trails of warm ecstatic sensation everywhere they touched until she was trembling from head to toe, hardly able to catch a breath. Not trembling outwardly, but with internal waves of heart-stopping sensation.

Their bodies gleamed under the rippling surface. However gently they moved, the water kept threatening to overflow on to the tiled floor.

"We shall be in trouble if we cause a flood," Charlotte whispered.

"At this moment, I don't care," said Karl, barely coherent. "You look like a moon goddess, and this waterfall of golden hair... Ah, I shall drown in you."

"In each other," she echoed. "I have been drowning in you since the first moment you looked at me."

She rotated to face him, her spine arching as the water buoyed up her outstretched legs. He drew her down hard against him, causing a small tide to lap over the rim of the bath.

Karl's long, sleekly muscled body shone – all she could see of him that wasn't covered by her own. The rest, she felt moulded to her. His slender, strong thighs. The very warm, firm evidence of his desire left her thrilled and breathless: her source of eternal, sensual delight.

He was pressing raptly against her, moving, teasing, but she needed him inside her now. Where they both belonged. Joined.

His eyes were half closed, gleaming and sultry. His head tipped back as she enclosed him within herself... or tried. A bathtub was not the easiest place to do this – she slipped, and he caught her arms, but she was slippery with rose oil and fell forward, went right under with her face on his chest, then righted herself, spluttering. They wrestled, laughing and groaning, until they found their way.

Then the world went scarlet behind her eyelids. Exquisitely subtle and slow at first, barely causing a ripple... and after a time – not long, for the water was still hot – writhing together in uncontrollable spasms of ecstasy.

Blood swirled in the water as they bit and fed on each other. A rose-coloured tide splashed over the rim of the bath tub, pattering on to the tiles. Waves tilted back and forth as they subsided, spent, lying lazily against each other with their limbs intertwined.

Karl's lips rested on her hair. She ran her tongue along his collarbone, taking the last drops of blood.

Desire is never about a single encounter, a single explosion of pleasure, she thought. *It's a hunger that burns and burns. Makes us insane with the need to consume each other over and over again, to be joined constantly, because this is where we belong.*

"Would you really have killed me?" he asked. His wry but

serious tone ambushed her. "When I tried to end Stefan's life?"

"Oh, don't ask that now."

"When better? Whatever you say, I shall be content. I'm just curious."

She believed him, only because she knew him so well.

"Would you have killed *him*?" she riposted. "I meant it in the heat of the moment, but... I think I would have thrown myself over Stefan like a shield and felt the cleaver bite into my own back, rather than harm you."

"We were all unhinged at the time," Karl said thoughtfully. "Despite that, we each did what was necessary to avoid the worst outcome."

"Sense prevailed."

"And love."

"Karl, the vow we made... I should feel anguish at the very thought, and I do, but it's awe-inspiring. Terrifying yet full of wonder. All the same, is it right to decide how our story will end?"

"We can make all the pacts we want," said Karl. "The universe may have other plans."

"The universe can do what it likes. I don't care, because this moment matters more than eternity, more than any supposed afterlife. *This moment*."

She bit into his throat again, tasting the compelling richness of his blood. Karl gasped. She kissed him with his blood on her lips. The water swirled red, pooling on the floor and staining the white towels. Someone entering might think they'd walked into a murder scene.

"*This* is heaven," she said.

"Paradise," he echoed. "This is why we live."

ACKNOWLEDGEMENTS

For all their help with inspiration, feedback and general support, I would like to thank Aliette de Bodard, Kari Sperring, Keren Gilfoyle, Jenny Gordon, Tricia Sullivan, Anne and Stan Nicholls, Storm Constantine, Jane Johnson, Juliet McKenna, Ian Whates, Sam Stone and David Howe, Chelle and Kevin Bullock, and my American namesake, the "other" Freda Warrington.

And of course, always, my husband Mike.

I also wish to thank my agent John Berlyne, my editor Natalie Laverick and all at Titan Books and Forbidden Planet, for being wonderful. I can't express how delighted I am – twenty years after *A Taste of Blood Wine* was first published – to be given the chance to write a brand-new book in the series. Karl, Charlotte, Violette et al. have long been my favourite characters and always will be. I'm determined this won't be the last you see of them!

As you'll know from my previous Blood Wine books, I've long found inspiration in the music of Stevie Nicks and the romantic, eerie, gothic atmosphere she creates, particularly with songs such as "Sisters of the Moon" and "Outside the Rain". In continued tribute, many of the chapter titles were inspired by snatches of her lyrics. I doubt she will ever know it – but thank you, Stevie!

My usual modus operandi, when setting scenes, is to use real places and then play with them, inserting locations that aren't really there but could be, even to play fast and loose with the terrain and with snatches of fictionalised history that *could* have happened.

(For example, dissenters really did try to shoot Mussolini...)

So before you write to tell me there are no such buildings as Bergwerkstatt or the Ballet Lenoir in Lucerne, no Hotel Blauensee, no such cinema or beer hall, no house in Algiers as Bayt-al-Zuhur, and so on... I know! While I've done my best to be historically accurate, any mistakes are mine so please forgive my use, or misuse, of artistic licence.

If you'd like to learn more about my work, please visit www.fredawarrington.com. From there you can read all about my other novels, contact me, reach my blog and find me on Facebook, Twitter and other sites.

Oh, and as the saying goes: "Save an author. Write a review!"

ABOUT THE AUTHOR

Freda Warrington was born in Leicestershire, UK, where she now lives with her husband and mother. She has worked in medical illustration and graphic design, but her first love has always been writing. Her first novel *A Blackbird in Silver* was published in 1986, to be followed by many more, including *A Taste of Blood Wine*, *Dark Cathedral*, *The Amber Citadel*, and *The Court of the Midnight King* – a fantasy based on the life of the controversial King Richard III. As well as the *Blood Wine Sequence* for Titan Books, she writes the *Aetherial Tales* series for Tor. Her novel *Elfland* won a Romantic Times award for Best Fantasy Novel. She can be found online at www.fredawarrington.com and on Twitter @FredaWarrington.

A TASTE OF BLOOD WINE
Freda Warrington

1918. A First World War battlefield becomes the cosmic battleground for two vampires, as Karl von Wultendorf struggles to free himself from his domineering maker, Kristian.

1923. Charlotte Neville watches as her father, a Cambridge professor, fills Parkland Hall with guests for her sister Madeleine's 18th birthday party. Among them is his handsome new research assistant Karl – the man Madeleine has instantly decided will be her husband. Charlotte, shy and retiring, is happy to devote her life to her father and her dull fiance Henry – until she sees Karl…

For Charlotte, it is the beginning of a deadly obsession that sunders her from her sisters, her father and even her dearest friend. As their feverish passion grows, Karl faces the dilemma he fears the most. Only by deserting Charlotte can his passion for her blood be conquered. Only by betraying her can he protect her from the terrifying attentions of Kristian – for Kristian has decided to teach Karl a lesson in power, by devouring Charlotte.

A DANCE IN BLOOD VELVET
Freda Warrington

For the love of her vampire suitor, Karl, Charlotte has forsaken her human life. Now her only contact with people is when she hunts them down to feed. Her thirst for blood repulses her but its fulfilment brings ecstasy.

The one light in the shadows is the passion that burns between her and Karl. A love that it seems will last for eternity – until Karl's former lover, the seductively beautiful Katerina, is rescued from the Crystal Ring. For nearly fifty years she has lain, as dead, in the icy depths of the Weisskalt. Now she wants to reclaim her life... and Karl.

In despair, Charlotte turns to the prima ballerina Violette Lenoir, an ice maiden who only thaws when she dances. Charlotte is fascinated as she has been by no other human, longing to bring joy to the dancer. But her obsession opens the floodgates to a far darker threat than the vampires could ever have imagined. For Violette is more than human and if she succumbs to the vampire's kiss, it could unleash a new terror...

THE DARK BLOOD OF POPPIES
Freda Warrington

The ballerina Violette Lenoir has fallen victim to the bite of the vampire Charlotte. Her fire and energy have fuelled a terrifying change and a dreadful realisation; that Violette has become Lilith, the demon mother of all vampires.

Haunted both by what she has done and by Violette's dark sensuality, Charlotte and her immortal lover Karl are drawn towards the dancer and the terrible destiny that has fallen on her shoulders. But other, far more dangerous shadows are gathering around Violette. To the vampire Sebastian and to the dark heirs of Kristian, she threatens to wreak havoc with their plans to bring all of mankind under their dark wings.

Innocently embroiled in the endgame, courtesan extraordinaire Robyn Stafford finally meets her match as she is torn between the two ultimate lovers: Sebastian, and Violette…

For more fantastic fiction, author events, exclusive excerpts, competitions, limited editions and more

VISIT OUR WEBSITE
titanbooks.com

LIKE US ON FACEBOOK
facebook.com/titanbooks

FOLLOW US ON TWITTER
@TitanBooks

EMAIL US
readerfeedback@titanemail.com